More Praise for

The American Outsider

"The novel's descriptions of the plight of hunted and captive dolphins are heartbreaking...Equally evocative are the depictions of Japan..." –BlueInk Review

"This 5-star literary execution is not only entertaining but written with incredible agility and insight. Inevitably, readers will come away with a new appreciation of the struggles to protect animals in our modern society." –*Reader Views*

"Finely crafted tale of love and adventure that brims over with heart." –IndieReader

"A vibrant story that is highly recommended for its review of obsessions, relationships, and struggles with panic attacks and love." –Midwest Book Review

The American Outsider

a novel

HOMA POURASGARI

Linbrook Press

Published by Linbrook Press
www.linbrookpress.com

ISBN: 978-0-9779780-4-5 (hard cover) | 978-0-9779780-3-8 (trade paperback) | 978-0-9779780-2-1 (ebook)

Library of Congress Control Number: 2022946279

Publisher's Cataloging-in-Publication Data

LCSH: Women veterinarians--Fiction. | Dolphins--Japan--Taiji--Fiction. | Dolphins--Effect of hunting on--Japan--Taiji--Fiction. | Animal welfare--Japan--Fiction. | Animal rights activists--Japan--Fiction. | Japan--Social life and customs--Fiction. | Japan--Civilization-- Fiction. | LCGFT: Romance fiction.

LCC: PS3616.O867 A44 2023 | DDC: 813/.6--dc23

First trade paperback edition printing January 2023

To my Parents

The American Outsider

CHAPTER 1

Another damn bloody nightmare. Looking around her one-bedroom Santa Monica apartment, Tessa Walker stared at the purple glow of her clock; her flight to Tokyo was in five hours. She rubbed her sleepy, gray eyes and turned on the Y-shaped alphabet light on her nightstand before getting up to go to the bathroom. She tied her ash blonde hair back to splash cold water on her face.

Her chest felt tight, and she had trouble breathing. *No, no, no, no, not another panic attack,* Tessa thought. She curled up into a ball on the floor by the tub, and her ears filled with familiar sounds of distress. "Stop. Please stop," she pleaded.

She covered her ears to block out the cries of dolphins. In her head, she saw images of Japanese fishermen driving them into a cove to slaughter them. She heard their screams when she woke up; she heard their screams when she went to bed.

Every year from September to March, the blue waters of Taiji, a fishing village in Japan south of Osaka, turned red from the massacre. For months, Tessa had been preparing to fly there to protest the killings. Several of her activist friends who lived and worked in Japan warned her that the Japanese consider her *gaijin*, an outsider, and *gaijin* have no right to interfere in the country's affairs.

Her activism began when she was sixteen after a trip to visit her widowed aunt Harriette and half-Japanese cousin Natalie, who lived in Taiji. Natalie was Tessa's age and had stayed with Tessa and her family in California several times when they were growing up. So when Tessa was invited to Taiji, she jumped at the opportunity.

Her first trip to Japan made an impression on her that she would never forget. Amid sightseeing in the region, she also witnessed a grisly scene. On a walk by herself, she made the mistake of wandering off into a bay where she saw Japanese fishermen luring dolphins into a cove and stabbing them to death with spears. Tessa saw the dolphins splash frantically and screech as they tried to escape. The once-blue waters turned into bloodbath. Adults and baby dolphins—all slaughtered. Some were left trapped in nets until the next day. When Tessa asked her aunt why these fishermen were so cruel, her aunt reprimanded her for sticking her nose where it didn't belong and made her promise to never go there again or she would be on the next flight home. Harriette failed to explain that the fishermen considered these creatures pests because they ate all the fish. Other fishermen captured and sold show-quality dolphins. Tessa had called her parents to ask how she could help these dolphins, but they also told her to stay out of it. She was a guest there, and she should follow the rules.

Feeling helpless, Tessa repressed her memories for years. But now, at age forty, all the memories engulfed her like a tsunami. Tessa had been seeing a therapist to help get rid of her nightmares.

After months of sessions, she learned that the only way to stop them was to do something about the injustice.

Tessa took a slow deep breath, got up off the bathroom floor and made her way to the kitchen. She thought back to that August day a few weeks earlier when she had told her father that she was going to Japan.

"Why Taiji?" her father had asked her when he found out that Tessa was planning to go to Tokyo, Kyoto, Taiji, and Osaka for two weeks in September.

Tessa was seated on the patio of her parents' four-bedroom house off of Montana Avenue, an upscale neighborhood in West L.A. She sipped on her lemonade as turmoil brewed inside her.

"I mean, we have plenty of animal abuse in our own home country," Jeff shrugged. At seventy-four, he was a successful real-estate broker with a muscular body and a buzz cut. He didn't like the idea of meddling in other countries' affairs even though when he served in Vietnam, he followed orders without asking questions. He was eventually discharged due to his symptoms of post-traumatic stress disorder. Years later, he realized that he was unhappy about some of the decisions his superiors had made.

Tessa stared at him in disbelief and blurted, "I like dolphins. There are many causes in the world, and I chose this one. It's not possible to stand up for everything if you want to make a change. But if you chose one thing and see it through, then you have stood up for something."

"Then tell me this, what about Iceland, Norway, or Denmark? They abuse whales and dolphins."

Sure that her father was about to lecture her, Tessa set down her drink on a wicker table and got up to leave. "I was not in Iceland, Denmark, or Norway. I was in Taiji when I witnessed it firsthand, and you and Mom have never supported me on this."

Folding his arms in front of his chest to register his disapproval, Jeff glared back and said, "So this is your way of rebelling?"

"No, this is the only way I can put a stop to my nightmares. Did you think that I would just forget it? I was sixteen," she said, tears streaming down her face. She wiped them away. "You weren't there to see it. I was heartbroken, and there was nothing I could do."

"And now that you're older, you're. …"

"Now that I'm older, I'm going to do something about it and there is nothing you can do to stop me," she interjected. She thought about how she was going to use her scuba diving skills to film the killings and put them on social media, even though she knew that the slaughter of dolphins was already featured in the documentary, *The Cove*. More than ten years had passed since the film came out, but the killings continued. Tessa felt that people needed to be reminded again of how dolphins are tortured. Since her Aunt Harriette had died long ago and her cousin had moved to New Zealand, Tessa was planning to stay with her activist friends and pursue her cause.

"How are you planning to do this? Walk around with signs of bloody dolphins before you get arrested? Believe me, you don't want to end up in jail in some foreign country." Jeff knew what that was like. He had been imprisoned and beaten in Vietnam.

"You know Dad, I thought you would be happy for me, standing up for something that I believe in so strongly," she said and started to leave.

"I'm worried about you."

"I'm a grown woman. I don't need you to take care of me." Tessa had long been fiercely independent. She had a rewarding career as a veterinarian at a homeopathic pet hospital. It took ten years of education, including four years to earn a bachelor of science degree, four years of veterinary school, and two years specializing in aquatic medicine to achieve it, and she wasn't about to let that knowledge go to waste. She also volunteered at the Pacific Marine Mammal Center in Laguna Beach where she treated rescued sea lions and other cetaceans.

Tessa was not the only veterinarian who felt intense empathy for suffering animals. Extensive scientific studies showed that veterinary professionals were at risk for compassion fatigue. Having to daily encounter death and illness, they sometimes relived traumatic events, which might occur as nightmares or flashbacks and cause serious psychological distress.

Her father's harsh but loving concern did not dissuade her from pursuing her goals. He said, "You may not have a husband in sight, but you're still my child. Nothing will change that no matter how old you are."

"Oh, yes, the inevitable question on your mind: Why don't you get married and have children? I was married, or have you forgotten?"

"No, I haven't forgotten that rotten ex-husband of yours. But that doesn't give you an excuse to give up." Jeff had always wanted a large family with children and grandchildren. But his wife could not bear more children after Tessa was born. And with Tessa turning 40 today, his wishes for grandchildren were dissipating.

Her mother came out to the patio with a platter of carved watermelon. Carol was the peacemaker in the family. As if to reprimand them, she said, "What's all this ruckus about? Are you two arguing again?"

"Never mind. I was just leaving," Tessa said, huffing.

"But you just got here. And I made you a birthday cake." At 5-feet 8-inches, 71-year-old Carol looked like an older version of Tessa. She had been an activist for many causes until she married at age 30 and had Tessa a year later.

"I would if Dad would stop picking on me." Even though Tessa loved her father, they constantly butted heads because their thought processes were so different. He was a conservative, owned a gun and hunted. Tessa was a liberal and an animal rights activist and she hated guns.

"Jeff, please!" Carol said.

"Then you talk to her," he suggested and then addressed Tessa. "Tell your mom what you're planning to do."

"Already know. Let it go," Carol replied. Unlike Jeff, Carol had always given her daughter breathing room. Part of her regretted not supporting Tessa when she told her about witnessing the dolphin slaughter. She was glad that Tessa was now planning to do something about it.

"Fine," Jeff threw his hand up in the air, knowing that his daughter would not listen anyway. "I'm not saying another word."

Now, about to embark on her journey, Tessa was still fuming because of her father's lack of understanding, even when he knew about the dolphin abuse. In Japan, many residents didn't know about the killings because their government hushed it up. And those who knew believed that foreigners should not pass judgment on what they considered Japanese traditions.

Taiji residents claimed that it was their tradition that pushed them to slaughter the dolphins. This inhumane treatment of mammals may have been acceptable when humanity didn't know better, but today people better understand the pain they are inflicting on harmless sea creatures, Tessa thought as she made tea to calm her nerves. Perhaps the world had not changed much. People were supposed to know better—to be wiser and behave more humanely. And yet, legal and illegal hunts continued to take place all over the world in the name of tradition, sport, entertainment, and trophy.

She turned on the faucet of her bathtub, threw in jasmine-scented soap, and plopped down on a comfy armchair across from the TV while waiting for the tub to fill. Flipping from one channel to the next, she couldn't stop thinking about the dolphins. She knew that the way Japanese fishermen slaughtered them was no different than the way mega food industries in the U.S. slaughtered chickens, cows, pigs, ducks, and other animals. She did speak out about their inhumane treatment and pushed to bring awareness about where food came from, but the plight of the dolphins in particular kept tugging at her.

Nine years ago, she attended a lecture given by Lori Marino, a neuroscientist and biopsychologist, who studied the behavior of captive dolphins. According to Marino, dolphins can recognize themselves in a mirror, which shows self-awareness. She further explained that they are intelligent, have individual personalities, and can suffer psychological trauma. Therefore, their slaughter and captivity raise ethical questions.

What if they are smarter than us? Tessa thought as she stepped into her tub to see if she could relax. She laid there and closed her eyes. Her luggage was already packed.

Tessa belonged to an organization called, The Dolphin and Whale Guardians. They paid half her travel expenses to Japan to advocate for the dolphins. Not all animal rights organizations had that kind of funding, but this one was supported by celebrity activists who couldn't join a protest in a foreign country but would gladly pay for others willing to stick their necks out.

Before leaving for her trip, Tessa taught herself some useful Japanese phrases, such as "Good morning," "Thank you," "Excuse me," "Where is the bathroom?" and "I am a vegetarian." Tessa went through numerous travel blogs and took notes about the areas she wanted to visit. Then she studied the daunting subway maps with their numerous lines and how to travel by train. She downloaded map and translation apps on her phone and converted some of her currency into yen. With all its advanced technology, Japan was still a heavily cash-based society.

Tessa also carefully prepared for the protests so as to not bring attention to herself when going through customs. Some activists were immediately sent back by Japanese authorities before even setting foot in the country. So even though she was planning to take her laptop with her, she stored all the protest information and plans in the cloud, used an anonymous voicemail, and had a virtual private network service to hide her online identity.

She had wired a modest sum of money from The Dolphin and Whale Guardians supporters to her friend and fellow activist, Akira Nakano, in Tokyo so that she could distribute it to other activists to cover expenses for upcoming protests. It was easier to get financial support for activism in the U.S. than in Japan.

The Japanese government frowned upon protests, even when they were peaceful. In 2013, the government bypassed its constitution and added a state secrets law, similar to the U.S. Patriot Act, which allowed the government to crack down on protests and activists under the pretext of preventing domestic terrorism or preventing designated harmful activities. The following year, about 8,000 protestors had gathered in Tokyo's Shinjuku Central Park to denounce the new law, which took away many of their rights. However, it was a relatively small protest, considering that Japan had about 127 million inhabitants at the time. In Japan's collective society, people were educated from childhood to work toward a greater good. They were taught conformity and social harmony as opposed to the Western ethic of individualism and free expression. They learned to not criticize authorities and as such, many did not take part in protests.

CHAPTER 2

The wheels of Japan Airlines flight JL061 glided onto a runway at Narita International Airport, and Tessa was glad that her 12-hour flight had come to an end. Akira was at the airport to meet her. Eight years younger than Tessa, Akira had delicate features and silky black hair with red highlights. Born in Japan and raised in the U.S., she spoke English and worked in Tokyo as an independent private tour guide. The two met seven years before in Los Angeles at an animal rights rally and became fast friends.

"How was your flight?" Akira greeted her with a hug. It wasn't typical for people to hug each other in Japan, but Akira was not a typical citizen. She had strong views and had to learn to curb them if she wanted to work in Tokyo.

"Not too bad," Tessa said, with a tired smile. "Thank you for meeting me here." Tessa might have been fine navigating the airport by herself because most everyone spoke English, but once outside, finding her way around would become complicated because fewer people spoke English. Thankfully, Akira was there to guide her on her first night, and a taxi ride would have been costly.

"Of course. Here, let me help you with your bags."

"Thanks, but I'm good," Tessa said, putting her duffel over her luggage to make it easier to roll through the airport. "It's not that heavy. I packed light."

"Do you want anything from the airport?" Narita International had many interesting shops, great food everywhere, and places to relax and chat on the phone. A visitor could easily spend hours there and never get bored.

"Actually yes. I need to pick up the portable Wi-Fi I ordered," Tessa said, unzipping a small pocket on her bag and pulling out a receipt.

Akira glanced at it and said, "I think I know where to go."

Tessa followed her and, after picking up her device at a booth, the two started toward an area to catch N'EX—the Narita Express train that connected the airport to urban stations. It was one of the cheaper and easier ways to reach a destination.

"Hungry?" Akira asked.

"No, not really."

"Me neither. I just thought—you know—you might be." Akira was painfully thin, thinner than Tessa remembered.

A capable scuba diver and former instructor, Tessa had an athletic body. "I just need a shower and sleep."

"I can give you that," Akira said, heading down the escalator with Tessa to catch the train.

After the train from the airport, two transfers, and several blocks of walking in a light drizzle, the two reached Akira's apartment. It was located on a quiet residential street in Jiyūgaoka, a trendy neighborhood in the southeastern part of Tokyo, minutes away by train from tourist destinations, such as Shibuya, one of Tokyo's busiest districts. Akira's place was on the fourth floor of a five-story, modern building. Tessa was impressed that she lived in such a high-class neighborhood. At the *genkan*, an entryway where shoes are removed, Tessa put on a pair of slippers that Akira had laid out for her. The one-bedroom apartment had bamboo floors, a kitchenette, and a sliding glass door that opened to the balcony, which overlooked the street. Near the entrance was a tiny room with a toilet and sink along with a separate bathroom with a Japanese soaking tub and shower. Tessa noticed an extra pair of slippers at the door of the toilet room and another at the door of the bathroom.

From her last visit as a teenager, Tessa knew that the Japanese changed out of their home slippers into toilet slippers because they considered toilets unsanitary, and they wanted to prevent their house slippers from getting wet or dirty. When they exited the toilet area, they left the toilet slippers exactly where they were so that it would be convenient for the next person to slip them on. Foot size was inconsequential—it was the user's problem to figure out a way to squeeze into them. For Tessa, who had big feet, drank lots of water, and peed often, the slipper etiquette became a nuisance. Nevertheless, Tessa had learned this rule quickly when her Aunt Harriette yelled at her during her first visit. She could still hear her nagging, nasal voice in her head: "Tessa, how many times do I have to tell you, no toilet slippers around the house?"

Akira's apartment had a few eclectic pieces, such as a lacquered, green vintage table with a statue of Buddha on top and an Edo period Tansu chest—a traditional legless two-door chestnut cabinet from the 1700s that represented a peaceful time in the country. There was also a separate bedroom and a small walk-in closet.

"This is nice. It's possible to afford an apartment like this on a tour guide's salary?" Tessa asked. She knew that most apartments in Tokyo were much smaller. Akira's was about 900 square feet, whereas most young singles lived in 220-square-foot rentals.

For many Americans, Akira's place might not be considered upscale, but in Japan, it was. Considering the expensive properties, the high rate of poverty, and the fact that Japan was a patriarchal society—women's salaries were half of men's on average, and even then, many were only hired part-time—Akira was fortunate to be able to support herself and have a sizeable, modern apartment in one of the city's most sought-after neighborhoods.

"No. Not really. I inherited it from my grandparents," she said. "I opened up some space in my closet and the living room chest for your things."

"You didn't have to do that. I could've lived out of my suitcase for a few days. It was nice of you just to put me up."

"Happy to do it. This," she said, pointing at a red sofa, "opens up into a double bed, and I have towels, sheets, and pillows in that chest."

"Thank you," Tessa said. "I think I'll shower and try to get some sleep so that we can get an early start tomorrow."

"I have clients tomorrow and Friday. Why don't you do some sightseeing? And when I'm done with my work, we can go over our plans for the demonstration," Akira said, opening up the sofa for Tessa.

"Maybe I'll go check out the aquarium where we're planning to protest," Tessa said.

"Actually, we're going to be at the Shibuya Crossing instead," Akira said. The famous Shibuya Crossing, also known as the Shibuya Scramble Crossing, is located in front of the Shibuya Station's Hachicō exit. The intersection consists of ten lanes of traffic, seven crossroads, and potentially hundreds of pedestrians spilling onto the street and walking from all directions as they push through the crowds to cross.

"I don't understand," Tessa said as she unfolded one of the sheets and laid it on the sofa bed. "I thought that we were going to protest in front of Maxell Aqua Park Shinagawa."

"I tried but couldn't get the permit for it," Akira replied, helping Tessa with the sheets.

"That's too bad," said Tessa, frustrated. "The protest would really have an impact if we demonstrated in front of a place that exploited sea life."

Akira had more experience with activism and was more patient than Tessa. "Our goal is to bring attention to the horrible manner in which fishermen hunt and slaughter the dolphins. It's a start," she said. "We have a long road ahead of us to convince the public that there's also a moral and ethical issue at stake."

Both women were well aware that dolphins' brains were complex and sophisticated. They also knew that dolphins have problem-solving abilities and are possibly the second-smartest creature next to humans; evidence showed that they may even suffer when losing a family member.

"Alright then. Tomorrow I'll go to Shibuya to get a feel for the area and figure out how we're going to do this."

"Yes, but for now, try to get some sleep. If you want anything from the kitchen, help yourself," Akira said and showed her where things were and how to use her electric kettle. "I'm going to get ready for bed."

Tessa helped herself to some herbal tea until the bathroom was free. She grabbed two white towels and her pajamas and took a shower. When she got out, she got into bed and texted her best friend, Karianne Metzler, who she had known since childhood and now lived in Japan. "Hi. I'm in Tokyo. Can't wait to see you. I know you had mentioned that you're busy for the next few days, but how about getting together when I return from Osaka? I'll text again soon to confirm date and time. BTW: I brought your favorite chocolate-covered wafers from Trader Joe's."

When Tessa woke up in the morning, she read Karianne's reply: "Would love to see you. How about two weeks from now, on Wednesday? And don't forget my cookies ☺—K."

"Perfect! We're on. I'll get in touch with you again on my way back from Osaka," Tessa responded.

Akira emerged from her bedroom, wearing an almost uniform-like navy button-front dress. She had pulled her hair into a perfectly neat bun and added a red clip in front to keep her bangs off her face. Most Japanese women spent a lot of time on their hair and clothing. They made sure to look pretty and feminine, and Akira was no different.

"Hey, remember my friend, Karianne Metzler?" asked Tessa. "I was just texting her. She works at the U.S. Embassy here."

"I remember her. We spoke for a long time at your dinner party a few years back. I liked her. I thought that she worked at the embassy in Vancouver."

"She did, but she married a Japanese diplomat. They now live in Tokyo."

"I would like to see her again," Akira said.

"Then clear your calendar for Wednesday, the day before I go home, because her schedule is tight, and that's the only time we can spend with her."

Akira looked at her schedule on her phone and said: "Shoot. I have a client on that day."

"Well, you two can hang out when I'm gone. I'll group text both of you so that you have each other's phone numbers."

"Thanks, I would like that," Akira said and glanced at the oven clock. She had an hour to eat and leave to take the subway to meet up with a visiting American family at their hotel. "What would you like for breakfast?" she asked.

"I'm good, thanks. I'll have something later," Tessa said. She was without makeup and dressed in black jeans, a belt, a silver necklace, and a pale peach shirt. Her hair was frizzy from sleeping on it damp.

Akira took out a small fruit salad and ate half of it.

"That's all you're eating?" Tessa asked as she finished folding her bed covers.

Unlike Akira who was small and svelte, Tessa was curvy and loved to eat. She also preferred pants to skirts as did many women who lived in Los Angeles. It was easy to throw them on with a shirt and leave home with a cup of coffee in one hand while driving. A lot of L.A. residents' time was lost as they sat in traffic for the majority of their lives. But in Japan, even though people worked extremely long hours, they ate a healthy diet and didn't eat or drink while walking, driving, or doing other activities.

"I'm not that hungry," Akira said. She had gained two pounds and was determined to lose them.

In Japan, it was important to conform to social norms, so there was a lot of peer pressure to stay slim like everyone else. If someone gained weight, their friends would let them know that they were getting fat. "Please help yourself to anything in the fridge," Akira said, thinking that perhaps Tessa was uncomfortable eating her food.

"I think I'll wait and grab something from one of the street vendors I've heard so much about," Tessa said, and then handed Akira a package.

"What's this?" she said, admiring the white and pink floral wrapping.

"Something small to say thank you for putting me up for a couple of days."

Japanese gift-giving and receiving was a complicated affair. Etiquette dictated that when receiving a gift, it should not be opened right away. Instead, the receiver should open it later, when alone. If a gift-giver requests that a gift be opened right away, the receiver should ask if the giver is sure. But Akira didn't follow this etiquette with her close foreign friends unless they were in the company of other Japanese. It was also important to not tear apart the wrapping paper or the bow. So, she carefully unwrapped her gift and found a delicate olive and ivory cable-knit scarf.

"Thank you! This is beautiful," she responded, her hands feeling the texture of the knit.

"You're welcome. I made it out of vegan wool."

"Vegan wool?"

"It's made of desert plants that need little water. No animals are hurt in the process and it's sustainable."

"It feels just like wool!"

"There are different types of yarn made out of the plants. Some feel like cashmere."

"I love it. What a genius idea."

"If you look carefully, you'll find your initials at one of the corners," said Tessa, who enjoyed knitting. She had already started to knit another scarf in gray while she was on the plane.

Akira turned to look at the oven clock. "I have to head out to work. You want me to show you how to get to the train station? I'm going that way."

"Definitely," Tessa said, taking a swig from her water bottle. They were off.

Fifteen minutes later, the two walked to the Jiyūgaoka station, and Akira showed Tessa how to get to central Tokyo. Tessa bought a Souica card—a prepaid e-money card that could be refilled by machine. After pressing the "English" button, Tessa put in 1,000 yen, about $10. She could now use her card to board the JR-East train, subways, and buses without having to buy a ticket each time. She boarded the train for the twelve-minute ride to Shibuya.

CHAPTER 3

Toshiro Yokoyama and his friends were having lunch at the Royal
Garden Café on a ginkgo-lined street near Gaienmae Station. The
scene was a tranquil departure from the busy and fast-paced
Shibuya Crossing. On his fifth beer, Toshiro was laughing and
making jokes with his best friend Souji along with three other
former college pals. He was also staring at a pretty blonde woman
wearing a silver necklace and sitting two tables away.

Toshiro was charming, and his laughter contagious. When he
smiled, his face would light up. He never had to work hard to get
a girlfriend; girls were drawn to him like moths to flames. They
always made the first move. So when his friends teased him about
the fact that he was "the girl" in a relationship, his ego was hurt.

"What do you mean? I'm as masculine as any of you," he said.

"We didn't say that you weren't, but it's always the girl who
makes all the moves to get you. She's the one who asks you out.
She's the one who attempts the first kiss and, for God's sake, you
even got proposed to by two different girls," said Souji, who, with

his course, black hair and short stature, was always a bit envious of his handsome pal.

"Jealous?"

"You bet. But even so, we dare you to do something completely out of character."

"Like what?"

"Hmm. Let's see," Souji replied as he scouted the area and noticed Tessa sitting by herself. "See that blonde woman over there?" he said, pointing his head in her direction.

"Yeah, what about her?"

"I dare you to go over and ask her out."

"I have a girlfriend!"

We know. Everything about her is perfect, Souji wanted to say, thinking of Kaiya with her long, silky, black hair, porcelain skin, and small nose. Souji was in love with Toshiro's girlfriend, and he took every opportunity to get him into trouble with her to break them up. "Okay, fine. I dare you to walk up to her and kiss her."

"What?" said Toshiro, not quite believing his friend's challenge.

"You heard me. You march right up to her, grab her tight, and give her a kiss. And I mean a real kiss, using the tongue and all." Souji leaned back in his seat, his legs stretched out in front of him. He had known Toshiro since they were in second grade together and had gotten him into trouble a few times over the years, like the time he convinced him to drive his dad's Aston Martin before he had a driver's license or when he had convinced him to throw a party when his parents were out of town.

"That's crazy. I'm not going to do that."

The others were overcome by laughter.

"See, what did I say? He has no guts to make a move on a girl," taunted Souji. "If you do this, you're the man."

"Fine! If I do this, you have to stop calling me 'the girl.' Because I don't think any of you would have the guts to do what I'm about to do."

They all looked at each other with surprise and nodded in agreement.

Tessa was busy writing a postcard and occasionally glared at the noisy young Japanese men at a nearby table, who should know better than to be so loud while others were dining. Then she figured that they were just obnoxious and immature. They were all extremely well dressed in casual but fashionable designer clothing. Tessa thought that one of them, with a layered haircut that came down to the nape of his neck and high cheekbones, could be a model or an actor. They all looked to be in their 20s. And experience had taught her that most guys who hadn't reached their 30s were simply unseasoned. She went back to her writing.

Dear Bruna,

This morning I was at the Shibuya Crossing to check out the site where Akira and I would be protesting in a few days. Did you know that more than 2,500 people cross the Shibuya intersection every three minutes? Wish you were here to share the experience. Oh, and I bought a vegetarian *okonomiyaki* (a savory pancake) from a street vendor. Delicious.

Feeling self-conscious and disturbed by the noisy group, Tessa decided to move elsewhere. *What jerks*, she thought as she got up when suddenly, the young man with the defined cheekbones approached and embraced her. His lips covered hers in a long passionate kiss. She felt violated. She broke free from his grip and slapped him hard.

His face was red. *It was worth the kiss*, he thought. Pointing at his friends, he said in English, with a Japanese accent, "Sorry, my friends there said that I was square and I wanted to show them…"

"I don't care what they said," she yelled at him. "What you did was unacceptable. You're lucky that I'm not calling the police." She then quickly walked away, feeling humiliated. And yet, a part of her had enjoyed the kiss. When he had pulled her toward him, she had noticed that he was several inches taller than her, which was unusual since many Japanese men were short. She felt things that she hadn't felt in a long time.

What's the matter with you, Tessa? she thought to herself. *You can't possibly be so desperate that you actually enjoyed kissing a complete stranger.* Perhaps it was the three years of not having been with anyone that made the kiss so wanting, so incredibly amazing. Or maybe, it was the fact that he was easy on the eyes with his long, auburn bangs swept to one side, boyish face, and brown, almond-shaped eyes. Yet she was angry at the same time.

I hate that guy, she told herself as she boiled with anger and pushed through a dense crowd of locals and tourists.

After a fifteen-minute walk, she ended up in Hyakkendana, a quiet area on Shibuya's back streets. Akira had told her that if the crowds ever got to her, this was the place to be. She had given her directions to get there and where to eat. Hyakkendana, meaning "100 stores," used to be the busiest area in Tokyo fifty years earlier. Now, Shibuya, with its futuristic architecture, neon signs, and television screens mounted on tall buildings, was the busiest area. Hyakkendana contained shorter buildings and was frequented by locals, so it appeared aged, serene, and humble. Tessa walked under a big red *torii*, or gateway, marked "Hyakkendana," passed by several retail shops, and saw an old building tucked in an alley that Akira directed her to. She went in and up a flight of stairs and found SinKaya, a tavern with a black-and-white sign. Without her friend's directions, this place would have been hard to find.

The tavern's owner, Sin-San, prepared the local cuisine of the Mount Fuji region. Seated behind the counter were a few customers who seemed to be regulars as they chatted with Sin-San. Tessa also saw a Scandinavian couple asking about worthy attractions in Shibuya. She took a seat on a dark cushy bench behind a wooden table and followed the chef's recommendation of ordering *hoto*—udon noodles with vegetables in miso sauce—and pairing it with a white wine from Koshu Valley, a region outside of Tokyo bordered by Mount Fuji and the Japanese Alps, which is known for its grapes and wineries. The warm cozy atmosphere, the hot soup with sweet vegetables, and the rustic aura of the place improved her mood. As she sat there finishing her correspondence, her boiling anger dissipated into a simmer.

Toshiro and his friends' poor conduct was uncommon in Japanese culture. They were usually more reserved and respectful and did not speak loudly. However, they all had been drinking more than they should have and had reached the point of being unable to conduct themselves properly.

Watching Tessa leave, Toshiro stood there with butterflies in his stomach and a heart that pitter-pattered. With all the girlfriends from different cultures that he had in his lifetime, he had never felt this way before. He felt that it was too bad that the kiss hadn't lasted longer and that she wasn't nicer so that he could have gotten her number. But an older woman like that was too stiff and serious. At 29 years old, he was used to girls ten years younger who laughed at his jokes and said silly things; they were girls who spent hours on their hair, makeup, manicures, pedicures, and trendy clothes. But the woman he had kissed possessed a natural beauty without a need for makeup and painted nails. Even her air-dried hair complimented her light complexion and charismatic eyes. Although she looked older than him, he was attracted to her.

During the kiss, his body had trembled. It had been so out of character for him to kiss a stranger. He found himself lost in her beautiful eyes when she rebuked him. When he headed back to his friends, they all asked, "How was it?"

"It was perfect," he answered with a silly smile and dreamy eyes.

"I guess it was worth the slap," Souji said.

"So worth it that I would do it all over again." Toshiro felt an unfamiliar emotion in him that he hadn't felt before about anyone.

"You wish," Souji said. "A woman like that would have no interest in hanging out with someone your age."

After her encounter with Toshiro and several more hours of sightseeing, Tessa returned to Akira's place and let herself in. Akira was still at work, and Tessa needed to rest from all the walking she had done. Her feet were sore and her body ached. She wished she could take a day to rest up, but her participation in the demonstration was essential, and missing it was out of the question. So she set her phone's alarm clock, fluffed her pillow, and fell asleep on the sofa.

Ninety minutes later, the soft music of her alarm woke her up. It was still light outside, and she felt refreshed and ready to work. She opened her laptop, signed into her Twitter and Facebook accounts, and began posting about the upcoming protest in Shibuya and asking her followers to help make it go viral. She emailed American journalists who lived in Japan to ask if they could get the word out. She knew this was a longshot; she had emailed them while she was in the U.S. and did not get responses, but she had nothing to lose by sending them a reminder. Maybe, if it was a slow news day, radio or TV stations would come out and cover the story. Even if she could get one of the local journalists to write a short article about the protest, it would be something; and something was always better than nothing.

CHAPTER 4

Carrying her handbag, which held a hidden folder filled with pamphlets, Tessa went to Maxell Aqua Park Shinagawa. She would have never purchased a ticket and contributed to the profit margin of any place that kept marine creatures in captivity, but the ticket was given to her by a friendly tourist who didn't have time to go. Tessa had used Akira's printer to make pamphlets about the cruelty that sea creatures endured in captivity. She was planning to discreetly leave them around the park for visitors to read.

Once inside the park, she noticed that the design of the indoor area was set to create a soothing atmosphere for the visitors, which was also a terrible environment for the captured marine life. The dark interior was dimly lit with small yellow, green, pink, orange, and blue lights. The inside of the tanks and enclosures, however, was brightly illuminated by artificial lighting. These lights were irritating for the creatures because, in their natural ocean environment, there are no artificial lights—only subtle, natural lighting from the sun and moon. The night before, she had listened to China Global Television Network's news show, which reported how organisms depend on the sun and moon to regulate their behavior. Without natural lighting, they become confused, which causes them to move around erratically.

Tessa observed that in a larger tank, a glass tunnel with visitors walking underneath it, giant stingrays, manta rays, and sawfishes moved round and round because there was no room to do much else, whereas, in the ocean, they could travel for miles. In another tank, a school of electric blue acara moved aimlessly in circles, and a guitarfish lay quietly on the bottom even though, as ocean bottom dwellers, they usually hunt for their food and perform impressive acrobatic movements out of the water, such as jumps and pirouettes.

An avid listener of NPR, Tessa followed an interview with Dr. Jonathan Balcombe, the director of animal sentience at the Humane Society Institute for Science and Policy. During the interview, he pointed out that fish have conscious awareness, feel pain, and some can recognize human faces. As a member of People for the Ethical Treatment of Animals, also known as PETA, Tessa learned from the organization that divers often spray poisons into the aquatic environment to stun the fish and capture them. Half of them die, and the 40 percent that survives the poisoning, die in transport; only 10 percent make it to their destinations. The biggest and most well-maintained aquarium can't compare to the open ocean, according to PETA.

So, knowing that all sizes of fish have conscious awareness, feel pain and love, and recognize human faces, Tessa marveled sadly at how they could be treated so poorly. She wandered into a jellyfish room. These invertebrates were trapped inside cylindrical tanks. Some of the tanks were too full, and the creatures kept bumping into each other. Continuous lights flashed inside the tubes, making the jellyfish look pink, yellow, green, and other colors. Tessa knew that, just like human beings, jellyfish needed quiet time at night to help them rest and conserve energy. If disturbed, they would be less active the next day. Throughout the day, people took pictures of them with their cellphones. Children kept tapping on the glass containers, agitating the jellyfish. Tessa wondered how humans would feel if they were captured, put in tanks, and then stared at by other lifeforms.

In another room, all the viewing enclosures were small. She saw a sea lion and seal that had no room to move. She also saw lethargic penguins with droopy heads hanging toward the ground.

Tessa walked over to an area with rows of bleachers encircling a pool that was too small for the dolphins, whales, and porpoises trying to swim around inside it. The tanks where they were kept after shows were even smaller. An article on Ric O' Barry's Dolphin Project, a website created by a former dolphin trainer, reported that dolphins suffered undue stress from being held in small, sterile enclosures and from being forced to be with other mammals and entertain visitors. He revealed that many captive dolphins are regularly treated with ulcer medication or antidepressants to alleviate their stress. Even the largest aquatic facilities would not be able to duplicate a dolphin's natural habitat in which they usually live wild and free.

The handouts Tessa intended to distribute would make visitors think twice before purchasing their next ticket. The pamphlets read:

Dolphins and orcas live in large social groups and swim freely up to 80 miles per day at the speed of 20 miles per hour in the open ocean. Trapped in a tank, moving in circles, and performing meaningless tricks stresses dolphins and causes neurotic behavior. The Whale and Dolphin Conservation Society says that in the wild, orcas live for approximately 70 years and dolphins live for about 40. In captivity, their lifespans shorten drastically. Dolphins, orcas, and porpoises use echolocation to send out soundwaves that produce echoes in the environment. They use the echoes to navigate, hunt, and protect themselves from predators. According to Ric O'Barry's Dolphin Project, a website created by a former dolphin trainer, when these sociable mammals are in captivity, they have to lower the frequency of their communications because they are confined to tanks. This reduction in vocalization is unnatural. As a result of sound deprivation and boredom, dolphins and other cetaceans often attempt to commit suicide by banging their heads against the walls of their tanks. Those that live, lead stressful lives.

After distributing the pamphlets to visitors, Tessa left before the dolphin show started because she could not bring herself to watch it. She imagined that the audience members would aah and ooh as the dolphins did their tricks, but what they didn't know was that the dolphins were deprived of food. In the ocean, they would consume 22 to 50 pounds of live fish per day. Tessa had read in a HuffPost online interview with Gail Woon, a former dolphin trainer, that in captivity, food was withheld until the dolphin learned a trick. Dolphins had to get used to a diet of dead fish and undergo rigorous training against their will. Most American aquariums, water parks, and places that charged customers to swim with dolphins trained these voiceless creatures the same way. For the first time, Tessa began to question her presence in a foreign country when her own country behaved just as badly.

But no. She had to do this. The U.S. had strict animal-rights protection laws and numerous organizations spoke out against animal cruelty. Japan, however, lacked comparable protection.

Japan's guidelines on animal welfare did not apply to dolphins and whales when it came to large-scale commercial hunts. The way Japanese fishermen slaughtered dolphins was beyond inhumane. Tessa had to be here. It was personal. For her, it had all started in Japan, and it would have to end here.

Tessa thought about her volunteer work at the Pacific Marine Mammal Center. She loved donating her time there and contributing to the goal of healing, rehabilitating, and releasing sea mammals instead of keeping them in captivity. And today, watching so many creatures in enclosures was a difficult pill for her to swallow.

Distraught and saddened that there wasn't more that she could do, Tessa left the aqua park. At least she had left brochures, and hopefully, some of the visitors would read them. She took the subway from the Shingawa Station toward Shinjuku Gyoen National Garden in western Tokyo. To clear her head and regroup, she needed a serene place to get away from it all. There was so much chatter in her brain: her father admonishing her, her guilt that she had just abandoned those poor dolphins, and her aunt telling her long ago to stay out of it. After exiting the subway, Tessa bought a vegan bento box at the station and once she got to Shinjuku, she headed for the garden. It was spread over 144 acres and had a traditional Japanese garden with a koi pond and bridges; a French garden with its symmetrical design and tree-lined paths; and an English landscape garden with expansive green lawns.

At the Japanese garden, Tessa watched butterflies drink the nectar of flowers. She fed the fish in the koi pond and stood on a bridge to take several shots of the picturesque scenery. Less shaken, she headed to the French garden she had heard so much about and began sauntering down a sycamore-lined path. She sat on a bench and pulled out her beautifully wrapped bento box, chopsticks, and jasmine tea. Inside, the box cradled an artistically arranged mini-feast of multigrain rice, white rice, marinated tofu, and colorful vegetables. It almost looked much too pretty to eat. As she enjoyed her meal and drank her fragrant tea, Tessa took in her surroundings. A mother pushed a toddler in a stroller and carried her younger child in a strap wrapped around her. An elderly man sat at a bench and sketched the landscape. Two trendy-looking girls wearing miniskirts and hats chatted and sniggered. A group of middle-aged women used fanciful umbrellas to keep the sun from aging their flawless complexions. Showing off one's legs by wearing miniskirts was common in Japan, but showing one's shoulders and cleavage was taboo. Wearing hats and using umbrellas was favored because having a fair complexion was important and desirable for many Japanese women. Tessa, on the other hand, loved the sun and a good tan. *Funny, how everyone's perspective is so different*, she thought. When she finished eating, Tessa placed her trash in a plastic bag and put it in her handbag. In Japan, it was rare to see public trash cans. People carried around small plastic bags to put their trash in until they could discard it at home.

To outsiders, Japan's trash etiquette is complex and one of the reasons why landlords do not like to rent apartments to foreigners. For example, garbage is separated into many different categories: combustible, non-combustible, recyclable, metal, ceramic, glass, oversized trash, and so on. They even give households calendars as to which day of the week and what time of the day they are allowed to dispose of their trash. There are even quizzes on how to dispose of waste on YouTube because foreigners often get it wrong. Japanese take their rubbish disposal quite seriously and if someone does not follow the rules, they get mad. Luckily for Tessa, Akira was there to help her sort it all out.

As Tessa continued people-watching, she noticed a Japanese couple holding hands and walking in her direction. *How nice*, she thought. But as the two got closer, Tessa's smile faded. There he was, the man who had kissed her, along with a much younger-looking girl. Even though Tessa had enjoyed the kiss, she was still angry about what he had done. Tessa got up and moved toward him, planning to get back at him for embarrassing her. She felt that she needed to teach him a lesson. Taking long strides, Tessa quickly approached him.

When he saw her, his eyes widened in surprise. But before he could utter a word, she grabbed him and gave him a long kiss, thinking this would embarrass him in front of his date. He let go of his girlfriend's hand and wrapped his arms around Tessa and kissed her back. Once again, she felt her space was violated. His grip was tight around her, and she fought every feeling within her as she pushed him away. She turned to his date and said, "Sorry, but he had it coming. It wasn't personal, and I have no feelings for him." What Tessa didn't know was that the girl didn't understand a word she had said. Tessa walked away, leaving Toshiro and his girlfriend, Kaiya, dumbfounded.

Kaiya was the daughter of a wealthy businessman. Both her parents and Toshiro's hoped that one day they would marry. Although Toshiro enjoyed being with her, he was not yet ready for marriage.

"Who is she?" Kaiya asked him.

"I, uh, I don't know," he stammered and grabbed her hand. "Some crazy woman, I guess."

"And yet, you kissed her back. I really don't understand you, Toshiro," she said, releasing his hand and giving him an angry look.

"I don't know her. This wasn't my fault," he shrugged, scared to explain what he had done the day before.

"Go to hell," she said and walked away.

"Wait! Let me take you home."

Kaiya didn't bother looking back when she said, "I'll take a taxi." Kaiya knew Toshiro's reputation with women, but she hoped that she could change him and make him settle down.

Later that day when Toshiro went home to change before heading out to his office, he could not stop thinking about Tessa. He mused that she looked older than he and, judging from her accent, might be an American. He preferred younger Japanese and European girls. She intrigued him, but he had no idea how to contact her. He figured that he would never run into her again, but what had started as a dare turned into an uncontrollable fixation. She was bold, confident, and mature. He knew that what he was feeling was nothing but a temporary obsession. And she even wasn't his type. Boyishly dressed, she was beautiful, yet plain and not all that feminine. So why was he so taken by her?

That evening, Tessa sat on the floor behind Akira's coffee table working with poster boards, markers, and flyers for the upcoming protest. She thought about her run-in with the handsome stranger, flattered that a twenty-something guy was interested in her. Not that she wanted him; he was way too young for her. Even if he had been her age, she didn't want to fall for someone here since she was going home in less than two weeks. She tried to put him out of her mind and focus on the protest. *Tomorrow the protestors will be gathering near the busiest intersection in Tokyo*, Tessa thought as she went back to working on the signs and the flyers they were planning to hand out.

Akira was in her bedroom changing from her work clothes into a pair of comfortable pants and a T-shirt. She headed into the kitchen to make herself a cup of tea and noticed that Tessa was already preparing for the protest.

"Would you like some tea?" Akira asked, starting some mint tea in a glass teapot for herself.

"No, thanks. I'm good," Tessa responded. She was using a red marker to color blood against a dolphin's skin.

"I thought you were going to wait so that we could do that together," Akira said.

"There's plenty of work left. We still have to come up with ideas for the flyers," Tessa answered without looking up.

"I already made the flyers and passed them out at college campuses," Akira said, looking at Tessa's drawing. "Gruesome!"

"You think so? I was thinking that it needs more wounds and blood to make it look more authentic," Tessa said, looking up. "We need different flyers geared toward different demographics: parents, students, young professionals."

"Okay, Okay. But how are you feeling? Still jet-lagged?"

"Nope," Tessa replied and returned her attention to her drawing.

"Something's bothering you?" Akira asked, folding both arms firmly over her chest. Tessa seemed to be unusually focused and didn't want to chat at all.

"No. Just jitters about our march this weekend," she said. She was holding a marker in her left hand and moving it swiftly back and forth on the paper to put the final touches on before starting a new poster.

"Don't worry about it. I've done this before. We'll be fine," she said. She poured tea into her cup and walked over to sit on the sofa.

Tessa continued with her painting. "You know, Japanese men?"

Akira's ears perked up. "Yeah, What about them?"

"Do they treat women well?"

"It depends. If they're in love, yes. If not, they cheat. I mean after marriage sometimes they change. They expect more and give less."

"You're a great help." Tessa gave her a sideways glance, "That can describe any man. How do they treat foreign women?"

"Why? Don't tell me you have fallen for a Japanese guy already?" Akira jokingly said. "You've only been here three days."

"No. I was just curious about your culture, people, and relationships," she said, trying to sound as casual as possible.

"I don't think so," Akira said, staring at Tessa inquisitively. "You met someone, didn't you? C'mon, who is he?"

"No one. Let's move on to tomorrow and the dolphins."

"Uh-uh, you're not going to get away that easily. You say you want to learn about our culture and people. Well, here it is. Once we know you well, we ask you about everything. Where are you going? What did you eat last night? Where did you go shopping? What time?"

"Really?" Tessa asked, astonished. She was a private person and kept most things to herself.

"Yes. No privacy. So, who is he?"

"My gosh, Akira, no one. Just some guy who grabbed and kissed me without asking."

"Whoa, back up a minute. You're sure he was Japanese?"

"I think so," she said, frowning.

"Well," Akira said, "Japanese men are the quiet type. They don't show their emotions, let alone grab a stranger and kiss them."

"Mmm, we don't do that in America either. I think he had one too many drinks. He tasted like beer." She went on to tell Akira what had happened.

"No way, no way," Akira uttered, eyes widening. "I have to meet this guy."

"I doubt I will see him again. And anyway, he was with another girl," she said, sounding disappointed. But why be disappointed? She had no interest in him. She was there for a single purpose, and any guy would just be a distraction that she did not need.

"I know this Chinese girl one floor down. She's a tarot card reader. Let's go see her." Akira believed in New Age practices of connecting to other people through energy and psychics. Her newest interest was meditation and out-of-body experiences.

"Are you nuts? If she's so good at reading people's fortunes, she would read her own and become rich."

Akira clucked. "You know they can't read their own fortunes—only those of strangers."

"Yes, suckers willing to lose their hard-earned money."

"You're too cynical. C'mon, if anything, it'll be good fun."

"I'm not going, and I have already forgotten about what we were discussing. Let's work on these for an hour and then go eat."

CHAPTER 5

Dinnertime. Four subway stations and fifty minutes later, Tessa and Akira reached Tsukishima, or Moon Island, a manmade island in the Chuo district. A meld of Japanese and Western culture in the center of Tokyo, the Chuo Ward was made up of modern structures, like high-end housing, retail stores, and restaurants, as well as historical features, such as shrines, old Japanese houses, and back alleys with little cafés and shops selling local wares. Akira wanted Tessa to experience the cuisine at Kishidaya, a famous neighborhood *izakaya*. *Izakaya* was often translated as "gastropub," though the literal meaning of the word translated as "stay sake shop." The historical Kishidaya began as a liquor store a century ago but now was a popular, informal tavern with an all-female staff. After an hour, Akira and Tessa were finally seated at a U-shaped fifteen-seat counter. Diners noisily chatted just like in any Japanese pub, which were louder than more conventional restaurants or coffee shops.

"Shall I order for you?" asked Akira.

"Thank you, would you?" responded Tessa, since everything was written in Japanese.

After explaining to Tessa what she was ordering, Akira asked a server for two whiskey highballs and the house specialties: *gyū-nikomi,* a beef tendon stew, for her, and *nikomi udon,* a miso noodle soup, fried tofu, assorted vegetables, and egg for Tessa.

Tessa looked around her. Trapped in time almost 100 years ago, the pub had no frills. Patrons put their jackets on wall hooks. On the counter, there were *jujube* wooden cups filled with chopsticks. Black and white strips of paper with Japanese words written on them were taped to the walls.

"What are those?" Tessa asked Akira, but before she could answer, the man next to her said, "That's the menu. First time here?"

"Yes," she answered in surprise, happy to hear an English-speaking voice. "Lucky for me, my friend's here to translate."

"I can help you out. My name is Ethan," he said, extending his hand to shake hers. He admired her blue-gray fitted sweater and thought it looked pretty on her.

"Hi, I'm Tessa," she said, shaking his hand. In his 30s, he had blond wavy hair and looked like a football player, even though he was wearing a business suit.

"It's quite small here, and I'm a big guy. If I move and bump into you, I'd like to apologize ahead of time."

"No worries," she said, turning to face Akira, who looked very interested in getting to know him.

"This is my friend, Akira. Akira, this is Ethan."

"Nice to meet you, Akira," he said, slightly nodding his head to bow, as is customary when meeting someone in Japan.

"Likewise," Akira said. "You work nearby?"

"Yes, I work for QZMZ. I am in charge of web design and maintenance."

QZMZ Inc. was an extremely successful Japanese-owned clothing retail company with stores not only in Japan but also in France, Germany, Australia, Switzerland, and Denmark, with plans to expand to China, Austria, and the United States.

"I used to work for QZMZ Australia long ago," Akira said. "I was in charge of inventory control."

"Were you? Then you and I have a lot to talk about," Ethan said, taking a sip of his whiskey and eyeing the way her cherry highlights commingled with her shiny black hair.

"It's been a while. I'm a tour guide now. Less pay, but better hours," She said, sweeping her bangs to the side.

"Yeah. Working for a Japanese company can be stressful."

And I don't miss it, Akira wanted to say.

Letting Ethan take the lead to talk about his work, Akira thought it best not to bring up her experience of working for a Japanese-owned business. She often worked overtime without pay and was made to feel guilty about using her vacation days. The Japanese came up with the term *karouchi*, which meant death by overwork. It was legally recognized in Japan as a cause of death, and Akira understood why. The country's average wage was below $40,000, but was much higher if in IT, finance, or management.

Akira knew that she would have better job security if she signed a contract, but in return, her employer would expect extreme loyalty and time commitment. Work would have to take precedence over friends, family, and leisure time. And raises were hard to come by; contract employees weren't rewarded on merit but seniority and often had to work late after others went home.

Ethan seemed to share many of Akira's unspoken sentiments about the state of Japan's economic situation, saying, "Poverty is on the rise here and the middle class is slowly disappearing, even if the government tries to portray the country as economically stable and prosperous."

Akira added a nod and a "yes" here and there, but she didn't feel completely comfortable expressing her feelings about the government even though she agreed.

Tessa sat there silently, listening to them. She was happy that they had hit it off. But she was in-between the two and felt like a third wheel. She asked Akira to switch seats with her so that Akira could sit next to Ethan.

Now closer, Akira asked Ethan, "You're here by yourself?"

"Oh, no. My friend went to use the bathroom."

From the way he looked at her, Akira could tell that he liked her, and the feeling was mutual. "So, you have a girlfriend?"

He laughed. "No, I'm on my own. No girlfriend. Not yet, anyway."

The night is young, Akira thought. "Me neither. That is, I'm on my own, too."

Ethan's friend returned from the bathroom. When Tessa saw him, she spat out some of her drink and sputtered "Shit!" and then covered her mouth.

Toshiro looked nervous but grinned. "We usually greet people in the evening by saying *konbanwa*," he teased.

"You two know each other?" Ethan asked.

"Yes. No. Well, ..." The two of them replied in unison, then cleared their throats.

Akira turned to Tessa and whispered, "This is the guy you kissed?"

Tessa nodded her head and looked embarrassed.

"*Yaozaaa*, he is hot," she said, making a sizzling noise that only Tessa could hear.

Dressed in a dark purple suit, white shirt, and black tie, Toshiro looked debonair and not at all like the tipsy guy who had grabbed and kissed her. "Can I get anyone a drink?" he asked. Since he was busy staring at Tessa, he hadn't even noticed that everyone's glass was still half full.

Toshiro ordered a whiskey neat to calm himself. Why was he attracted to this woman? And why did he keep running into her? He decided that this time he wasn't about to let her get away. This must be fate. Meeting a stranger three times in two days couldn't possibly be just an accident. "So, how do you all know each other?" Toshiro asked Ethan.

"We only just met," he said and introduced him to Akira. "And you already know Tessa, except that neither of you has told me how you know each other."

So her name is Tessa. I have kissed this woman twice and just learned her name. Tessa—what a pretty name, Toshiro thought.

Tessa was flushed. All she could think of was the last time they had kissed in front of his date.

Toshiro nodded his head to Akira and then looked over to Tessa, "Finally, I get to know your name." Not knowing that Akira already knew how they had met, Toshiro decided to take the tension away and said, "We met at a gathering through acquaintances but never met formally."

Tessa gave him a look of appreciation for not embarrassing her.

Their food arrived and Akira said, "Have you guys ordered?"

"We were just about finished before the two of you arrived," replied Ethan. "Too bad for us. I think they're expecting us to leave soon so that they can turn over our table."

"Now that is too bad," Akira said, flirting with her eyes.

"Maybe we can get together when you're done with your dinners? There's a place called Rainbow Karaoke, not too far from here. What do you say?" Ethan offered.

"Oh, no thanks," said Tessa. "We have an early day tomorrow. And besides, I can't sing."

"We can't either," Ethan replied. "It'll just be good fun. C'mon, how about it?"

Before Tessa could refuse again, Akira jumped in: "That sounds great." She took out her cell phone and typed in the name of the karaoke place to see where it was located.

Tessa said, "You guys go. I'm really tired and going to turn in early."

But Toshiro gazed into her eyes and insisted, "Please come. We'll make sure you'll have a nice time. Promise."

Maybe it was the way he looked at her or the soothing tones of his voice that coaxed her, but she found it difficult to say no. "Fine. I'll come, but only for a few songs. I mean it when I say that I have a terrible voice."

He chuckled. "We'll see the two of you at 9."

Ethan said, "We should go. There are a lot of people waiting for a table."

Toshiro downed his drink and they left.

Akira turned to Tessa and said, "Do you have any idea who he is?"

"Who? Toshiro?"

"His father is one of the five owners of QZMZ. It's a multibillion-dollar company. How in the world did you land this guy?" Akira asked.

"I didn't land anyone," she said, frowning. "I already told you about the unfortunate way we met. He has a lot of growing up to do, and I'm too old to teach him. He needs to figure out things on his own." She picked up her whiskey glass and took a swig.

Akira noticed Tessa's shaky hand and pushed further. "Maybe so, but you look good for your age. You're fit and have no wrinkles."

"My body has nothing to do with it. He's too immature," Tessa said.

"You know what they say about men in their 20s and women in their 40s? Great sex!"

"First of all, I just turned forty last month. And second, you don't know how old he is. And third, it's never going to happen, sex that is."

"Oh c'mon. Have a little fun," Akira said, looking mischievously at her friend.

"Change the subject, will you?" Tessa responded, getting irritated with Akira.

"Okay, Okay. So, I'm guessing about seventy-five people are going to show up at the march tomorrow. At least that's what I told the officials when I filled out the forms for a permit."

"Wish we could get a lot more people," Tessa said, slurping her miso soup. "Mmm, this is so good."

Akira did not hear her. Her mind was too busy plotting. "You know, Toshiro and his family?"

"Oh, we're back to him again?" Tessa dropped her spoon into her soup.

"No, no. I was just thinking. His family is often on the society pages of the paper. And his father, Riku Yokoyama, made the cover of several business magazines."

"So?"

"So, we can use him," Akira suggested.

"What are you talking about?" Tessa asked, noticing a young couple that just got seated across from them. They seemed to be bickering, and it reminded her of when she and her husband would argue whenever they went out to dinner.

"If we can convince him to join us at the protest tomorrow, we may actually get some media coverage," Akira said.

"Oh no, I don't want to use him," Tessa said with a panicky tone. She did not want to have anything to do with this man and wished that they had gone elsewhere for dinner. She did not know why, but her gut told her to stay away from him.

"Why not?" Akira said and shrugged. "We could get a lot of attention for our cause."

"I don't like using people. It's just not right."

"Listen to me for a minute. Imagine the publicity we could get if members of the media show up." Akira didn't get her. All along Tessa had been telling her how important the demonstration was and now, given the opportunity to make it count, she was turning it down because she didn't want to use someone. What was all that about? Tessa didn't act as though she cared for Toshiro. So what was the big deal?

"I know, but no." She crinkled her nose.

"Okay. But think about it. It may do us some good."

After dinner, they met Toshiro and Ethan at Rainbow Karaoke inside the Shibuya Modi building, a giant, brightly-lit mall with lots of escalators, hip stores, and eateries. A white brick wall marked Rainbow Karaoke in the colors of the rainbow led to the reception area, which was brightened by stripes of multicolored lights above their heads. Toshiro and Ethan paid at the reception desk. The place had an artsy, urban feel to it. Tessa noticed a wall with colorful letters: "No Rain ... No Rainbow," and a row of multicolored metal chairs. Behind an ice cream and soft drink bar was a wall-to-wall poster of New York City. There were twenty-seven private karaoke rooms divided by a hallway and decorated with plants, ornate lampposts, and wooden benches.

Toshiro led the way to their room. On their way, Tessa was surprised to see a white wall painted with a caricature of a dancing Elvis Presley with writing that said, "Everybody Let's Rock." Musicians sometimes used these rooms to practice. Toshiro told them that each room was unique and pointed at one of the larger rooms that had guitars, drums, and a digital keyboard.

Once inside their room, they chose drinks from a large menu and Toshiro used a wall phone to order them. The room was outfitted with a wide-screen TV, a microphone, sound equipment, and an olive leather sofa resting against a blue-and-white-horizontal-striped wall with white lights flashing against it to create a clublike atmosphere. Ethan scrolled through a tablet with a menu of songs and chose Whitney Houston's "I Will Always Love You." To make Tessa feel more comfortable, they decided to do a sing-along, but Tessa simply mouthed the words.

Toshiro put his arm around her shoulder and said, "You cannot cheat. You have to sing with us."

Her heart seemed to possess nervous energy. She removed his arm from her shoulder and began singing, hoping to turn him off. "And I will always love you … ooh ooh I … will always love you …" she sang, unable to hit the high notes and sounding completely ridiculous. Instead of Toshiro losing all interest in her, they all started laughing so hard that Ethan's drink came out of his nose. Once everyone had a few more drinks and started feeling tipsy, no one even noticed how poorly Tessa sang. Eventually, they all sat next to each other, leaning their heads back against the sofa. Ethan and Akira started making out, which was awkward for Tessa and Toshiro.

Toshiro asked Tessa, "Do you want to go for a walk?"

"It is getting rather late, and I have an early day tomorrow," she replied. "You mind walking us toward the Shibuya Station?" It was around 11 pm, and the last subway line was at 12.

"Ethan has a car; he can give us all a ride," Toshiro offered.

"Thank you. Maybe another time." She wasn't about to get into the car of a stranger, especially one who had been drinking.

Toshiro turned to the other two and said, "I'm walking Tessa to the station. You guys want to come along?"

Tessa could tell that they didn't want to, but Akira nodded yes anyway. Tessa was a guest, and Akira wasn't about to abandon her.

Heading toward the station, Ethan and Akira lagged and held hands. Toshiro walked with his hands in his pockets. After Tessa had moved his arm away from her shoulder, he decided to back off and get to know her. Tessa walked with her arms folded across her chest and contemplated asking him to attend the protest. *No,* she protested to herself, *she couldn't use him like that. But his presence at the demonstration would be so helpful.*

Toshiro noticed Tessa deep in thought. "Something on your mind?"

"Oh, no, well, actually, um, I was wondering if you're free tomorrow?"

"Yes, why?" he responded without hesitation, knowing it wasn't true. He had promised to spend the day with his family and had no idea how he was going to get out of it, but for Tessa, he would find a way.

"Akira and I … never mind."

"What is it? Just say it."

"I don't know if you're interested. Well, there is this protest," she confessed, as her voice faded.

"A protest? What about?"

"Not sure you'd be interested." Part of her hoped that he would say no, and another part of her needed him to say yes because it would be so good for her cause.

"Tessa, what is it that you're trying to say?" he asked, a bit frustrated, not quite understanding why she was struggling to communicate.

Akira, who was now walking just behind them with Ethan, jumped in and said, "Sorry, I didn't mean to eavesdrop, but we've put together a demonstration against Taiji dolphin drive hunts. Do you want to participate? You too, Ethan."

"We sure could use your and Ethan's help holding signs as we march from Shibuya to Harajuku," Tessa added with more confidence now that Akira had stepped in.

Ethan declined. He was catching a flight in the morning to Osaka to meet up with friends.

"A protest about the killing of dolphins?" Toshiro asked. He hadn't heard anything about it.

"You know, don't feel pressured to do this," said Tessa. "I'm sure you have things to do."

Toshiro squeezed her arm and replied, "No, I am interested. I'd like to hear what you have to say."

"Well, it isn't really a night-on-the-town kind of conversation." Tessa felt that most people did not like to get into serious topics while having fun.

"Tell me. I'd like to learn."

"You know Taiji and the problem with the dolphin drive hunt and how they are killed?"

"I read about it years ago, but had forgotten all about it." He didn't know what else to say. Japan was a country with plenty of restaurants where people ate all sorts of creatures.

"Then maybe you know about the documentary called, *The Cove*? It's about how dolphins in Taiji are driven into a cove by fishermen and killed."

"I've heard about the killings and documentary but have never seen it."

"As far as I know, the Japanese media does not cover the hunt," explained Tessa, "In fact, when Caroline Kennedy was the U.S.

ambassador to Japan, she said the drives were inhumane, and lots of Japanese criticized her on social media, saying that the dolphin hunts were a tradition."

Bolstered by a new confidence, Tessa spoke with energy and passion. "The dolphin captivity industry subsidizes these hunts and pays a lot of money so that they can get show-quality dolphins."

"How are they killed?" Toshiro asked with intense curiosity.

"Entire families used to be beaten to death," said Tessa. "But because of all the negative reactions around the world, many fishermen are pulling the dolphins underneath plastic tarps, so no one can see or film the actual slaughter. They claim that the new method of execution is humane, but now they kill them by pushing a sharp metal spike into their necks to sever the spinal cord to produce what they call 'instant humane death,'" Akira said, making quotation marks with her fingers.

"That doesn't sound very humane," Toshiro said, shaking his head.

"It is not, and they know it," Tessa said. "Now, instead of the entire cove turning red from the dolphins' blood, the fishermen push wooden corks into their wounds to prevent the blood from spilling out. There is film footage from hidden cameras showing the dolphins slapping their tails in agonizing pain until they die."

Toshiro winced, dismayed that this was going on in his country and that the government allowed it.

"Some can't even slap their tails because the fishermen tie them with ropes to prevent them from escaping. Then they drown them by holding them upside down in water," Akira inserted.

"Those that are spared are usually the young ones that are show quality," Tessa continued. She was beginning to show how upset the situation made her. "Even the babies are not spared. Some activists reported that the fishermen laugh out loud as the dolphins suffer."

"I did not know this," Toshiro said, frowning and getting goosebumps all over his body. He had read about the killings, but he had also heard the fishermen's argument that the drives were done humanely and killing the dolphins was a tradition essential to their livelihoods.

"When they forcibly hold the babies underwater," said Tessa. "The whole pod, or rather the group of family and friends that live together, fights to save the babies, but it's no use. The fishermen have the upper hand."

Ethan said, "I saw *The Cove* documentary. It's really horrible how they are mistreated."

"I've never seen it," Toshiro said, but the description made him feel cold and disturbed.

"Tomorrow after the protest, we're having a private showing for high school and college students at the Hyatt hotel," Akira added. "Why don't you come and see it?"

"Yes, sure," he said. Toshiro was ambivalent. He was worried that once he saw it, he would stop eating all seafood. He loved seafood.

"In *The Cove*, you can see how fishermen stab the dolphins with sharp hooks and haul the still-living dolphins onto their boats," explained Tessa. "The dolphins thrash about in their own blood, and their screams fill the air."

"That's horrible," said Toshiro.

Tessa continued. "The Japanese government was not too pleased when *The Cove* documentary came out, and it sided with the fishermen. I read an article in *The Washington Post*, reporting that the mayor of Taiji had powerful connections to senior leaders.

Because of that, the town had plenty of support for the hunts and was able to withstand international criticism."

Ethan jumped in, "Some dolphins are still alive and moving when they are hauled to the slaughterhouse."

"I wonder why nothing is being done about it," Toshiro replied.

"Many organizations are working to end this," Akira said.

Tessa noted, "You look disappointed, but your country is no different than ours when it comes to the inhumane treatment of animals used for food. Different groups support different causes. My cause is the protection of dolphins and whales, though, for these next two weeks, I am focusing on dolphins."

"What about the whales?" Toshiro asked.

"Some species are endangered yet killed inhumanely," she replied. "Fishermen often use grenades and harpoons to kill the whales. These explode inside their bodies, but it doesn't always kill them instantly."

Tessa went on, "The international whaling commission has banned commercial whaling, but it still happens all the time. And by the way, killer whales are actually dolphins."

"I did not know that."

"Most people don't," Tessa replied.

Toshiro was glad that he had met Tessa. She was different than his other friends, who were mostly self-absorbed and frivolous. Tessa was interesting, passionate, and confident. Toshiro had never been passionate about much. And most of the women he had dated were insecure about their looks, always needy, and desperate for compliments.

Tessa thought Toshiro was nice and after taking a closer look at him, she realized that he wasn't as young as she had originally thought, though he sometimes acted like a boy rather than a man. She had run into him twice during workdays, seemingly living a carefree life. She wondered if he ever worked. And if not, did his parents support him? She remembered her first husband, who was lazy and had lived off of her. She didn't want to even consider dating someone who had no goals and wasted his life away.

"Here we are," Tessa said when they reached the Shibuya Station.

"You're sure you don't want us to give you a ride? Ethan's car is parked not far from the station," Toshiro said.

Before Akira could respond, Tessa interrupted: "Oh, no. We're good. Thanks." She didn't know what they would expect from them after dropping them off. Akira and Ethan were already all over each other, and Tessa had no intention of getting that close to Toshiro. And what if Akira invited them up to her place? Then what? No, it would be too awkward.

Ethan gave Akira a long kiss and promised to call her.

Tessa shook hands with Toshiro and said, "See you tomorrow at the protest."

As they began to part, Toshiro stopped and said, "You forgot to tell me the location of the protest."

Tessa reached in her handbag and gave him a flyer.

He looked at it and said, "I guess you come prepared. How did you know I would say yes and join you?"

"I didn't, but I hoped that you would," she said, winking. "*Oyasumi nasa.*"

"Goodnight," Ethan said, waving.

"*Oyasumi,*" Toshiro said, bowing slightly.

CHAPTER 6

The day was sunny without a cloud in the sky. Hundreds gathered in Shibuya near the Hachikō, a noted statue of an Akita, known for his loyalty to his owner. Japanese and international activists of all ages held signs and banners written in their native languages and with pictures of trapped dolphins. Most of the signs said, "Say no to dolphin slaughter, say no to aquariums, say no to captivity."

Akira led the protest with a bullhorn in hand. Behind her, Toshiro and Tessa held up a horizontal banner that said, "Stop the slaughter of dolphins" in Japanese and English. A teenage girl was wearing a dolphin costume; a Japanese man in his 70s held a big dolphin balloon; those who didn't want to be identified wore surgical masks. Seven police officers protected the activists with their whistles and red sticks to wave traffic away from them. At the end of the protest line, a police car with flashing lights slowed down the traffic that followed. Pedestrians stopped to see what was happening. Some glanced over as they walked by. One Japanese onlooker flipped them the bird, and Tessa wondered if most of the country's citizens felt the same way. Toshiro was there to support Tessa. If she hadn't been here, he would not have shown up. Photographers and videographers documented the protest, both amateurs and professionals.

Six activists were interviewed by a Japanese newspaper, including Tessa and Akira.

Tessa went on the record saying, "We're here to give a voice to the dolphins abused by the Taiji fishermen."

Akira added, "We must put a stop to the brutal slaughter of these cetaceans."

An American journalist living in Tokyo arranged to meet them the next day for an exclusive interview regarding the protest.

When the demonstration was over, Tessa, Akira, and Toshiro left to grab a late lunch at a sushi restaurant, recommended by Akira.

"Thanks for helping us out," Tessa said to Toshiro. She offered him and Akira chocolate mint patties, and they each took one.

"I didn't do much. I just held the banner with you," he said while admiring her. As the patty melted in his mouth, he realized that he had never tasted one of these candies before and he relished it. A new woman, a new taste. Both were excellent.

"All the same, you really came through for us, and lunch is on me." *He either doesn't care or he has no idea that I used him*, Tessa thought. She felt bad for not being up front with him. Earlier that morning, she and Akira had tried to contact bloggers, newspapers, and TV stations to let them know that the son of Riku Yokoyama was going to be at the demonstration. They had hoped it would entice the media to do some coverage, and their plan had worked. But this was the last time she was going to use him. Tessa was actually starting to like him.

"You can treat Toshiro, Tessa, but I can pay for my own lunch," Akira said. She fixed a few strands of her black hair that had escaped her ponytail.

"No, Akira. You have been so kind to me, letting me stay at your place. Please let me do this," Tessa insisted as she followed Akira and Toshiro. They seemed to know where they were going. Tessa's fair skin had a rosy glow from protesting in the sun.

"You already gave me a beautiful scarf."

"Oh, it was nothing. I'm treating and that's that."

"*Arigato!*"

"*Dou-itashi mashite*," Tessa responded.

At the restaurant counter, Tessa was mesmerized by how the meals were served. Invented about sixty-seven years ago by Yoshiaki Shiraishi, a restaurant owner who had trouble staffing his kitchen, a conveyor belt system transported the sushi from the kitchen to diners the same way an automated toy train would go around a track. Customers could grab what they wanted from the belt and, if they couldn't find what they were looking for, they could order it from a screen in front of them. Minutes later, a bell would ring and their order would arrive on the belt.

Tessa grabbed a *tamagoyaki*, an omelet made with a mixture of eggs, sugar, and soy sauce. Toshiro took the scallop *nigiri*, sushi rice with raw scallops. Akira put in a special order for *gyudon*, a bowl of rice with beef and onions. Even during an off-hour, all the seats were taken.

"So Tessa, is being an activist something you do full time?" Toshiro asked.

"Actually, I'm a veterinarian and work for a pet hospital in Los Angeles, treating small animals. But I also specialize in marine mammal medicine and volunteer at a rehabilitation facility," she said, wearily thinking about the long hours she always put in.

Besides wanting to help save the dolphins and whales, visiting Japan was also a much-needed vacation.

"Ah, no wonder you're so passionate about dolphins," remarked Toshiro.

"You know, Tessa doesn't have a boyfriend," Akira said to Toshiro.

Tessa glared at her so that she would shut up.

"What? I'm just stating the truth," she said, spotting her *gyudon* on the belt after the bell rang.

"Can we talk about something else, please?" Tessa said, picking up her *tamagoyaki* with a pair of chopsticks.

Toshiro smiled. *So, no boyfriend?* he thought. He believed that he had a good chance of winning her if he played his cards right and did not push too hard.

"Toshiro, what kind of work do you do?" Akira asked.

"I'm the regional manager of QZMZ. I oversee the operations of our Tokyo stores," he answered before downing a piece of raw scallop.

"What's your workday like usually?" Akira pushed brazenly.

"I visit our stores, solve problems, and get suggestions from managers. I prepare reports such as manager evaluations, feedback, or profit and loss reports," he said, pausing, to see if his response satisfied Akira. She seemed to be waiting for more information, so he continued. "I sit in meetings and have teleconferences with regional managers working in other cities. I also meet with our general manager and share ideas about how to improve things. Sometimes I have to hire, demote, or fire managers."

Toshiro felt awkward since he made himself sound more important than he actually was. The truth was that his father and colleagues did most of the work. If he ran into a problem at a store, he would pass it off to an entry-level employee. He had his assistant, Ena, visit all the stores to make sure everything was running smoothly, collect feedback, and prepare performance reports for each manager. He asked someone from the accounting department to prepare the profit and loss reports for each store and give them to the general manager; he didn't even look at them. If he had to fire or hire someone, he asked Ena to do it. He rarely attended meetings and never got into trouble for it because he was the son of one of the owners. Anything that Toshiro forgot to do, his father or the general manager would cover up for him. Toshiro could work harder, except that he didn't need the money, thanks to his grandparents, who had left him a sizable inheritance.

Tessa decided to change the subject. She didn't want to spend the rest of the time drilling him. "Akira, I thought the protest went well today, didn't you?"

Akira replied, "I wasn't expecting that many people. I think there were about 150—twice as many as expected."

"Plus, we have about 300 students committed to showing up at the Hyatt," Tessa said. The meeting room was paid for by generous, anonymous celebrities from Los Angeles.

"Three hundred? How did you guys manage that?" Toshiro asked in awe.

"It was all Akira. She's been handing out flyers to college students and seniors at high schools. Many RSVP'd."

Most Japanese citizens had a significant sense of responsibility. When they made a promise to show up, they would do so, unlike Americans who often assume that they won't be missed at a casual event.

"I didn't do anything extraordinary. I think I just got lucky. Younger people are more interested in animal welfare than older generations."

"You're being too modest," Tessa remarked.

"Akira, you should get a job in marketing. You seem to be good at it," Toshiro remarked.

"Thank you, no. I love being a tour guide. I set my own hours," she said, looking at her watch. "We should get going. It's almost 4. It'll take twenty-five minutes to get to the Hyatt, and then we have to set up and be ready by 5:30."

They arrived at the meeting room of the Grand Hyatt Tokyo in Roppongi Hills, an area in central Tokyo with vibrant nightlife, art museums, and luxury hotels. The room they had reserved had been set up theater style. Akira and Tessa spoke with the person in charge of showing *The Cove* and several ushers who had volunteered to help and went over their speeches.

Once the students took their seats, Akira stood at the podium and thanked everyone who had helped spread the word about the protest and attended the event. Tessa spoke as well and assured the audience that the international community was very interested in bringing an end to the dolphin hunt drives.

The film started, and Toshiro, Tessa, and Akira took their seats. Partway into the screening, Tessa glanced over at Toshiro, who looked pale. Toshiro wasn't feeling well at all, but forced himself to sit through the entire film. He was having a hard time handling all the blood and torture depicted in the documentary. Before it came to an end, he excused himself, headed to the nearest bathroom, and threw up. He regretted being there. He was too upset about what he had seen—fishermen banging against metal poles to confuse dolphins' sonar and lure families into a cove. He was haunted by the dolphins' screams as they were slaughtered. It was just as horrible as Ethan had said, and he wished that he didn't know anything about it. For the first time, he started thinking about where the food on his plate came from, how the creatures were killed, and how long they suffered. Many people eat beef, poultry, and seafood, but they order it at a restaurant or buy it at a grocery store. No one thinks about or sees the actual kill, and he wished that he had not either. When he finally emerged from the bathroom, Tessa was outside waiting.

Are you alright? Tessa asked, visibly concerned.

"I'm not feeling all that well. I think I'm going to go home," he said, the color drained from his face.

"Why don't you wait? Akira and I can go with you to make sure that you get home safely."

"I'll be fine. I'll call you," he said, leaving abruptly.

Akira came out of the meeting room and asked, "What's going on?"

"I'm not sure. Toshiro wasn't well and took off. I think the documentary affected him more than I expected."

"That's too bad, but the film just ended and we have to go back for the question and answer session."

Tessa took in a deep breath, let it out, and said, "Okay. Let's do this."

After wrapping up the Q&A, Tessa and Akira headed home. Tessa tried calling Toshiro, but the call went straight to his voicemail. "He's not answering. I'm worried," she told Akira.

"If he's not feeling well, he may have gone to bed."

"I don't know. I hope that nothing happened to him on the way home."

"Why don't you try him again in an hour or so?"

Tessa nodded and made some calming lavender tea for Akira and herself. "I feel good about what we did, but why do I feel so lousy?"

"You're just concerned about Toshiro. He'll be okay," Akira said, heading to the bathroom to freshen up and change. She was going out with some friends.

Fifteen minutes later, Toshiro texted and said that he was home and everything was fine. He said that he needed to take a nap because a couple of his friends were coming over later. He promised to call her tomorrow.

"You see? Akira said. You were worried for nothing. Why don't you come with me and my friends for drinks?"

"Thank you, but I'm just going to make some calls, work on my blog, and just relax."

"Okay. I'll be back soon. I'm tired, too."

"Have fun," Tessa said, knowing full well that there was no way Akira was going to come back early. She was a party girl and enjoyed drinking and socializing.

CHAPTER 7

Sunday. Lazy day. With the first protest over, Akira and Tessa could unwind, albeit in different ways. Akira was out with friends until three in the morning. Tessa stayed up past midnight to work on the vegan cashmere scarf she had started to knit on the plane. The two slept in until the sun was out and brightened the rooms.

"Hungry?" Akira asked Tessa. She had forced herself out of bed, showered, and was contemplating what to wear for that day's interview with Jessica, the American journalist. She opted for a red-plaid pleated skort and short-sleeve, high-neck, cream blouse.

"I am, but we don't have much time. And we can eat when we meet with Jessica," Tessa replied from behind the bathroom door, throwing on a pink and ecru striped button-down shirt. She added navy slacks for a polished look.

In a few minutes, they were off.

Akira lived in a neighborhood that felt like Sunday every day. Unlike the rushed life in most of Tokyo, Jiyūgaoka moved at a slower pace. It had a European atmosphere with cobblestone walkways, chic boutiques, creative restaurants, and bakeries displaying mouthwatering treats.

Their meeting was to take place at Kosoan, a century-old Japanese tea room. A set of flat, circular rocks led the way to the wood tea room fronted by a Japanese garden. After removing their shoes, Tessa and Akira went inside. The atmosphere was serene and quiet. The hostess smiled and silently took them to a low table by a window, which overlooked the garden. They were about to sit down when they saw Jessica walk in and remove her pumps. The flame-haired thirtysomething reporter looked sharp as she sported a wine-cropped jacket and matching high-waist wide-leg pants. Akira and Tessa greeted her and all three took their seats on blue cushions on the floor, which was covered with tatami mats. Jessica and Tessa assumed a traditional cross-legged position. Akira sat *seiza*-style, kneeling, a traditional position for native Japanese that was difficult for foreigners if they weren't used to it.

Almost in a whisper, an elderly female server took their orders.

Jessica worked for ITO, an independent daily paper offering news in Japanese and English. It had about 350,000 subscribers and was named after the newspaper's first publisher, Chiharu Ito.

She took out her white iPad to record Akira's and Tessa's answers. The three women spoke in low voices to not disturb the quiet environment of the tea room.

Jessica began: "So Tessa, are you a full-time activist or do you have another job?"

"I work at Charles Avery Homeopathic Pet Hospital in Los Angeles as a small animal veterinarian, and I also volunteer at Pacific Marine Mammal Center. I use my specialty in aquatic medicine to help diagnose and treat sea lions and seals that have been rescued."

"And what made you come to Tokyo?"

"I was in Taiji when I was sixteen, and I wanted to come back to see more of Japan and to save the dolphins," Tessa responded.

"Taiji? Not many people go there on their first visit," she commented, raising her eyebrows.

"I was visiting a cousin who used to live there."

Tessa began to recount the horrors she had witnessed when she was sixteen and what she had learned about dolphins over the years. "So you see, I had to come back. I had to figure out a way to help save them."

A tea boy shuffled over to their table with a floral-patterned wooden tray to serve their food and drinks.

"And you, Akira? Do you have another job besides being an activist?"

Akira, who had been listening quietly, said, "I'm self-employed, working as a tour guide."

"Why are you doing this?" Jessica asked, taking a spoonful of matcha soup made with stewed red beans and rice flour balls.

"I grew up in the U.S., and some of my friends were members of different animal rights groups. Then one day, I accompanied one of them to a meeting. I had no idea what was happening to our whales and dolphins. I decided to do something about it."

"You are 100 percent Japanese?"

"Yes. Both my parents are Japanese, and we left Tokyo for the States when I was five. I came back here when I was twenty-four for work," she answered, pouring syrup over her *anmitsu*—agar jelly with beans, Mochi, and fruit—and taking a bite.

"Tessa, what is it that you're trying to accomplish here?" Jessica asked. "I mean, you're not going to be able to stop the fishermen with a handful of activists. Fishing is their livelihood."

As she lingered over her *wagashi*, or Japanese sweets, Tessa wished that she knew what Jessica was writing and hoped that the interview would present her cause in a positive light. "Dolphins are not fish. They are mammals."

"It does not matter that they are not fish," pointed out Jessica. "They are still captured by fishermen."

"Actually, in Japan, it does matter," explained Tessa. "There are laws in Japan that protect mammals from cruelty. But because dolphins are mistakenly classified as fish, these laws aren't applied to them."

"I see," Jessica responded.

"In 2019, London's Action for Dolphins and Japan's Life Investigation Agency, two nonprofit organizations that advocate for the humane treatment of animals, filed a joint lawsuit against the governor of Wakayama asserting that, because dolphins are mammals, the cruelty inflicted on them is illegal under Japan's own laws."

"What was the verdict?"

"The high court said that individuals do not have the standing to challenge the hunts. But since dolphins are mammals, the Japanese fishermen are violating the law. Meanwhile, the authorities look the other way."

Jessica pressed on. "Maybe so, but how are you planning to make a change?"

"I'm here to support Akira and other Japanese activists who want to save the dolphins. We're trying to make enough noise to get the government's attention."

"And are you going back to the U.S now that the protest is over?"

"No, I'll be participating in several other protests in Kyoto, Taiji, and Osaka. Well, in Taiji, an activist friend of mine and I are not actually involved in the demonstration. We will be there just to observe the Japanese activists and take photos."

"And then what?" Jessica grilled her, thinking that many famous activists who had come before Tessa were only able to make a dent. Tessa wasn't even that well known, and the only reason she had piqued Jessica's interest was that Riku Yokoyama's son had also participated in the demonstration. In fact, when Jessica had asked Toshiro for an interview, he declined, explaining that he was there to support Akira and Tessa.

"I'm not expecting an overnight change," Tessa said, shrugging. "I'm hoping to eventually open up a dialogue with the fishermen and show them the kind of pain they're inflicting on the dolphins. For example, they sever the dolphin's spinal cord with a rod and then stick a cork in them to stop the bleeding. And as a vet, I can tell you that this method, which they call humane, is inhumane and prolongs an agonizing death because stopping the blood forces the dolphins to live longer while suffering."

"But you're an outsider. There's no way they would listen to you," Jessica objected.

"That is true, but they may listen to Japanese activists. If we can get the younger generation involved, change may be possible."

"What do you think, Akira?" Jessica inquired. It wasn't that she wanted to discourage them, but she had to write an objective article that represented both sides.

"I have to agree with Tessa. The problem is that children in Taiji and other towns are taught from a young age that it is perfectly fine to slaughter dolphins and whales. In Denmark's Faroe Islands, parents bring their children to play with slaughtered piolet whales, cut them open, remove their teeth, and take pictures with them. This is unacceptable."

"Piolet whales?"

"Piolet whales are dolphins. All dolphins are whales, but not all whales are dolphins," Tessa said.

"I see," Jessica said. "There are a lot of towns in Japan with populations that are shrinking as residents move to cities for jobs. Do you think that this will happen in Taiji?"

"Yes, there is a strong possibility. The town needs to create more employment for their residents," Akira replied, wiping off a drop of syrup from her lips. "One way would be to figure out ways to attract tourists. I mean tourism is not the only option, but it can help generate jobs. However, slaughtering dolphins in such a horrific way sends a wrong message to visitors."

"Tessa, has anyone given you a hard time since you've been out here?" Jessica asked. The Japanese were kind and understanding most of the time to visitors in tourist areas. But in residential areas, some Japanese didn't like foreigners or felt comfortable speaking broken English. Others had difficulty trusting outsiders.

"Not so far. A Japanese man did flip us off yesterday," Tessa admitted, "but that was just one person. I don't believe that's the sentiment of everyone here."

"Is there a place where readers can find out more about where and when these protests take place?"

Tessa gave her the name of her Facebook account, which listed the events.

Jessica took more notes, and then picked up the bill.

"Oh no," Akira said, "let's split it." In Japan, it is customary to split the bill regardless of who ordered what or what it cost.

"Don't worry. It's a business expense and my paper will cover it."

Jessica interviewed them for another twenty minutes, took a photo of Akira and Tessa for her article, and thanked them for their time before leaving.

"I'm glad this is over with. I was very nervous," Tessa said, picking up her bag to leave.

"Me too," Akira added and followed suit.

"When we get back, I need to work on the Kyoto demonstration. It's in five days," Tessa said as she walked over a series of stepping stones.

"Let's hang out for a while. I have to go back to work tomorrow, and I won't have much time to spend with you."

"I'd like that. I just thought you have things to do."

"They can wait. C'mon, let me show you little Venice."

"Little what?"

"You'll see."

They walked through Green Street. It was lined with rows of sakura trees, or cherry blossom trees, which flowered in spring. Shops selling household goods, food, clothing, and books bordered the street. People walked about and relaxed on benches; children played; others rode bicycles and scooters. Tessa was taking it all in as she followed Akira's lead. They came to a small outdoor shopping mall architecturally reminiscent of Venice, Italy. Called La Vita, the picturesque spot had a bridge set over a small canal with a stationary gondola floating in it. A brick building with a bell tower and Roman numeral clock, black iron lampposts, and replicas of late-1400 Venetian buildings with arched windows set a scene that conjured visions of the Mediterranean City of Bridges.

"This is amazing," Tessa commented. "It does look like Venice, not that I've ever been."

"It's different. We copy things a lot. We copy British architecture, European clothing designs, and French food, and then we add our own flare to it to make it our own."

"I still prefer the authentic Japanese atmosphere, but I'm glad that you showed me this. It's so pleasant and relaxing here."

They began walking back toward the subway station. Akira wondered if she would ever hear back from Ethan. She desperately wanted a boyfriend.

Tessa thought about the fact that she hadn't had a single nightmare since she had arrived in Japan. Maybe she was slowly starting to heal.

Back at Akira's place, Tessa's cellphone rang. It was Toshiro, and she was glad to hear from him.

"How are you?" she answered, taking a seat on the sofa.

"Doing okay, thank you. How are you?" he inquired. He was at home relaxing in his robe, looking out the window of a five-bedroom house that once belonged to his parents.

"I was worried about you yesterday. What happened?" Tessa asked, propping up a pillow behind her back.

"I wasn't feeling well. I'm much better now." He was too embarrassed to tell her that he had thrown up several times after the film. He didn't know why it had affected him so, but he decided last night to put the whole thing behind him and not think about it.

Tessa thought it odd that he didn't want to share what was wrong with him, but she let it go. "We had an interview with an American journalist today."

"Did you? How did it go?"

"So-so. She was drilling us, but I guess that's her job."

"Hopefully, she'll write something nice. I gave an interview once long ago and I have regretted it ever since. They twisted my words and took everything out of context," he said, settling into a comfortable chair.

"What was the interview about?"

"It was about my dad. Everybody is always interested in knowing more about him and my family."

"Ugh. I hope that ours turns out better."

"Don't worry about it. It's done. What're you doing tomorrow?"

"Not sure. I haven't figured it out yet."

"It's my birthday, and I would like to invite you to my parents' house," he said. He spoke as though he had known her for years and she was obligated to say yes.

"At your parents' home?" she asked, with wide eyes. She wondered why he didn't instead ask the girl she had seen him with. Wasn't she his girlfriend? She didn't want to give him the wrong idea and show interest by asking who she was. Although Tessa liked Toshiro, she did not want to have an intimate relationship with him. He was just a guy she had met in Japan under strange circumstances, and he had been kind enough to support her cause.

"It's just a small gathering. So what do you say?" He tried to sound casual about it, but he really wanted to show her off to his family and friends.

"Um, I'm not sure I would feel comfortable coming to your parents' home. I'll tell you what: why don't we hang out for an hour or two on Monday? We'll celebrate your birthday before you go spend the evening with your family."

"It would mean a lot to me if you would accompany me," he insisted. All his friends were coming over with their dates, and Kaiya stopped talking to him since that day at the park when Tessa had kissed him. Of course, he could have probably asked any number of other girls, but he didn't want to take just anybody to his family's home. Tessa was special, and he was quite attracted to her.

Tessa didn't want to go, but she couldn't think of a single excuse to get out of it. "Sure, why not?"

"Pick you up at 6:30?"

"Text me the address and I'll meet you there," insisted Tessa.

"Why not let me pick you up?"

Because I don't want this to be a date, she wanted to say. "Because I'm more comfortable this way."

"No problem." He didn't want to push his luck. He was just glad that she had agreed to come. "I'll meet you in the lobby of my parents' condo at 7."

"Got it. Dress code?"

"Casual chic."

Great. I've got nothing chic, she thought. "See you then. And thank you for the invite," she said, about to hang up.

"Oh, wait! I don't even know your last name."

"Walker."

"Tessa Walker," he repeated and then changed the subject. "What about your friend we had lunch with?"

"What about her?"

"I've forgotten her name."

"Akira Nakano," she said, wondering why he was asking about Akira. Maybe his friend Ethan was interested in her, though he seemed like a guy who slept around.

"Akira Nakano," he said out loud so that he would remember her name. He didn't know anything about Tessa and this was his way of learning more about her and her friends. "I'm curious—how did the two of you meet?"

"We met at an animal rights rally in L.A. seven years ago and we have been friends ever since," Tessa replied. "What about you and Ethan? Are you good friends?"

"Not really. We work together. He wanted to grab a bite to eat that night when we ran into you and Akira."

"Is he seeing anyone?" Tessa asked, thinking of Akira.

"I know where you're going with this, but you should let your friend know that he's bisexual."

"Really? I did not see that coming!"

They talked awhile longer, feeling comfortable with each other. Had he lived in Los Angeles, they could've become good friends, Tessa thought. Although he seemed to want more than just a friendship.

After hanging up with Toshiro, Tessa told Akira about Ethan's sexual preferences. Akira was surprised.

"If there was a woman in his life, I would try to win him over. But he also likes men. There's no way I would be able to compete with another man."

"I am sorry. I know that you liked him," Tessa said, frowning. She wished that she knew someone nice for Akira.

"I'm not hurt or anything. Just glad that I didn't sleep with him," Akira said, shrugging it off. If she had a thousand yen for every frog she had kissed in her life, she would be able to buy herself a Chanel bag.

"So what else did Toshiro say? You guys seemed to talk for a long time," Akira asked. She hadn't been eavesdropping, but she could hear Tessa's muffled voice through her closed bedroom door.

"Well, he invited me to his parents' home for his birthday."

"Wow! He likes you." Akira was impressed. It wasn't every day that an outsider got invited to a Japanese home.

"I wish he hadn't. He said to dress casual chic, but I have nothing to wear. What am I going to do?"

"You can't go casual. This is his family. They'll probably have some important people there," Akira insisted.

"He said that it was a small gathering."

Akira furrowed her brows. "No matter. Let's look through my closet and find you something that will knock their socks off."

"This isn't a date," Tessa said with a serious tone. "I'm just there as his friend."

"Does he know that?" Akira asked as she pulled out two dresses, two skirts, a blouse, and a sweater out of her closet.

"Yes, of course. That's why I didn't want him to pick me up. I'll be taking a taxi," Tessa said, removing the hairband that was now giving her a headache.

"What time do you have to be there?"

"Seven o'clock."

"Better leave early. Subways are packed, and traffic is bad during that time. And the Japanese are extremely punctual. If you're there on time, you're already late. They usually show up at least fifteen minutes early," Akira said, sounding much more excited than Tessa. *Lucky girl*, Akira thought. She would love to go to a dinner party.

"Boy, I did not know that. What else do I need to know?" Tessa asked, sounding worried. She sat on Akira's bed.

"Take a hostess gift with you, like fruit or candy. You don't need to bow when you meet his parents. They don't expect it from Americans. Just shake hands with them. And when asked for your opinion, think carefully before you answer," she said, rummaging through her drawers to look for shawls that would coordinate with the outfits that she had pulled out.

"Why can't I just say what I think?"

"Here, we have concepts called *honne* and *tatemae*," explained Akira. "*Honne* refers to our true feelings and opinions, and *tatemae* refers to what we present in public." She put the shawls on her bed and sat next to Tessa.

"So the Japanese behavior that we see is not real?"

"Well, we show our true feelings and opinions to those who are closest to us, but not strangers," Akira replied.

"Then, if I think someone likes me, that may not be the case. It could be that they are just being nice because that's the expected behavior."

"Something like that. People just don't want to hurt others' feelings. And when we're in a large group, we try to avoid conflict by not expressing what we really think."

"Good to know. What else Yoda? Teach me more," she asked eagerly.

"I'm not exactly Yoda; I just want to give you a few pointers so that you can survive dinner."

"Ugh. Now I'm not sure if I want to go."

"You have to go. You promised, and you must keep your promise."

"Is that one more thing I need to learn?"

"Once you say yes, you must show up. You cannot cancel unless you're dying."

"Okay. No more lessons," Tessa protested, covering her face with her hands. "I'm feeling nauseous."

"Don't worry. You will be fine," Akira assured her, though she didn't have any idea how difficult it was for foreigners to adapt to her culture, rules, and traditions.

"I brought a few items, including a box of chocolate from Compartés in Los Angeles, in case I got invited somewhere and needed a hostess gift. You think it would be okay if I gave it to Toshiro's parents?"

"Compartés? Fancy schmancy," Akira replied, recalling when a friend of hers had brought her a small box. The chocolate was cubed and topped with colorful designs.

"A client gave it to me for treating his veiled chameleon right before I came here."

"What was wrong with it?" Akira asked. She was always interested in Tessa's stories about her patients.

"Whenever it would try to climb, it would fall. I ran some tests and found out that his calcium was low and his bones were brittle. So, after a couple of months of giving him medication and making sure that a special light bulb was used so that he could better absorb calcium from his diet, his health improved. Its owner was really appreciative."

"The chocolates would make a great hostess gift," said Akira. "We all like treats from someone's hometown. Just make sure that there's enough for everybody to share. It should be wrapped in see-through paper and put in a bag that you carry in. When you're ready to give it to his parents, take it out of the bag and present it to them with both hands," Akira lectured.

"There are twenty pieces of chocolate in there, and Toshiro did say it was a small dinner party."

"Perfect. I'll help you with the wrapping. Here, presentation is as important as the gift. Each wrapping color has a different meaning. For example, green means eternity and good luck, purple means celebration, red is used for funerals or sexuality, white means holiness, and black means death or bad luck."

Tessa felt overwhelmed. There were just too many rules. What if she messed up? Would they think less of her? And would she be spending the entire night focused on etiquette? She simply was not ready for this dinner party. "Anything else I need to know?"

"When you present it, you say, '*Tsumaranai mono desu ga*,' which translates to: 'This is a trivial thing, but please accept it.' It's a humble expression."

"Will you write it down so that I can memorize it tonight?" *Learning Japanese is more difficult than memorizing medical terms*, Tessa thought.

"Sure. You can also say it in English, and if they don't understand, Toshiro will translate."

"Thanks," Tessa said but frowned.

"Don't worry too much. As a foreigner, you are not expected to know all the rules of etiquette. So stop looking upset."

"I'm frowning because I just realized, your clothes will never fit me. You're much skinnier," Tessa said, sounding panicky.

"I'm not that much skinnier. Just try them." Akira pushed one of the skirts toward her.

Tessa put it on, but she couldn't get the zipper all the way up. She tried the blouse, but her breasts made it look more revealing than she desired. "Let's face it, I'm fat!" she cried.

"Stop it. You're beautiful. Here, try this one," Akira suggested, passing her the outfit. The dress was a size too large for Akira; it fit her loosely whenever she wore it. At one point, she had considered giving it away because it just didn't compliment her boyish figure.

Tessa looked at it skeptically. At least the material seemed to be stretchy. When she put it on though, it was the perfect black dress, conservative yet sexy. It had long sleeves, conformed to her body contour, and fell two inches above her knees, showing off her long legs.

"Finally, I see a smile on that pretty face of yours," Akira remarked when she saw Tessa admiring herself in the mirror.

"Thank you! You saved me," she exclaimed, feeling relieved. Why was she so tense? Probably because she was out of her comfort zone. She never really liked dinner parties anyway. Tessa was a casual person who preferred a potluck.

"Anytime. Now you need accessories to make the dress pop!"

Tessa borrowed Akira's single-strand pearl necklace. In her luggage, she had a simple vegan-suede garnet clutch and a pair of matching pumps she had purchased at Neiman Marcus.

Akira jotted down the address of her hairdresser. He worked in a small salon and understood English. The salon also had a manicurist. "Tomorrow I'll call and make an appointment for your hair and nails."

I wish I had said no, Tessa wanted to say. But what good would it do to complain? She had to suck it up and go. It was just one night and not the end of the world. "Thank you. I sure do appreciate all of your help."

"You're welcome. Now, do you want me to find you a place that will do your makeup?"

"Oh, no. Thanks. This is already taking up too much time. I need to work on the Kyoto protest. This whole business with Toshiro will eat up a good chunk of my day."

"It's a good experience, Tessa," Akira said, hiding behind her closet door and changing into her sleepwear. "Most women would dream of an opportunity like this."

"You know me. I'm not like most women," Tessa said, getting off the bed.

"I can't disagree with that. Neither am I, but even so, I would love to be invited to a party at the Yokoyamas."

"Then you can go in my place," Tessa joked.

"I would, but I don't think I'm the one Toshiro wants," she said, seeing her friend's disapproving look.

That night, Tessa stayed up late to finish the scarf she had worked on the night before and decided to give it to Toshiro. She could always make another one for herself when she got home.

CHAPTER 8

On the warm September night of the dinner party, Toshiro met Tessa outside the lobby of his parents' condominium, which was located in a modern high-rise in Azabu, an area that boasted some of the priciest and most-coveted real estate in Tokyo.

"You look beautiful," said Toshiro, setting eyes on Tessa. Dressed up, she looked completely different, and he liked both the old and the new. He admired her curves, her silky layered hair, the hint of glitter in her smoky eyeshadow, and her kissable cranberry lips.

"Thank you. And you look quite handsome yourself. Happy birthday. *Tsumaranai mono desu ga*," she responded. She handed him his delicately wrapped gift. She thought that tonight he somehow appeared more mature in his black-and-white-checked cashmere suit. His skin glowed, and there was a twinkle in his eyes. For the first time, Tessa could envision herself dating him, though she still didn't want to start something that would have little chance of success.

He beamed. He was touched that she had memorized a phrase that most visitors did not know how to say. *"Domo arigato.* Shall we?" he asked as he put his arm through hers and escorted her into the lobby. A uniformed doorman greeted them and used his key to access the elevator. While waiting for the doors to open, Tessa took in the Zen-like lobby: a large copper waterfall wall cascaded over onyx stones and a tiered fountain spilled into a koi pond that divided the area, furnished with clean-lined teak chairs and tables and floor-to-ceiling bamboo trees.

The elevator lifted them to the penthouse on the 52nd floor. The doors opened to reveal black-and-white-inlaid marble floors and four separate entrances: main, kitchen, servants, and emergency. Near the main entrance was an aubergine velvet chair in the shape of a half-moon. It was set against a milky wood-paneled wall and a console topped with a bronze sculpture of a sleeping woman's head.

Toshiro noticed Tessa staring at the sculpture. "It's a replica of Constantin Brâncusi's famous *La muse endormie*—the sleeping muse," he explained. "My mother commissioned a sculptor to make it for her after she was outbid for the original at a Christie's auction."

Toshiro and Tessa were among the last guests to appear. A formal butler greeted them and took Tessa's shawl. A musician played Mozart piano sonatas on an ebony Fazioli grand piano situated by floor-to-ceiling windows that overlooked Tokyo. A bartender mixed drinks behind a laminated cherrywood bar and eight servers wandered around offering guests hors d'oeuvres on silver trays.

Wearing a Dior button-down white silk blouse and matching skirt, Toshiro's 48-year-old mother, Minako, looked youthful with her pixie haircut and side-swept bangs. She and her distinguished husband, Riku, who was a good twenty-five years older, were showing Riku's rare stamp collection to a similarly aged well-dressed gentleman.

"Those are my parents," whispered Toshiro to Tessa, pointing them out. "And you might be interested to know that the man with them is billionaire Junichiro Fujimoto, who owns sea-themed water parks and aquatic research centers all over the world."

Tessa gulped, looking alarmed.

Toshiro's three friends, whom Tessa saw on that fateful day at the Royal Garden Café, were also there with their fashionable, cute, twenty-something dates. The Yokoyamas spotted their son near the main entrance and walked over to greet him. But when they saw Tessa, his mother whispered to her husband, "Who is that?"

"Someone who shouldn't be here," he replied, looking over his half-glasses, which did nothing to soften his stern face. His black and silver hair was parted to one side, and he was dressed conservatively in a single-breasted camel suit. Round-faced and thin-lipped, he didn't look anything like his son. With his square jaw and full lips, Toshiro resembled his mother.

Minako stiffened a bit, not sure why her son was there with an older woman instead of his age-appropriate girlfriend, Kaiya. More importantly, Kaiya was a native Japanese and Minako could relate to her better than to an outsider.

"Happy birthday," his father said, mustering a smile.

"*Tanjoubi omedetou*," his mother repeated in Japanese, barely making an effort to smile.

"Thank you. This is my friend Tessa. She is from Los Angeles."

"Good evening," Tessa said, noticing Minako's gorgeous turquoise Fabergé egg pendant. She offered her hand to shake.

If they were shocked that Toshiro's date was an older American woman, Tessa didn't notice. They simply said, "Hello, welcome to our home." His mother shook Tessa's hand. She could understand why her son was attracted to her. Tessa was striking, with her large eyes, bowed lips, and long legs, even if she was the wrong woman for her son.

With both hands, Tessa gave her the hostess gift wrapped in rose cellophane paper, the way Akira had taught her, and said, "*Tsumaranai mono desu ga.*"

"Thank you. This is very kind of you," Minako said, surprised that Tessa knew something about their Japanese etiquette. *Toshiro must have taught her*, she thought. *What a foolish boy to be playing like this with his life when he should be settling down with Kaiya.* She invited Tessa into the living room and asked, "What would you like to drink?"

Tessa wanted a glass of wine, but when she saw Minako drinking water, she said, "Sparkling water, please."

Minako directed one of the servers to bring Tessa a bottle of Ferrarelle. "Please have a seat," she said, pointing to a curved, silk-upholstered sofa.

The two-story penthouse, decorated by an exclusive interior designer, had eight bedrooms and a butler overseeing two chauffeurs, two full-time housekeepers, two cooks, and all the business of running the home.

Toshiro's father excused himself and gave Toshiro a look. "There is something I need to discuss with my son." In his office, he confronted Toshiro. "Why did you bring her here?"

Astonished by his father's reaction, he answered, "She's my friend. You don't even know her. Why don't you like her?"

He picked up one of three newspapers sitting on his highly polished mahogany desk. Splashed on the front page of a local paper was a photograph of Toshiro and Tessa holding a long banner with a bloody dolphin drawn on it. The banner read, "Please help stop the slaughter of Taiji dolphins." "Did you think

I wouldn't find out? What is the meaning of this? And it's in the other papers, too."

"I was just helping out. These dolphins. …"

"Stop!" his father said, holding out his hand in protest. "I don't want to hear it. Fujimoto-san's company has been named and condemned in these articles. I had to calm him and invite him to dinner as a gesture of goodwill."

Junichiro's company was a lucrative business that captured dolphins and showcased them in sea-themed parks or sold them for $100,000 to $300,000 each to other parks around the world. The newspaper articles that covered the protest could harm his reputation and business.

"Maybe we can open up a dialogue about how to change things," offered Toshiro.

"Not one word from you, you hear?" shouted his father. "Did you ever think that she is using you to promote her cause?"

"What do you mean?" he asked, red-faced and tense.

"For a smart guy, you sure act stupid. People in the media know that you are my son. Why do you think that the dolphin story made the front page of major newspapers? She used you to bring attention to her cause. Wake up, son, and see her for what she is."

"No! She would never do that. I volunteered to help out. If you only knew the torture these dolphins endure."

His wife knocked on the door and came in. She said to her husband, "Fujimoto-san is looking for you. Please leave your discussion for another day."

"This is not over," he said, pointing his finger at his son. "We will talk about this later." Riku Yokoyama tolerated foreigners but did not trust them. His father, a Japanese-American, had told him stories about how his grandparents, both American citizens, lost their families' land, homes, and businesses when President Roosevelt issued an executive order on February 19, 1942, ten weeks after the Japanese bombed Pearl

Harbor, authorizing the military to forcibly move all Japanese people residents—regardless of their nationalities—to internment camps. His nineteen-year-old parents and grandparents, along with other Japanese-Americans, suffered immensely in the camps. They endured difficult living conditions and abuse by military guards.

Riku, who was born years after his grandparents and parents moved to Tokyo for job opportunities, was not about to let his family's suffering be forgotten. He wanted his son to stay in Japan and marry a Japanese girl. He believed his family should stick to their own kind. Although he operated businesses in foreign lands, he wanted his son to be by his side at home.

Toshiro walked out of his father's study and looked for Tessa. He wanted to leave, but the party was in his honor, and he didn't want to embarrass his father in front of his guests and make him lose face. The concept of saving face was ingrained in Japanese culture. Americans typically feel relatively comfortable speaking openly to those in positions of authority, such as teachers, bosses, parents, or honored guests. By contrast, native Japanese tend to be indirect and avoid arguments with those in positions of authority to prevent publicly embarrassing them. In fact, Japanese people seek to make authority figures look good and well respected in front of others by not challenging them, even when they were wrong.

"Is everything okay?" Tessa asked when she noticed the tension in Toshiro's face. Toshiro's mother had just questioned Tessa, but when Tessa had assured her that she and Toshiro were just friends, his mother seemed to relax.

"Yes, all is good. Would you like a drink?" He put on a fake smile.

"Thank you, but your mother got me a Ferrarelle."

"No, I mean a real drink like a stiff bourbon?" he hissed.

"How about you tell me what's going on?" It was clear to her that she was not welcomed there, and she felt that Toshiro should have known not to invite her.

"It's nothing."

"Okay, but if you want to talk about it, I'm here for you," she said, but wished that she hadn't come. *C'mon Tessa, you're old enough and have put up with a lot of shit dates. Suck it up for an hour or two.*

After getting a drink at the bar, Toshiro started to relax. He spotted his friends and introduced Tessa to them.

Souji was surprised to see Tessa there. He wondered where Kaiya was. "Are you …" *the girl Toshiro met a few days ago*, he wanted to say, but Toshiro interrupted him by shaking his head and shooting him a cross look.

"So Souji, how was the Mori Building Digital Art Museum?" Toshiro asked, knowing that his pal had visited it earlier in the day. The all-digital museum combined science and art to create an atmosphere that moved people emotionally, physically, and spiritually, arousing all of the senses. Using computers, projectors, and lights, colorful installations gravitated in and out of rooms, appearing and changing form on the walls, floors, and ceiling as they interacted with other works. It was like being in dimly lit rooms full of various artworks that constantly moved, surprised, and mesmerized visitors.

"It was amazing. You absolutely have to go see it. Take your American friend Tessa with you. She would really enjoy it."

"So, how old are you now, old man?" one of his friends teased him.

"Thirty. I know, I'm getting old." Some of his friends were a few years younger.

So that's how old he is, Tessa thought, *ten years younger than I. I thought he was in his mid-20s.*

From across the room, Junichiro glanced over at Toshiro and decided to wish him a happy birthday. But when he saw Tessa, he gritted his teeth and sneered. He turned to Riku, "You invited her?"

"No, my son invited her. I am sorry," he replied. "I had no idea that he was bringing her. I thought he was coming with Kaiya, his girlfriend."

Tessa excused herself and went to the bathroom, and Toshiro went into the dining room to check out the seating arrangement. He noticed that one place card had Kaiya's name on it and that he was designated to sit at the head of the table next to his father and Junichiro. He switched the cards and put himself at the end of the table and asked the butler to discard Kaiya's place card and make a new one with Tessa's name. He then shuffled the place cards so that he would be next to Tessa and close to his friends and their dates.

When Tessa came out of the bathroom, Toshiro was waiting for her. He knew that she didn't know anyone all that well, and he didn't want to leave her alone.

A server announced that dinner was awaiting them in the dining room. Ten guests made their way to the table, which had half a dozen chairs on each side. The yellow, gray, and white marble Italian dining table had mirrored crocodile legs and taupe, silk dining chairs. A delicately handcrafted chandelier shaped like thin ice crystals hung above their heads. In the middle of the table was a Swarovski vase arranged with pink roses and lavender.

Each place setting had hand-painted placemats topped with crystal chargers. Each setting had place cards with pictures of bonsai, and at the head of the chargers were intricately folded napkins and ivory chopsticks, pointing left and resting on chopstick holders. Were it not for the Japanese accoutrements,

Tessa felt as though she was dining at some aristocrat's home in Paris.

Once the guests were seated at their designated spots, Minako was not pleased. Earlier she had dictated the seating chart to the butler. But what happened? Why wasn't Toshiro seated across from her husband? And why were all the guests scattered in a way that did not make sense? She realized that Toshiro must have made the switch because Kaiya's name on the card was now replaced with Tessa's. Riku also noticed that his son was sitting far away, but thought that it might be for the best. He didn't want to further upset Junichiro by placing his son and Tessa too close to him.

The guests kept the conversation light, talking about the weather, their work, and their travels. But Tessa could feel the tension in the room even if she didn't speak Japanese. Everyone had been expecting to see Kaiya, and Tessa stuck out like a sore thumb. Toshiro, sitting next to her, passed her an assuring look to communicate that everything was going to be fine.

The servers handed out warm towels.

"The menu is *kaiseki ryori*, multiple dishes served in small portions," Toshiro told Tessa.

Tessa nodded as she wiped her hands.

She had read about it in her guidebook. *Kaiseki ryori*, a traditional multicourse meal, used to be a simple way of eating. But over time, it became an elaborate way to serve food, and the upper class adopted it as a fashionable way to dine. The dishes were presented in a set order: amuse bouche, main course, rice, misu, pickles, and dessert. The number and content of the plates were at the chef's discretion. Tessa wondered how many dishes were going to be brought out and if the chef would make anything vegetarian that she could eat.

The waiters served wine and bite-size appetizers on black square plates with red edges for each guest. Each course was arranged like a fine work of art.

Before starting the meal, everyone said, "*Itadakimasu.*" The word was somewhat similar to the American version of saying, "thank you for the food I am about to receive." However, in Japan, the word *itadakimasu* went a step further. The term expressed gratitude to mother nature, farmers, delivery workers, the cook, and everyone else who had made it possible to bring the food to the table as well as all the animals and plants that were sacrificed to make the meal.

Tessa sipped her *umeshu,* plum wine, and said, "Interesting taste. Kind of sweet and yet sour. I like it and can't wait to try the food. It looks delectable," *with the exception of sashimi*, she wanted to say. She didn't like the texture of raw fish.

Toshiro was glad that the food pleased her. Because he brought her to the party as a surprise, he never asked his mother to tell the chef to prepare vegetarian dishes for her. Now he regretted putting her in an uncomfortable situation.

Tessa savored everything except the sashimi. The other guests cleaned off their plates, as was customary. The Japanese didn't like wasting food and it was rude not to eat everything off the plates, but Tessa did not know this. Because of Japan's dense population and scarce natural resources, parents taught their children the concept of *mottainai*—to feel regret over waste. Tessa didn't know that etiquette dictated that she either finish her meal or offer her sushi to Toshiro instead of leaving it uneaten on her plate.

Toshiro was the perfect host. As more dishes arrived, he described them to Tessa, "This is *suimono*, clear broth to cleanse the palate. It's made with soy sauce, sake, kelp and shitake dashi, wild parsley, and mung bean sprouts."

"You know, I have passed by many places serving Japanese food, but the ingredients were written in *kanji*, and I was hesitant to try them. Thank you, for explaining the dishes."

"You're welcome," he replied, squeezing her hand, which did not sit well under the stare of the Yokoyamas.

When one of the main courses arrived on a rustic-looking, charcoal-colored plate, Toshiro told her, "This is sea urchin, abalone, and marine snail, all cooked alive."

Abalone was an expensive dish because it was difficult to catch at sea and difficult to prepare, so it was served only on special occasions.

"The presentation is beautiful," she said, looking at the colorful dish. "But I'm starting to get a little full and need a break," she said. She was fibbing because she didn't want to tell him that there was no way that she would ever knowingly eat any creature cooked alive.

Toshiro whispered in her ear, "If you don't like something, just pass it to me. I'll eat it."

Tessa heaved a sigh of relief. And as more courses arrived, she ended up giving her wagyu, duck loin, and custard made with chicken to Toshiro. He ate all of it without complaining. *He must've been starving*, Tessa thought. Meanwhile, she could see his mother looking at her out of the corner of her eye. Tessa wondered if she was angry that she was not eating all of her food.

The last course before the dessert consisted of a bowl of herbed white rice, miso soup, and vegetables. Souji noticed that Tessa was not eating much and said, "If you don't want your rice, I'll take it."

"It's yours," Tessa said, "Thank you for helping me out." She couldn't tell if she was too full or too nervous to eat.

"You're welcome. I love white rice."

Riku looked over at Souji, shaking his head. With the exception of Kaiya, he didn't like any of Toshiro's friends. They had no manners. But it was his son's birthday, and Riku wanted to indulge him.

Tessa noticed that Junichiro Fujimoto seemed to be scowling at her. She tugged at Toshiro's sleeve and whispered, "Why is that man who owns the sea-themed parks giving me a dirty look?"

"Oh. Mr. Fujimoto. That's how he is when he doesn't know someone," Toshiro lied. He didn't want to explain that Junichiro knew exactly who Tessa was after seeing her photo in the newspapers.

After the final course, the servers brought everyone peach sorbet, after which the guests were ushered to the family room. On one wall was a large painted portrait of the Yokoyamas seated on two traditional wingback chairs with Toshiro standing behind them when he was twenty-five years old. Two smaller paintings of Riku's and Minako's parents and grandparents hung on each side of the portrait.

Toshiro sat in the family room on one of the sofas with Tessa next to him. Tessa felt that she would never want to live this way. The place reeked of opulence and arrogance. Sure, it was fun to be there for an hour or two, but she needed warmth and comfort, and this penthouse did not emanate either of those.

The servers brought in an award-winning Tencha tea from the city of Uji, followed by a lavishly decorated, round, three-tiered birthday cake adorned with green stars. They all sang happy birthday in Japanese: *otanjoubi omedetou, otanjoubi omedetou, otanjoubi omedetou, otanjoubi omedetou.*

Singing happy birthday was a foreign concept introduced to Japan after World War II. Birthdays were seen as a personal and private matter. More focused on the group than the individual, native Japanese celebrated their birthdays on New Year's Day because they believed that they all became one year older on that day.

After finishing their cake and tea, the guests addressed the servers, saying, *"Gochisousama deshita."*

"Gochisousama deshita translates to 'It was a great feast and great deal of work,'" Toshiro explained to Tessa. "Guests say it after they finish to express gratitude for their meal. Long ago, people could only get their food by hunting, fishing, and harvesting. Guests said *gochisousama* to express their appreciation and tell their hosts that they recognized it was a great deal of work to prepare the meal. People also use this phrase at restaurants. If it is an open kitchen, they thank the cook; otherwise, they thank the server or the cashier."

And since it was the norm for the Japanese to not open their gifts in front of everyone, the guests thanked the Yokoyamas, wished Toshiro a happy birthday again, and said their goodbyes.

One reason that gifts are not opened in front of everyone is if someone buys an inexpensive gift, they might be embarrassed that their gift was not as lavish as the others. Or, if someone had brought an extravagant gift, they might not want everyone to know that they had spent a lot of money on it.

"Aren't you going to open your gift?" Tessa asked Toshiro after the guests had left.

"Are you sure you want me to open it?" he asked.

"Yes, absolutely," she said.

His parents joined them in the family room, waiting for Toshiro to open his gift, curious as to what Tessa had gotten him. Minako asked one of the servers to bring them more tea.

Toshiro removed his gift from the bag. He looked at a tag on the box that said, "For Toshiro," written in Japanese characters.

"Did you write this?" he asked, reading the tag.

"Yes. Akira taught me how to write your name in Japanese. Sorry about the poor penmanship," she said.

"No. It's perfect," he responded, taking great care to untie the navy linen ribbon without tearing the ribbed, ivory wrapping paper.

From the box, he removed the pale-gray vegan cashmere scarf with fringe at the ends. He felt its soft and luxurious texture against his fingers.

"I made it for you. It has your initials on it," she pointed out.

The tense muscles on the Yokoyamas' faces went unnoticed by both Toshiro and Tessa, who were too focused on each other.

"How did you do this in such a short amount of time? I hope that you didn't stay up all night."

"Well, not all night," she smiled. She was glad that she had made the extra effort to finish the scarf instead of getting him a generic gift.

"Thank you so much. I love it," he said, sounding touched.

"You're welcome. Glad you like it."

His parents hated the fact that Tessa had made something especially for their son. *They must be more serious about each other than they are letting on*, they thought.

A server brought in a silver tray of tea, served everyone, and left.

Toshiro neatly folded Tessa's gift wrapping and gift and put them back in the bag.

Riku addressed Tessa: "So, how is your visit to Tokyo, so far?" He really didn't care about her, but he wanted to learn more about her plans and motives.

"Wonderful. I really like it here and wish I could stay longer," she said, smiling.

"What do you do for a living?" Toshiro's mother asked.

"I'm a veterinarian. I treat small animals and aquatic mammals," she explained with her hands folded primly in her lap. She felt like a student being interrogated at the principal's office. *Boy, I wish this night would end soon*, she thought.

"Oh," said Minako. She recalled buying a Chihuahua a few years back because she thought it was cute but never took it to a vet. When she tired of the dog, she gave it to a pet shelter.

"Are you here for pleasure?" Riku poked.

Tessa had no idea that Riku recognized her from the newspapers. "Yes. I have always wanted to visit Japan," she responded, evading the truth about the main reason for her trip. *"Honne"* and *"tatemae,"* Akira had warned. This was definitely *"tatemae,"* otherwise she would have expressed her true feelings.

"I understand that you are an activist. Do you enjoy it?" Toshiro's mother blurted, hoping to get more answers out of her. She had also seen the photo of Tessa and her son and was as unhappy about it as her husband.

How on earth did she know that I'm an activist? Did Toshiro tell her? Tessa wondered. Not wanting to give too much information about herself, she kept her answers short. "Yes, I do," she said, clearing her throat.

"How long will you be staying in Tokyo?" Riku inquired. He wanted to see if she had long-term plans.

"A few more days, and then I'm traveling to Kyoto," Tessa said, hoping to allay his fears about her relationship with Toshiro. If she didn't want to get involved with Toshiro before, she was now determined to carry out her resolve.

"Have you ever met Kaiya? We thought she would be here tonight, with Toshiro that is," his mother said, hinting at Kaiya's relationship with her son.

Toshiro grit his teeth. His parents were rude and intolerable, and he wasn't sure how much longer he could contain himself before bursting into a fit of anger.

"I don't believe I have," replied Tessa. *Unless Kaiya was the girl holding Toshiro's hand in the park*, she thought.

"She is Toshiro's girlfriend. We're hoping that one day soon they will get married." She looked at Tessa's face for any type of emotion but couldn't read her.

"I think it's time for us to leave," Toshiro finally said. "We're both very tired." He got up and Tessa followed suit. He wore the scarf that Tessa had given him, carried the bag it came in, and held Tessa's hand to irritate his parents and make them think that they were going to spend the night together. "I'll pick up the rest of the gifts on another day."

"Toshiro, why don't you stay the night? We hardly ever see you. We can have the chauffeur take Tessa home," his father suggested, forcing a smile.

"Ah, not tonight." *I think I have had quite enough for one night,* he thought. "Thank you for a great birthday," he said, picking up Tessa's shawl from the guest closet and dragging her out with him before she could thank his parents for dinner.

On the elevator ride down, Tessa didn't say a word. As soon as they were outside his parents' door, she released his hand.

"I'm sorry about my parents," Toshiro said.

Tessa kept quiet and pushed the elevator button for the lobby.

"Look, I said I'm sorry. Why are you giving me the silent treatment?"

"Because it's your birthday, and I don't want to ruin it for you more than your parents already have. Let's talk about this another time."

"No, let's talk about it now," he insisted as the door to the lobby opened.

"Would you please call me a taxi?" she said stiffly, noticing that the doorman was watching them from a few feet away.

"I'll give you a ride home."

"I came here on my own, and I will leave on my own."

"Please let me take you home," he pleaded.

Tessa didn't want to make a scene in front of the doorman as Toshiro pushed the button for the parking level. Neither spoke until they reached Toshiro's white Nissan 370Z. He opened the car door for her, and she reluctantly got in.

Toshiro drove out into the street. Tessa gave him Akira's address.

"We need to get this out in the open. Let's talk it out," he said, making a right turn.

"Fine. Just remember, you were the one who started this."

"Started what?" He asked, turning his head slightly to look at her and then shifting his eyes back to the road.

She gave out an exasperated sigh. "The girl I saw with you, Kaiya, she is your girlfriend?"

"Was. She broke up with me that day that you kissed me."

Tessa blushed. "I'm truly sorry. I shouldn't have done that."

"Neither should I have grabbed and kissed you, but then maybe we would have never met." Toshiro had been dating Kaiya for the past two years. He liked her. She was kind and sweet, but he wasn't ready to marry her.

"Where do you think this is going?" Tessa asked. She knew that he liked her. He was always looking at her when he thought she wasn't paying attention. Toshiro may have been thirty years old, but he behaved like a schoolboy with a crush.

"What are you talking about?" he asked, glancing at her.

"Do you think of us as a couple?" she asked, frowning and folding her arms in front of her chest.

"No. You're my friend and I like being with you," he answered, avoiding eye contact.

"We are not friends. A friend would have never put me in such an uncomfortable position," she snapped, her shoulders stiff with tension.

"I wasn't thinking," he admitted.

"And that's the problem with you. You don't think. You just do. Did your parents even know that you were bringing me tonight?" She felt a headache coming on. The night had gone much worse than she expected.

He looked at her sheepishly. "No. I didn't tell them."

"You should have been honest with them. Your poor judgment affected me."

"How?"

"How? You made me go through all this—getting my hair and nails done, doing my makeup, borrowing clothes, hiring a taxi, and going to a dinner where I was not wanted."

"And shouldn't you have been more honest with me?" he retorted, remembering what his father had suggested about her intentions earlier.

"I never lied to you."

"Really? You used me. You knew that if I came to your protest, you would get more media attention. Isn't that why you asked me?"

She was flabbergasted. "That was … that was … Akira's idea. And I'm sorry."

"But you went along with it," he said, raising his voice. "My parents saw our picture in the paper."

Shit! "That's why they disliked me so much and were asking me questions about being an activist." Tessa had been so busy all day, prepping for the next protest and getting ready to go meet Toshiro that she hadn't seen the photos. And Akira had been with her clients all day.

"They don't dislike you. They just don't know you," he said, speeding through town, minutes away from Jiyūgaoka. Even though he was upset with her for using him, he actually enjoyed participating in the protest and helping to save the Taiji dolphins.

She paused to collect her thoughts. "May I make a suggestion to correct two wrongs?"

"What?" he asked, stopping at a red light.

"Go makeup with Kaiya, take her home to your parents, and make sure they know that there's nothing going on between us."

"Why are you doing this?"

"Toshiro, I like you. And because I like you, I don't want you to get hurt. I'll be going home soon, and you need to stay away from me. I'm an activist. And it was obvious tonight that your parents don't approve of me," she said, looking into his sad eyes.

"Can't we just hang out while you're here?" he asked when he reached Akira's apartment.

"I don't think that's such a good idea," she said and kissed him on the forehead. "Happy birthday. Good night." Tessa knew that the more time she spent with him, the harder it would be to break it off.

He sat in his car and watched her leave, hoping that she would turn around and look at him. But she never did.

CHAPTER 9

By the next afternoon, Tessa had already put the disastrous birthday party behind her. She realized that all her worries, concerns, and preparation for the dinner party—learning the proper things to say and do, choosing the right gift and gift wrap, dressing conservatively, and not expressing her true feelings—did not matter. The Yokoyamas had made up their minds to dislike her before they had even met her.

Tessa had discussed this with Akira in the morning, and Akira reminded her that she had come to Tokyo to help save the dolphins, not worry about the opinions of others. "We are in this together for the long haul, and we both need to develop thicker skins if we want to survive adversity," Akira told her. Tessa agreed and after Akira left for work, she went back to working on the Kyoto protest, promoting the cause on social media and making new contacts.

Still in her pajamas, Tessa decided to take a nap and then do a bit of sightseeing before Akira got home. The doorbell buzzed as she laid down. She wasn't expecting anyone. *If they are looking for Akira, they'll come back*, she thought. It buzzed again and again. Tessa went to the balcony to take a quick look down at the persistent intruder. It was Toshiro. *The guy doesn't give up*, she thought. Tessa was about to walk away before he could see her, but he lifted his head.

"Hello," he said, admiring her bedhead of soft wavy hair, which was pushed behind her ears.

Surprised by his presence, she began firing questions at him: "What are you doing here? How did you know which apartment to buzz?"

"There is only one Akira on the directory. I figured that would be your friend. Akira Nakano. That's her name, isn't it?"

She stared at him with narrowed eyes. "Yes, but …" *you shouldn't be here*, she wanted to say before he interrupted her.

"May I come up?"

"No, you may not come up." She began to move away from the balcony.

"Please? Look, I have flowers," he said, raising his arm to show her a bouquet of yellow roses.

Flowers have different meanings in Japan and the U.S. For example, yellow roses mean jealousy in Japan and friendship in the U.S. But since Tessa was an American, Toshiro opted for the yellow roses.

She shook her head. "You're crazy, you know."

He smiled.

He reminded her of the dolphins she was trying to protect— friendly, sociable, playful. "Okay, I'll buzz you in," she said, reluctantly.

A minute later, he was at the front door. She let him inside and said, "You should've called first."

"And would you have answered?"

"Probably not," she said, admiring him discreetly. He was wearing an olive suede jacket and smelled like *oud* mixed with clove and cinnamon, giving him a masculine, sexy appeal.

"Then what would've been the point?" He gave her the flowers.

"Thank you. This is nice of you," she said, cutting the ends of the roses and arranging them in a vase filled with water. "What's the occasion?"

"No occasion. It's just a peace offering. I don't want you to stay mad at me," he said, looking at her white robe and wondering what she looked like underneath it.

"I thought I made myself clear last night." She knew that he wanted her from the way he was looking at her. And in all honesty, she was starting to lose her resolve. She hadn't had sex for three years and wouldn't mind a one-night stand. The problem was that he was not just a one-night stand. Tessa knew that if the two of them ever got it on, problems would ensue.

"You said good night, not goodbye," he answered, taking off his jacket and getting comfortable on the sofa.

"Oh, do make yourself at home," she said sarcastically. She went to sit on a kitchen stool.

"I would like to be your friend," he blurted, leaning forward, his hands in a prayer position, pointing in her direction.

No, you don't. You want to get into my pants, she wanted to say. "And how would Kaiya feel about this?"

"Will you leave her out of it? First, my parents and now you, pushing me to be with her."

"My apologies. Still, the two of us hanging out—not a good idea." She shook her head and tightened the belt of her robe to cover her thin pajamas.

"Give me a chance to be your friend." He didn't know why he liked her so much. It was just a gut feeling that she was "The One."

"I'll be going home soon," she said.

"We can keep in touch and talk from time to time."

Talk? She knew that he wanted more. He wasn't even being honest with himself. Maybe once he got to know her better, he would stop liking her—she hoped. She wasn't the easiest person in the world to get along with, especially at forty when she was so set in her ways. She sighed. "May I get you some tea?"

"I thought we'd go out for a walk or something," he offered, hoping that she would give in to him.

"I was planning to do some sightseeing."

"Then I'll be your guide."

On one hand, she thought it was wrong to lead him on, but on the other, she welcomed visiting Tokyo with a native. "Okay, let me go change," she said and disappeared into Akira's bedroom.

"You're still working on more protests," he said, rummaging through the papers on the coffee table.

"Yes," she said, pulling a white V-neck T-shirt over her head and throwing on a pair of black jeans with a cropped mustard jacket. This is what she usually wore to run errands and she wasn't about to dress up or put on makeup for Toshiro. Okay, well, maybe just a quick gloss on her chapped lips. "I'm going to Kyoto in two days to help out a group of activists."

"You're demonstrating in Kyoto?" he asked, surprised.

"Yep, and after that, I'll be off to Taiji and Osaka." It had been a quick trip and she knew that once she was on the plane heading home, she was going to crash from exhaustion. But it will have all been worth it.

"Are you planning to come back to Tokyo?"

"After Osaka, I'll be back in Tokyo for two days and then I head home," she answered as she came out of Akira's room.

He stared at Tessa. Her messy hair rested loosely past her shoulders, and her alluring eyes looked in his direction, expressing comfort and kindness. *She was plain yet so pretty*, he thought.

Tessa felt uncomfortable under his scrutiny and said, "Is what I'm wearing alright? I can go change."

"No. You look great," he assured her. "I like your leather jacket. Who designed it?"

Tessa shrugged, and said, "No idea, but it's not real leather. It's vegan leather."

"Vegan leather?" he asked with wide eyes. Veganism and anything vegan had not really caught on in Japan. He knew what vegan leather was, he just didn't understand why anyone would want to wear something fake.

"It's faux leather. I like animals. I don't want to kill them and wear their skin."

"So, it's acrylic, then?" he asked. If he cringed on the inside, he did not show it. He was used to luxury materials, such as high-end silk, cashmere, and suede.

"I'm not sure," Tessa said. "Some are made of apple peels, cork, pineapple leaves, papaya, and other recycled materials."

"Well, it looks great on you," he reiterated.

"Thank you. You know, the scarf I gave you for your birthday is also vegan. It's made of desert plants." Tessa knew goats were farmed because of their wool. When demands were high for cashmere wool, farmers sheared goats during wintertime and the animals died because they had little fat to protect them from cold weather.

"Amazing! It feels just like cashmere," he said and reached in his jacket pocket, took out a folded newspaper, and presented it to her.

"The interview! When did it come out?" Tessa asked excitedly.

A picture of Akira leading the protesters with a bullhorn with Tessa and Toshiro holding a banner a few steps behind her had made the front cover of ITO with a caption that read, "Activists protest the slaughter of Taiji dolphins. More on page 8."

"Today. I take it Akira hasn't seen it yet?"

"No. She left early to meet up with her client," Tessa said as she riffled through the paper and found her photo with Akira at Kosoan Teahouse. "An interview with Dr. Tessa Walker and Akira Nakano." She began reading.

The article went on to say that hundreds of animal rights activists paraded from Shibuya to Harajuku on Saturday to speak out against the slaughter and captivity of dolphins. It quoted Tessa and Akira on the brutality of dolphin killings and the need to stop them, but also included the viewpoint of the fishermen, claiming, "Dolphins are an essential part of our tradition and livelihood, and we will not yield to international pressure."

"May I keep this?" Tessa asked, noticing that the article seemed to tilt slightly in favor of the fishermen. She planned on reading it later and reflecting on what Jessica had written.

"Yes, of course. I already have a copy at my house."

"Thank you! Let me grab my camera and backpack and leave a note for Akira."

When they got outside, Toshiro gave Tessa a spare helmet.

"We're riding on that?" she said, gawking at a sleek black motorcycle.

"What's wrong with it? I designed it myself," he told her proudly.

"Nothing's wrong with it. It's beautiful. I just wasn't expecting to. … Did you carry the roses while riding?"

"I sure did."

"How in the world did you manage that?"

"It's easy. I just don't drive as fast. I've done it many times before."

"I'll bet," Tessa said, shaking her head.

"No. You have it all wrong. Sometimes I take flowers to my parents."

"Ah," she said, donning the helmet. The guy was full of surprises, but if he thought for a moment that he could fool her into thinking she was special to him, he'd better think again.

Tessa hopped on the back of his motorcycle and held loosely onto his jacket. But he rode so fast that she was forced to wrap her arms around his waist for the next twenty minutes until they got to Harajuku, a district of Shibuya, north of where Akira lived. Unlike in the rest of Tokyo, here the younger generation freely expressed themselves by wearing funky clothes. Toshiro parked his bike and the two headed toward the famous Takeshita Dori, a long street with colorful decorations and signs, trendy shops, used clothing stores, and food stalls catering to Tokyo's teen culture as well as tourists. As they walked down the sloped street, Toshiro stopped in front of a sign written in both Kanji and Rōmaji.

The Japanese have three writing systems: Kanji, Hiragana, and Romaji. Kanji is based on the Chinese written system. Hiragana is a simplified form of Kanji. And Rōmaji is a Latin script used to write Japanese. Tessa was able to read the Rōmaji sign, *Purikura*, but had no idea what it was. She noticed a pink circle with an arrow pointing downward as Toshiro led her down a series of steps.

"Where are we going?"

"To *purikura*, a photo sticker booth. I'm going to show you a bit of Japanese culture."

What the heck is a photo sticker booth? she wondered. Tessa was familiar with photo booths. She and her friends used them in malls and shopping arcades when they were younger. But this place was different. They could hear piped-in music getting louder as they approached the basement, which was filled with mostly young girls dressed in "Lolita fashion." She had seen it in Shibuya and asked Akira about this peculiar way of dressing. Akira told her that in Japan, it was popular to dress like an innocent doll. Lolita fashion was a mixture of styles from the Victorian and Rococo periods, incorporating lace, ribbons, ruffles, aprons, chunky heels, and petticoats. It enabled girls to break away from ordinary, everyday clothing.

There were at least fifteen photo booths. Toshiro explained, "Some of the booths fit five or six people; some are labeled 'Cinderella,' or 'Beautiful,' and others have different virtual animated characters you can take pictures with."

"What's over there?" Tessa pointed at a long line of girls.

"They're waiting to rent a costume. There are makeup tables, changing rooms, and an area where you can find scissors to cut your pictures and give them to friends."

Toshiro and Tessa stood inside a booth, drew a curtain, put money in a slot, and posed for the camera. Then Toshiro sorted through the digital photos and added virtual backgrounds, costumes, stickers, animation, and writing to them. Tessa was impressed by how great she looked in the pictures after he edited them. Toshiro looked good, as well. But then again, he was ten years younger.

"Here, it's yours," Toshiro said.

"What about you? Don't you want a copy?" Tessa didn't mind keeping the pictures. She knew that when she got home, she would be reminded of their time together in Japan.

"I had one sent to my email. Now, let's go get some ice cream."

Not really in the mood for ice cream, she suggested, "Let's share."

Toshiro ordered a wasabi ice cream, but there was no place to sit. In Japan, people do not walk and eat, so the two stood in a corner to savor the treat. Tessa took a few spoonfuls of the sweet and spicy dessert and let Toshiro have the rest. "Would you mind if I pop into that store while you finish your ice cream?" she asked, pointing to an accessory store.

"Sure, sure. Go ahead."

She went into the store, which had all sorts of knickknacks: colorful plastic sunglasses, wigs, temporary tattoos, earrings, and wallets. Tessa took her time browsing until she saw an orange wig and tried it on. It made her look like an orange popsicle. Toshiro walked in, saw her, and laughed.

"I think I'll buy it."

"You can't be serious. Why hide your beautiful hair under this funny-looking thing?"

"Because it's fun and when I'm in a bad mood at home, I'll put it on to cheer me up," she told him, taking it to the register and paying for it.

"Would it be okay if we stop by QZMZ? It's a couple of stores down. I just want to poke my head in and say hi."

"Of course. I love shopping." She was curious about the type of merchandise QZMZ carried.

"Our Harajuku store is the smallest one. The flagship store is in Shibuya and is three stories high."

"I prefer smaller stores. They are more intimate," she said as they arrived in front of a store with a blue QZMZ sign written in English and Japanese calligraphy. When they walked in, all the employees were busy at work stocking shelves and racks, organizing piles of clothes, helping customers, and ringing up sales. But as soon as any of them eyed Toshiro, Tessa could see the panic on their faces. The manager stopped what she was doing, approached Toshiro, and bowed at thirty degrees with eyes lowered to the floor as a sign of respect for her boss.

Toshiro nodded slightly and began talking to her in Japanese. Tessa wondered why they all looked so scared.

Toshiro turned to Tessa and said, "This is Mio Himari-san, the store manager." Addressing Mio he said, "This is my friend, Dr. Walker."

Mio, about Toshiro's age, gave a deep bow and when she straightened up, Tessa shook her hand, and said, "Hi. Nice to meet you." She hated formalities and any system of hierarchy, even if it was part of the culture. Although the employees at her job addressed her as Dr. Walker, the atmosphere at her office was relaxed and friendly.

Mio smiled and said with a heavy accent, "Very nice to meet you."

Toshiro said, "Tessa, why don't you have a look around while I speak to Himari-san?"

Tessa nodded and walked away, wondering about how Toshiro behaved so differently at the store. He had turned into someone she did not recognize, someone formal and stiff. She preferred the casual Toshiro.

As she browsed through the store, bustling with young customers, Tessa noticed that everything was perfectly folded, and the clothing racks of blouses, skirts, and pants were coordinated by size, style, and color. Two mannequins wore unmatched unisex ensembles that were youthful and fashion-forward; the shelves carried knockoffs of the latest shoes and handbags. Tessa found a sleeveless, red georgette dress with a handkerchief hem. A salesperson showed her to a dressing room.

Meanwhile, Toshiro talked to Mio Himari, asking her how busy they were and how much they had sold so far. He asked her what items were doing best and if the window display enticed the customers to come in. Mio was not happy that Toshiro was there. She didn't like surprise visits. Normally, Toshiro's assistant, Ena, would call ahead to let Mio know that he would be coming over. Toshiro rarely stopped by and if he did, he would show up with Ena. But today, he wanted to impress Tessa and show her the importance of his position even if he didn't care much about work.

Tessa decided to purchase the dress, and the cashier rang her up.

"I think you made a mistake. That dress was 13,000 yen, but you only charged me 6,500," she informed the cashier, whose understanding of English was limited.

Toshiro said, "There was no mistake. I told her to charge you the wholesale price."

"Oh no. I would gladly pay the full price. I don't need special treatment," Tessa replied, feeling uncomfortable as she noticed the unhappy look on the manager's face.

"The cashier rang it up already," he said, scribbling on the back of his business card, and giving it to the cashier. He said something to her in Japanese, and then turned to Tessa, "Okay, we can go now."

"Are we going to come back to pick up the dress?" Tessa asked, walking outside.

"It'll be delivered to Akira's apartment."

"Thank you, but you overwhelm me, Toshiro. I could have carried it," Tessa complained.

"You're welcome. Don't worry about it. It's her job," he said, matter-of-factly.

"You mean she has to deliver clothes to customers at the end of her shift?" she asked in surprise.

"No, but I am her boss and she'll do what I ask," he responded arrogantly.

If he thought that he had impressed her, he was wrong. Tessa appreciated that Toshiro wanted to treat her well. But she wondered if he was used to snapping his fingers and having people jump. She felt sorry for the employee who was now tasked with the extra chore of delivering her dress. On top of that, the manager didn't look too happy that Tessa had gotten a discount. "Are your salespeople on commission?"

"No. But each manager has to sell a certain amount by the end of each day, and if they don't meet their quotas several days in a row, they need to explain why."

"I see," she said. She was glad that she was not in sales and wished that she had paid full price to help the manager's sales.

After browsing in more stores and watching girls in their wild outfits and boys with pink hair, Toshiro suggested that they leave so that he could show her the Sensoji Temple before it got dark.

The Sensoji Temple was the oldest Buddhist temple in Tokyo and a landmark in Asakusa, northeast of Harajuku. Located on the banks of the Sumida River, Asakusa was a historic neighborhood with a traditional Japanese ambiance. Tessa gazed at a massive red gate with a 12-foot-high lantern in the middle.

"This is the Kaminarimon entrance gate," said Toshiro. He pointed to two red alcoves on either side of the red gate each of which had a statue inside. "The god of thunder is on the left and the god of wind is on the right."

Tessa tried to take a picture, but the area was crowded with Japanese and foreign visitors bumping into her and excusing themselves.

"There is a legend that in the 7th century, two brothers went fishing in the Sumida River and found a golden statue in their nets," explained Toshiro. "They put it back in the river, but the statue kept returning to them. It was the statue of Kannon, the goddess of mercy. The two brothers and a local landowner decided to build a small temple for this goddess. Over time, the temple turned into the grand Sensoji Temple."

They walked around the gate to a street lined with outdoor shops selling crafts, souvenirs, toys, clothing, and snacks.

"This street is called Nakamise and has been here for two centuries. It connects the first gate to the second one, Hozomon, and past that is the temple."

"Mind if I look through some of the stalls? I want to get a few souvenirs."

"Sure."

Tessa found two *yukatas*, or summer kimonos, for her parents and *geta*, Japanese wooden slippers, for her good friend Bruna, also an activist. There were many food stalls and she was starting to feel hungry. She bought two *yakiimo,* Japanese baked sweet potatoes, and gave one to Toshiro.

"This is so good," Tessa remarked after biting into it. I've never had anything like it." The potato was crunchy on the outside with a sweet, creamy, and velvety texture on the inside. She wondered how they baked it because hers never came out like that.

"These are made in stone ovens, which affect the cooking process and flavors. They release heat slowly, sealing in the steam produced by the water in the sweet potato."

"Well, no wonder mine never comes out like this. I just stick mine in an oven."

"If you were here when the weather turns cold, you would see old open-back trucks carrying sweet potatoes in cast-iron ovens on hot stone beds. They sing: '*ishi ya-kii-mo, ishi ya-kii-mo, hokka hokka dayo,*' meaning sweet potato, sweet potato, hot steaming hot."

"I would absolutely love that! I want to get more of these."

"Save your appetite," Toshiro said. "Let's go to my house for dinner."

"Thank you, no. After this, I want to go to Akira's, take a bath, and go to sleep."

"You can do all of that at my place."

"I don't think that's such a good idea."

"Please?" he begged.

"Let's go see the temple and you can explain to me how to cleanse my soul and make a wish," she said, changing the subject. While planning her trip to Japan, she had read a travel blog about soul cleansing at temples.

The two walked to Hozomon, the temple's main gate. Toshiro bowed and said, "This is the line between the earthly world and sacred grounds. And we bow again once we pass through and are on the temple ground. This is a sign of respect to the Buddha and to let him know that we're going to pray."

"Are you a Buddhist?"

"I practice Shintoism and Buddhism. In Japan, Shintoism and Buddhism have evolved throughout the years and now they coexist."

"I have read about Buddhism, but I know nothing of Shintoism."

"Shintoism is the native religion of Japan in which there are many *kami*, or deities; Buddhism follows the teachings of Buddha and it is the path to enlightenment."

"You have two religions then?"

"Like many native Japanese, I'm not religious; I'm spiritual. There is a saying in Japan: 'The Japanese are born Shinto and die Buddhist.' You see, there is no afterlife in the Shinto religion."

Tessa looked lost, so Toshiro elaborated. "It takes time for foreigners to understand. Buddhism and Shintoism are interwoven into our daily lives. During special holidays, we may visit a Buddhist temple, a Shinto shrine, or both. Now, let's keep going, and if time allows, maybe we can visit the Asakusa Shrine, which is on temple grounds."

Tessa looked around, trying to take it all in; she noticed a stately red, gold, and white pagoda.

Toshiro continued: "If someone has a hat, they should take it off. We walk on the sides of the road leading to the temple. The center is the path for the Buddha to walk on."

The center may have been the path for the Buddha to walk on, but the place was swarming with visitors walking everywhere. And because there was not much they could do about it, the temple monks were tolerant of many such faux pas.

"That pagoda, do you know how tall it is?" she asked. The structure had five stories of elegant tiers. Each tier had an overhang that gracefully curved upward at the corners. She stood in silence, amazed at her surroundings.

"It's 175 feet tall and was rebuilt in 1973, after World War II when it was completely destroyed by the ..." *Americans*, he wanted to say and stopped himself.

"Sorry," Tessa said as if reading his mind. Even if she had nothing to do with it, it was awkward to hear.

Toshiro's father never let him forget history's deadliest air raid, the firebombing of Tokyo by the United States on March 9, 1945, which destroyed half of Tokyo's residential and commercial neighborhoods, killed at least 100,000 civilians in a single night, and left one million homeless. The Japanese later called this "Night of the Black Snow" because of the ashes from the burned bodies and buildings blanketing the ground.

"That was long ago before you and I were even born. Anyway, back to *gojunoto*, which means a five-story pagoda. The levels, from bottom to top, represent the five elements of Japanese

Buddhism: *chi* or earth, *sui* or water, *ka* or fire, *fu* or wind, and *ku* or void."

"Can we go inside?"

"It's closed to visitors. It is my understanding that it serves as a graveyard," Toshiro explained. "The bottom floor contains memorial tablets of families and individuals. People can see the inside at special times during the year by asking permission and proving that they have family there."

"What's on the other floors?" Tessa wondered.

"Buddha's ashes and relics are on the top floor. They were received from a temple in Sri Lanka," Toshiro said, and continued walking. He enjoyed being Tessa's tour guide because he was in charge and she was like a child, curious about everything.

"The Buddha's ashes?" Tessa asked with wide eyes.

"I see why you're surprised. One would think that Buddha's ashes would be in Nepal, where he was born, or buried at the Bodhi tree in Bihar, India, where he found enlightenment, but his ashes and relics were divided among various countries," he said, stopping in front of the temple in an area dedicated to fortune-telling.

Toshiro showed Tessa how to pick out her fortune. Against a wall, there was a cabinet with at least 200 small drawers.

Toshiro said, "You put 100 yen in this money collection box to pay for your fortune. Then you pick up one hexagon metal container from the shelf, shake it, turn it upside down, and a wooden stick will poke out with a number in Japanese on it."

Tessa did as she was told. Toshiro then helped her match her number to a number on one of the drawers. Tessa pulled out her *omikuji*, or random fortune. The fortune was written in both Japanese and English.

"If you don't like your *omikuji*, you can tie it to that wire rack over there," Toshiro said, pointing to a red square-shaped stand with horizontal wires running through it, "and the gods will take your bad fortune away."

She read her fortune and said, "I actually got a good one, so I'm keeping it." It was about business, life, and love. Her favorite prediction was: "You will succeed in your endeavors." And even though she didn't believe in fortune-telling, she wanted to take the paper home as a memory of her visit.

From there, the two moved toward a billowing cloud of incense coming from a *jokoro*, an urn, which was so large that about a dozen people could encircle it. Visitors gathered and lit incense to make personal wishes. Toshiro and Tessa each bought a stick. Tessa was about to light hers using the fire of another stick, but Toshiro stopped her.

"If you do that, then you will be taking on another person's sins. Use the temple fire to light it. And when you're done, place it in the center and wave the smoke toward you."

Tessa did as he said and watched him light his own stick.

"You see, when you light this, you're also inviting Buddha to make himself welcome."

"I see," Tessa said, thinking there were so many rituals in the Japanese culture that even if she lived there for years, she would not be able to master them.

"Do you want me to show you how to cleanse?" Toshiro said.

"I thought I was cleansing."

"You still need to purify and cleanse at the *chōzubachi* before making a wish at the temple," he said as they walked toward a cement trough filled with water and metal ladles with long wooden handles.

Toshiro showed her how to fill her ladle with water and rinse her left hand, then her right, and then put a little water in one hand and rinse her mouth and spit the water out on the ground. Then she had to rinse the handle with the leftover water in the spoon. After this cleanse of body and soul, it was time to pray.

The two walked up a series of steps to the front of the temple. "Now, you need a coin," Toshiro told her.

Tessa reached in her purse and took out a 100-yen coin.

"It is better if you use 5 yen."

Not yet familiar with the Japanese change, she sifted through her wallet.

Toshiro said, "It's the coin with a hole in the center."

Tessa pulled out a worn gold coin and said, "Why does it matter which coin I use?"

"The 5 yen is pronounced 'go-en.' 'Go' is a prefix and 'yen' sounds like 'en.' 'En' represents casual connections or relationships. People throw 5 yen to establish a good relationship with the deity at shrines."

"But we are at a temple."

"How should I say…it's hard to explain. You see, the coin represents good luck. People throw it in, hoping that they will meet new people who may bring them fortune or love."

"Ah, I get it."

"At a Buddhist temple, you bow once and put a coin into an offertory box for Buddha, since one of the teachings is to forgo monetary attachments."

"Okay, let's do this."

"Wait a minute; if there is a *waniguchi*, a temple gong, you ring it gently to greet the Buddha, close your eyes, put your hands together and pray, and bow once more when you're done."

They lined up behind other visitors and when they got to the front of the line, Tessa looked to mimic what Toshiro was doing. She was nervous and afraid to make a mistake, but if she did make a mistake, Toshiro never corrected her. And she prayed. She prayed that her nightmares would not come back to haunt her. She prayed that someday soon the brutal slaughter of the dolphins would end. She prayed for world wisdom and compassion. Toshiro prayed for answers. He prayed that he would someday stop feeling so lost and find his path in life.

"There is much to visit here, but we will not have time to do it all. There are two more things I would like to show you."

"Oh, how I wish I could have had a longer stay in Japan," Tessa said. Her work back home was demanding, and she was very lucky to have been able to take this much time off.

"Me too."

"You know, I noticed that many things are colored red."

"The color red is symbolic of celebration. It is the color of blood and brings energy, vitality, and fertility."

"What about the red buildings?"

"They are painted in red to scare away evil and bring peace and prosperity. The color represents strength, power, and wealth," Toshiro said and then guided her to a red one-story building. "This is Yokodo, a place where you can get a red stamp commemorating your visit here. The stamp is called *goshuin*."

"I'm not sure I understand this," said Tessa.

"Every time you visit a temple or shrine you can get a *goshuin*," he continued. "You pay a fee, about 100 to 300 yen, and you receive a card with a stamp and the date. You can even purchase a notebook and have a monk stamp your notebook."

Toshiro helped her pick out a floral notebook that opened up like an accordion. She paid 2,300 yen, about $23, to a cashier working behind the window. She then watched him pass the notebook to a woman wearing a blue uniform, who started to write in the book by dipping a calligraphy brush into a bottle of black ink.

Toshiro explained, "You see, the notebook you purchased is called *goshuin-chou,* which means honorable red-stamp notebook."

"What is she writing?" Tessa asked looking at her Japanese writing.

"She is writing the name of the temple, the word *houhai*, which means worship, and the date of your visit according to the Japanese calendar. It's all written in traditional Japanese calligraphy. She adds a red stamp on top of the calligraphy, which is the emblem of the temple to show that you visited here."

"I thought your calendar is the same as ours," she remarked, as she admired the impressive calligraphy.

"Yes, we do follow the Christian calendar, but we also have a parallel numbering system for years based on reigns of emperors."

Tessa put her *goshuin-chou* in her backpack, and the two walked side by side as though they had been good friends for years. Toshiro felt that he could spend a lifetime with Tessa and never get tired. Tessa, on the other hand, was fatigued. Between the time difference and all the running around she had been doing, her energy was starting to fizzle.

"Here we are," Toshiro said, stopping in front of the Asakusa Jinja Shrine. "At the entrance of a Shinto shrine, there is always a *torii*, a sacred gate, to separate the physical world from the spiritual world."

Tessa noticed that the large *torii* was also red. The shrine grounds were much quieter, and the building was much smaller and more understated than the Sensoji Temple.

"Here, you'll see how Buddhism and Shintoism are interwoven. Remember the legend of the two brothers and the land owner I told you about earlier?"

Tessa nodded.

"This Shinto Shrine is in honor of the two brothers and the landowner. Before the temple was built, Tokyo did not exist, and

Asakusa was a small fishing village. After the trio built the temple, much prosperity came to Asakusa. This shrine is also known as the *Sanja-sama*, Shrine of the Three Gods."

"Then they are considered gods in the Shinto religion?"

"They are not 'gods' the way many religions would interpret it. *Kami*, or deities, are not divine or omnipotent. *Kami* are imperfect and may make mistakes and behave badly. They don't live in a supernatural world. They live in the same world as humans. At this shrine, *kami* embody the souls of human beings of outstanding achievements."

"It sounds like they share similarities with saints."

"Perhaps, but *kami* have an extraordinary manifestation of energy, and that energy can be good or evil," explained Toshiro. "They can also be elements of landscapes, like lakes and mountains, or forces of nature, like storms and thunder."

"I think I would need to live in Japan for a long time to truly comprehend what you're trying to convey," remarked Tessa. "But now I can better understand the connection of the two religions."

"You see, I may pray at a Buddhist temple and then come here to pray and pay my respects at this Shinto shrine. And incidentally, at a Shinto shrine, the praying ritual is different than at a Buddhist temple. But that would be a lesson for another day," he said, noticing that it was starting to get dark.

By the time they walked back, some of the stalls were starting to close up.

"Are you still hungry?" Toshiro asked.

"I'm more tired than hungry. Let's get something quick and call it a night."

"Why don't you come over to my place, and I will make you a home-cooked meal?"

"You know how to cook?" She imagined that he always ordered takeout or went out to eat.

"I only know how to do a few things. But I do them well."

"Maybe another night when I'm not so tired," Tessa defered.

"What other night? You're not going to be around for that long. Please?"

"Okay, but I would have to leave right after we eat. I know it's bad manners, but I really need to get my z's."

"Z's?" Toshiro cocked his head. "What's that?"

"It's slang for sleep."

He then repeated to himself, "I need to get my z's," so that he would remember the expression. Tessa hopped on the back of his motorcycle and the two were off.

When they reached his house in Denenchofu, a ritzy area in the southern part of Tokyo, Toshiro pushed a six-digit code to unlock a sturdy stainless-steel gate. They drove up a dirt driveway, and Toshiro parked his motorcycle in the garage next to his white Nissan 370Z. Tessa got out and looked at the two-story, modern, rectangular, glass-and-wood house surrounded by 9-foot-high bamboo trees and illuminated by in-ground lights. They went inside through the front entrance and took off their shoes at the genkan.

"The house has five bedrooms and was designed by a friend of my father's who is a well-known architect in Japan," he said, giving her a tour.

"This is your house?" she asked with amazement.

"No, it belongs to my parents. They were going to sell it, but I didn't want to live with them. So they let me stay here until I figure out what to do with my life."

"You don't like what you do?"

He shrugged. "Not sure. I'm still trying to figure that one out," he said, sounding despondent.

Toshiro liked having fun and treated his work as a hobby. He went into his office and left whenever he wanted. If a friend called and asked him to hang out, he would take a long lunch break, even if he had deadlines. Sometimes he didn't bother going back to work.

"Here's the kitchen and the dining area," he said, trying to change the subject.

Tessa looked around the open space. The maple floors had wide planks and a white finish. Wooden stools sat behind a gray-and-white granite breakfast bar. The kitchen had a tall built-in beverage and wine fridge, a Viking stainless-steel double oven and gas range, and a Sub-Zero refrigerator. A staircase in the center of the house led to the bedrooms. The house suited him, Tessa thought. Although she hadn't yet seen the upstairs, the downstairs exuded a single guy vibe, a perfect setup for someone who had lots of friends over for drinks while watching sports on television.

"Please, have a seat on the sofa and relax while I cook," he said, pointing at a leather curved sectional situated behind a white lacquer coffee table.

Tessa sat on the charcoal sofa, facing the huge flat-screen TV. From there she had a view of the outside: bamboos, hostas with their heart-shaped leaves, pink, white, and orange cosmos, yellow and red chrysanthemums, and maple and Japanese larch that would turn yellow, orange, and red in a few weeks. She felt as though she were in the middle of a forest. "Mind if I turn on the TV?" She asked.

"No. Go ahead. Can I get you something to drink?" he offered as he grabbed a bunch of raw vegetables from his fridge.

"No, thanks. I'm good."

"Have some sake. It'll help get rid of some of the tiredness you're feeling," he insisted. He heated it and poured some for both of them.

"Thank you, I've never tried this brand before," she remarked, looking at the label of the bottle sitting on his counter. She took a sip. "I like it," she said, enjoying the dry warm sake with a hint of cherry.

"I thought you would. It's a popular brand called, *Otokoyama Tokubetsu Junmai*. You should be able to find it in America," he commented, washing some bok choy and throwing it in a pot of boiling water. He was making his specialty—ramen soup with tofu and vegetables.

Tessa flipped through the channels and found BBC World News. Relaxed, she listened to a segment on whales and dolphins, which explained how similar their minds were to human minds. They also reported on a dolphin in Indonesia that had recently died because it lived in captivity. The reporter said that the dolphin was alone and the tank was too small, so the dolphin kept banging its head against the wall out of frustration. The caretaker had been forced to sedate it so that it would stay calm, and it died shortly after it was captured.

"Is everything alright?" Toshiro asked, noticing a sudden sadness in her. Her shoulders were stooped, and her head fell forward as though she were crying.

"I'm fine. May I use the guest bathroom?" she asked.

"Sure. Past the staircase, and turn left. You're sure you're alright?"

She did not respond. Instead, she downed her sake and left the room.

He overheard the news she was watching. It was upsetting, but it didn't hit him as hard as her. Although Japanese people rarely ate dolphin meat ever since finding out it was toxic, a dolphin to him was no different than a cow, chicken, or octopus. Didn't they also suffer when they were killed? Yet people ate them. He picked up the remote and changed the channel so that Tessa wouldn't get more worked up. He put on an animated, romantic DVD.

Tessa dried her eyes and washed up. She didn't want to fall apart in front of him or be rude and put him in a bad mood. She came out and said, "Sorry. I, I didn't…you know…never mind me."

"Alright then. Dinner should be ready soon. I put on a video titled, *Your Name,* written and directed by Makoto Shinkai. It's a fantasy film in Japanese, subtitled in English. It won the Los Angeles Film Critics Association award and the Japan Academy prize. Hope that's okay."

"Absolutely. I love foreign films," she said, sitting down on the couch to watch.

By the time dinner was ready, he found her fast asleep. He put a pillow under her head, covered her with a blanket, kissed her on the forehead, and turned off the light.

Toshiro was glad that she was spending the night. And in fact, he was thinking about how to keep her at his house for the rest of the next day. She would probably want to leave and go change. So he decided to go buy her a change of clothes. Since it was late, retailers were closed. He could have gone to QZMZ, but he didn't want to have to explain why he'd been there so late at night if anyone noticed him—especially since his father didn't approve of Tessa.

There was a shop called Don Quijote, referred to as Donki, in Akihabara that was open late and was geared toward American tastes. Before taking off, Toshiro left Tessa a note in case she woke up, though he believed that her exhaustion and the sake had knocked her out.

In the morning when the sun streamed through the house, Tessa opened her eyes and wondered where she was and why she was there.

"Good morning," Toshiro said, holding a tea mug with an emblem of the University of Tokyo. He had a graduate degree in economics from there, which he rarely put to good use.

Tessa sat up and rubbed her eyes. "Did I? … "

"Yes, you did. You fell asleep on the sofa."

"Shit! Akira!" She rummaged through her backpack and pulled out her cell phone. Akira had texted and called her several times. She stood up, held her phone up high, and moved it in a circle to see if she could get reception.

"My username is James Dean. Put in the passcode 65921 to connect to my Wi-Fi," Toshiro said.

She looked at him inquisitively. He looked good in his black jeans and a black-and-red T-shirt. "James Dean, huh? Let's hope that you'll have a better outcome than him," she said, entering the passcode and calling Akira.

"Where've you been? I was worried sick about you," she said. She was on her way to pick up a British couple and their two boys from the Narita Airport to show them around the city during their layover.

"I'm so sorry. I had every intention of coming back to your place last night, but I fell asleep at Toshiro's."

"Really?" she asked, playfully. "How was he?"

"Oh no, nothing like that. I literally fell asleep."

"Oh," Akira said, sounding disappointed. "Well, there's still hope. Morning sex is always good."

"I'm going to ignore that and hang up. I just wanted you to know I'm okay."

"See you tonight? I mean, you know, let me know how your day goes."

"I will. Thanks for understanding." Tessa ended the call. She turned to Toshiro. "I'm so sorry for falling asleep after you did all that work to prepare dinner. And I really did want to watch the animated film."

"It was no trouble. Why don't you and I hang out today?"

"Thank you, but no. I really need to go take a shower, freshen up, and get some work done."

"You can use the guest bathroom and take a shower here."

"I want to change into fresh clothes."

"Come with me," he said, grabbing her wrist and leading her up the stairs to the guest bedroom.

To her surprise, he had laid out a new outfit, packets of white underwear and socks, and brand-new canvas shoes on the bed. "How did you...where did these come from?"

"I got them for you last night."

"Last night? Where? All the shops were closed," she responded, looking at him dumbfounded. "And how did you even know my size?" She stared at him, wondering if he had used a tape to measure her while she was asleep. *No, Tessa. That would be too creepy. He's not a creep.*

He passed her a mischievous smile, "I've had many girlfriends. I can size women by just looking at them. And I sort of guessed."

"I see," she said both mad and grateful. Mad because he was treating her like a Barbie doll, wanting to dress her. And besides, he was so full of himself. He must've thought that he had her eating out of his hand.

When he saw the look of ambivalence on her face, he said, "Look, don't misunderstand. I thought it would be good to hang out together as friends. And I need someone to practice my English with."

"Practice English, huh?" She shook her head. "Okay, if that's the only reason." She went to the bathroom and closed the door. There, she found the toiletries he had bought her: a toothbrush, toothpaste, shampoo, conditioner, and soap. She wasn't sure what to make out of the whole situation. She was worried that he was falling for her, and she didn't want to hurt him. She stripped off her clothes and turned the chrome shower handle.

Forty minutes later, she emerged from the room dressed in the clothes he had bought for her. She had blow-dried her hair and pulled it back into a ponytail. Her skin had a hint of almond and rose scent from the soap he had picked out. He was texting someone when she came into the kitchen, and she wondered who he was texting. Yet another girlfriend?

Toshiro looked up and put his phone down. He couldn't take his eyes off of her. She was so natural without makeup, fake lashes, or filler-injected lips, unlike some of the women he had dated. Even his ex, Kaiya, who looked perfectly fine, had nose surgery because she thought her nose was too flat and wide.

"Well?" she asked.

"Well what?"

"How do I look in the clothes you got me?" She twirled.

"Nice!" he answered, proud of himself that he had picked them out for her, and that she looked happy wearing them. "What would you like for breakfast?"

She was glad that he asked because her stomach was rumbling. "Any leftovers from last night?"

"You really want ramen soup?" he asked, surprised.

"What's wrong with that?"

"Nothing. I just thought you might want toast, butter, jam, and coffee—an American breakfast," he answered, taking out a container of last night's soup from the fridge to heat it.

"Sometimes I like real food for breakfast. Besides, you raved so much about your ramen yesterday that I must try it at least once," she admitted, leaning on the kitchen counter.

"It was good when it was fresh. But now, I don't know."

"I'm sure it's great. Why didn't you wake me up last night?" she asked, noticing two short glasses and two water bottles on the counter. "May I help myself to some water?"

"Please do! You looked so peaceful and comfortable. I didn't want to disturb you. Are you mad?"

She shrugged, "No. I'm just overwhelmed by your hospitality. Keep this up and I may never leave."

"You can stay. You'll have your own room and shower," he offered, excited at the prospect. He poured *sencha* into two cups and gave one to her.

"Oh, but I wouldn't want to share you with all your girlfriends," she teased.

He blushed, his face turning crimson.

Tessa went to the stove and turned it off. "You have a bowl?"

"Here, let me do it," he said, grabbing a bowl and presenting it to her.

She took a spoonful and blew on it to cool it off. "This is really good, chef Toshiro."

"Glad you like it. It's my specialty. By the way, do you have any more of those chocolate mint patties in that rucksack of yours?" He pointed at her bag, remembering how much he had enjoyed one on the day of the protest.

Tessa grabbed a bunch from one of the pockets and said, "You like those, huh?"

Toshiro smiled and said, "Yeah I do."

"Mind if I turn on the TV?"

"No, go ahead," he said, watching her make herself at home in his house. He felt that it was odd for him to like her so much. He didn't know much about her—her likes and dislikes, her character, or what kind of people she associated with. And then there was that age difference between them. So why her? Why now? He didn't have an answer, but he was certain that the chemistry between them was strong, and the harder he tried not to think about her, the more she occupied his mind.

"You know, this will probably be the last time we get to see each other," she said, turning to face him as he stood in the kitchen drinking his tea. "I'm taking the Shinkansen bullet train to Kyoto tomorrow early morning." It was a short trip, about two-and-a-half hours.

"Mind if I tag along?" he asked, thinking he could easily get a last-minute train ticket or catch a short flight out.

Tessa enjoyed his company, and with him around, it was easy to get around. She never had to worry about the language barrier, and he was a great tour guide, but she hated using him. "Don't you have to work? I mean, I'm surprised that you are here, spending time with me."

"I'm on vacation for two weeks."

"And you want to spend your vacation with me?"

"Yes. I have no plans, and I like hanging out with you."

Tessa sighed, unsure of what to say. "You can't travel with me. What if someone takes a picture of us again?"

"You're too worried. I will deal with it."

Tessa shook her head no. "I'm going to Kyoto, Taiji, and then Osaka. We can't travel together. I don't want to upset your parents."

"I'm not a child, you know. I'm thirty years old, and I certainly don't need their approval of how I should live my life."

Tessa took in a deep breath, rubbed her hands together, and stared out as she thought about what to do and say. He was so stubborn. "Sorry. I didn't mean to offend you. I'm just trying not to step on too many toes. What if you met me there?"

"A compromise?"

"Yes, a compromise. But let me know if this plan works for you..."

"Tell me."

"Satomi's meeting me at the train station in Kyoto."

"Who is Satomi?"

"She is an activist, like me. We'll be working together on the dolphin demonstration, and I'll be staying at her place. I should be there by 10 a.m. I need time to meet and greet and take my bags to her place. We can meet back at the Kyoto station by say, 12:30."

"That would be fine. I'll take a later train."

"And here's the thing. I can't have dinner with you."

"Why not?"

"We have a dinner meeting. Four of us will be going over our plan for the protest. Then I have to go back to Satomi's place, and we need to work on making signs and flyers."

"I have family in Kyoto and Osaka. I can spend my free time with them when you're busy."

"Are you sure you want to do this? I mean, you can go to France, Italy, or anywhere else. You know, just get out of Japan and explore." Tessa wished that she had time to travel more and see the world, but the majority of her spare time went to her volunteer job. And the pet hospital where she worked was already short-staffed. Her problem was that she was a workaholic.

"No, I'd rather be with you." When he was with her, he felt fulfilled and content and he didn't know how to make her feel the same about him.

He was like a stray dog, Tessa thought, following her everywhere, except that he wasn't stray. He came from a good family that afforded him many opportunities, but she didn't know how to dissuade him from having a crush on her. She didn't know how to get him to see what a great life he had. He had the means to do anything he wanted with his life, if only he applied himself.

"May I ask you a question?" he asked, taking a seat on the kitchen's wooden stool, "If it upsets you, you don't need to answer it."

"Go ahead," she said, curious. She joined him behind the breakfast bar.

"You know yesterday? How upset you got over the death of a dolphin?" He inquired, crossing his ankle over his knee.

"Oh, that," she said rubbing her nose. "I have a hard time dealing with loss and suffering."

"But as a vet, you see all sorts of animal abuse and there are times when you lose patients. How do you deal with it?"

She took a sip of her tea and said, "Doctors are not immune to grief. We do what is best for our patients, but that doesn't mean we are devoid of emotion. I remember my first patient, a Maltese that was bitten around the ribs by a coyote. I lost him on the operating table. After consoling its owner, I locked myself in the bathroom and had a good cry. I still cry each time I lose a patient. It never gets easier."

He furrowed his brows, leaned forward, and said, "You have a tough job. I don't know how you do it."

"It's not just a job for me. It's my passion. I want to save as many animals as I can," *even if it means getting arrested,* she wanted to say. "It's rewarding when you get to make their quality of life better."

CHAPTER 10

Outside the Kyoto Station, Tessa was met by Satomi, who had insisted that they walk because her place was not far, and it didn't make sense to take a taxi.

Most Japanese were frugal and didn't like to waste money even if it was a friend's. Japanese millennials, and even those who were older, like 26-year-old Satomi, had grown up in the age of the tsunami, nuclear disaster, and a stagnant economy. As a result, were thrifty, walked and took the subway or bus instead of taxis, and kept their spending in check.

On the other hand, Tessa noticed that Satomi had double eyelid surgery, so her eyes looked much larger than other Japaneses'. In Japan, eyelid surgery is more popular than liposuction or breast implants. Tessa guessed that this procedure must have been important to Satomi since it was probably costly.

It was a twenty-minute walk to Satomi's street, and Tessa had no choice but to roll her luggage the entire time. Satomi's building was old, run-down, and one of many that were packed close together. The pair climbed three flights of stairs and went down an outdoor hallway until they reached a worn brown door with a scratched metal knob.

"Welcome to my home," Satomi said, unlocking the door. "Hope you like it."

The apartment seemed to embody a traditional, authentic Japanese experience. The other homes she had visited were Westernized versions of the Japanese lifestyle, which Tessa preferred.

"I like it already," Tessa lied, trying to catch her breath from the climb up the stairs.

They removed their shoes before entering a narrow hallway. Satomi's place was smaller and dingier than the other places where Tessa had stayed. In the hallway was a 4-foot-high refrigerator, two gas burners, and a small sink. Every time Satomi wanted to chop vegetables, she had to put a cutting board over the sink.

The hallway led to a multifunctional room with a wall-mounted working desk, a TV, and an orange sofa bed. On the opposite side, there was a teensy, round rustic wood tub with a showerhead above it, a white curtain that wrapped around it, a shower faucet that was installed outside the curtain, a sink, and a separate room with a squatting toilet. It was situated at floor level and required squatting instead of sitting. Many old buildings in Japan had squatting toilets.

Oh shoot, Tessa thought. She dreaded using squatting toilets, but what choice did she have? She could always get a nice hotel room, except that she didn't want to offend Satomi, who had insisted that Tessa stay with her.

The combination workstation and TV room led to a bedroom with a double bed and a sliding glass door behind it, revealing a balcony.

Tessa smiled and removed her moto jacket. She was starting to understand the concept of *honne* and *tatemae* as she noticed Satomi's view: the wall of another apartment building. On the balcony were a weathered washing machine, a rickety table, two worn chairs, and a hanging circular rack for drying laundry.

In a way, Tessa was impressed by the home that Satomi made for herself. With only a high school degree, Satomi worked at her uncle's convenience store for $10 an hour. She supplemented her income by delivering food on her bicycle.

After their mid-20s, unmarried men and women were negatively labeled *parasaito shinguru*, meaning parasite singles, if they lived at home or off of their parents. But Satomi was independent and preferred to have a place of her own. Had she lived in Tokyo, she would not have survived on her income. However, in Kyoto, the cost of living was lower.

Tessa put her luggage in the closet and took out a lavender box that held a daisy-patterned makeup pouch with organic citrus hand lotion and organic fruity lip balms she had purchased at a boutique back in Los Angeles. "Just something small to thank you for letting me stay here."

"Thank you. Of course," Satomi said and left the room to put the box on her desk. Tessa followed her as she continued talking. "We have a meeting with other activists at 6:30 at Musoshin, a ramen restaurant in the Gion district."

"Okay. Are there geishas in the Gion district?"

"You mean *geikos*. Geishas are from Tokyo and *geikos* are from Kyoto, even if many people use the terms interchangeably. Both are experts in Japanese art, music, and dance, but *geikos* are considered superior, speak a Gion Dialect, and perform different songs and dances. Also, different rules apply to *giekos*. For example, they have to be trained at a much younger age than geishas."

"Interesting. I did not know that."

"Maybe you'll get to see a *maiko*, an apprentice *geiko*. After five years of training, a *maiko* becomes a *geiko*."

"I would love that," Tessa said, glancing at her phone. It was noon. "Sorry, but I have to run, I'm meeting a friend at the Kyoto Station."

"Oh, yes. You told me about that…Do you know how to get back?"

"I think so," said Tessa. "If all else fails, I'll Google a map."

"I'll walk back with you," offered Satomi. "This is your first day here, and I don't want you to get lost."

In Japan, most people are more patient with foreigners than they are with each other. If you are Japanese, they explain something to you once and expect you to immediately understand it or consider you stupid. But if you are a *gaijin*, they go out of their way to make sure you get things right. Of course, just like anywhere else in the world, there are also plenty of people who are not so accommodating. Tessa had witnessed it firsthand when she was at Toshiro's parents' house and when she was at the Tokyo train station and the person behind the ticket booth had been unnecessarily rude to her.

Satomi guided Tessa to the north side of the Kyoto Station, where she was supposed to meet Toshiro. "You want me to wait with you?"

"No, I'm good. See you tonight."

A few minutes later, Toshiro showed up at the station in a pair of jeans, a cream shirt, and an olive-green vest. Before leaving for Kyoto, he had spent time putting himself together and in the bathroom of the train station, he fixed his hair and made sure that his clothes looked neat and tidy.

Appearance is important in Japan, and if a person walks around with a shirt half tucked in or an improperly fitting blouse, it drives people crazy. The unkept person is considered *darashinai*, a slob, which is a severe insult. When applied to women, *darashinai* means a slut.

At the first sight of Tessa, Toshiro smiled. He had missed her and was already wondering what he was going to do once she went home.

"You only have a small backpack. No bags?" Tessa asked. Her eyes sparkled when she saw him.

"I put it in a locker. I'll pick it up after our sightseeing. So where do you want to go?"

"Well, I would like to see the Golden Pavilion I have heard so much about." Also known as Kinkakuji, the Golden Pavilion used to be the retirement villa of a shogun in 1397. According to his wishes, it became a Zen temple after his death.

"That's easy. It's about a forty-minute bus ride to the west side of Kyoto."

"Great. I'm glad you're here."

"Are you really? You're not just saying that?" he asked, surprised.

She nodded. He was starting to grow on her. "No, I mean it. I'm grateful that you're hanging out with me."

The bus ride was comfortable, unlike during the rush hour when the bus would be so packed that entering, exiting, and movements of any sort were a struggle. People would push their way in no matter how crowded the bus was or how uncomfortable it was to be touching other passengers.

Tessa looked out the window and saw a fragile old man on the sidewalk hunched over while carrying a heavy bag on his back. She felt sorry for him and wanted to get off the bus and help him. Tessa read somewhere that most Japanese lived a long life and often ran out of money about twenty years before their death.

She saw traditional Japanese homes, knickknack shops, and many cyclists. Compared to Tokyo, Kyoto had too many cyclists who rode both on the street and on the sidewalks, which was annoying for pedestrians who constantly dodged them. When it rained, some riders held umbrellas in one hand while maneuvering themselves through traffic with the other. It was interesting to watch them ride at a crawl without wobbling or losing their balance.

Tessa noticed that Toshiro was deep in thought, staring at his phone.

He was trying to figure out where they were going, what was there to see, and what to do afterward. "Are you interested in also seeing Ginkakuji and the Philosopher's Path?" he asked.

"I remember reading about them in my guidebook, but I can't recall all the details."

"Ginkakuji, also known as the Silver Pavilion, is a Zen temple. Philosopher's Path is named after one of the country's famous philosophers, Nishika Kitaro, who walked the route on his daily commute while practicing meditation."

"Do we have time to see both places?"

"If we spend no more than an hour at each, we could do it."

"Let's go for it," she said excitedly.

"And you won't be too tired tonight?"

"Nah, I'll sleep when I get home." Tessa was working on nervous energy. She was nervous about the upcoming protests. She was nervous that her efforts didn't seem to make a difference. She was nervous about starting to have feelings for Toshiro.

When Toshiro and Tessa reached their destination, they walked for a bit and entered the Golden Temple, so named for the top two floors covered in gold leaf. The bottom floor was made of wood and white plaster walls. A bronze phoenix sat on top of its pyramid-shaped roof. Toshiro took pictures of the temple and one of Tessa when she wasn't paying attention. Tessa snapped several photos of the Zen temple, which overlooked a large pond surrounded by gardens and trees with copper, red, and yellow leaves that complemented the impressive structure.

"Kinkakuji was burned down many times; the last time it was rebuilt was in 1955."

"It's lovely," Tessa remarked, noticing the reflection of the pavilion on the pond.

The two stood there for a while, taking in their breathtaking surroundings. Apparently, autumn arrived early, and Mother Nature painted the entire area with deep green, cinnamon, gold, eggplant, and bold red, interwoven to create a feast for the eyes.

"I wish we had more time to just sit here and soak it all in," Tessa said.

"We can stay here and skip the rest if you want."

"No," she said looking at her phone, "Let's leave in fifteen minutes so that I can see the other pavilion. Can we see the inside?"

"It's not open to the public," Toshiro said, looking in his guidebook. "It says here that statues of Buddha and Yoshimitsu are stored on the ground floor. The second floor contains a seated statue of Kanon, the god of mercy, surrounded by the statues of Shitenno, the Four Heavenly Kings, who are the protectors of temples. Relics of Buddha are on the third level."

As they started to leave, they saw a fortune bowl. Toshiro said, "You can toss a coin in there for good luck."

Tessa threw in a 100-yen coin, equivalent to one U.S dollar, and hoped that her fortune would include making a positive difference in the lives of dolphins. But this time she also hoped for something new and for herself: a rewarding love life. She didn't have Toshiro in mind, but she had to admit it was nice having a male partner to enjoy the sights with.

The two took a taxi to the east side. Thirty minutes later, they arrived at Ginkakuji Temple, and Tessa insisted on paying the driver. She felt that Toshiro had already done enough for her by helping her get around.

In Japan, couples often split the bill, or the man paid a bit more than the woman. If a man didn't have enough money, the woman paid.

They walked down a narrow street lined with quaint shops. A tree-lined path led the way to the temple grounds, which had a sand garden and a mound of sand representing Mount Fuji; past it was Ginkakuji.

"This is different," Tessa said, noticing that the silver pavilion had the same design as the golden pavilion, but the materials were humbler with a rustic weathered look.

"It belonged to the grandson of the owner of the Golden Pavilion. He was obsessed with art and as a result, the Silver Pavilion became the center of contemporary culture." Toshiro had been there before on a school excursion when he was eight, but he hadn't been back since.

"I'm curious…Why isn't it silver?"

"It is said that the grandson intended to create a silver pavilion, but he ran out of money. This building is made out of wood and is a good representation of *wabi-sabi*."

"What's *wabi-sabi*?" she asked, studying the faded black-and-brown building with white panels.

"*Wabi* describes quiet, rustic simplicity, and *sabi* means finding beauty in weathered characteristics. So *wabi-sabi* means taking pleasure in simplicity and natural materials, enjoying rough edges and imperfections."

"As opposed to enjoying a perfect brand-new building or furniture?"

"Something like that, except it could apply to other things, such as focusing on the serenity that comes with time or scars that become signs of experience. It could also represent enlightenment."

They walked around for a while. The place had a peaceful ambiance. Moss was prevalent everywhere, especially in the Zen gardens. On the grounds was the Togudo Hall, an architecturally influential building that shaped the look of present-day Japanese homes. Toshiro looked at his guidebook and said, "It says here that the Togudo has the country's oldest standing example of a tea ceremony room. It measures 4.5 tatami mats, which is the standard size of most tea ceremony rooms today."

"I don't understand," Tessa said.

"A tatami mat is a unit of measurement in Japan. Sometimes an ad for an apartment might say, it is 10 tatami mats, meaning it is 164 square feet. Each tatami mat is about seventeen square feet."

"Interesting. You know, it's so strange," Tessa commented as she looked around her. "Serenity is so prevalent in every place I have been to and yet…"

"And yet what?"

"Never mind." She shook her head. I don't want to ruin this moment."

"You won't. Say what you're thinking," he insisted. He wondered why Tessa was struggling to convey her thoughts.

Tessa stopped walking, paused to collect her thoughts, and said, "Buddhism is such a big part of your culture, yes?"

"Yes."

"And Buddhist monks follow a vegan diet because they want to do no harm, right?"

"Yes, what's your point?"

"Well, the cruelty brought upon the dolphins by those who follow Buddhism is unforgiving." For a week now, Tessa had been savoring Japan, soaking in the atmosphere, observing, and thinking about how there was so much goodness and harmony on the surface. But just like in any other country, she had to scratch the surface and go deeper to see it for what it was—a mélange of good and bad, happiness and sadness, cruelty and kindness.

"You can't let that go for a moment, can you?" Toshiro said with disappointment. "No break for you. Always an activist."

"You ask me what I think and when I share it with you, you get mad at me," she said, raising her voice.

"I'm not mad," he said, putting his hand on her shoulder, "I just think it's good to sometimes take a break and let things go."

But Tessa couldn't. The main purpose of her trip was to help save the dolphins, and she wasn't good at letting things go. Even when she was younger, if she had to solve a problem and couldn't find the answer, it would drive her crazy. She would pester her teachers and everyone else until she would get an answer. What she didn't realize was that sometimes there were no answers.

After their visit to Ginkakuji, they took a short walk to the Philosopher's Path. The stone path ended at Nanzenji Temple, established in 1291.

"Too bad you're not here during the cherry blossom season. This place is so beautiful at that time," Toshiro said, admiring hundreds of trees along the stone path.

"Oh, but it's beautiful now. We have nothing like it in our city. We'd have to drive a long time to reach a place that would resemble this," Tessa admitted, as she looked at the water running through the canal that divided their route in two. A few people were walking ahead of them; small, family-owned shops and cafés bordered the path.

"Do you want to go see the Nanzenji Temple?" asked Toshiro.

Tessa glanced at her phone. It was 5:30. "We won't have time. I have to meet Satomi in Gion before 6:30, and I don't want to be late."

"Sure," he said, "But we still need to walk for ten minutes before we reach the subway or take a taxi."

As they walked, Toshiro asked, "What are your plans for tomorrow?"

"The protest is at 1 p.m. and then I'll be hanging out with the other activists in the afternoon."

"Why don't I help out?" he asked. He desperately wanted to spend more time with her.

"Absolutely not. I don't want you involved. This is my battle. Besides, your parents already hate me for dragging you to the last protest."

"My parents don't hate you."

"I can tell when someone doesn't like me. At your birthday party, I could see that your parents were not pleased that you had invited me. I could see it in their cold looks at the dinner table."

"You're wrong. It just takes time for them to warm up to out— *"outsiders,"* he wanted to say, but as soon as he started saying that word, he regretted it. He wanted her to feel comfortable with him. "I mean to people."

"No, you meant outsiders. And I am an outsider. I will always be *gaijin* in your culture. Now you see why I said we could never have an intimate relationship," she said. When she saw the look of sadness on his face, she kissed him lightly on the cheek. "I am sorry. I really love hanging out with you and want us to be best friends."

He tried to hide his disappointment when he said, "I know that you're trying to protect me. But I'm a big boy and can take care of myself."

"True, but I still don't want you to come to the protest. I know I'm sticking my nose where it doesn't belong in a foreign country, but I love animals, especially dolphins. They're so intelligent and loving."

"I can see that you need your space. As I told you before, I have family here. I'm going to spend the day visiting them. You have my number. Call if you want to get together for dinner."

"I will. In fact, let's plan on meeting up," she said, looking at her phone. "Would tomorrow at 7:30 work for you?"

"Yes, it would," he said with joy in his heart. He had to learn when to back off and when to push if he was to have any chance with her.

"It's a date, then."

"I'll text you the name and address of the restaurant." He felt sad that his love was unrequited. It was as though she was throwing him crumbs. Would she ever fall for him? He reasoned that she liked him or she wouldn't have agreed to see him again. But to get her to love him was a challenge. All his life, girls had pursued him and now, the tables were turned. He felt bad for all the women he had hurt. He now knew what rejection was like. But perhaps in time, Tessa would change her mind and return his love.

Toshiro flagged down a taxi. When they reached Gion, he accompanied Tessa to help her find the meeting place. Tessa introduced Satomi to Toshiro and then he left.

"He's handsome and nice, too!" Satomi told Tessa.

"He's alright," she said, trying to hide her feelings. As soon as he had walked away, she missed him. What was happening to her? He needed to date younger women, in other words, of childbearing age. And what if she did get into a relationship with him? Would he want marriage? Children? She couldn't offer him any of that. She believed she was too damn old to be raising children even if nowadays many women started a family late in life. *Shut up Tessa*, she told herself. *Why are you jumping so far ahead? Nothing will happen. You two are friends.* Her thoughts were interrupted by Satomi, when she said, "We're early. You want to walk around?"

"Sure. Maybe I'll get lucky and see a *maiko*."

"Just keep your camera ready because they walk super-fast and you may miss a photo opportunity."

Packed with culture, tradition, and history, the town of Gion had narrow cobblestone side alleys and restaurants, some of which only catered to an exclusive clientele. The streets that were wider and full of tourists had wooden *machiya,* also known as merchant houses.

"Because taxes are levied based on the frontage instead of the size of the house, *machiya*, nicknamed 'bedrooms for eels,' were built as narrow one-or two-story wooden townhouses, less than twenty feet wide, but sometimes reaching 164 feet long," Satomi said.

Tessa looked at the row of attached, uniform houses. They had wooden railings and windows covered either with bamboo blinds or slatted wooden frames to give them privacy. She then saw something that looked like curved bamboo skirts attached to the lower walls of the houses. "What are those?"

"Those are called *inu-yarai*, dog barriers. They were made to prevent homes from getting soiled on by dogs or splashed with mud from passing cars. They are also to keep beggars from sitting on the walls."

"Clever!"

Satomi continued, "The first room of the *machiya* was where merchants received their customers, and the rest of the structure served as their living quarters, a tiny courtyard garden, and a workshop or warehouse. Many of these were converted to shops, restaurants, and hotels, and some were demolished and replaced by high-rises or modern homes."

As they strolled the charming streets, Tessa soaked up the atmosphere; she was captivated by everything she saw. Then Satomi halted in front of a building that looked just like another merchant house to Tessa.

"This is a teahouse or *ochaya*. Teahouses are not the same as tea rooms, and they don't actually serve tea unless it is incidental. An *ochaya* is a place where *geiko* and *maiko* perform. Some of the old teahouses have been turned into museums."

Satomi told Tessa that many of the restaurants on the narrower streets did not allow foreigners. Most wouldn't deny you a table to your face, but they would simply say, "Sorry we are full." A few have signs that say, "No foreigners."

"Really? That's a bit xenophobic, isn't it?"

"Many foreigners and tourists are loud, and some of these restaurants have their own Japanese clientele who don't like to be disturbed. You see, Kyoto is incredibly traditional, and *miyabi* is prevalent everywhere."

"*Miyabi*, what is that?"

"*Miyabi* embodies a philosophy of sophistication and refinement. It expresses the image of aristocratic culture and gracefulness."

"What about the teahouses?" Tessa asked.

"You would have to be invited the first time, otherwise you can't get in. Once you're in, you would need to schmooze if you want to frequent the establishment."

"Like some of the private clubs we have in the U.S." Tessa pointed out.

"Something like that. And it's quite expensive to see *geiko* and *maiko* perform. The invited guests spend thousands of dollars to interact with them and watch them dance and sing."

"Really?" Tessa asked. Then she noticed a small iron structure hammered to one of the walls. "What's that?"

"It's a tiny *torii* or gateway."

"It's an odd place for it, isn't it?"

"Often, men who have had too much to drink pee against a wall. But when they see a *torii*, they refrain as a sign of respect."

I guess they are rough around the edges and haven't caught on to the miyabi philosophy, Tessa thought. Or was *miyabi* nothing more than a pretentiousness that one finds in all cultures?

As they began walking back toward their meeting place, Tessa saw a *maiko* in her high *okobo*, or wooden shoes, and took a picture from a distance. She was so young and pretty in her bright-green floral kimono held together by a wide red obi, tied into a bow, which fell to her feet in the back, as opposed to the shorter sash that a *geiko* would wear.

Satomi was grateful that Tessa did not run after the *maiko* the way many tourists did. Disturbing a *maiko* or *geiko* was taboo. "Did you notice the place she walked out of?"

Tessa nodded.

"The place is called *okiya*—a lodging house where *geiko* and *maiko* live. They stay there to get trained. The *maiko* who makes the most money is the most desired and is favored by the house mother. The house mother is usually the owner and collects all the money. In exchange, she pays for all the girls' expenses— accommodations, clothing, wigs, hairdressers, makeup, and other things. Some of the money goes toward their training."

"Can a *geiko* ever live on her own?"

"She would have to be financially successful and before leaving, she would have to pay the house mother a sum of money."

"I'm so lucky to know you and Toshiro. You have both helped me to learn a great deal about your traditions. Thank you."

"You're welcome," Satomi said, checking her phone for the time.

They headed back to Musoshin. Three other activists—two men and one woman, all in their mid-20s had already arrived. Two of them did not speak English and Satomi had to translate. One of the boys, Haruto, spoke some English. Before going into the restaurant, they selected what they wanted and ordered it through a vending machine. Once they paid, they got a ticket and gave it to the host who passed it to the kitchen. Tessa noticed that all the tables were taken, but after a fifteen-minute wait, they were able to find one.

Once they began eating, their conversation turned to the protest.

"There will be others joining us at the protest?" asked Tessa.

"No," replied Satomi. "It will be just the five of us standing at a corner with signs and banners. Maybe you can make a sign in English when we get back?"

"Sure, I would love to. I wonder if there is a way to get more people to come to the protest. I made flyers when I was in Tokyo. I have them in my rucksack," Tessa said, pulling out a folder to show them to her.

"We can pass them out after we eat," Haruto said.

"Sure, and tomorrow, maybe Satomi and I can get an early start and hand out more flyers," Tessa offered. "Do we have any media coverage?"

"Nothing big. A few student journalists may come and write about it in their school papers," Satomi said.

In the meantime, Haruto was translating what they were talking about to the other two activists, who nodded in agreement. One of them said something in Japanese and Satomi replied.

Tessa felt at a loss for the first time. So far everyone she had hung out with spoke English, but now she felt left out.

Satomi noticed that Tessa was quiet and said, "They're saying we have to be careful tomorrow. They heard from some of their friends that the police will be there."

"So? We had the police in Tokyo. They were very helpful," Tessa said.

"They say that the government officials here are not happy about this protest. They don't want any negative publicity."

"But there are only five of us, not exactly a large group," Tessa said, raising an eyebrow.

"I know, but they're saying to be careful and stay away from confrontation," Satomi whispered, as though someone was listening.

Why are you whispering? Tessa wanted to say. Except for Tessa, everyone at the restaurant looked Japanese, spoke Japanese, and seemed to be too busy talking to their friends to be eavesdropping. "Well, no worries there. I don't speak Japanese. Or should I be concerned?"

"No, it's just a precaution to have an awareness of our surroundings."

After dinner, they managed to hand out many flyers, not only to the locals but also to the tourists. Two Australian boys promised to be there and a British woman in her 50s said that she was going to try to make it. Some Japanese locals who were curious about the demonstration read the flyers to learn more. But the highlight of the evening was meeting Erica, a teenage Japanese African–American animal rights activist and a social media influencer from San Francisco with 5 million followers on Twitter, Facebook, and Instagram combined. She asked a lot of questions and showed a genuine interest in their cause. She told Tessa and Satomi that unfortunately, she was leaving Kyoto for Osaka the next morning. Tessa let her know that there would be another protest in Osaka in two days. Erica said that she would likely be there to support her.

The following day, when Tessa and Satomi showed up at the protest, the other three activists were already there, and so were the police. The prior night, Tessa had worked on a sign in English, and that morning, she and Satomi had passed out more flyers at Kyoto University, hoping to get the attention of the younger generation. They knew that it was too late to promote the protest and that they should have done it much sooner. But even if they could get the interest of a few students, it would be helpful. The problem was, Satomi was new to activism and she hadn't planned out the demonstration that well. But fortunately, Tessa and Akira had made Japanese and English pamphlets to hand out to the public.

The pamphlet read:

According to Richard O'Barry, an animal rights activist, former animal trainer, and founder and director of the Dolphin Project, public oceanariums often claim that their purpose is educational and that their goal is to promote environmental conservation and respect for the environment and nature. However, tens of thousands of dolphins are brutally slaughtered every year. The government of Japan censors this data, keeping it from the media and the public. Your attendance at these public oceanariums financially supports the capture of wild dolphins and their horrific massacre.

The demonstration took place outside of the Kyoto Station where there was a lot of foot traffic. Satomi used a bullhorn and the others held out their signs. They started to grab the attention of people walking and driving by. A small crowd started to form and Tessa and Haruto passed out pamphlets. After two hours, the gathering had picked up momentum as more people showed up, and the demonstration lasted much longer than expected.

Tessa needed time to go home, change, and meet Toshiro. She was mad at herself for making plans with him. Her main purpose here was not a short-term romance.

"I'm sorry, but I have to leave soon," she said, anxiously.

"We all have to leave. Our permit is only for four hours and we have already gone over that time," Satomi responded and told the others to start packing. They were supposed to be finished up by 5 in the afternoon. It was now 6.

The activists gathered their water bottles, signs, banners, and whatever else was left of their belongings. Satomi's head was lowered as she organized her backpack when Tessa nudged her. Three male officers were getting out of a police car and heading in their direction.

Satomi was nervous and told the police, "I'm sorry for running late, but we are leaving."

"Do you have a permit for this protest?" a young officer with a narrow face asked in Japanese.

"Yes," Satomi said, searching her backpack for a copy and showing it to him.

He looked at it and showed it to his older partner, who said to Satomi, "You can all go, except her."

"But she doesn't speak Japanese. You need me to translate."

"I speak English," the younger officer said.

Satomi passed Tessa a fearful look, stepped aside, and stood at a distance, but did not leave.

Meanwhile, an Australian college student was filming the incident with a hidden camera.

A middle-aged officer was now asking all the questions, and the younger was translating. "Why are you here?"

"I was helping out my friend," Tessa said with confidence, even if she was quite scared.

"This is why you came to Japan?" He frowned.

"Oh, no," Tessa lied. "I'm on vacation."

"Which organization do you work for?"

"I represent The Dolphin and Whale Guardians," is what she should have said. "I work for a pet hospital. I'm a veterinarian," she answered, evading the question. She knew that he was asking about the activist organizations she was involved with.

"If you're on vacation, why were you protesting in Tokyo?"

She was surprised that he recognized her from the Tokyo protest and said, "I was helping. ..."

"Helping a friend," he said sarcastically, finishing her sentence. "Do you have other friends here who are activists?"

"Yes. I have many friends who are activists in the U.S. and here. Is that a problem?"

"Passport."

"What?"

"Your passport. Please hand it over," he said, holding out his hand impatiently.

Tessa pulled out her organizer, unlatched it, and gave it to him. Before coming to Japan, she was told that if the police ever stopped her, be compliant. Her friends had told her stories of women getting arrested in Japan, having their genitals searched, and being interrogated for more than ten hours a day for several weeks.

"Stay here," he told her and went to his car to verify what he already knew—that up until now, Tessa was a law-abiding American citizen. He knew that the activists had not done anything illegal. But he was under orders to question them anyway.

Tessa stood there with a grim face. She wanted to text Toshiro and let him know that she was going to be late, but her phone battery was drained. And anyway, she wasn't certain how late she was going to be. What if they arrested and jailed her?

After a long wait, the younger officer came over and returned her passport. "You can go," he said without any other explanation.

As soon as the police left, Satomi came to her and asked, "Are you okay?"

"Yes. They just asked me a bunch of questions. Not sure why. I have done nothing wrong."

"It's a scare tactic. The government wants to hide everything about the Taiji dolphins."

"I wish they were more open-minded about it," Tessa said, glancing at her watch. It was now close to 7 p.m. "I have to go. I am so late."

And when it rained, it poured. Once Tessa reached the subway, there was a problem that was slowing down all lines. A man from Tokyo in his mid-20s had jumped in front of a train at another station and committed suicide, Satomi explained to Tessa. So, the two took the bus, which normally took longer than the subway.

In Japan, many worked extremely long hours and were under constant stress. Those who couldn't handle it committed suicide by jumping in front of trains or hanging themselves deep in the forest near Mount Fuji. Some elderly people committed suicide as well because there was no one to take care of them. The concept of therapy was not as common as in America, and there was some stigma attached to seeing a psychologist.

Tessa was distraught when she learned about the suicide on top of everything else that had happened after the protest. She needed a drink, but more importantly, she needed to get back to

Satomi's place, plug her phone in a charger, text Toshiro, and freshen up.

Toshiro was mad. He had spent extra time fussing with his hair, polishing his leather shoes, and picking up a black jacket at the cleaners. He impatiently sat at the restaurant for thirty minutes with no sign of Tessa. Then he got a measly short text from her, telling him that her phone battery was low and that she would be there in thirty minutes.

Tessa was more than an hour late. She showed up in the red handkerchief dress that she had purchased two days earlier at QZMZ Harajuku. And even though she had been running late, she had taken a little extra time to look pretty and feminine for Toshiro. Her curled hair pulled up above her head and held together with a gold clip, the hint of makeup that made her skin glow, and a pair of dangling amber earrings revealed that she cared about how she looked tonight. "I'm so sorry. I completely lost track of time," she lied. She didn't want to tell him about being held up by the police.

He was irritated. It showed that he would always come second in her life. But he wanted to spend time with her. So, he accepted her apology and did not argue. "Why didn't you carry a spare battery with you?" he asked.

"I forgot to take it with me," she said, looking around her. "It's beautiful here."

They were seated outside on a *kawayuka*, a terrace on stilts, that overlooked the Kamogawa River. The tables and chairs were made of cypress, and the subtle lighting around them created a romantic atmosphere. Locals and tourists were filling up the other tables. Down below by the river, couples, families, and singles either sat by the flowing water or milled about as amateur acrobats and musicians performed, each vying for attention.

"How did the protest go?" Toshiro had been thinking about her all day, wondering if he should join her. But he decided not to because he did not want her to be mad at him.

"It was good," she said with a poker face. "There were a lot more people than we had anticipated. That's why we ran late. Well, that and the slowing down of the underground. So sad," she said.

Toshiro was surprised that Tessa had found out about the suicide. Satomi must have told her. "Any media?"

The Japanese often tried hard to hide negative events that took place in their country. They were proud of their homeland and didn't want to give visitors a poor impression of where they lived. So from the outside, everything looked perfect to tourists. But in reality, as in most places, nothing was perfect.

"I don't think the media were there." She didn't want to tell him the truth in case her name would pop up in some small paper about her getting harassed by the police. "I was too busy answering questions and passing out information to notice."

"I hope that all your efforts will make a difference someday. I couldn't do what you're doing," he said. Fortunately, the owner of the restaurant was a good friend of his aunt's or he would have had to abandon the table when Tessa hadn't shown up.

"Activism is not for everybody, and everyone's purpose in life is different."

Toshiro thought about what she said. He wished that he was more like her, knowing where he was going and having a passion in life. But he had kind of drifted through life without a purpose. He didn't put a lot of effort into his job and he didn't have a hobby during his time off. Not much excited him except for Tessa.

Tessa noticed that Toshiro was distracted and wasn't saying much. "What did you do today?" she asked.

"Oh, not a whole lot. I slept in. Watched some TV. Chatted with my aunt who works from home."

"What does she do?"

"She teaches English and helps students pass the TOEFL."

"The TOEFL?"

"It's like the SAT for foreigners. They need to take it if they want to study abroad."

A waiter in a white uniform walked over to take their orders. Tessa pointed at a picture on the menu to indicate what she wanted.

Toshiro said to the waiter, "Excuse me, one moment please," and then he looked at Tessa and said, "But you don't eat meat, do you?"

"No, but there's no meat in that photo."

"There is, but it's hidden. Would you like me to order it without the meat?"

"Please. Thank you!"

Toshiro ordered for her and ordered sukiyaki for himself.

"Should I order a bottle of Japanese Merlot?" Toshiro asked Tessa.

"Sure. That would be great," she said. *I deserve a drink after what I've been through,* she wanted to say.

"So," Toshiro said after their waiter left.

"So," Tessa mimicked him.

"Are you busy tomorrow? I thought we could do more sightseeing," he said, hoping that she would say yes.

"I'm leaving for Taiji tomorrow. We can meet in Osaka if you like."

"That's right, I forgot about that," he answered, discontented. "Would it be okay if I join you?"

"I would love that, but I will not be able to spend time with you."

"Not even a few hours?"

"I'm only going to be there for two days and then I'm heading to Osaka the following morning," Tessa said, thinking about how busy she was going to be once she got to Taiji. Not only was she attending a protest, she was also planning to scuba dive to film the dolphin hunt from under the water. The last thing she needed was Toshiro accompanying her.

"Maybe I can help you with the ..." *the protest* he wanted to say, but when he saw Tessa shaking her head no, he stopped.

"We have already been through this. I don't want you involved." He was so stubborn, she thought. He kept on trying even if she kept refusing him.

"I suppose you would be too busy to miss me."

"I'll miss you. As a matter of fact, I will miss you a lot," she said and meant it. Tessa was attracted to Toshiro, probably from the first day she met him. He treated her well and had been patient with her. Most men would have given up on her after so many rejections.

Toshiro smiled. It was worth the wait to hear Tessa say that she would miss him. "You mean it? You're not just saying that?"

"Of course, I mean it. Since I came here, you're the one I have spent most of my free time with. It will be hard to go back home without you."

"What if I come to the U.S. with you?"

She sighed. "You know that's not possible."

"We can make it work."

"Let's not talk about this, and let's just enjoy our time together for now." There was such a huge cultural divide between them. The more she learned about the dos and don'ts, the bigger of a headache she got. It would be too exhausting to abide by all the rules. At some point, she would end up offending one of his relatives or friends.

A silver-haired woman in a blue apron came over. She served Tessa's dish first—steaming hot tofu with vegetables sitting in a clay pot over a burner. She made Toshiro's meal in front of him. Tessa watched diligently, enjoying the experience even if she did not eat meat.

Toshiro kept quiet.

"What's the matter?" Tessa asked after the server had left.

"I want to pick you up at the train station in Osaka."

"That makes no sense because I have to meet with my friend Yoko, and then we need to put things together for the protest."

"Then what's the point of me coming to Osaka? I might as well go back to Tokyo tomorrow."

"I'm sorry. It seems that I've been saying that a lot lately. But I did come here for a purpose. Meeting you was not in my plans."

"So, what you're saying is that I'm imposing myself on you?"

She held his hands in hers, and Toshiro felt a strong warmth from her. "Far from it. I would have been lost in Japan without you. You have been a great friend to me and I don't want to use you."

"You are not using me. I choose to spend my time with you."

Tessa nodded and replied, "We can see each other on Monday evening. We'll have dinner and I won't schedule anything with anyone the next day," she promised.

"We'll hang out, just the two of us on Tuesday?" he asked, confirming that he was hearing her correctly.

"Yes. I have to leave Osaka Tuesday night for Tokyo. Are you okay with that?" Tessa had to go back on Tuesday because she needed time to pack, wrap things up with Akira, meet up with her best friend Karianne Metzler on Wednesday, and catch a flight to L.A. the following day.

He could tell that she genuinely cared for him. Sure, she wasn't in love with him the way he was with her, but things were changing in his favor and he was happy about it. "Yes, I'm okay with that," he said, using his chopsticks to dip his Wagyu beef into a raw egg before savoring it.

That night, after dinner, when they went for a stroll by the Kamo River, Toshiro took a selfie of the two of them making funny faces and laughing. He held her hand and Tessa didn't try to pull it away. She even kissed him lightly on the lips when he dropped her off at Satomi's apartment. Toshiro wanted to hang onto that moment forever. But nothing lasted forever. That's how life was, a series of unpredictable events, out of one's control.

CHAPTER 11

Throughout the train ride to Taiji, Tessa was texting back and forth with Toshiro. He shared pictures of himself and his cousin Hansuke having breakfast at Café Sky 40 inside the Umeda Sky Building, an Osaka landmark with a rooftop deck called the Floating Garden Observatory.

"I miss you. Wish I could be there with you."

"Miss you too ♡♡. Let's have a romantic dinner here when you get to Osaka," Toshiro texted.

"It's a date. Can't wait to see you," Tessa texted, grinning like a teenager.

What was happening? Tessa thought. She was getting distracted from her purpose in Japan and now found herself contemplating what-ifs. What if she decided to live in Japan? What if Toshiro came back home with her? What if they started a family together? Sometimes, she started to see herself in a relationship with him. But then she would recant, repeating to herself that he was too young and needed to lead a different life. She wasn't about to obligate him to an ordinary, mundane life. This conflict was gnawing at her. She decided not to think about it anymore because there was nothing to think about. She needed to concentrate on the task at hand.

Tessa had an American activist friend in Taiji named Jack who could help her do just that. Jack was twenty-four when she had met him four years ago at a Twitter meet-up in Los Angeles, and they had hit it off right away. At the time, he was tweeting about how ducks and geese had their feathers violently ripped from their bodies to make down pillows, quilts, and jackets. Two years later, Jack moved from L.A. to Japan to study veterinary science at Osaka University, where he met like-minded activists.

Taiji, a quiet seaside town south of Osaka, once under the radar, now attracted protesters from all over the world. The town had tightened security ever since *The Cove* was released in 2009. The fishermen's abuse of dolphins and whales made worldwide news, and foreigners, as well as many young Japanese citizens, were horrified at what was happening.

Ironically, many *gaijin* were not as horrified at the way animals were killed in their own countries, as many Japanese complained. Nevertheless, the *gaijin* came to speak out for the protection of the dolphins, and the majority of the Taiji residents didn't appreciate the outside interference. Many children who grew up with dolphin-hunting parents became hunters themselves. Because what they did was essential to their livelihood, they felt no remorse.

As a sixteen-year-old, Tessa had sensed that what she witnessed in Taiji twenty-four years ago was wrong. Now with science to back her teenage interpretation of what had happened, she had proof that dolphins experienced pain and trauma when torn away from their families and social circles. She knew that even a small fish in a bowl can recognize its owner's face, get depressed, and feel pain and loneliness.

Tessa was intent on sharing this knowledge with others. She decided that it is not enough to say "Well, it is our tradition, heritage, and food culture," and continue with the old ways. She questioned civilization's progress: If we refuse to use the knowledge that we have gained through science and history, then what is the point of humanity?

Jack had come to Taiji to film the protest. This time, neither he nor Tessa was participating in the demonstration, which would start on the streets of Taiji. Thirty or so protesters planned to march and hold signs with a van following to chant "save the dolphins" in Japanese from a speaker. The counter-protesters would march as well, keeping their distance and shouting their own slogans. Then the demonstrators would stop on the sidewalk that led to the Taiji Whale Museum, continue with their protest, and pass out pamphlets about the dolphins. Because this was strictly a Japanese protest, Jack and Tessa would support them from a distance, taking pictures, and posting them on social media.

Both Jack and Tessa had decided that Tessa should get in and out of Taiji quickly. Her scuba diving mission was dangerous, and Tessa didn't want the authorities to sense trouble. The protest would be a perfect distraction because if Tessa could film the slaughter without getting caught, and the authorities later found out about the filming and photos, they couldn't point the finger at her. The interloper could be any of the demonstrators, and by the time they could question everyone, Tessa would be on her way home. At least that's what Jack and Tessa hoped.

"How's your trip been so far?" Jack asked, running his hand through his brown hair, thinking that Tessa had not aged since the last time he saw her. She even dressed the same: a T-shirt and jeans, her hair pulled back into a bun.

"It's been interesting, to say the least. Many unexpected turns of events," she said, thinking about meeting Toshiro and her encounter with the police.

"Any problems in Tokyo or Kyoto?" he asked with a look of concern. He was tall with muscular arms and thick thighs and he reminded Tessa of the Incredible Hulk with his imposing stature and warm, fuzzy personality.

"No problems in Tokyo, but for a second, I thought I was going to end up in jail in Kyoto." She told him how the police had questioned her.

"Good thing they let you go. I didn't have many problems when I joined up with other activists last year, but you never know with these things. You have to have your wits about you at all times to wiggle your way out."

"Lucky you! It could also be that you don't belong to a particular organization. I heard that two activists from an Australian organization were arrested at the airport and deported before they had a chance to see Japan."

"I do belong to an organization. I just don't advertise it."

"Me neither," Tessa admitted. "Let's hope that things will go smoothly tomorrow."

"It will," Jack said, but deep down, he was concerned. He had searched hard to get scuba diving gear and a heat-retaining rash guard that would fit Tessa. He had planned out where she would be dropped off, take pictures, and hide the gear once she was done. If caught, they would all get into serious trouble, but it had to be done. The world needed to be reminded over and over about the cruelty that was inflicted on these creatures.

"So is there a place where I can drop off my stuff?" Weeks ago, Tessa told Jack to get her a hotel room, but he insisted that she stay at his friend's house.

"We're both staying at Hiroke's house. He is a good friend of mine. We met at Osaka University. He only has one room, but we will each have separate mattresses on the floor," he said, as he started walking toward his friend's parked car.

"Thanks, but no. I'll get a hotel room," Tessa said. Not only did she feel uncomfortable bunking up with two men, but she was also starting to get weary of staying in tight spaces. In fact, she had already made arrangements to stay at the luxury Intercontinental Hotel Osaka.

"No, he is expecting you. That way we can stick together in case something goes wrong."

Like Tessa, Jack had interesting friends—activists, tattoo artists, treasure hunters, and writers as well as entrepreneurs, lawyers, and accountants. Tessa was curious about what Hiroke would be like, but she wasn't curious enough to want to stay at his place.

"Nothing will go wrong. I'm an expert scuba diver," Tessa said without flinching, but inside she was a nervous wreck.

"Even so, I would feel much more comfortable if we were all under one roof. And anyway, my friend is waiting for us at his home."

Tessa gave in since it was only for two nights and he had a point about sticking together. "Thank you," Tessa said, reluctantly.

"Let's take a drive, and I'll go over our plan," Jack said, putting Tessa's carry-on and bag in the gray Suzuki Celerio he had borrowed from Hiroke.

Driving through the streets of Taiji, Jack pointed out where the protesters would start their march.

As they passed through town, Tessa saw some of the same places that she had visited with Natalie. She spotted the restaurant where she had first eaten sushi rice, seaweed, vegetables, and sashimi. She remembered that she hadn't liked the slippery texture and had wanted to spit it out. Among the rows of small houses that they drove by was her aunt's former house. Nothing about the outside had changed; all the houses in the area looked dated. It had the same old white paint, battered wooden roof, and weathered mailbox. Just seeing the house brought back an assortment of memories.

"You okay?" Jack asked because Tessa seemed lost in another world, not speaking at all. She told him about what she had witnessed long ago.

"Sorry. This place brings back a few good memories and a lot of bad ones. I can't wait until I'm back on the Shinkansen."

"I understand, but Tessa, what you're planning to do is dangerous and I need to make sure that you can handle it," he said, looking worried. "If you're going to fall apart on me, don't do it."

"I'm okay. I was just having flashbacks."

"Then get ready for some more of them because we're going to park the car and walk around."

"I can handle it. Let's do it," she said, more to assure herself than him. She had to have a pep talk to remind her that backing down was not an option and that she was there for a cause worth the risk.

A few minutes later, Jack pulled into a parking space facing the front of the Taiji Whale Museum. "You and I will be here taking photos and filming."

Tessa recognized the museum where as a teenager, she saw the dolphin show and cluelessly cheered when the dolphins performed their tricks. She was reliving horrible feelings; she felt both cold and disgusted.

Jack began driving again until he reached a parking lot. The two got out, and Jack grabbed his backpack. They began walking as he took out a pocket-sized tape recorder.

"What's that noise?" Tessa asked, listening to a continuous swooshing sound.

"It's white noise, in case there are any listening devices around us."

"I don't understand."

"There are closed-circuit cameras in certain areas, some with microphones. When we get to Hiroke's place, I will show you a map of where the cameras are that my activist friends put together," he said and held her hand in his.

Raising an eyebrow, she asked sarcastically, "Are we a couple, now?"

"Yes, temporarily for the cameras. We don't want the police to find out that we were scouting the place. I want us to come across like a couple taking a romantic walk by the water."

"Hardly. Bloody water is not exactly romantic," Tessa said as they crossed the street and walked over to a short bamboo railing. Beyond the railing was a white gravel shore that led to the infamous cove.

"Ten days ago, before the hunting season started, kids were swimming in that water," Jack said.

Tessa recalled swimming in that water with her cousin Natalie and her friends. She hadn't realized that the water would be stained with blood a week later. These days, the fishermen would section off the water with a tarp so that the dolphins' blood wouldn't flow into outside areas, but it still didn't prevent seepage, which indicated that the slaughter was underway.

Jack said, "See the metal pens in the water? They are captivity tanks. A net is attached to the metal frame and is suspended downward to trap the captured dolphins. Those are the ones they're going to train."

"The last time I was here and didn't know any better my cousin and I swam over to the pens and stood on one of the platforms on top of the pen to watch the trapped dolphins," Tessa said, noticing a huge net that would be used to capture dolphins the next day.

Tessa knew that when the dolphins were separated from their pods, they lived in fear. If there was a strong storm, they were stuck in the nets as they were tossed around in the ocean until the storm subsided, which could take days.

There was a complete lack of compassion from the fishermen, trainers, and people who sold them. During their capture, they were yanked by their fins, flukes, or rostrums. And after going through a gruesome training period, many were exported to other countries and imprisoned for hours on end in tiny crates without room to move. *If for a moment, people would put themselves in the position of these dolphins, death would be a welcomed exchange,* Tessa thought.

"I'm sorry. It must have been horrible for you," Jack said, noticing Tessa's somber face.

Tessa wiped a lingering tear from the corner of her eye and said, "Thanks for helping me do something about it."

"You're welcome. Let's continue walking," he said. Minutes later they approached a fenced area marked in Japanese and English: "No Trespassing. Danger. Look for falling rock," and "Unapproved posters are not permitted."

"I don't remember the fences and signs being here," Tessa noted, "but it's been so long, and I probably just don't remember."

"No, you're right. After *The Cove* came out, they put these up to keep intruders out. The slaughter of dolphins has been a dark stain on Taiji's image."

They left the area and walked north, until Jack stopped and said, "This is where you will get dropped off tomorrow."

Tessa looked at the mountain that sloped upward at least 1,500 feet and wondered if she would have to climb it to get to the other side. But Jack took her to a dirt road that led to the shore, located on the other side of the mountain behind the cove and out of view. It was a hidden area where the water splashed against the rocks. "Is this where I'll be getting into my gear?"

"Yes. Everything will be set up for you here," he said, pointing to a small grotto, large enough to hide cameras, equipment, and clothes.

"Who is setting it up?"

"There are a lot of people helping to put together this dive. They prefer to remain anonymous if you get my drift," he winked.

"Okay. No names. But how do I get back to your friend's place?"

"You'll leave all your gear here, change back into your clothes and walk back the same way you got here."

"You're not going to wait for me?"

"I'll stay with you until you enter the water, and then I'll leave."

"So, once on the road, I just keep walking until I get to Hiroke's house?"

"No. A black Honda Civic with a purple sticker on the passenger window will pick you up and drop you off a mile away from Hiroke's house. Then all you would need to do is to keep moving on a straight path until you reach his place. I will put a Japanese flag on his mailbox, in case you forget where he lives."

Hiroke wasn't an activist, but he knew his way around Taiji. A writer from Osaka, he spent several months in Taiji to work on a book. His tiny apartment was almost bare: a *shoji*, or bamboo-and-rice-paper-paneled partition, divided it into two rooms. One room had a small refrigerator, a stainless-steel sink, and a portable kitchen counter, the top of which was used to prepare food; the bottom held kitchen utensils, dishes, and cookware. In the center of the room was an *irori*—a square sunken hearth that served as a fireplace and stove. On the other side of *shoji* were two shelves filled with books and a desk piled with papers, pens, and a laptop. A small section of the room was devoted to hydroponics, and in the closet sat neatly piled soft *shikibutons*—lightweight, foldable mattresses along with neatly piled blankets and pillows.

Jack introduced Tessa to Hiroke.

"Nice to meet you. Thanks for letting me stay here for two nights," said Tessa shaking his hand. With nothing to eat since breakfast, she was starving and could smell food simmering over the firewood and charcoal.

"You're welcome. Jack's a good friend and any friend of his is a friend of mine," Hiroke said. He was twenty-eight, tall, and thin with a dragon tattoo on one arm that he covered when he went out because according to Japanese social norms, tattoos belonged on gang members, prisoners, and criminals.

"I hope you're hungry," Jack said, "Hiroke is a great cook. He's vegan and, after eating his food for the past few days, I'm thinking about converting."

Hiroke smiled and said, "Dinner is ready."

"Is there a place where can I freshen up?" asked Tessa.

Jack showed her the shower room and the toilet room.

Tessa noticed that the sink was located on top of the toilet.

"When you wash your hands, the water gets recycled into the toilet tank," Jack explained when he noticed Tessa staring at it.

"Clever!" Tessa remarked. She looked inside her bag for a wrapped box of caramel salted fudge that she had purchased in Los Angeles and presented it to Hiroke.

"*Domo arigato,*" he said.

"*Douitashimashite,*" Tessa replied and then turned to give Jack a bottle of Jack Daniels, "I know this is your favorite drink because it has your name on it. You can share it with Hiroke."

"Oh, Hiroke doesn't like to drink," he said teasingly, not wanting to share.

"Yes, I do," Hiroke replied, making Tessa laugh.

Jack, Hiroke, and Tessa sat on cushions around the *irori*. In one corner of the hearth, there was a kettle of hot green tea and on the opposite side was a clay pot of vinegared rice. In the center, a large circular copper pot was suspended from the ceiling over the fire. Cooking inside of it were clamshell and button mushrooms, soba noodles, scallions, *mizuna* or Japanese mustard greens, vegetable dumplings, pumpkin slices, and white yams, all simmering in *kombu*, or dried kelp broth. Three skewers of tofu and eggplant, perched on top of the pot, sizzled and roasted.

"I have never seen a hearth before," *except in a museum*, she wanted to say.

"They're not that common anymore. But you can still find them in some houses on farms, in rural areas, and in guesthouses," Jack said.

"Nowadays, some homes have *kotatsu*, which is like a hearth except that it's an electric heater built into a low sitting table framed by a heavy blanket," Hiroke added as he served everyone. "During cold weather, families sit cross-legged underneath the blanket to keep warm; sometimes they even sleep there."

Tessa, who was usually quite interested in learning about Japanese culture, just wanted to eat; her stomach growled. Hiroke put his hands together in a prayer position. Jack and Tessa followed suit and repeated after him, *"Itadakimasu."*

Hiroke said, "I hear that you're a veterinarian. How do you like it?"

"I like it most of the time. In fact, a few months ago I had to operate on a seal that had fishing hooks stuck inside of him. On the train ride here, I received a video from one of my work colleagues showing that the seal had recuperated and was released back into the ocean. It's times like those that are so gratifying."

Hiroke finished his vegetable dumpling and said, "So the pet hospital where you work is near the water?"

"Oh, no. This was at Pacific Marine Mammal Center in Laguna Beach. I volunteer there."

"How do you find time for yourself between work, activism, and your volunteer work?" Jack asked, picking up a piece of tofu with his chopsticks.

"I don't. I mean, I try, but saving animals is my priority. This vacation is my first vacation in seven years."

"Then, I'm lucky that you're here to help me out," Jack said.

"Thank you! It's a cause I would not miss. But enough about me," she said, enjoying her meal tremendously. "Hiroke, Jack is right. You are a great cook."

"*Sonna koto nai kedo ureshii desu. Arigatou!*" said Hiroke, which translated as, "Not at all, but it makes me happy to hear you say that. Thank you."

Tessa only understood the word thank you. However, she got the gist of what he was trying to say because when she was in Taiji as a teenager, her Aunt Harriette told her that the Japanese did not accept compliments right away because a compliment should, at first, be rejected. Humility was an important part of Japanese culture, and saying thank you right away would mean that you're saying thank you for noticing how great you are. So a response to a compliment was sometimes met with *Sou ka na*? Is that so? Or other versions of the phrase.

"Did you marinate the tofu and the eggplant?" Tessa asked.

"Yes, I did. I'll give you the recipe."

"You must have read my mind. I hope that someday you will come to L.A., and I can return the favor."

"Maybe I will," he said.

"You have to try the vegan custard pudding he's made for dessert. It's so much better than that store-bought kind," Jack commented as he ate his soba noodles.

"I can't wait," Tessa said and smiled as she brought her soup bowl to her mouth and slurped the same way Hiroke did. She had read that in Japan, slurping is a compliment to the chef, indicating that the delicious food is much appreciated.

"Jack tells me that you're a writer. What are you working on right now?" she asked, sitting the bowl down.

"I'm writing a book about growing hydroponic food in your apartment, and I will include vegan recipes."

"But aren't the apartments in Japan small?"

"Yes, but people can do vertical hydroponics and share with their neighbors. For example, one person can grow vegetables and the other person can grow fruits. They can trade."

"What a great idea!"

"It's sustainable and you don't have to kill anything to feed yourself. Some of the vegetables we ate for dinner were from my hydroponic garden. Let me show you my plants."

On the other side of the room partition, Tessa saw two hydroponically grown plants with LED lights shining on them—tomatoes and string beans. He showed her beans sprouting in jars, several jars of mushrooms that he was growing, and mustard greens and scallions sprouting roots in water. "I cut the top part of the scallions and leave the rest in water until they grow back again. I'm planning to plant more vegetables and fruits."

"I'm impressed," Tessa said.

"The soup broth was made from kelp I collected near the water two days ago. And don't worry, I wasn't anywhere near the cove. I got it from an area far away from here."

Tessa smiled and nodded.

"You see these mushrooms I'm cultivating?" asked Hiroke. "They are packed with protein. So there is no need for dolphin and whale meat."

"Well, many people are carnivores and pescatarians," responded Tessa, "You will have a hard time convincing them to get their protein from mushrooms."

"True, but I'm hoping that they would at least reduce their consumption of land and sea animals. Take dolphin and whale meat, for example. Both are filled with mercury, yet the townspeople here still eat it," he said, walking back to the hearth.

Jack had already brought out three small glass dishes of custard and poured everyone more green tea.

Tessa tried the custard and enjoyed the blend of flavors on her palate. "How did you make this?"

"I make it with soy, almond milk, cornstarch, turmeric, vanilla pods, and sugar. The trick is having lots of patience, using low heat, and precisely measuring the ingredients. If the measurements are off even a little bit, it throws it off the balance."

"Just like the chemical balance in a fish tank," Tessa commented, recalling a woman who called Tessa at the pet hospital wanting to know why her fish were dying one by one. Tessa advised her to purchase test strips to check the pH balance and minerals in the aquarium. It turned out that the nitrate and pH balance was off and too much fertilizer was being used to feed the live aquatic plants in her tank.

"Correct, except that I don't like fish tanks. Fishes should roam free in their natural environment," Hiroke said.

"Agreed," Jack added, finishing off his custard.

The rest of the evening was spent with Jack showing Tessa the closed-circuit camera map and reviewing their plan for the next day. Hiroke fixed their beds on the floor and then retired to the other side of the partition to work on his book.

"Thank you for a perfect evening. Goodnight," Tessa said. The evening may have been perfect, but now she was left alone with her thoughts and no one to distract her. She wondered what would happen the next day and if she would succeed. She worried about having problems with her equipment, such as her oxygen tank not working or her camera failing her. She questioned whether she could handle watching the slaughter without being able to do anything to stop it. *Shut up Tessa*, she told herself. *Just go to sleep.*

CHAPTER 12

After a long night of tossing and turning, Tessa fell asleep at dawn, only to be nudged awake a couple of hours later by Jack. Feeling listless, she managed to push herself up to shower and throw on a bathing suit, a navy slouchy hooded tunic, and a pair of loose-fitting sweatpants that Jack had given her to wear. Jack had purchased the clothes at a thrift store and was planning to donate it.

"I still don't understand why I can't wear my own clothes."

He gave her a cup of strong coffee and said, "Because I need to get rid of the clothes when you're back in case someone notices you walking in them."

Tessa drank the coffee, but not even the caffeine helped clear her foggy mind. She hoped that the fresh air would wipe away her fatigue.

"Everything is ready for you in the car," said Jack. "We should head out if we want to make it to the protest on time."

Tessa nodded, grabbed her camera, and got into a white Prius. "New car?" she asked.

"A friend of mine rented it from Osaka, and I put on a fake license plate just in case someone spots the car."

"Who would spot it?" she asked, now more alert and concerned.

"No one. It's just a precaution. Now, let's go over our plan once again."

"You will drop me off and help get me set up. Once I'm done filming and taking pictures, I will leave my gear at the same location where I started and walk away. Someone will pick me up shortly after that."

"Remember, once you get to the end of the dirt road, turn left."

"Got it," Tessa said, trying to hide her fear. Until then, she had been worried, but now her worry had turned into nausea. What if something went wrong? What if the authorities caught her? Would they all get into trouble? *Stop it, Tessa*, she told herself. *You already made this decision when you were in the U.S. Finish what you started.*

"There is a hat, a black wig, and sunglasses in the dashboard. Go ahead and put them on."

"What for?"

"Again, it's just a precaution in case someone sees you when you're walking."

"What about you?" she asked, reaching in the dashboard, thinking he stuck out more than she did.

"I have a baseball cap, a dark short wig, and glasses in my backpack."

"I see," she said, feeling like a spy in a clandestine operation. She put on the disguise. From a distance, she looked Japanese.

"There are already several activists, hiding behind trees, close to the cove, filming the mistreatment of the dolphins by the fishermen. So don't be a hero and film above the water."

"Believe me, I'm no hero," she said, pulse racing and hands shaking.

"You're okay?" Jack asked, glancing over at her and noticing the color fading from her face.

"Yes. I'm a little nervous, but this is how I always feel before something important is about to happen."

"You're sure? Because if you have changed your mind, I understand."

"No. I haven't changed my mind. Let's do this."

He explained the timing of everything: how long she would be taking pictures, what time she would have to return and change, and what time she would have to start walking away. They had to stick to the plan as closely as possible.

Tessa reached in her pocket and took out a pocket knife with a brown handle and held on to it.

"What's that?" Jack asked.

"It's my pocket knife. I don't go scuba diving without it."

"Why would you need a knife?"

"It's my rabbit's foot when I go diving."

"I hope that you're not planning to kill someone with it," he laughed.

She smiled and shook her head at his ridiculous comment. "My father gave it to me. It has his initials on it: JMW, Jeff Miles Walker. Miles was my grandfather. My dad said it always brought him success, and when I first started diving when I was seventeen, he gave it to me for good luck."

After walking on the same dirt road they had used the day before, they arrived at the rocky shore on the other side of the mountain behind the cove, hidden from the view. Tessa removed her hoodie and pants and put on a black-and-blue rash guard that looked like a very fitted onesie to keep her warm; on top of that, she wore a wet suit.

"Here is your dive computer," Jack said, handing her a gadget that looked like a black scuba-diving watch. It was used to show the length of time a diver spent underwater, the current depth, the maximum depth during a dive, and how much time a diver could safely remain at a particular depth.

Tessa put on the apparatus and removed her wig and glasses.

"Make sure you follow it precisely so that you make it back in time."

Jack helped her with her scuba gear, including a buoyancy compensator, which looked like a vest and held the tanks on her back. The equipment helped her descend or ascend by adding or releasing air. He attached a regulator-octopus to her tank. The regulator had a hose attached to a mouthpiece for breathing underwater. The octopus was a backup for the regulator.

Tessa put on her dive fins. Jack gave her an underwater plastic housing to protect her video camera and a snap-on coil to connect her to her camera so that she wouldn't lose it. The area she was diving in was hidden from the fishermen's view; after she moved from the shore into the water, Jack handed Tessa her camera.

"Remember to come back to this location. I have put a plain purple flag and a blank orange sign here so that you can easily find it again."

"Okay, I will," Tessa said as she dipped in and out of the water a few times, adjusting her goggles and making sure everything was comfortable on her.

"Good luck."

Tessa nodded and dove into the water. She went down thirty feet and swam closer to the fishermen. Once underwater, she could see four captive dolphins in pens. Now closer to the site of the slaughter, she rose closer to the surface. With good buoyancy and the ability to hover effortlessly in different positions, she was able to film the cetaceans underwater. The dolphins were agitated and confused as they jumped in and out of the water, flapping their tails, and whistling in distress. Some were already injured and bleeding, and she saw a spotted dolphin sink to the bottom of the cove because it had no fight left in it. Horrified, Tessa yelped and covered her mouth.

When certain species of dolphins die, water replaces the air in the body causing them to sink. Decomposition causes gas to build up in the body, and it resurfaces.

Tessa continued filming. Her watch indicated that she had a little more time. She took a dangerous risk and surfaced to take shots of the fishermen. They were too busy butchering the dolphins to see her. She wanted to go there and take their spears away and free the dolphins, but she couldn't. Some of the dolphins converged, awaiting their doom. One of them suffered an injury to its upper jaw and as it bled, two of the fishermen grabbed its flukes and dragged it into their boat, causing more injuries to the defenseless creature. Tears streamed down Tessa's face, blocking her visibility. *Stop it. Stop crying. There is no time to waste. Stay objective. You need to get out of here*, she told herself. Tessa was afraid that her emotions would lead her to do something rash and blow everyone's cover. She dove underwater and headed back, passing again by a captivity area with penned dolphins.

Tessa noticed a female free diver trying to pry them loose. She had always admired these free divers, who were able to hold their breath for long periods and swim underwater without any gear, but she also knew that the free divers' time was more limited because they needed to surface for air. Tessa swam to help her out even though she was running out of time and oxygen herself.

She went to one of the four pens, nodded at the free diver, and started cutting. Tessa's knife was sharp and easily cut through the thick netting. They managed to cut all four nets, leaving a gap for the dolphins to escape. They silently shook hands before the free diver swam off.

Tessa started to put her knife into one of her vest pockets when it slipped out of her hand and sank to the ocean bottom. *Damn, I just lost my lucky knife. Forget it. You must leave*, she told herself. But she suddenly realized that part of the net was wrapped around her oxygen tank. She tried to reach behind her and free herself, but it was no use. She tried to get rid of her oxygen tank, but the latch on her vest was stuck and wouldn't budge. *I sure as hell could use my lucky knife*, she thought. Panic took over her as she wriggled, hoping to free herself. *This is it*, she thought. *This is where I will die and no one will know until someone finds my corpse.* Trapped and feeling hopeless, she had to accept her fate. Her heart pounded hard against her chest, and her breathing became shallower as the dolphins she had set free passed by her and swam toward the free diver. They circled the diver, behaving erratically. She turned to see what was wrong and noticed that Tessa was stuck. The dolphins were asking the diver for help. She swam back to rescue Tessa, untangling the net from her tank.

Tessa had seen dolphins helping humans in films, but she had never actually experienced it firsthand. She was so grateful to them and the diver. The dolphins swam away and Tessa offered her octopus to the free diver, who took a breath with it and went on her way.

Tessa had no oxygen left when she ascended near the rocks by the shore, where the purple flag and orange sign were posted. A less-experienced diver might have died. But after years of scuba diving, she had learned to reduce her air consumption to make her oxygen last longer.

She got out of the water, removed her gear, and threw up. The reality of how close she had come to dying and watching the dolphins suffocate at the hands of the fishermen sickened her. How could anyone be so cruel? If people could witness the slaughter, there would be no way that they could ever support oceanariums and swim-with-the-dolphins programs. So much horror. So much pain.

Tessa followed Jack's instructions, but no black Honda Civic with a purple sticker appeared. She realized she was late and had possibly jeopardized everyone's plans by taking the extra time to free the dolphins. *No, I did the right thing,* she told herself. She continued walking until the Honda finally showed up. The worried Japanese driver who didn't speak English had been circling the area for awhile, hoping to run into Tessa. She got into his car. He dropped her off a few minutes away from Hiroke's house and gave her a map that he had drawn on with a blue pen, marking where she was and where she needed to go. Following the map was easy enough, as it pointed straight in the direction of the house. When Tessa reached the house, she noticed the Japanese flag and wanted to cry, but when she saw Jack, she held back her tears.

If he was upset that she was late, he didn't say anything. Jack could see from Tessa's chalky white complexion, grim face, and red eyes that what she had witnessed had been overwhelming. He tried to cheer her up. "You did it!" he exclaimed.

She was too emotional and couldn't talk. She was about to burst into tears.

"Come here," he said, stretching out his arms. She sobbed for a long time in his arms before she said, "I'd better go change and clean up my face. We have a protest to attend."

"You don't have to come, you know."

"Oh, yes I do. I need to be there."

"Okay, I'll wait for you in the car." This time, the white Prius Jack drove in the morning was gone and he was back to using Hiroke's car.

"I need my camera."

"You will get it later. You can use my spare."

Tessa was unhappy about that. She felt naked without her camera. She always had it with her. Unfortunately, there was nothing she could do but wait. "I can use my phone's camera."

On the way, Tessa told Jack about the free diver, losing her knife, and getting stuck underwater.

"Tessa, do you have a death wish? What did I tell you?"

"Not to get involved, but I couldn't look the other way. I wanted to help."

"You do not listen well, do you?"

Tessa shrugged.

"You are one lucky son of a B, you know that? Did you recognize the diver, at least?"

"No. I have no idea who she was."

"Well, do me a favor, and don't talk about any of this to anyone."

Tessa didn't realize that the free diver was not an activist. She was part of the fishermen's crew and had gone rogue. After years of helping to kill dolphins while she was young, she could no longer stomach it. Instead, she had bought herself a boat and took tourists to watch dolphins in their natural environment. Just like many Japanese activists, the free diver wanted the slaughter to stop, and cutting nets now and then was her way of dealing with the sorrow and remorse that tugged at her heart every day.

When they reached the demonstration on the sidewalk near the Taiji Whale Museum, about twenty protesters were there. Some of the activists had already left. A parked van had a banner stretched across it with a picture of dead dolphins and a slogan in Japanese and English, "Raise your voice, end the cruelty." There was a table with pamphlets spread across it. Behind the table were a man and a woman in their late 20s with photos of bloodied dolphins behind them. A woman wearing a blue T-shirt embellished with a picture of two dolphins swimming in the water spoke using a bullhorn, and the others echoed her sentiment. Some handed out pamphlets to Japanese and foreign spectators.

Jack and Tessa stood apart from the opposition, made up of twelve people, who were shouting back. Four police officers were there to stop the three-hour protest from turning violent.

Jack said, "We're going to let the Japanese activists do their job. We're just observing and filming. If someone pushes you, don't push back. Be cool."

Like all activists who had been at it for a long time, Jack knew that intruders often attended demonstrations to provoke trouble. Sometimes they were sent by the government to break up protests, arrest activists, and put fear in them. At other times, the opposition was just angry and would shout vulgarities or get violent to start a fight.

"Don't worry. I will keep calm," Tessa assured him. She didn't need to know Japanese to understand the opposition's hostile tone from their screams.

An angry man approached Tessa and said, "Why are you here? Go home, *gaijin*."

Tessa ignored him, which made him even angrier. Then he pushed her.

Jack, who spoke Japanese, told the man to get lost. Jack was bigger and could have easily crushed him. The police came over and separated them. "Go over there. Go over there," they told Tessa and Jack, who did as they were told.

"There are other foreigners here. Why did this man pick on me?" Tessa whispered in Jack's ear.

"Not sure." *It seems that he doesn't like you*, he wanted to say, but instead said, "It seems that he doesn't like us. A personal vendetta, perhaps?"

"But I've never seen him before. Have you?"

"No. Maybe. I'm not sure."

"Which one? No, maybe or you're not sure?" Tessa pressed.

"I don't know. I might have run into him in the past, but I have no recollection. You know how it is at these demonstrations. Sometimes you rub someone the wrong way."

Some of the onlookers were residents of Taiji. Many likely didn't appreciate the activists getting in the way of their livelihood. And yet, the demonstrators from other parts of the country continued chanting and holding up signs displaying dolphin slaughters. Jack continued filming. Tessa took pictures with her cellphone and posted them on her social media account right away. The description read, "I'm in Taiji at a protest. The police are here and the situation is tense. One of the locals called me an 'outsider' and told me to go home."

The demonstration continued for two more hours until it was time to leave. The activists rolled up their signs and packed up their things. Tessa and Jack walked over to thank them for caring and wanting to change things in their country. The man who had pushed Tessa earlier had disappeared. The crowd began to disperse. The four policemen left as well. The locals went back to their homes and lives as though nothing had taken place. *It would take a lot more than one protest to change their way of thinking,* Tessa thought. One step at a time, she reminded herself.

CHAPTER 13

The next day, while on the train from Taiji to Osakako where the Osaka Aquarium Kaiyukan was located, Tessa texted Toshiro to confirm their dinner plans. He told her that he missed her; she said that she missed him too and was looking forward to seeing him at the intercontinental hotel where she was planning to stay that night. Reflecting on the horrifying slaughter in Taiji, she thought that spending time with Toshiro would be a good distraction for her. It was nine in the morning, and the seat next to her was empty. She was glad for that because it allowed her time to think in solitude.

Taking the underwater photos was a nightmare because, except for the few dolphins that she helped rescue, she couldn't actively save the rest. If she had tried, she would have been arrested. She felt heartless, but she had to keep her emotions out of it to accomplish her goals. And the magnitude of her repressed emotions from the previous day was now catching up with her. Until that moment, she had been surviving on nervous energy. But now, left alone with her turbulent thoughts, she sensed an unsettling feeling that she wished would go away.

Her scuba gear had been hidden in the small grotto, and later one of the activists had picked it up and returned it to the diving school before anybody could notice that it was missing. Her camera was returned to her when she returned from the protest, but the photos and videos of her dive were wiped clean so that they couldn't be traced back to her.

"But I need to post those pictures on my blog and my social media accounts," Tessa had complained to Jack.

"I put them on the Cloud. You can use my anonymous laptop to retrieve and post them, but I recommend that you don't take credit for them under your real name."

"No. I post under a different handle. You know it?"

"Yes, FreeMyDolphins. I just wasn't sure what you were planning to do. Lots of people were involved in our plan, and I want to make sure that no one gets arrested."

"Don't worry. I mostly repost things under my real name, but I rarely take credit for anything." Under her real name, Tessa deliberately had few social media followers. She usually posted material that people already knew. But that would soon change.

Before reaching Osakako, Tessa stopped at Tennoji, one of Osaka's largest transportation hubs surrounded by seven malls along with a temple, park, museum, and dining and entertainment district. Tessa didn't have time for any of that. She just needed to change trains to get to the Bentencho Station and from there, she would have another transfer before reaching Osakako. She used her pocket Wi-Fi to access the internet and was exhilarated to see the results of her anonymous posts. The videos and photos she had taken had gone viral. By noon, the internet was buzzing with comments, and several journalists were digging in to find out who had filmed the gruesome event so they could get an interview. Besides Tessa's closest activist friends, Erica, the Japanese African-American Tessa had met in Kyoto, also knew that Tessa was the photographer by questioning her sources. But Erica had no intention to disclose what she knew.

I did it! I no longer feel helpless, Tessa said to herself. With the help of a group of caring people, she had again managed to bring attention to the dolphins' plight. It had been smart to go incognito, Tessa thought.

Yoko arrived early at the Osakako station, a short walk from the Osaka Aquarium Kaiyukan where the protest was taking place. Two of her friends were already setting up while Yoko waited to meet Tessa.

Tessa reached the Chuo line tired but fired up. She badly needed a rest, but there wasn't time for that. *Strike while the iron is hot*, she said to herself, noticing a young girl staring at her. She remembered how Yoko had described herself to her—shoulder-length black hair with purple ends, a baseball cap, and a gray suede jacket with red leather sleeves. Tessa noticed her camera dangling from a strap around her shoulder. She wore a pair of white-rimmed cat-eye glasses and bright red lipstick, not exactly a look that would be approved by Tokyo residents. But out here in Osaka, people went out of their way to be different. There was a friendly rivalry between the two cities: Tokyo was formal and neat; Osaka was casual and somewhat sloppy. People here dressed less conservatively and were more relaxed, and the streets were not spotless as in Tokyo.

"Hello. Nice to meet you," Yoko said as she approached Tessa and shook hands. Yoko felt intimated by her—an American who carried herself with confidence and was much older than 21-year-old Yoko. Tessa's clothes were simple and classic—navy pants, a baby blue shirt, and a tailored jacket. She reminded Yoko of her seventh-grade English teacher. She and Tessa had had many telephone conversations to plan the protest, but they hadn't met in person until that day.

"Well, shall we?" Tessa said when she noticed Yoko staring at her. Why was she staring? Tessa thought. She had dressed appropriately—if anything, Tessa should've been the one staring. But Tessa grew up with many funky friends with nose and tongue piercings, belly rings, tattoos, spiky hair, the whole shebang.

Yoko was staring more out of curiosity than anything else. All her friends and coworkers were Japanese. "Yes, we go. Only five minutes," Yoko said with a thick Japanese accent. She raised her hand and displayed five fingers in case Tessa didn't understand her. Although she spoke English, her vocabulary was limited.

They followed the signs to the aquarium.

"I wish I had more time to visit Osaka," Tessa said.

"Come back and visit us," Yoko said. "How long you in Japan?"

"Today is my thirteenth day, and it all has gone by so quickly. I love your country. It's so beautiful out here—the architecture, the people, the streets, the gardens, and the food. Almost nothing has disappointed me thus far."

"I must come to America to, how do you say, com, comp...?"

"Compare?"

"Yes, compare," Yoko replied. She had never been outside of Japan. It was too costly. Yoko lived at home with her parents, worked at a clothing store, and spent her free time with her dog and boyfriend, who was rarely available because he worked long hours like most of the Japanese population.

"And when you do, I'll show you around. By the way, Akira said to tell you hello when I see you."

"Thank you. I call her." Yoko and Akira were good friends and spoke to each other regularly.

When they reached the outside of the aquarium, there were only two other people there to represent their cause: a man and a woman only a couple of years older than Yoko who spoke even less English. "Hi, hello, how are you?" was all they could manage. But no matter. *It's my problem that I hardly know any Japanese,* Tessa thought. The two were seated on folding chairs behind a table and in front of easels displaying photographs of the cove, bloody waters, and captured dolphins. Two more empty folding chairs were at the table, but Tessa and Yoko never got to use them. Around fifteen people stopped by. Tessa spoke with the English speakers, passed them pamphlets, and explained the mistreatment of the cetaceans at entertainment venues. She told them one of the ways to stop the cruelty was to stop buying tickets to those places.

Members of the aquarium administrative staff came out from time to time to observe the activists. They looked uneasily at these demonstrators, who were hurting business and promoting negative publicity. But there was no need for their concern because soon four policemen approached and asked to see their permit for the assembly.

"I'm sorry. I forgot to get a permit," Yoko said, lying. She had tried but had been denied. She was a rebel, however, and decided to put together an information table outside the aquarium grounds anyway.

One of the policemen approached Tessa and asked for her identification. She showed him her passport. He paged through it carefully and then asked her to put her wrists behind her back and handcuffed her.

"I don't understand. Why am I being arrested?" she asked.

The policeman said nothing as he lowered her head into a police car. Then he handcuffed Yoko and put her in a different car.

Some of the people who had stopped by to learn more about the dolphins were filming the arrest, and the police were using their hands to cover up their cameras. Luckily for Tessa, they missed Erica, who was filming everything with a camera outfitted with a zoom lens.

At the police station, the officers put Tessa in an interrogation room with bare walls, a table, and three chairs. Two investigators took turns grilling her.

"Did you take these photos?" asked one investigator with beady eyes. Among the many photos that he showed her were images of a pair of human hands forcing a baby dolphin underwater, a dolphin bleeding in the water as a fisherman inserted a rod into its spine, and a dolphin sinking to the ocean bottom.

"I would like a lawyer."

Tapping his finger so hard on the table that it shook, he shouted, "Did you take these pictures?"

"No!" Tessa said angrily. She did recognize her handiwork but hoped that they couldn't prove it. If they could, she, and those who had helped her, would be in more trouble for her lies.

"These photos were taken from under the water. Do you own scuba diving gear?" He asked, pacing the room.

The other officer, with a kinder face and a milder manner, looked uncomfortable with Tessa's harsh treatment.

"No."

"Weren't you a scuba instructor in the U.S?"

"Yes. Long ago. I don't do that anymore," Tessa responded. *How the hell did they know that?* she thought.

Unbeknownst to Tessa, she had made an archenemy of Junichiro Fujimoto, even before he spotted her at Toshiro's birthday party. Right after Jessica's newspaper article in *ITO* about the Tokyo protest, he had her investigated and found out that her efforts would defame his name and livelihood. So, he learned everything about Tessa—what she did for a living, her activism in the U.S., and her extracurricular activities, such as scuba diving.

The internet provided a tremendous amount of information about Tessa's endeavors. Junichiro found out about her social media accounts from the newspaper article in *ITO* and posted investigators at each protest who tried to get her into trouble. They had pushed the police to question her in Kyoto and sent someone to start a fight with her in Taiji. And though Tessa hadn't been participating in the Taiji protest, one of Junichiro's investigators reported that someone had cut through the dolphin nets and four of them had escaped. Junichiro was livid because he had purchased those particular dolphins to sell to buyers in Dubai for more than one million dollars. He had therefore used his contacts to push for Tessa's arrest. He had a gut feeling that she was involved. He knew that she used to be a scuba diving instructor. She had to be the one who had cut the nets; at least that's what he had hoped. If so, he could put her away for a long, long time. His problem was that many activists had been present in Taiji when Tessa had been there. It could have been any one of them. Some activists who were still in Taiji had been questioned, but no one knew who cut the nets.

Beady-eyes studied Tessa in silence, rubbing his chin and thinking. He hoped to intimidate her before he spoke again: "What were you doing in Taiji?"

"Observing, just like the rest of the activists," she retorted, but she worried that Jack and the others who helped her would also get into trouble. Going scuba diving had been her idea, and Jack had agreed to help her out.

"And you never participated or helped them?"

"I was told not to get involved in a local protest. I did as I was told," she answered calmly.

"Who gave you the film?"

"I don't understand." *Which film is he talking about now? He is fishing. Keep your cool.*

"You did post the film about the dolphin drive on your personal social media account, didn't you?"

"Yes."

"Who sent the film to you?"

"No one. If you paid attention, you would have noticed that the posts didn't originate from me. I simply shared what others posted."

"But you do have your own posts," he remarked, his eyes glued on her, watching her every twitch, hoping that she would make a mistake and admit that she had lied.

"Yes," she responded, staring right back at him. "Those are from the demonstrations I participated in. I'm very upfront about it."

"I need a list of all of your activist friends," he said, passing her a sheet of paper and a pen.

"That's personal. I'm not willing to give you that." She felt as though she was being interrogated by the Gestapo. Luckily, she had thought to save only the numbers of her friends, family, and the few activists she knew in Japan on her phone. She had stored the rest of her activist friends' phone numbers in a secure, heavily encrypted online site. She was well aware that when people traveled, their rights were taken away during security checks, and security reserved the right to look through their personal information without a warrant. So she carried as little information as possible with her.

"You do it now," beady-eyes shouted.

Then kind-face said something in Japanese to beady-eyes, and the two left the room.

What is going on? Tessa thought. Were they playing good cop, bad cop, or was kind-face actually a nice person? But, she decided, it was best to keep her guard up. She felt frightened and uncertain, but it didn't appear that she would receive help any time soon.

The two officers returned. Kind-face gave her bottled water, but she refused to drink it. What if they were trying to fill her up with water and then refuse her the use of the bathroom unless she confessed? What if they wanted her DNA? She was unfamiliar with arrest procedures in Japan. They had denied her a phone call and a lawyer. That, in itself, baffled her.

"For you. Drink." Kind-face pushed the bottle toward her. He stared at her dry lips.

"No thank you. I'm not thirsty," Tessa replied, even though she was parched and would give almost anything for a cold glass of water.

"Let's talk about the nets," beady-eyes said.

Shit! Did they have a video of her? But how? Underwater surveillance? Nah, not possible. The knife! They must have found it. Damn! she thought frantically. But she coolly replied, "I don't understand."

"Don't play dumb with me. You cut the nets to the pens, and four dolphins escaped."

"You keep accusing me of actions I did not commit. You don't believe anything I say. I'm not talking to you anymore," she shrugged.

He put both hands on the table and leaned toward her, so close that she could feel his breath on her. "Oh, you will talk. Because if you refuse, I will move you from detention to prison."

Kind-face looked worried, but Tessa did not flinch. Even if they had found her knife, it had her father's initials on it, not hers. But what about her fingerprints? Would they still be on it? She had no idea. And anyway, if they had proof of any wrongdoing, she would be in prison by now. "Kindly remove your face from mine and treat me in a civilized manner."

Beady-eyes moved away, stared at her harshly, and said, "Do you have family in Taiji?"

"Not anymore," *but I'm sure you already know that*, she wanted to say. *They probably know everything about me down to the color of my underwear*, she thought.

"You have family in Taiji. No?" He had pulled up her records from when she had visited Japan as a teenager. In the section that indicated where she would be staying, she had put Harriette's address. For relationship, she had handwritten, "aunt."

"Did. She passed away."

"Was she also an activist?"

"No." There was no need to go into details about her past and her estranged relationship with her father's family.

"Your aunt had a daughter around your age. She is alive and living in New Zealand. Did she use her contacts to help you?" The police had checked Natalie's records and had gotten in touch with her. They found out that Natalie was married with three children and didn't keep in touch with anyone in the U.S. or Japan.

"I haven't talked to her since I was sixteen."

"You're lying. We know that you filmed the dolphin drive. We know that you cut the nets. You know how to dive. You were an instructor," beady-eyes reiterated with tight lips. He was angry at himself for underestimating her resolve and being unable to break her.

Tessa raised her voice to match his: "I'm not lying." *Two can play this game*, she told herself.

They had searched high and low for her gear and found no trace of it. They had questioned Jack and his friend Hiroke, but both said that they had no knowledge of it. Orders had trickled down from Junichiro Fujimoto to the police department head, the supervisors, and finally, the investigators to convict this woman and silence her.

"Is this your swimsuit?" They had gone through her luggage collected from the train station locker and discovered no evidence except clothes, undergarments, a bag of toiletries, a box of cookie bars, and a bathing suit. In her backpack, they found evidence of what was already obvious—her attendance at different protests was marked on her calendar. As far as her camera went, there was nothing but some tourist photos and the photos of the protest that she had already admitted attending. So far, they weren't able to tie her to any illegal activities.

"You went through my things without a search warrant?" she asked, eyes widening.

"We have a warrant," he lied. In Japan, officials often got a search warrant after they went through a suspect's belongings. "Answer the question."

"Yes, it's mine. I didn't know it was a crime to own a swimsuit," she responded boldly. She had to show them that she was tough and that they couldn't crack her. But what Tessa did not know was that they had torn apart people much stronger than her. They knew how to get a confession even if it was coerced and false.

"We know that you used it under your scuba diving gear," he continued harshly.

"I already told you that I don't own scuba gear," she said, tired of repeating herself. All she wanted was to go home, take a hot bath, order room service, and relax in a bed. *Oh, shit! Toshiro!* She had forgotten all about him during the interrogation.

"Why did you bring a swimsuit, then?" he blurted, throwing it in front of her.

"For the same reason that anyone brings a swimsuit—to go swimming. I just never got around to it. I am planning to go for a swim at my hotel tonight. You may come and watch to make sure that I'm telling you the truth." She was so relieved that she happened to be staying at a hotel with a swimming pool and that she had washed her swimsuit with lavender soap the night before to clean out the saltwater.

He sniggered. "You aren't going anywhere. You will be here tonight and tomorrow and the days after until you tell us the truth."

What was he saying? That they were never going to let her out? This couldn't be. She wanted to cry. *Hold yourself together Tessa*, she told herself. "I would like to see a lawyer."

Unfortunately for Tessa, in Japan, people were guilty until proven innocent without immediate access to a lawyer. Officials often held a suspect for much longer than the forty-eight hours declared on the U.S. government website. Sometimes, it took weeks to drill and threaten suspects to force them to confess.

In the meantime, they aggressively questioned Yoko and fined her for not having a permit. Because this was her first offense, the police let her go once she paid the fine. When Yoko was released, she called Akira and told her what had happened. Yoko let Akira know at which police station they were holding Tessa.

"Okay, go home," Akira told her.

"I cannot just leave her there," she pleaded, her body tense, her face scrunched up. "This was my fault. She doesn't speak any Japanese and she is probably petrified."

"There's nothing you can do because they're not going to let you talk to her. Leave the police station and go home. I have to make a call and will get back to you."

As soon as Yoko hung up, Akira remembered that Tessa had sent her Karianne Metzler's phone number a few days ago. She remembered that Karianne worked at the U.S. Embassy representing U.S. interests abroad, so Akira figured that she might be able to help. Karianne answered Akira's call and listened to her explain Tessa's detainment in Kyoto and Osaka.

"Two times?" Karianne asked.

"They were just scaring her off in Kyoto and let her go. But this time, she's in real trouble. I didn't know who else to call," Akira said, nervously. In all the time she had been an activist, she had never been jailed. She couldn't even imagine what it would be like to be interrogated by authorities in a country where she didn't know the language. *Poor Tessa!* she thought.

"You did the right thing. I'm actually in Osaka with my husband, visiting his family," said Karianne. "I'll look into it."

Both Karianne and her husband had connections—one phone call to the right person would take care of things. Karianne was friends with many U.S. members of congress. Born into a wealthy, powerful, political family, her husband knew people with connections to the Japanese imperial family, Supreme Court members, and the prime minister. Karianne was determined to get her friend out as quickly and smoothly as possible.

Yoko was angry at herself for being so irresponsible. She should never have dragged Tessa into a protest without a permit. What was she thinking? She was so mad that she wanted to bang her head against the wall as she took the subway to her parents' house. And as soon as she was home, she went on her anonymous Twitter account to tweet about what had happened to Tessa and alert her followers. She thought that if she could create enough noise, the police would have to let Tessa go. When she signed into her Twitter account, she noticed a message from Erica with a link to a video of their arrest. Erica had already posted the video on her anonymous social media accounts, hoping it would go viral and all her activist friends would see it.

Yoko watched the video. The entire event had been recorded from the moment people had slowed down to watch the Taiji dolphin drive hunt protest to when the police had approached Tessa and Yoko, handcuffed them, and pushed them into their cars. Yoko edited the video to put more emphasis on Tessa's arrest and posted it on her anonymous Mixi, a Japanese social media account, and Twitter account. Because of Yoko's activism, a few journalists and U.S. media outlets followed her, as well as a couple of American celebrity activists.

Meanwhile, Karianne arrived with a brown leather briefcase in hand to visit Tessa. They sat on the opposite sides of a table in an otherwise empty room. She held Tessa's hands, noticing her red eyes and the dark circles beneath them. She asked, "Are you okay?"

"I'm, I'm, sorry to drag you in here. They have been drilling me for a long time. Do you know what happened to Yoko?" she asked, lips trembling.

"Akira said that they fined her and released her."

"That's comforting to know, but I don't understand why they kept me and let Yoko go. I have done nothing wrong. It was Yoko who forgot to apply for a permit and didn't tell me."

"We only have twenty minutes to talk. Be careful of what you say. The walls have ears." In Japan, officials listened in on all conversations when relatives visited, but they were not supposed to when the conversation was between a client and a lawyer or consul. Even so, years of working at the U.S. embassy taught Karianne that it was wise to take precautions.

"Okay," Tessa said and nodded.

"We are working on getting you out. If it doesn't happen today, we're going to get you out by tomorrow," she assured her.

"Tomorrow?" Although this wasn't Tessa's first detention at a police station, it was her first in a foreign country, and she was petrified. Her father had been right when he warned her, "Believe me, you don't want to end up in some foreign country's jail." *Suck it up, Tessa. This is all part of being an activist,* she told herself. A few years back, Tessa and a group of activists were arrested in Los Angeles for blocking the entrance to a drug research Laboratory that tested on animals.

"They will not harm you. I think that they just want to scare you and send you on your way home."

"But my flight leaves from Tokyo in three days. I still have to pack up the rest of my belongings from Akira's home," she said, lowering her head in defeat. Tessa had left the souvenirs she bought, a small load of laundry, and a few items she didn't need to carry with her at Akira's place. She was embarrassed because she felt like a burden. In the U.S., she was proud and independent, but here, she was at a loss.

"Hey, look at me," Karianne said. Tessa slowly lifted her head, tears running down her face. Karianne continued, "You're going to be okay. I will get you out. I asked a high-profile lawyer to look into your case. He said that they have nothing on you and he is putting pressure on them to let you go."

"Thank you!" she managed to say before feeling a lump in her throat.

"You're welcome," Karianne responded, reaching in her briefcase and pulling out a tissue.

Tessa wiped her eyes and said, "I am sorry to ask you this but, but. ..." she stammered.

"What is it? I will do whatever you ask. You're like my sister," she said recalling when they were kids having play nights over at each other's houses, dancing and jumping up and down, making popcorn, and watching movies.

"They, they took away my cellphone. If I give you the phone number of a friend, will you call him and apologize on my behalf for standing him up for dinner?"

"He should be the least of your worries." *So much like Tessa, always concerned for others,* she thought.

"Please? He is important to me and I always seem to disappoint him."

"A lover?" Karianne blurted out and smiled mischievously.

"Not in this lifetime. I have enough trouble taking care of myself."

"You can always make room for love. Isn't that so?" she said. Noticing the look of concern on her friend's face, she added, "Don't worry. I will call him."

It was already two hours past the time she was to meet with Toshiro. She didn't want to involve him in this, so she added, "Please don't tell him that I'm in jail. Just let him know that an emergency has come up and I will get in touch with him once it's resolved."

"No problem. Anything else?"

"No, that's it. Thank you for helping me out. I'm really sorry for putting you through this."

"Listen, I know all about the Taiji dolphins and the way they are massacred. Privately, I fully support you, but publicly, I have to be careful about what I say," Karianne said, carefully choosing her words. When Tessa and Karianne were kids, they had made up their own language so that people would have a hard time eavesdropping. If Karianne were just a visitor, it would have been illegal to speak in a secret code. But since she was acting as a liaison, she had some leeway.

Tessa winked at her. "I appreciate your support."

"Unfortunately, this is the end of your protests here. At least for this trip. I think there is someone who knows your every move. It seems unusual for you to get harassed by the authorities in Kyoto and arrested in Osaka in the same week," Karianne said. When she saw the look of apprehension on her friend's face, she squeezed her hand reassuringly before getting up to leave. "I will get you out. That's a promise!"

In a smart charcoal gray suit and burgundy pinstriped shirt, Toshiro waited for Tessa at Adee, a stylish, romantic bar on the 20th floor of the Intercontinental Osaka Hotel. It had a laser waterfall screen and spectacular city views. A scotch and soda later, he asked the front desk if they would ring Tessa's room; they said that she hadn't checked in. At first, he got worried, but as more time passed, he started to get angry, thinking that she had stood him up. *Forget it,* he told himself, *I've never waited this long for anyone.* He called up Hansuke and asked to meet him at Bar Masuda in Dotonbori, an area with intense nightlife.

Toshiro turned off his phone once he reached the three-story bar. *Let her chase me for a change*, he thought. This was the second time Tessa was doing this to him and he felt stupid even bothering to wait for her. Tessa always prioritized everything else over him. *It didn't feel right to be constantly at the bottom of the pile*, he thought as he took a seat behind the counter on the first floor and ordered a 160-proof John Crow Batty Rum. He wanted to get blitzed, which he was when Hansuke arrived. His cousin knew right away that something was wrong; he hadn't seen Toshiro that drunk since college.

"C'mon, let's get out of here," Hansuke said with his pitch-black hair swept to one side, covering one of his eyes. Toshiro was staying with him while in Osaka.

Slurring his words and tapping the red leather barstool next to him, Toshiro said, "Come join me. What do you want to drink?"

"I think you have had enough for both of us."

"What will it be?" the bartender asked.

"Another one of these," Toshiro pointed at his drink, "And one for my cousin. And keep them coming. I'm thirsty."

The bartender looked at Hansuke with an expression in his eyes that said, he's had enough. Take him home.

"We will not be staying," Hansuke told the bartender, glancing over at two attractive young women looking their way.

"I said, sit," commanded Toshiro.

"What happened?" His cousin did as he requested to keep him from shouting.

"Women is what happened. Never fall for them. They stick their hand in there," he said pointing at Hansuke's heart, "and rip it out."

"You know, there is a great club called Owl near the Umeda Station. Why don't we go dancing?" He lied to get him out of there, intending to take Toshiro home.

"Dancing? Now, why didn't I think of that?" Toshiro said, staggering out of his chair, tripping, and almost falling when Hansuke caught him. "Let's invite those two ladies to come with us," he said, pointing his head toward them.

"Oh, there will be plenty of girls where we're going. Let's get out of here," Hansuke said.

On the drive home, Toshiro closed his eyes, feeling dizzy and nauseous. And when Hansuke finally parked his car, Toshiro said, "Hey, this isn't a club. Where are we?"

"We're at my house. We can go dancing tomorrow when you're good and sober."

"You lied to me. You're just like her," he said, trying to get out of the car, but he kept falling back into the seat.

"C'mon, you need sleep," Hansuke answered, helping Toshiro to the house and guiding him to the guest bedroom, where he passed out.

Late in the morning, Toshiro opened his eyes to find he was still in the same clothes he wore last night. His hair stuck out in all directions, his head pounded, and all he could think of was aspirin and water. Hansuke was in the kitchen, making a concoction of herbs for him to detoxify.

"What is that? Toshiro asked.

"Drink up. It'll help you," Hansuke said, dressed for work.

Toshiro took a drink. "Blah, this tastes awful."

"Here's a glass of coconut water to replenish the electrolytes you lost last night," Hansuke said, pushing it toward him, "and some ginger in case you feel nauseous."

Toshiro chewed on the ginger until he started feeling better. "Don't you have to go to work?"

"They know I'm be going in late," said Hansuke, who owned a startup tech firm. He looked at his watch. It was 11 a.m. "I wanted to make sure that you'd be alright."

"Sorry to make you late for work," he said, feeling irresponsible. He should have never had that much to drink over a woman, especially a woman who didn't give a damn about him.

"Go take a shower. I'm making breakfast. I laid out clothes for you on the bed," Hansuke said, treating Toshiro like a child even though Toshiro was two years older.

While Toshiro showered, Hansuke took out some bowls to serve sticky rice, *natto*, or fermented soybeans, miso, and *yakizakana,* or grilled fish.

Toshiro came out with a towel around his neck, his hair dripping water. He had changed into Hansuke's brown slacks and a cream color sweater. "Do you have a hairdryer I can borrow?"

"Middle drawer of my bathroom. Have to go to work. You're going to be okay?" Hansuke liked his only cousin. They didn't get to spend time together as much as he wanted to, but he considered him a good friend.

"I think so. I'm starting to feel better."

"Have some breakfast. Then just lock up when you leave."

"Thank you!"

"You're welcome," Hansuke said, grabbing his messenger bag and leaving.

Toshiro filled up on miso and rice and then remembered that he had turned off his phone. He turned it on and saw a voicemail from a number that he did not recognize and a text from his friend, Souji. He listened to the voicemail: "Hi, this is Metzler. I'm a friend of Tessa's. She asked me to let you know that she had an emergency and is sorry that she wasn't able to make it to dinner. She will call you." In Japan, people don't refer to each other by their first names unless they are friends.

Toshiro called Tessa and when she didn't answer, he called back the woman who had left him the message.

"*Konnichiwa*, Metzler *desu*, good afternoon. This is Metzler," she answered. Karianne was on the shinkansen heading back to Tokyo because of work.

"Hello. You left me a message about Tessa."

"Ah, yes, she was really upset that she couldn't make it to dinner, but it was beyond her control."

"May I ask what was the emergency?" he inquired with concern. What if she were lying somewhere in a hospital? He would never forgive himself for turning off his phone and getting blitzed.

"You'd better ask her," Karianne suggested.

"Where is she?" he asked, his body feeling weak and numb.

"I dropped her off at the Intercontinental. She should be there if you want to talk to her." She gave him Tessa's room number.

"Is she okay?"

"She is fine. I'm sorry, but I have another phone call coming in," Karianne lied so that he wouldn't ask any more questions.

"Thank you," Toshiro said. He dialed the hotel and asked for Tessa's room, but the front desk said that she wasn't answering her phone.

Next, Toshiro read the text. "You need to see this," Souji said and added several links. Toshiro clicked on the first one and there they were, Tessa and Yoko getting arrested by the police. "Oh damn. Tessa!" He clicked on the next link. It was a report from an American news station explaining that an American protesting the Taiji dolphin drive hunt had been arrested in Japan and that the U.S. Embassy was negotiating to get her out. The third link showed that some activists had cut the nets and let four dolphins escape. And finally, the fourth link led to the footage that Tessa had filmed during her dive, which showed that not much had changed in Taiji to the chagrin of activists around the world. All their demonstrations had not produced the result they had hoped for.

Toshiro tried Tessa again and still no answer. He quickly washed the dishes, locked up, and took the subway to the Intercontinental.

Earlier in the day, Karianne and a lawyer managed to get Tessa released. Tessa's lawyer told her that she would not be allowed back into the country, but he was filing an appeal to the district court to revoke the ministry of justice's decision. He told her that she had to leave Japan the next day on Japan Airlines flight JL062 at 7:30 p.m. Once at the airport, she would need to exchange her ticket for a new one. Japan Airlines employees working behind the ticketing counter were expecting her. Tessa had jotted down the information on a yellow sticky note and stuck it to the outside of her original ticket.

"They wanted an official to escort you to the gate, but I told them that that was not necessary. So, they are holding me accountable for your departure," Karianne told her.

"Thank you! You have my word that I will be on that flight," Tessa promised.

Karianne helped Tessa pick up her luggage from the police station. Tessa confided in her about her scuba diving ordeal. Karianne's driver dropped her off at her hotel. Tessa gave Karianne a box of the cookie bars she had asked for and thanked her profusely before hugging her. The two promised each other to keep in touch.

Checking in at the hotel, Tessa had to explain why she hadn't shown up the day before for her reservation. She made up a story about having a family emergency in the U.S., missing her flight, and arriving late. The young woman working behind the desk made copies of her ID and credit card and gave her a key card.

The first thing Tessa did when she got to her room was plug in her phone to see if she had any messages. Toshiro's texts from the night before said: "Where are you?" "Why aren't you here?" "Call me." "I'm mad at you." "I'm leaving." Her parents had expressed how worried they were, and her friends from the U.S. wanted to know what was going on. Akira, Satomi, Jack, and Yoko had also texted her. They told her that social media was in a frenzy over what happened.

Tessa was flabbergasted when she signed into her Twitter account. Her followers and likes were increasing by the minute, and she had so many replies that she couldn't possibly respond.

American and international media had requested interviews. Follower after follower asked if she was alright and if she needed help. She shook her head at the insanity of it all and then realized that it was Erica who had taped her arrest, which had gone viral and gotten her all this attention. It was as though Tessa had become a celebrity overnight, and she hated it. She just wanted to bring attention to the cause, but if this is what it took, so be it.

Tired, hungry, and thirsty all at the same time, she opened the bar fridge in her room and inhaled a candy bar, a bag of chips, and two bottles of mineral water. She tried calling Toshiro, but his phone seemed to be having an issue—when she tried to leave a message, it cut her off. She tried texting him, but her phone indicated that the text had not gone through. After several tries, she gave up and responded to all her other texts and returned her parents' calls to let them know that she was alright. She then took a much-needed shower.

Toshiro eventually arrived at the hotel. Without a key card, he hitched an elevator ride with other guests, including a young couple who got off on Tessa's floor. He knocked on Tessa's door, but no one answered. He knocked harder.

Tessa looked through the peephole and then opened the door. She was in a white bathrobe and slippers, and her hair was wrapped in a towel. "Hi," was all she could utter.

"Hi? Hi? That's all you have to say? Why weren't you answering your phone?" He reprimanded her. His eyes shot daggers at her.

"I must have been in the shower when you called. I'm sorry. I feel like such a shit, but there was nothing I could do," she answered, unwrapping the towel from her head and drying off her hair.

"Your friend called me. She said that you had an emergency. What was it?" he asked, playing dumb. Even with her hair wet and looking so ordinary, he was still attracted to her. What was it about her that drew him to her? Her big eyes? Her shapely body? Her personality and confidence? Her kindness toward animals? Or the whole package? He had no idea, but somehow, he always seemed to forgive her no matter how much she hurt him.

Great. So, he doesn't know, thought Tessa. Maybe the Japanese media hadn't covered what happened. "It was. ..." She frowned, trying to come up with an excuse, "It was personal."

"Personal?" he shouted, "I waited more than an hour for you."

"Look, I'm exhausted. Can we talk about this later, after I get some sleep?"

"We talk now," he said, forcefully. "You owe me an explanation."

She turned her back to him, thinking about how to explain herself out of this one.

He took his phone out of his pocket, clicked on the link, went around to face her, and showed her the video of her arrest.

She winced, guilt written all over her face.

"You spent the night in jail and didn't even bother to ask for my help!"

"Well, you see, um, Yoko forgot to get a permit for the protest. We both got arrested. They let her go, and I thought that they would let me go too, but they kept me overnight."

"That doesn't make sense. Why would they keep you overnight for such a small infraction?"

"I don't know. To scare me off, maybe? I am an American meddling in your country's affairs. I'm sure your government is not too thrilled about it." She didn't want to tell him about filming the dolphin drive.

He stared at her for a long time. He considered turning around and leaving. She loved her dolphins. She loved her cause. He was certain that she didn't love him. Why was he trying so hard to get her to want him? "The other night when you showed up late in

Kyoto, were you arrested there as well?" He asked, his face sad and grim.

"Not exactly. The police came by our table. They briefly questioned Satomi and let her go. They grilled me longer, but didn't arrest me."

"What kinds of questions did they ask?"

"What was the purpose of my visit to Japan? Was I in contact with other American activists in Japan? Was this my first trip here? What did I do for a living and so on."

He let out a loud sigh. "Why? Why do you do this?"

"If you have to ask, then you don't understand me at all."

"I'm trying to understand you. Do you actually think what you're doing makes a difference?"

"Maybe not today, maybe not tomorrow, but if we continue, things will change. We have already made a big difference. In California, Sea World stopped buying dolphins from sources that abuse them. Some aquariums have been pushed out of business. We're starting to make a dent."

"Do you love me?" he asked bluntly. He was tired of tiptoeing around the question.

"I, I, care about you," she said in surprise. It was an unexpected question to which she didn't have an answer.

"Do you think that someday your feelings could turn into love?" he asked, hoping that she would say yes.

She shrugged. "I don't know. I have to leave your country by tomorrow night. So, there is no point in us talking about this." Karianne had been able to negotiate an extra day so that Tessa could get her belongings from Akira's place and say goodbye.

A heavy grief filled his heart when he said, "Stay."

She closed the distance between them. She hadn't felt anything toward anyone in a long time, and she was fine with that. But why was she falling for this stranger? She put her arms around him and said, "I can't stay even if I wanted to. Your government has asked me to leave Japan."

He put his lips against hers and parted them to taste her, to show her how much he loved her. She responded willingly as she wrapped her arms around his neck. And after a long moment, he untied her robe; she took off his jacket and loosened his tie. He finished undressing as she lay on the bed, waiting for him. And in an instant, he was on top of her, inserting his fingers inside her to see if she was ready. He kissed her neck and worked himself down. "Now," she said. He did as she requested and entered her. All his dreams from the moment he met her were fulfilled. He had wished for this day for so long, he thought as he moved inside her, working to bring them both to a climax. "I love you," he told her.

She didn't know what to say.

When he noticed the sorrow on her face, he added, "It's okay if you don't love me. Just promise to stay with me forever."

They made love several times, never leaving the bed until they both fell asleep. When he opened his eyes, it was the next morning. Tessa had already packed her things. She was seated on a chair staring outside at the high-rise buildings towering the shorter ones as though they were trying to reach the blue skies. The sun was beaming its rays, and Tessa was thinking about Toshiro and how close the two had become in such a short time. She felt deep regret about having to leave. Tessa was mad at herself for wasting so much time and pushing him away each time he had tried to love her, but maybe it was better this way. Their differences in culture, language, and background were too overwhelming to overcome. If she had so many problems getting along with American men, her relationship with Toshiro would be even worse. They had nothing in common, yet she felt a deep connection to him—the way he cared for her, the way he loved her unconditionally. No, she couldn't. She had a well-established career and family and friends in Los Angeles, and he had his parents, career, and friends in Tokyo. Long-distance relationships never worked, and she couldn't ask him to leave Tokyo. It wouldn't be fair.

"Hey," he said, looking at her lovingly. He heard a knock on the door.

"Hey," she said. "I ordered breakfast."

A short, black-haired server with a white uniform pushed in a trolley with their food. He set the table with white linen and silverware. Tessa signed the bill and he left.

"How did you sleep?" Toshiro asked.

"Okay, I guess. You?" she answered, removing the covers on their food. She had ordered *udon* noodles, which came with side dishes to mix in. Not exactly breakfast food, but this would be her last day in Japan, and Osaka was known for *udon* noodles.

He got off the bed and went to her, holding her from the back, his heart beating hard against his chest, his chin resting on her shoulder. Would he always be this nervous around her? He couldn't let her walk away. He had planned for the two of them to spend time at the Umeda Sky Building at night, holding hands, looking at the city lights, taking pictures together, being romantic, and reveling in a date night. He wished he had more time with her.

She leaned back against his chest, not wanting to part. She was running out of time. After the massacre of the dolphins—parents and pups—and seeing so much blood, she looked forward to a break. A break from the killings. A break from so much cruelty. Toshiro was her light in the darkness. Tessa had planned on swimming at the hotel pool, getting a massage and facial, and having a quiet dinner with Toshiro. But now, none of that would ever pan out. Osaka was the city she would never get a chance to see as an adult. Tessa was glad that she had accomplished her goal of bringing attention to these intelligent mammals. Although Toshiro had started as a distraction she had tried hard to avoid, she was now finding herself torn between her cause and the man she was starting to love.

They ate a little, but neither had much of an appetite.

"Why don't I come with you on the Shinkansen?" Toshiro asked.

"That's not a good idea. I have a feeling they are watching me and the last thing you need is another photo of the two of us. I don't want to give your parents another excuse to hate me. Get on your flight and go home." She paused and wiped a tear from her eye. "And I will get on the train before my flight leaves for home."

"I'm going to come to the U.S. and be with you. Our company is opening a new office in Los Angeles and. ..."

She shook her head no. "We need to say goodbye."

"But I'm in love with you."

"And I have never felt for anyone the way I feel about you, but there is just too much working against us."

"Like what? I don't understand. Please?" He pleaded with her.

She looked at the clock on the table and grabbed her luggage. She was an activist and always would be. He was like the rest of the population, going about his day, wanting to meet the love of his life, get married, and start a family. She didn't want him to be dragged into her endeavors and estrange him from his parents. "I have to go. Wait for me to leave before you come out." She kissed him one last time. *I love you*, she thought, but couldn't bring herself to say it.

"We can't end like this."

"You must forget about me and move on." She opened the door and rolled her luggage out.

He had a feeling it would come to this, so while she was sleeping, he got up and took a look into her purse, where he found her business card and her flight information.

After leaving the hotel, he took the subway to Hansuke's place. He wrote his cousin a thank-you note for taking care of him, packed his things, and headed to the airport to catch a flight to Tokyo, hoping to talk to Tessa before she left.

Tessa took the Midosuji subway line to Shin-Osaka Station and headed toward a shop, where she bought a few magazines and a Melon Creamy Soda—a Japanese drink that tasted like honeydew melon and bubble gum. The journals were to keep her mind busy during the two-and-a-half-hour ride on the Nozomi line. The drink, though too sweet and unusual for her taste buds, was a reminder that she was still in Japan, that she had the time of her life even if she did get arrested, that she had made a dent in preventing the slaughter of the dolphins, and that she had found love in the least likely place.

What a mess, she thought as she headed to Tokyo. Who had been following her, causing her problems, and pushing to get her arrested? Now with time to think about what had happened, she was glad that she continued to gain followers on social media. It meant that she could reach a wider audience for her cause. She checked her social media accounts and email and responded to several journalists who were interested in interviewing her. She looked at her activist friends' Twitter accounts and noticed that the video taken of her arrest had been retweeted three hundred thousand times and was still being shared.

Unfortunately for Junichiro Fujimoto, all his efforts to stop Tessa backfired. She had never been a real threat to him. She was small—minuscule. But he made her a hero by getting her arrested. Junichiro's losses, however, had begun way before Tessa came into the picture. In 2015, the publicly funded World Association of Zoos and Aquariums, or WAZA, suspended the Japanese Association of Zoos and Aquariums, which consisted of eighty-nine zoos and sixty-three aquariums, and threatened to expel them unless they stopped buying Taiji dolphins. JAZA reluctantly agreed to WAZA's terms, and as a result, many Japanese sea-themed venues, including those that belonged to Junichiro, pulled out of JAZA and continued to use Taiji dolphins. However, pulling out of JAZA hurt his businesses because his aquariums were no longer able to cooperate with other international member organizations for breeding and trading programs. Also, aquariums, water parks, and zoos that were WAZA members stopped buying Junichiro's dolphins. Now with Tessa's video going viral, he was going to hurt even more.

CHAPTER 14

Back at Akira's apartment, Tessa told her about all that had happened as she packed. Akira was somber; she wanted to spend more time with her friend. They had little time left and had to make every minute count. They headed for the Tokyo district of Yanaka for a late lunch. It would be Tessa's last excursion in Japan. She wondered if she would ever be welcomed back. She loved the culture, the people, and the hustle and bustle of Tokyo. She also loved Osaka for its casual atmosphere and Kyoto for its rich history, temples, and scenic parks. Maybe someday, Taiji would join the age of enlightenment, the fishermen would end their cruelty, and tourists would visit this historic town. Even if it seemed that the world was picking on Taiji when other towns also inflicted pain on helpless creatures, Tessa hoped that Taiji would set an example for other towns to follow.

In Yanaka, the girls strolled down narrow, winding cobblestone streets past intimate cafés and restaurants, artsy shops, mom and pop stores, a small cemetery, an outdoor market, and temples.

Uniformed schoolchildren sported sturdy, fashionable backpacks. Locals were always surprised to see American tourists in their neighborhood.

"Those backpacks are called Randoseru and are quite expensive. Some cost nearly $1,000. The schools require them, and their grandparents usually buy them."

"Why are they so pricy?" Tessa asked, looking at the red-and-black leather backpacks.

"They're handmade and supposed to last the students from grade 1 to 6. There are cheaper ones made of synthetic leather, but even those are costly."

"And they only come in those colors?"

"No. you can find them in different colors, but some schools require their students to wear a particular color."

Tessa felt as if she had stepped back in time—children roaming without supervision, traditional one-or-two-story buildings, quiet streets with lots of trees, and a slow pace of life. Stopping at a family cemetery, Akira explained that people were no longer opting for family plots due to the high cost. Some cemeteries were even closing because caretakers were laid off.

"What happens to the remains, then?" Tessa asked.

"For a fee and according to the family's wishes, the remains may be relocated or cremated."

Tessa noticed wooden slabs sticking out of many of the gravesites. "What are those?"

"They are grave markers. A sponsor, usually a family member, pays for the wood to be blessed by the priest. See the writing on them?"

"Yes, what do they say?"

"It is the name of the deceased and the person or company sponsoring it."

"There are so many of them."

"Yes, it is believed that the more wooden slabs a dead person has, the faster he gets to heaven," Akira responded.

"What happens if someone doesn't have a family or anyone to pay for it?"

"The government cremates them and either does a mass burial or recycles them as building materials."

"I thought the Japanese were big on ancestor worship and visiting graves."

"You mean the yearly celebration of the Bon Festival, where the Japanese pay their respect to their ancestors?"

"Yes. They don't do that anymore?"

"Some do. Like I said, the cost is a big factor and sometimes children of the deceased who have moved away don't want to bother going back to their hometown for this."

They reached their destination, Ueno Sakuragi Atari, a historic spot in which tourists could view the original architecture of homes built in the 1930s, now housed shops and eateries. A green water pump remained as a reminder of the period.

"The Yanaka Beer Hall," Tessa read the sign written in English.

The two went inside but walked through it to a courtyard in the back, where Tessa noticed a kiosk named OshiOlive with tables and chairs near it. An elderly couple sitting near a Japanese maple tree were enjoying their tea and rolls stuffed with fruit and sweet cheese.

"Do you want a balsamic vinegar drink?" Akira asked when they approached the vendor.

"Balsamic vinegar drink?" Tessa asked with wide eyes, wondering how that would taste.

"I'll order one for me and a rice vinegar one for you so that you can try both."

"Okay," Tessa said hesitantly, wondering how acidic it might be.

When their drinks, served in schooners, arrived, Akira suggested that they take them back to the Yanaka Beer Hall so they could get lunch.

The two returned to the hall and grabbed seats at a wood table. They ordered various vegetarian dishes and shrimp. Tessa tried the balsamic drink, which tasted much better than kombucha.

"You like?" Akira asked.

"Strangely, yes. I didn't think I would, but I could get addicted." She smiled for the first time since she had been back in Tokyo. "I'm going to miss it here."

"And I will miss you. A friend of mine told me that she knows who took that video of you that went viral."

"Erica?"

"Yes! How did you know?"

"I didn't. I guessed that it might be her. She has a lot more connections than any of us. And when I first met her in Kyoto, I noticed that she had an expensive camera; you know, the kind reporters use."

"My friend also knows who has been getting you into so much trouble."

"Who?"

"Mr. Fujimoto."

"Mr. Fuji-who?"

"Fujimoto. He sells dolphins to aquatic venues all over the world at $300,000 a pop. He also owns aquatic venues and research laboratories that conduct experiments on marine creatures. You have become a big problem for him."

"Why me? You guys were there, too."

"You are an American and stick out. You were attracting too much attention to yourself."

"Ugh," Tessa uttered in frustration and then paused.

When Akira noticed Tessa's narrowed eyes and the puzzled look on her face, she asked, "What is it?"

"I think I met him. In fact, I'm sure of it now."

"How?"

"I was introduced to him at Toshiro's birthday party. He is a good friend of Toshiro's parents. That's why his parents dislike me so much."

"He must have been keeping an eye on you ever since."

A young server wearing a fashionable yet traditional *hachimaki*—or bandana—wrapped around his head delivered their food. Tessa didn't recognize some of the vegetables, but every single dish, though small, was delicious. She was so glad that Akira ordered for her. The tourists around her had simpler dishes because that's all they knew how to order. But it wasn't just the unusual food choices that made the meal so special. Akira shared her customs, traditions, and small but significant details that many tourists would miss during a visit. Akira made her feel at home. Tessa was going to miss not just the country, but also all the goodhearted people she had met along the way.

"I was wondering, whatever happened to Toshiro?" Akira asked, picking up a still-sizzling shrimp with its head attached.

"We saw each other in Kyoto and Osaka, and as much as I loved being with him, a part of me wishes that we never met," Tessa admitted, serving herself from a vegetable plate. She didn't eat anything with a head or eyes.

"But why?"

"Because now there is this gap in my heart. A gap that didn't exist when I first came here, and I was fine with that. And now, even though I have many friends and family, I feel empty and alone."

"Then why not try to make it work?"

"My work, volunteer job, and activism leave little time for anything else," Tessa said shaking her head. "I need to get back to my life, and he needs to get back to his."

"And just when I was starting to like him, too." Akira did think that Toshiro was overly impulsive, grabbing Tessa in public for a kiss, showing up at her apartment uninvited, and trying to steer her away from her work as an activist. But on the other hand, she felt that Tessa lacked balance. Toshiro might be good for her. Tessa needed to shake things up, and he might be the one to help her do it.

"Sometimes we connect with the most unlikely people in our paths, but we never get to see them again," commented Tessa. "Life is strange in that way."

"It sure is."

"We should go. I promised Karianne I'd be on the 7:30 evening flight."

"*Gochisousama deshita*," said Tessa to the servers, thanking them for the feast and their hospitality. With tears in her eyes and a heavy heart, she hugged Akira, thanking her for all her kindness and support, and headed for the airport.

At the Japan Airlines desk, Tessa traded in her ticket and took her place at the security screening line, when a familiar voice greeted her from behind. She turned in surprise and said, "What are you doing here? I thought we agreed..."

"I couldn't let you leave without seeing you," Toshiro said, studying her face, trying to memorize every detail about her.

"How did you ... ."

"Know which flight and time? I looked into your handbag last night." He had been waiting for a long time to catch a glimpse of Tessa. And after an hour's wait, he had spotted her by her usual garb: black moto jacket, trendy tattered jeans, and the same canvas shoes he had purchased for her from Don Quijote the night she had fallen asleep at his house.

"You went through my things? Didn't anyone teach you not to look inside a lady's handbag?" Still, as she studied his boyishly handsome face, she was glad to see him one last time.

"All is fair in love and war," he blurted.

"Your English is improving. But seriously, you have to go. What if someone sees us together?" She didn't want anyone to connect him to her. The Japanese government ordered her to leave. The last thing she wanted to do was to drag him down with her.

"I don't care," he said, grabbing her hand and pulling her out of the line.

"Stop. What are you doing?"

He found two empty chairs. "Sit."

"I have to go," she said, staring at him as if he had lost his mind.

"Marry me," he uttered.

She collapsed into a chair, startled.

He sat down next to her, grabbed her hands in his, and asked impatiently, "Tell me, what is your answer?"

She waited for a few minutes to gather her thoughts, before she said, "Marriage is just a piece of paper."

"I don't understand."

"An earnest commitment doesn't require a piece of paper. Besides, I've already been married once. I don't want to do it again." If she were to get involved with someone, she wanted someone closer to her age, who had already been married once, and hopefully had learned a thing or two.

"I'm sorry," he said, gaping at her. "Did you say you were married? You never. …"

"I didn't think it was important," she said, knowing full well that she didn't tell him on purpose. Her divorce had been so bitter that she didn't want to relive it by talking about it.

"Well, it is. How long ago was this?" he asked. His smile was replaced by tense, narrowed lips.

"More than ten years ago," she responded, refusing to give the exact time because it dated her, making her feel old. It was eighteen years ago when she first married. She would have been twenty-two and Toshiro twelve.

Toshiro gazed at her inquisitively, waiting for more details.

"I was married. We had too many problems, and I was willing to work them out, but he wasn't. He left me for someone much younger," she said, reflecting on the last conversation she had had with her ex: *Please stay with me, I cannot live without you.* But he told her that he was in love with someone else.

Toshiro noticed the look of pain on Tessa's face and said, "In all the time we were together, you never said anything. You never talked about him."

"You and I met twelve days ago and didn't even know anything about each other until ten days ago when we went to the karaoke place. And anyway, it's too painful to talk about him." She had felt betrayed and unworthy when he dumped her for someone else and she promised herself never to allow anyone to touch her heart in that way again. For three years, she had kept her promise until she met Toshiro. He was a pleasant surprise. Falling for him was unintentional, but it happened, and she had no idea how to deal with it.

"You still love him?" he asked, noticing that she was deep in thought.

"No, I have no feelings for the guy," she said. "He's just someone who caused me a lot of grief and I want to forget about it and move on."

He placed his hand on his heart. "I love you."

"You're infatuated with me. There's a big difference." Tessa thought that if she could just convince him to get on with his life, she too would get over him once she was back in Los Angeles.

"Infatuated, what is that?"

"It means that you think you're in love with me, but you are not thinking clearly. In a few weeks, you'll forget all about me and you'll go back to your old life." Tessa was afraid to take a chance on him. Everything was new between them, but once the newness wore off, would he come to his senses and discard her for someone younger?

"I don't want my old life." Toshiro thought his life before Tessa was boring. She made him realize how important it was to have a purpose and passion in life. True, he hadn't yet found his purpose, but he sure as hell found his passion in Tessa. She had aroused feelings inside him that he hadn't experienced before. He had pretty much lived his life without risks, but now he was ready for something new.

"Then make some changes in your life," Tessa responded. She didn't want to be the center of his universe. Toshiro needed to ask himself some hard questions. What was it that made him want to get out of bed in the morning? What fired him up should not just be another person. But then again, love was the root of everything—love for self, for a child, parent, sibling, spouse, friend, career. It was love and passion that made people want to get up in the morning. If no one cared strongly about anything, then what was the point of living?

"I'm trying to do that, and I have decided I want to be with you," he explained.

An announcement came over the speakers that her flight would be boarding soon. She got up and started walking back toward the line, moving her carry-on alongside her. He held her wrist.

"I have to go or I'm going to miss my flight," she said, knowing that if she spent any more time with him, she would lose her resolve. Her heart was beating fast and she felt nervous. No, she told herself. Her friend Karianne would lose face if she wasn't on that flight.

Glancing at his watch, he said, "You have time. Wait!" He then grabbed her and hugged her for a long time, not wanting to let go.

When he finally released her, she said, "We had fun, you and I, but I need to go home and you need to get back to your life." As she walked away, she thought, *Don't look back. Don't look back or you'll change your mind.* She didn't think it possible, but she had fallen in love with him, though she wasn't certain of his feelings. He said that he loved her, but someday, their age difference might get in the way and he would leave. But no matter how hard she tried to convince herself not to look back, her heart betrayed her as she turned around and saw him standing there, watching her. Against her better judgment, she turned around, walked back up to him, and said, "Okay, here's the deal."

"The deal?"

"Yes, the deal. The promise. We'll spend six months apart. We can't contact each other. You will go on dating and spend time with your friends and family, and I will do the same. If at the end of six months, we still feel the same about each other, then we'll figure out a way to be together."

"You feel the same about me?" He asked, his face beaming again. *She loved him!*

"Seriously?" she asked, with her hands on her waist. "Out of everything I just said, that's all you heard?"

"You love me?" he asked, shaking, nervous.

"Yes, but. ..."

"No, buts."

"But you need to keep your promise to stay away and go out with friends, party, meet girls."

"Why? You're the only woman I want."

"Because we both need to take a step back to be sure." Tessa was looking for the kind of love that, no matter how bad things got, they could work it out together.

He stood there, looking at her, thinking. Maybe they both needed space to see if this was going to work. Maybe if she wasn't leaving, he would not have proposed to her. He had walked into that airport ready to give up everything for her, and she had filled his mind with doubts. No. There was no doubt. He was certain that he loved her.

When he didn't respond, she said, "How about it?"

He scratched between his brows and replied reluctantly, "Okay, but you're wrong about us. This is true love."

"We'll see." She smiled and gave him a peck on the lips. She glanced at her phone's calendar and looked up six months from that day. "Okay on March 20 of next year. Are you going to mark your calendar?"

He shook his head. "Not necessary. I will remember it. How do we do this? Do I call you?"

Tessa paused for a moment to collect her thoughts before she said, "No. No phone calls. In downtown L.A., there is a wishing tree in the Japanese Village Plaza in Little Tokyo. People write their wishes on pieces of paper and tie them to the tree. Meet me by the wishing tree if you still love me."

"Downtown L.A. Wishing tree. Japanese Village Plaza. Little Tokyo. Got it."

Then he had a realization. "You mean like the Tanabata festival, celebrated on the day when the lovers Orihime and Hikoboshi meet?"

"Yes. Except that we'll be meeting on the first day of spring." Tessa attended the Tantaba festival in Los Angeles two years ago with several of her friends and learned about the history behind it. The legend of Tanabata is a story about a weaver princess and a cow herder who fall in love. Once married, they neglect their duties, so the princess's angry father splits up the couple, allowing them to meet only if his daughter continues her weaving, and then only once a year on the seventh day of the seventh month. Each year, on that day, when the couple gets together, anyone who writes their wishes on *tanzaku*—red, blue, white, black, or yellow strips of paper—and hangs them on the branches of a bamboo tree at a Tanabata Festival, gets their wishes granted.

"At what time will we meet?"

"How about 4 p.m?"

"On March 20, the first day of spring at 4 p.m," he repeated. "But…"

"Why is there always a but with you?" he complained.

"But," she emphasized, pointing her finger at him, "if one of us doesn't show, there is no need to call the other and explain. We will just part ways."

He tried to visualize the tree. He told himself that he would look it up when he got home. "I will be there by the wishing tree, waiting for you."

He looked at her with such deep affection that it tore her apart when she took hold of her luggage. "Go home," she said, walking away. Several minutes later, she looked back and he was gone. She wondered if she would ever see him again.

CHAPTER 15

The nightmares ended. Tessa returned to her mundane routine. She visited her parents once a month and spent time with her friends on Saturday nights. During her sixty-hour workweek, she cared for animals at the veterinary hospital—diagnosing illnesses and determining the best treatments. Any free time she had was divided between her volunteer work, exercising, hanging out with family and friends, errands, and her activism. She continued joining other activists on Facebook to protest the capture of whales and dolphins. They initiated an online petition that had been signed by hundreds of thousands of people. The petition was addressed to The World Association of Zoos and Aquariums' council and requested that their members cease keeping dolphins and whales in captivity. It read:

Please sign this petition to help put a stop to the capture of whales and dolphins. They do not belong in small concrete tanks in which they can only swim around in circles. They belong to the oceans—not chlorinated pools. They are starved until they perform tricks. Many die in captivity. Although some places have agreed to stop breeding dolphins, they still keep many aquatic mammals in tanks. More needs to be done. They are social creatures with families and deserve to be free.

Over the years, after much effort by activists everywhere, Mexico City banned dolphinariums. Vancouver Aquarium also announced that it would no longer keep dolphins and whales in captivity. Tessa hoped that someday all aquariums would follow suit.

One day, she took a few hours off from work to give a talk at a private middle school in West Los Angeles about why marine mammals didn't belong in tanks. She had videos, charts, and photographs to get her point across. She hoped that by the time the talk was over, the students would have questions and concerns that they would share with their families and friends. She believed that the best way to influence a new generation about the cause was to educate them.

At first, the class of thirty seemed restless in their seats. But once Tessa began the presentation, she captured their attention.

"Are dolphins as smart as dogs?" one boy asked.

"Yes. Dolphins are considered the second most intelligent nonhuman species on earth; orangutans are first. Some researchers refer to dolphins as cousins of apes."

"Are dolphins like humans?"

"According to Dr. Shimi Kang, a Harvard-trained doctor and researcher, there are many similarities between humans and dolphins. They have a high IQ, are quite social, show compassion, and are connected to their families and dolphin communities. They even respond to names."

"What kind of names? Like Letitia or Michael?" another boy—obviously the joker of the bunch—asked. Everyone laughed.

"Something like that, except that since they can't talk, they whistle." Tessa's frank and simple approach appealed to the young students.

"So, each whistle signifies a different name?" asked a girl in the back of the room.

"That's right. They're called signature whistles, meaning each dolphin has a distinct whistle to identify itself. That's how they greet each other. Dolphins remember each other's distinct whistle for decades even if they don't get to see their family or friends for a long time."

"That's so cool," she responded.

"It is. In fact, dolphins are the only nonhuman species discovered to date that call one another by name."

"How do they talk to each other?" asked a round-faced boy.

"They may use their body language by flapping their tails to let others know that there is danger or they jump up and out of the water to let their friends know that there is food. They whistle to communicate distress or socialize. They also have many other whistles that scientists and researchers are still studying."

When she concluded her lecture, the class cheered. Judging from the students' reactions, it seemed that Tessa's lecture had a positive influence on them. She passed out materials for the students to take home. They each received white poster boards, colored markers, glue, and glitter. She told them that they could use the materials to make a fun art project. She also handed out picture books about dolphins and whales.

Tessa had obtained the money to purchase those materials in an unusual way. Weeks before her presentation, a man visited her at work and handed her an envelope with $25,000 inside, claiming that he was representing a philanthropist who wanted to support her activism efforts.

"Who is this philanthropist?"

"I'm sorry, but the person prefers to remain anonymous."

"Why me? There are many organizations out there that could use this money."

"I don't know. I was told to give you this money. Your friend Akira received the exact sum."

"She did?"

"Yes, and she accepted it. You can call her to confirm."

Tessa called Akira, but it went to voicemail.

"May I get back to you after I have spoken to my friend?"

"I'm sorry, but I need you to accept this or the offer will go away."

Concerned and worried about where the money came from, Tessa was hesitant to take it, but he insisted that the money was legal.

The whole situation had been bizarre. But as much as she wished that she hadn't accepted the money, she also was glad to be able to use it to purchase materials for the class. It even enabled her to hire a public relations assistant who had experience promoting animal-rights activism. Although things were going well with her activism, work, friends, and family, Tessa still felt lonely.

She missed Toshiro, wishing he were there beside her, as she listened to her car radio playing "I Drive Myself Crazy," by N'Sync. Tessa kept wondering if she would ever see him again. Regretting that she had pushed him away, she wished that she could call him. But a promise was a promise. One month had already gone by; what was another five? The time would pass by quickly if she kept busy. The first week was the hardest, not just because she missed Toshiro and her friends in Japan, but also because she made the mistake of sharing her experiences with her father.

It all went down shortly after her return from Japan when her parents invited her to dinner. With a bag of souvenirs in one hand, Tessa opened the front door with her spare key and went in.

"Hello?" she yelled so that she wouldn't startle her parents.

"In the kitchen," Carol yelled out.

Tessa set down a bag on the kitchen counter and said, "Presents for you and Dad." Inside were two *yukata*, or unlined summer kimonos, that she had purchased at one of the shops near Tokyo's Sensoji Temple.

Carol's wavy dark-blonde hair was held up with a turquoise hair clip. She was attractive and quite fit for her age. Tessa hoped that she would look just like her mother when she got older.

"Thanks, darling. You have perfect timing. Dinner's ready. Tell your father to come and eat. He's in the back, building a brick pizza oven."

Tessa laughed. "He can't sit still, can he?"

"Well, you know your father. I've given up on encouraging him to relax," she smiled, showing off the wrinkles around the corners of her eyes. Carol was not one for surgery. She believed that her wrinkles represented the wisdom she had acquired throughout the years.

"It keeps him young, you know." Tessa walked toward the back of the house, pushed open the French doors, and yelled, "Dad? Dinner's ready."

"Tessa! How was your trip?" he said, brushing the dirt off of his clothes and hands. He had been worried sick when he had heard about her arrest on the news. But then Tessa had called to let him know that all was well. He was going to yell at her, but Carol had calmed him down.

"You will lose her if you continuously pound on her. She's not a child you know," Carol had said.

"Come inside and I'll tell you all about it."

He adjusted his floppy khaki sun hat and went to clean up before going into the dining room where his wife had set the round walnut table with floral-patterned china, crystal water goblets, and silver utensils. "There is no better time to use the good stuff than the present," Carol had often repeated. She placed her homemade vegetarian lasagna and garlic bread on the table next to a Caesar salad.

"Mom, you made my favorite dish!" Tessa said, kissing her on the cheek.

"And we have tiramisu," her mother added, knowing that it was Tessa's favorite dessert.

"She went all out for you," Jeff said, happy to see Tessa and still grateful that the authorities had released her.

"Awe, thanks, Mom. You spoil me."

"I missed you while you were in Japan," Carol said, cutting the lasagna.

"You mean, you were worried about me when I was there," Tessa replied, serving the salad and passing around the garlic bread.

"So, what happened?"

"Well, I got detained in Kyoto, but the police let me go. But later I got arrested in Osaka and had to spend one night in detention."

"You got into trouble in two cities?" her father interjected with a raised voice and his jaw dropping. He had only been aware of her arrest in Osaka.

"Close your mouth, Jeff, and stop giving her a cross look." Many years ago, Carol, who had been to jail once or twice herself back in the day, had participated in a protest when a big oil company was planning to put up a pipeline under a large parcel of land that belonged to a group of homeowners.

"Don't tell me what to do," Jeff insisted. "You would think that after her first run-in with the law, she would stop interfering."

"Let her finish her story," Carol said, obviously impatient. She looked over to Tessa. "Go on."

"In Kyoto, the police took my passport to check if it was legit, harshly questioned me, and then let me go," she said, intentionally failing to mention how scared she had been.

"Well, that's not so bad."

"Yes, it is," Jeff blurted, "She's lucky that they were nice enough to let her go."

"Let her finish her story."

Tessa continued. "The second time, I was in Osaka. My friend Karianne at the U.S. Embassy helped get me out. I had to cut my trip short because I was asked to leave the country the next day." She then explained what she had gone through. She even told them about scuba diving in Taiji.

"Foolish girl. If you hadn't received help, you would be rotting in prison right now," her father said.

Carol's face turned chalky white. She swallowed and tried hard to suppress her emotions. It was over, and she wasn't about to yell at her daughter for endangering her life. "Well, the most important thing is that you're home and safe."

Jeff got up and poured himself a glass of bourbon. What was Tessa thinking filming the underwater slaughter? And cutting the nets to help free four dolphins? If she had been caught, no one would have been able to help her, with or without connections. Tessa was difficult to reason with. Even when she was a child, she rarely listened to her parents. "I hope that you learned your lesson and will end this."

"End it? After all the work I've put in? Why not join me next time?"

"You're going back to Japan?" Jeff gripped his glass so tight it nearly shattered all over the dining room's hardwood floors.

"Not anytime soon, but I am a member of The Dolphin and Whale Guardians, which supports activists in Japan."

Jeff sighed. He always thought that Carol was too soft on Tessa when she was growing up. And now Tessa was too old to be told what to do. He always wanted a quiet life for her—a good husband and children. Instead, his daughter was divorced, lived alone in a one-bedroom apartment, and had a passion to save dolphins. He just didn't get it. He liked hunting and didn't see anything wrong with killing animals—land or marine.

Tessa was glad that she had gone to Japan. Had she not accomplished her goals, the nightmares wouldn't have ended, she wouldn't have been able to bring so much attention to her cause, wouldn't have met Toshiro, and wouldn't have learned so much about Japanese culture and people. Yet, as she explained away to her parents all that had happened to her, the reality of it slowly sunk in. Her father wasn't completely wrong, but she wasn't going to admit it. Tessa had no right to protest in another country when there was so much wrong in her own country. People still hunted for the fun of it, animal testing continued, and many animals were killed or tortured in the name of science. Yet she still believed it was her duty to protect the voiceless dolphins. Yes, she was a *gaijin* meddling in Japanese affairs, except that the dolphins belonged to the ocean. They had no nationality. They didn't deserve to be tortured or killed.

In November, two months after returning from Japan, Tessa started to feel antsy. She wished for the separation to be over soon. She was walking with her Brazilian friend, Bruna, at the Third Street Promenade outdoor shopping mall in Santa Monica when she blurted, "I miss him." Tessa tried hard to keep busy and not think about him, but somehow, he crept back into her thoughts.

"Then call him," Bruna said, pulling back her dark hair into a bun to stop the sweat from forming on the back of her neck. She was wearing a loose-fitting sundress and the Japanese wooden slippers Tessa had brought her from Tokyo. The relentless sun beat down on their heads; the air was thick without a hint of a breeze; an unshaven young street musician played his guitar.

"No," Tessa said and walked into Anthropologie—a fashionable women's clothing and décor shop—to escape the outside heat. She removed her dark sunglasses and pushed back her hair from her face. It was frustrating to experience such hot weather when it was almost December. Not even her white linen dress kept her cool. That was the thing about Los Angeles, 75 percent of the time it had one season—summer.

"Why not?" Bruna asked, enjoying temporary relief in the air-conditioned store.

"I want to make sure that I am the one he wants," she answered, picking up a straw hat, trying it on, putting it back, and picking up another one.

"He told you how he felt when you were in Tokyo. You know, that hat doesn't look good on you, try on this cowboy hat."

"That was then and this is now. He may be with some pretty young thing and if that's the case, good for him." Tessa tried on the hat but didn't like that one either.

"You're really that insecure?" Bruna replied as she shuffled through an overfilled rack of clearance items.

"No, but. ..."

"But what?" she stopped and looked her friend in the eyes, waiting for an answer.

"He could do better," Tessa said, trying on several more hats and not caring for any of them. Things just didn't look as good on her now compared to when she was in her 20s. Why would thirty-year-old Toshiro want her when he had so many choices?

"So can you. Except that he wants to be with you and you want to be with him," Bruna remarked, noticing that Tessa had just as much trouble in choosing a hat as she did in choosing a man. "Indecisive is what you are. Never sure of anything. Make a decision and just go with it."

"I don't need to. Time will tell. We are talking about Toshiro? No?"

"Hats, Toshiro, everything. If you ask me, he is the adult and you're the adolescent," she said, as they exited the store. Bruna wished that she had someone like Toshiro in her life, who would love her unconditionally.

"What do you mean?"

"At least he knows exactly what he wants. You're the one who can't even realize a good thing when it hits you on the head," Bruna blurted.

"You're wrong. I love him as much as he loves me. I'm just struggling with our age difference. I wish I were younger than him or at least that I was his age," she admitted, reaching in her purse and taking out a few dollars to give to the musician playing his guitar.

"You know, no relationship is perfect even when there isn't much of an age difference. There are hurdles and obstacles, and it's best not to focus on them. But be that as it may, I shouldn't be passing judgment on you. You have to do what feels right for you."

"Thank you for understanding," Tessa said, looking appreciative.

"Of course. You two clearly love each other. What're another four months? It's not going to change your feelings for each other."

"True. I just need to be patient." Tessa agreed. Like Bruna, she too spotted Sloan's when she said, "But for now, I need instant gratification, and a hot fudge sundae will do me good."

"I'm not going in there. I'm trying to lose 3 pounds, and if you drag me in there, I'll lose my resolve, and it'll be all your fault."

"Three pounds? That's nothing. Stick with me, and a week of daily eight-mile runs will get rid of them," Tessa said, grabbing Bruna's wrist, and heading toward the confectionary store.

CHAPTER 16

Shortly after Tessa's departure, Toshiro received mail from an organization called Students in Support of Dolphins, or SSD. He must have gotten on their list when he had participated in the Tokyo protest with Tessa, he reasoned as he removed the contents of a large white envelope. There were photos of bloodied dolphins along with a letter asking for a donation. The letter addressed a TV interview with Diana Reiss, a professor of psychology and dolphin expert, whose work focused on the cognition and communication of dolphins and other cetaceans, and included a quote from Dr. Reiss's interview: "Although people eat animals for food, there is a real change in their approach to try to do it humanely. In the case of Taiji, Japan, we're talking about highly evolved mammals, which are considered to be the cognitive cousins of apes, being killed in the most horrific way imaginable, being treated worse than laboratory rats, to be honest. These are mammals like we are. They breathe air and they give birth, they have very large brains;

in fact, their brain size relative to their body size is second to ours, and they do a lot with these brains; they are very evolved."

Toshiro never thought much about dolphins before he met Tessa. And like many others, he had no idea that they were abused. He called up his lawyer and asked him to make an anonymous donation to SSD. And for the first time in his life, he felt as though he was doing something that mattered. Tessa had finally gotten through to him in terms of helping others, whether humans or animals. He imagined that once he got his career in order and freed himself of his parents' control, he could be more involved in the protection of dolphins, not just by donating money, but also by participating in demonstrations.

He thought about Tessa and how much he missed her. Toshiro followed her suggestion and tried to date other women, but it was useless. He tried to put her out of his mind when his friend Souji set him up on a date, which ended after one drink. He tried when he went to a karaoke bar with a date and friends, but he left after the first two songs. He tried when he invited a pretty girl to his place, but ended the evening early. It was hopeless. Six months, a year, ten years, or an eternity of time and space between them would not stop Toshiro's genuine love for Tessa.

The best remedy to survive this forced separation was to work—and work he did. This time, he was determined to make something of his life and take his career seriously, especially since he was planning to devote himself to Tessa and start a family with her. But what if Tessa forgot all about him? What if she fell in love with someone else? No, he wasn't going to drive himself crazy with such thoughts. He shifted his attention to the work at hand.

As a regional manager, Toshiro's job entailed supervising all the QZMZ store managers in Tokyo and reviewing their daily sales to make sure that all the locations were earning sufficient revenue. He had to visit each store once a month and talk to each manager to motivate them and make sure they had the needed tools to succeed. Toshiro would also teleconference with other regional managers and exchange ideas. He prepared profit-loss statements for all the Tokyo stores and presented them to the general manager, who answered to his father, Riku Yokoyama, a part-owner and the chief operations officer. Toshiro had the potential to be a general manager but didn't want the responsibility or the workload. In fact, he often delegated his work to entry-level managers who were more than willing to help out and get more experience. Now he was willing to push himself to move up.

Toshiro worked extra hard and only got a few hours of sleep a night. He made sure that all the stores under his supervision were exemplary. His father was worried about him. He used to complain about his son's work ethic, but now Toshiro was working around the clock, and he wished that his son had more going on in his life. Impressed by how much Toshiro had been laboring, Riku decided that it was time for Toshiro to marry the right girl and give him the grandchildren he deserved. He wanted him to have a girl who would not embarrass his family the way Tessa had done. *An activist. What a joke*, he thought. He also didn't approve of her nationality. He still remembered Americans' distrust of his family when they lived in the U.S. many years ago. There was no way that he would ever let his son marry an American. Sure, he did business with them, but that was where it ended.

Riku was ecstatic that Tessa was now out of his son's life. One day, he stopped by Toshiro's office to see him. "How are you, son?" he asked, his glasses perched on the bridge of his nose. Today, his facial muscles were more relaxed, and he did not look as harsh as he usually did.

Toshiro, looking business-like in a starched, white button-down shirt and fitted gray slacks, looked up from piles of paper stacked on his desk and said, "Doing fine. Something you wanted?"

"Your mother and I, well, we've been thinking that you work too much."

"I thought that's what you wanted. You always said that I needed to step it up and be more responsible, and now you're complaining?"

"Nooo, I'm not complaining. I appreciate your hard work, but I was thinking, perhaps you should come over for dinner tonight, say at 7?"

He gave his dad a puzzled look, "Is it a special occasion?"

"No, no special occasion. Your mother misses you and we haven't been seeing a whole lot of you lately."

"Okay. See you at 7. Anything else?" he asked when the phone rang.

"No, I guess you need to answer that. See you tonight."

After his father left, Toshiro picked up the phone. "Hello?"

"It's me. Just wanted to let you know that it's all been taken care of," the caller said.

"Any problems? Did they ask any questions?"

"The check to SSD is done. The cash donations to Akira and Tessa went fine as well. Akira wanted to know who made the donation, but I didn't tell her. Tessa, on the hand, was afraid to take the money because she didn't know where it came from. But my friend in Los Angeles convinced her that it was from a trustworthy source."

"Good. Thank you!"

Toshiro showed up at his parents' house, carrying a bottle of Johnny Walker Blue Label, one of his father's favorite brands. His mother opened the door to greet him, and when he entered, he was not happy to see his ex-girlfriend there. Her layered black hair reached her small waist and she looked smart in a black dress, a long Chanel multistrand necklace, and fitted leg warmers that came to her thighs. Toshiro hadn't talked to her since they broke up a month ago when he realized that he was in love with Tessa. Now, there she was, invited by his parents.

"Hi," he said sheepishly, feeling guilty about how things had ended.

"Hello," Kaiya answered. Her affection for him was written all over her face. She wanted to go up to him and run her hands through his soft brown hair and trace his kissable lips with her fingers the way she used to. If he hadn't met the American, they would have still been together. She wondered how he could throw away their two-year relationship for a girl that he had just met?

"Thank you for the whiskey," his father said from the bar, "Can I fix you something to drink?"

"Bourbon, please." He needed it desperately so that he could calm down. He hated his parents for trying to meddle in his affairs. Toshiro was a grown man. Why couldn't they realize that?

Dinner was cordial. Toshiro decided not to make a big deal about his parents playing matchmakers. Tessa had told him that she wanted him to go out with other people. He wanted to see if he still desired Kaiya, but he was also afraid to hurt her all over again. When they broke up, she cried hard, and he still felt terrible for causing her pain. He wanted to be honest about his feelings and tried to let her down easy. But tonight, he could see that she was still in love with him.

An assistant to the CEO of a mid-size talent management firm, Kaiya didn't have much passion about anything except getting married, starting a family, and quitting her job. She wasn't interested in politics, sports, or humanitarian work. On rare occasions, she'd read a book or pick up a newspaper, but would soon lose interest. Her time was split between work, friends, personal grooming, and shopping, and when Toshiro first met her, he was fine with that. He was traditional and wanted a housewife, and Kaiya fit that profile perfectly until he fell for Tessa.

"Before you got here, Kaiya was telling us that she is getting a promotion where she works," Riku said proudly.

"Is that so? Congratulations are in order! Does that mean that you are now the CEO?" Toshiro teased.

"No. The CEO has three assistants. I was number two and have now moved up to number one. The first assistant left her job so that she could spend more time with her family.

"Well, good for you. You should be proud of yourself."

"Thanks! Mom wants to celebrate by taking me to Australia for a week, but I'd much rather go to Rome."

"Rome is lovely this time of year," Minako added, "Just don't forget to take a jacket because it gets much cooler at night." It was mid-October, and in Rome, it was still warm and sunny during the day.

"Thank you for your advice, Yokoyama-san. I will do that."

Toshiro could tell that Kaiya was trying to get back in his life by being nice to his parents. So, he decided to play along for the night, but that's where it would end. Actually, after seeing her, he thought that he should give dating another try and see where it would take him. And as much as he hoped that it wasn't true, Tessa was probably dating too. That's the promise they had made—to see other people.

Not long after Tessa's departure, Akira arranged to meet up with four other activists at a café inside the Tokyo train station to brainstorm ideas for the next demonstration. On her way, she reflected on the generous, anonymous donation she had received weeks earlier. An impeccably dressed Japanese man had rung her doorbell and told her that he represented a philanthropist who had taken an interest in her activism and presented her with an envelope full of cash. Dumbfounded, Akira accepted the money and asked if he would divulge the name of the donor so that she could show her appreciation. The stranger had said that the person preferred to remain anonymous. Akira expressed her gratitude for the contribution before leaving for her meditation retreat to India. And when she got back from her trip and returned Tessa's call, Tessa asked, "But who would do this?"

"Don't look a gift horse in the mouth. Whoever did it, doesn't expect anything back. I'm allocating a portion of the funds to Satomi, Jack, and Yoko so they can continue to push forward in their efforts."

"Still, I should have had a good mind to refuse it. I mean, why wouldn't this person send a check to an animal rights organization? Why send it to us?"

"I wish I had an answer, but I'm using the money to help our cause. Maybe someday, we'll know who is behind it," Akira said.

"I guess so," Tessa reluctantly replied.

Tessa's connection to Toshiro and her arrest brought in a lot of good publicity for activists in support of dolphins, and though everything had looked bleak at the time, Akira was now thankful that something positive had come out of it.

Back in her office, Karianne Metzler was glad that Tessa was safely back in the U.S. The reality was that the authorities were not able to prove that Tessa had done anything wrong. They had no evidence tying her to the filming of the dolphin slaughter or the torn nets. It was Yoko who had forgotten to get the permit. Or did she? Karianne pondered this as she sipped on a strong cup of

Italian coffee, which tasted as bitter as the incident. She had a feeling that Yoko had not forgotten anything. She probably hadn't been able to get a permit to protest in front of the aquarium and decided to do it anyway. If that was the case, it was a foolish decision. It almost cost Tessa time in a Japanese jail. Karianne was upset that she didn't get to spend much time with her friend and wondered if the Japanese government would ever allow Tessa back into the country.

Tessa's quick departure had disappointed Toshiro's friend Souji as well, not because he was fond of her but because Tessa's presence meant that he may have a chance with Kaiya. He had liked Kaiya for some time, yet he never made a move. Kaiya used to be good friends with Souji until he made the mistake of introducing her to Toshiro. He never thought that the two would fall for each other. Even before Toshiro, Souji had been too afraid to ask Kaiya out; he didn't want to risk their friendship and believed that she was out of his league. Now, with Tessa out of the picture, he knew that Kaiya would try to get Toshiro back. She was in love with Toshiro, and Souji needed to move on and find another girl.

CHAPTER 17

Staring at her computer screen at work, Tessa had been avoiding a major dilemma since yesterday, but her attention was interrupted by Brian, a veterinary technician with beautiful green eyes.

"I'm going on a break," he said, "Need anything before I go?"

"No. I'm good. Thanks."

"What are you staring at?"

"I wasn't staring. Was I staring?"

"I don't know. You seemed preoccupied."

"Did you know that dolphins have a lot in common with humans?" she said, evading an answer.

"I'm sorry, what?"

"I was just updating a pamphlet I wrote about dolphins before you came in. I was reading it out loud."

"Okay," he said. He wondered if Tessa was avoiding something or if she was just in the mood to ramble. After all, it had been a slow day without much to do.

"Never mind. Go ahead and take your break." She knew that what she said must have sounded strange, but she just wanted his attention elsewhere instead of on her.

"No, I'm interested. May I see?" he asked, now more curious. He leaned over the computer to look at what she was working on.

For a minute, Tessa forgot about her problem and said, "I wrote here that the genomes of dolphins and humans are nearly the same."

Brian nodded and continued reading. He learned that like humans, dolphins like to play and form strong social bonds. "Fascinating!"

"You're making fun of me! Okay, go."

"No, I mean it. Would you give me a copy when you're finished?" he asked, as he started to walk away.

"Yeah, sure," she said, surprised that he was interested.

She continued with her updates. She wrote that unborn human and dolphin babies look similar and develop in the mother's uterus. Like humans, some dolphin mothers talk to their fetuses.

"Ugh, I can't avoid this any longer," Tessa said to herself. She got up, grabbed a bag from the pharmacy, and headed to the bathroom.

On the toilet, Tessa stared at the pregnancy test kit and pondered her future. Two months had passed since she and Toshiro had said their goodbyes, and life had moved on as usual except that she had missed her period, which was nothing out of the ordinary. She always had irregular periods, but she was never this late and, on top of that, her clothes felt snug. She wasn't overeating and made the time to run, swim, and lift weights after work. She should have had her period by now. The last one ended when she was in Tokyo. Panicking, she peed on a pregnancy stick. It was positive.

"Shit!" she said to herself. She threw the stick in a trash can and covered it with a bunch of paper towels. Still in the bathroom, she called her doctor to make an appointment and then called Bruna to tell her what happened.

"Are you sure?"

"No. Will you come with me to the doctor's office? I'm really afraid," she said, pacing back and forth in the tiny bathroom. Earlier that morning, she couldn't button her jeans, and her breasts were almost popping out of her favorite shirt. So instead, she threw on pants with an elastic waist and an oversize shirt that she normally wore around the house.

Bruna, an account executive at a brokerage firm, shifted her weight forward in her ergonomic office chair, and said, "When is your appointment?"

There was a knock on the bathroom door.

"Be out in a minute," Tessa yelled from behind the door and then shifted her attention back to Bruna. "This afternoon at 4:30. Someone canceled and they were able to squeeze me in."

Bruna glanced at the clock on her desktop; it was almost 2. She usually left work at 5 even if the market closed at 1, Pacific time. "Okay. Give me the address and I'll meet you there. Is it far?"

Tessa texted the address while speaking with her. "No, it's actually near your office in Century City."

"Alright. See you soon," she said.

Tessa opened the bathroom door, and there was Terry, an assistant with spiky blue hair and a nose ring.

"You're alright?" Terry asked, noticing the grim look on Tessa's face.

"Oh, yes. I'm fine, thank you. It's all yours," she said, stepping away.

"I put Mr. Martin in room two." Mr. Martin was a red-eared terrapin with an upper-respiratory infection.

"Thanks," Tessa said, heading in. She didn't like it when turtles were kept in captivity because most of the time it shortened their lifespan by half or more.

In the meantime, Bruna worked for another two hours before calling it a day. She decided to walk to the doctor's office, a ten-minute trip to a towering medical building.

As soon as Tessa saw her, she got up to hug her, her eyes welling up with tears. Tessa looked unstylishly sloppy in her pull-on pants compared to her friend, who wore a fitted skirt suit, stockings, and pumps.

"Don't worry. It's going to be alright. Between the doctor, you, me, and your parents, we'll sort it all out," Bruna offered.

A nurse came out and called Tessa's name.

"You want me to go in with you?" Bruna asked as Tessa got up.

"I'll let you know," she replied, too shy to undress in front of her friend and have her see the doctor examining her.

The nurse gave Tessa a gown, asked a few questions, and marked the answers on a chart. When she left, Tessa changed into the blue paper gown, climbed a step, and sat on a brown-leather exam table covered with a thin sheet of paper. Minutes later, the doctor and a nurse walked in.

"How are you?" Dr. Cantor asked. He was in his 70s, silver-haired and pudgy.

"That depends on how pregnant I am," she said.

He smiled and said, "Go ahead and lie down." He gave her a pelvic exam and the nurse took a blood sample. She also had to have a urine test. Then came the long wait. Finally, the doctor and the nurse came back.

"The urine test shows that you are pregnant."

"How could this happen? You told me previously that I was not producing mature eggs and I had little chance of getting pregnant," Tessa protested, remembering when she and her then-husband were trying to conceive a child. He now had three kids from his young wife, and Tessa had been fine without children.

"It looks like you are producing mature eggs. I remember telling you that the possibility of getting pregnant was slim to none. But now, I guess you could say that you have won the lottery," he chuckled.

"That's a matter of opinion," she replied, looking upset. If only she had been smarter about this and used protection, except that she never thought about bringing contraceptives to Japan, since she didn't expect to be intimate with anyone.

Dr. Cantor studied his patient's unhappy face and said, "You know, you have choices. It's still early enough for you to have an abortion, but, if so, you must make a decision quickly. If you decide to have it, there are always adoption agencies."

Tessa knew that if she decided to have the baby, there would be no way that she would be willing to give it up.

The nurse took an ultrasound to see how far along she was. Tessa looked at the monitor in awe and said, "Is that?..."

"It sure is. You're eight weeks pregnant. Do you see this over here and that over there?"

Tessa stared, trying to figure out what she was pointing at. "Uh-huh, I guess."

"You're having twins."

"Twins?" Tessa's eyes were glued to the screen. How irresponsible she had been for not going to the doctor sooner. But how could she have known that she could even get pregnant? She got dressed after the nurse and the doctor left. She kept repeating to herself, "Twins!"

"Tessa, you're okay?" Bruna asked when she saw her friend in a daze.

She nodded.

"And? Are you or are you not?"

"I'm having twins," Tessa blurted, as they left the doctor's office.

"Twins? No way! Do twins even run in your family?" Bruna uttered.

"My mom has an identical twin who lives in Chicago, and I have twin cousins on my dad's side," Tessa said as they rode down the elevator.

"Did you find out the babies' sex?" Bruna asked, thinking how great it would be if one of the twins was a girl and the other a boy.

"Too soon to tell. They said if I wanted to, I could find out in eighteen weeks." She didn't want to think about their gender because she wasn't sure if she would go through with the pregnancy.

"Any thoughts as to what you're going to do?"

Tessa shook her head no, still in a fog. Twins! When they turned ten, she would be fifty-one years old.

"Coffee?" Bruna asked, trying to distract Tessa and bring her to the present.

"Hm? Yeah, sure," Tessa said, mindlessly as she paid for the parking. A valet brought over her white Audi Q7 SUV.

Tessa drove the two of them to the nearby Westfield Century City shopping mall. As they strolled the outdoor center, they stopped at one of the many kiosks where Bruna got a bag of potato chips and a double espresso and Tessa got an herbal peach tea. They found a wooden bench and sat down and watched the shoppers milling about. Tessa took particular notice of the mothers pushing their babies in strollers and thought that she probably didn't want to be one of them. But she also knew what her babies looked like in her stomach. They had taken on a human shape. She never should have looked at the ultrasound. *Damn it! Tessa calm down,* she told herself. Stress is not good for babies.

"Is Toshiro the father?"

"Yes."

"Are you sure?" Bruna asked, tearing open her bag of chips.

"Yes, I'm sure. I haven't been with anyone for three years and he was the only person I had sex with."

"You're going to tell him?"

"No," Tessa replied staring at Bruna's chips and espresso. "Chips with coffee? Are you pregnant too?"

"Yeah, it's a strange combo. Want some?"

"No thanks," Tessa responded. She wondered what kind of cravings she might have. So far, she didn't crave anything in particular.

"He has the right to know. You can't make this decision by yourself."

"I can't do that to him. I can't expect him to change his whole life for me. I know him. He would want to leave everything and come here," Tessa said, removing the lid from her paper cup and blowing on the tea.

"And what's wrong with that?"

"I don't want him to be with me out of guilt or obligation."

"If he loved you before you became pregnant, he would love you now," Bruna said, hopefully. But what if Toshiro was one of those guys who didn't like kids?

"It's not fair to him. I don't want him to stick around just because I'm pregnant," Tessa said, staring at Bruna's nice figure. Tessa already felt fat and figured it would be a long time before she would get her shape back.

"And it's not fair to *not* tell him. He has a right to know," Bruna said, brushing off the salt and grease from her hands.

"No, I can't do it," Tessa said, passing her friend a napkin.

"That's tough. I mean being a single mom, that is, if you decide to keep the twins. Are you?"

"Am I what?"

"Are you planning to go through with the pregnancy?"

Tessa shrugged, "If it were still an embryo, I might have considered an abortion, but this fetus has toes, fingers, and a nose. I don't know. Maybe it's not a bad thing that I'm pregnant late in life." Tessa believed that abortion was a personal choice and that women everywhere struggled to make a decision.

"What do you mean?" Bruna frowned.

"Well, I'm not exactly twentysomething. Maybe this is the only chance I will get to be pregnant." She knew that having a child at her age could cause complications, but maybe it would be worth the risk.

"True."

"This is going to change my whole life. I would need help. I would need more money to support them. I just don't know." Tessa thought about the times she had butt heads with the authorities because of her activism. She wouldn't be able to take chances like that anymore if she kept the babies. She would have two mouths to feed. She would continue her work as an activist, but she would have to be more cautious and not break rules.

"You don't have to decide today. You heard the doctor; you still have time. C'mon, let's go shopping," Bruna said, grabbing Tessa's wrist. They went from store to store. Bruna bought a skirt at Nordstrom, hand lotion at L'Occitane, and red lipstick at Sephora. Tessa was not in the mood to shop but tagged along anyway.

She was a mother-to-be. Tessa thought about the way fishermen carelessly stabbed pregnant dolphins to death. What was the difference between them and humans? Elephants cried when their families were killed. Cows displayed fear and anxiety when their calves were taken away to be slaughtered. Dolphins whistled anxiously when captured and separated from their families. She rubbed her stomach and thought about the twins living inside her.

Bruna watched Tessa wandering from one makeup aisle to the next, lost in her thoughts. And from the way she touched her belly, Bruna knew that she had made up her mind. "You're going to keep them, aren't you?"

"Yes. I have some savings and I'm going to ask my parents for help."

"You can ask for my help, too. I'm so excited. I'm an aunt," Bruna said, spritzing on a fruit-scented eau de toilette on her wrist and applying it to her neck.

Tessa smiled and said, "They're not out, yet. It'll be a while before you're an aunt."

"All the same. Are you planning on letting Toshiro know?" Bruna insisted, applying a sample lotion to her hands. She could just live in Sephora and never have to pay for anything, she thought.

"If he shows up in four months, I will not be able to hide my secret."

"What if he? …"

"Doesn't show up?"

"I was going to say, what if he doesn't want to be a father?" Bruna said, trying a tan eyeshadow.

"I'll be fine with that. It is my choice to keep the twins, and I'll take care of them," she replied. But deep down, she hoped that Toshiro would want her and the twins as a whole package.

"You'll need a larger place."

"I'm going to start looking to buy a house," Tessa said, picking up a bottle of floral-scented perfume, smelling it, and putting it right back down. The smell made her nauseous.

"So, you're not going to wait until you talk to Toshiro?"

"It'll take time to find something that I like. Hopefully, by then, he will be here, and we can make a decision together, that is if he wants to be part of our lives."

"And if he doesn't want to be a dad?"

"I'd still buy a place. Maybe rent out one of the rooms to help pay for the mortgage."

"Good for you," Bruna said, proud of her friend, her strength, and her resolve, and yet, she was also scared for her. Being a single parent was not an easy task.

CHAPTER 18

Some twenty dates and three months later, Toshiro was still thinking about Tessa. In fact, she was all he ever thought about. He even called her a few times, but then hung up. *No, if I want this to work, I have to stay away,* he told himself. He had been anonymously following her on Facebook, Twitter, and her blogs to see what she had been up to. There were pictures of her at different schools working to teach a new generation to treat all lives with compassion. There was a video of her at a demonstration in Los Angeles and another in San Diego. And then there was a blog post about similarities between dolphins and humans. As he followed her every move online, he also educated himself about aquatic life. He wished that he could express himself freely the way she did without repercussions. It was torture not being near her, and if it weren't for his work and his friends, he would lose his resolve.

"Toshiro, there are so many nice girls around you," his father said to him one day. "Why don't you marry one and give me a few grandchildren?"

"Maybe someday," he responded, "But it has to be with the right girl."

"Are you still interested in that American?" his father asked, noticing a picture of Toshiro and Tessa on Toshiro's desk at work.

"She's just a friend," he said, smiling at the photo in front of him. They had taken a selfie at Kyoto's Kamo River. The two of them were making funny faces and laughing hard.

His father readjusted the glasses on his face and said, "If you keep a picture of the two of you on your desk, it means that you're more than just friends, especially since you don't have pictures of other girls. What will people think?"

"Why should I worry about what people think?"

"You're my son. We have to protect our family name. The American is not good for our image. Mr. Junichiro Fujimoto…"

"Mr. Fujimoto? How does he figure into my life? I don't even like the man."

His father changed the subject. "Don't you want a girlfriend? Someone from our own culture?"

Japan was a homogenous society, even with the numerous ex-pats who lived there. Japanese families did not easily accept outsiders, and Riku Yokoyama was no different.

"Tessa was right. You do hate her," Toshiro said, getting up from his desk, sticking his hands in his pockets, and looking out the window with his back to his father. His father was simply intolerable.

"I don't hate her. I don't even know her. She's just not right for you, don't you see?"

Toshiro turned around and said, "Why is that, Dad? What is it about her that you don't like?"

"For starters, she is too old. How old is she? Almost forty?"

"What does that have to do with anything?" Toshiro frowned.

"Your mom is forty-eight. She had you when she was eighteen. This woman will not be able to give you children."

"How do you know that?" And anyway, it doesn't matter. We could always adopt."

Riku shook his head and walked out. He wished that Tessa had never entered his son's life. And to pour salt on an open wound, she was an activist. People in his position usually kept quiet about controversial subjects and went about their days. They were not tied to political parties and did not support one religion over another. Everything came down to business and the best deal. That was all that mattered. Kaiya was the perfect match for his son— she was pretty, young, Japanese, and came from an honorable family. Why couldn't his son see that? He was too blinded by the American.

Souji had given up trying to get Kaiya's attention because he knew that she still had her eyes on Toshiro. And so, he got himself a new girlfriend. She had short hair with bangs and a round face. Sure, she wasn't Kaiya, but she would have to do for now. To show off his girl, he made plans with a large group of friends, including Toshiro and Kaiya, at a karaoke *izakaya*. The place had no frills, was crowded, and patrons sat on the floor behind long rectangular tables. Like many others, there was a two-hour time limit for each table and dishes were shared, as was the bill, even when some drank more than others. People showed up in large groups and had to pay a seating charge, called *otōshidai*, of 3,000 yen per person, about $30, similar to a cover charge in the U.S., though in Japan, patrons also received *otōshi*, a small appetizer. This *otōshidai* was not exclusive to this *izakaya*, and some bars and establishments where alcohol was served had an average table charge of 300 to 700 yen per person, which was like tipping the staff for taking up a table since tipping was not part of the Japanese culture. There was an extensive selection of warm and cold sake, a limited beer menu, and comfort food, such as *karaage*, or deep-fried chicken, *korokke*, a mashed potato croquette, and beef *yakitori* roasted on a skewer.

Seated next to Toshiro, Kaiya tried hard to engage him in conversation, but he didn't seem to be in the mood to talk. Some of the guys were already drunk, and their dates were busy chatting away. Souji and his girl were on the stage, microphones in hand, slurring the songs scrolled on the TV monitor. Toshiro was quiet, his sentiments occupied elsewhere. Envious that Souji had found himself a girl, Toshiro wished that Tessa could have been there beside him. Today on her blog, he had learned that because of many activists' efforts, some tour operators had stopped selling tickets to theme parks that imprisoned dolphins. Toshiro was still learning from Tessa every day, even though she was miles away. He wondered if she knew she had such a powerful effect on him.

"Toshiro? Toshiro?" Kaiya nudged him to get his attention.

He was startled. How long had she been calling his name? He had no idea.

"Is everything okay? Where are you?"

"Sorry. I had work on my mind," he lied. He liked her and perhaps he would have eventually married her had he not met Tessa.

"Do you want to do a duo?" she asked.

Toshiro looked at the stage. Souji and his girl, both somewhat drunk, were attempting to sing John Lennon's "Imagine." "Uh, not tonight."

Kaiya's face registered disappointment.

He tried to muster a smile. "I guess I'm not good company."

"It's okay. Maybe we can hang out this Sunday." She missed him, their walks at serene parks, their picnic lunches, bar-hopping, and dancing at clubs. She never should have broken up with him. It had been a mistake, and she was going to correct it.

"We can do that," he said, feeling alone. He needed someone in his life, and Kaiya could be the friend he could lean on, especially now that Souji was busy with his girlfriend. But he didn't want to use and hurt Kaiya, so he added, "As friends. Would you be okay with that?"

She nodded yes. As much as it pained her that their intimate relationship had been reduced to a simple friendship, she still wanted to try to change it. She knew that it was going to be a slow process, but he was worth the wait.

CHAPTER 19

Toshiro and Kaiya squabbled all morning about going to the Maxell Aqua Park Shinagawa to watch the dolphin show. They stopped at the entrance, where Toshiro stood his ground. "We can do anything you want, just not this."

Kaiya would not be dissuaded since she already purchased the tickets online. It was obvious from her appearance that she had spent an inordinate amount of time putting together her look for Toshiro: Her friend who was a hairstylist had come to her house, added cappuccino highlights to her hair, cut it in layers with fringe, blow-dried it perfectly straight, and used a curling iron to create soft waves. After going through twenty changes of clothes, Kaiya had settled on a mauve knit minidress, lace socks, and black shoes with chunky heels. Her makeup, which took more than an hour to apply, was flawless and made her look as though she was ready for a magazine photoshoot. "You used to be fun. What happened to you?" she said, playfully grabbing his hand and pushing him toward the park's show stadium.

Unlike Kaiya, Toshiro had carelessly put on a plain sweater, jeans, and sneakers. After all, this was not a date since Kaiya was just a friend. "I really don't want to do this."

"It'll be fun, c'mon," she said, dragging him by the hand. "The show will be starting soon, and we need to take our seats.

"Let's go to Odaiba instead. We can go to the Mori Digital Art Museum, which would be much more interesting than this," he said, reluctantly taking a seat next to Kaiya on the stadium bleachers. He recalled something that Tessa had told him: "If people would stop going to aquariums and water parks, then it would not be lucrative for fishermen to capture dolphins."

"You've changed, you know. We used to like the same things. I feel like we're miles apart."

"You're right. I have changed," he replied, getting up.

"Where are you going?"

"I can't do this. I'm sorry," he said, walking toward the exit with Kaiya trailing behind him.

"Are you crazy? I paid good money for these tickets."

"I'll reimburse you."

"That's not the point. I deserve an explanation. You're acting weird," she said, frowning.

Outside, Toshiro said, "I'm sorry, this is not going to work."

She paused for a moment and stared at him. "This is not about us. This is about Tessa, isn't it?"

"Maybe."

"Don't say maybe. She has filled your head with nonsense."

"It's not nonsense. If you would just stop focusing on yourself for a moment and realize that you could make a difference in the world, you would be a happier person."

"You're judging me?" she asked with her hands on her waist. "You think you're better than me because you want to protect dolphins?"

"That's not what I'm saying. I'm just asking you to keep an open mind. The next time there is a dolphin hunt in Taiji, go watch and then come back to me and say that you agree with what they're doing. They're torturing these mammals to find show dolphins."

Kaiya didn't know what to say. She didn't understand him. She never thought about animal rights. She followed rules, did as she was told, and never got involved in anything because that's how she was raised. Like most Japanese, she just accepted things as they were. None of Kaiya's friends cared about activism and neither did Toshiro until he met Tessa.

"We've grown apart. I don't even know you anymore, and it makes me sad," she admitted, looking at him as her eyes welled up with tears. She was still in love with him. She wanted the old Toshiro, fun and carefree. But that was not going to happen, she thought as the two walked toward the subway, each heading to their own home.

Toshiro found it more and more difficult to stay away from Tessa. After arguing with Kaiya, he realized that things would never be the same between them, not even as friends. So he decided to break his promise and go see Tessa. His company's office in Los Angeles had opened up last week and he could work there for a while. QZMZ needed a general manager who would oversee the openings and the operations of its stores in Los Angeles. In fact, if the retail stores did well, he would be in charge of their entire U.S. operation with plans to expand to San Francisco, Seattle, Houston, Chicago, New York City, and Boston. To say that his father was not thrilled would have been the understatement of the century.

When Toshiro went to talk to him in his stately office, his father was seated behind an ornately carved mahogany desk concluding a conference call with general managers from all over the world.

Toshiro barely got the words out about his intention before his father curtly replied: "No. I need you here." Riku's eyes seemed to pierce through Toshiro. His white starched French cuff shirt, solid gold cufflinks, and custom-tailored suit begged respect and a deep bow from others.

"I want to work for this company, but I want to live in Los Angeles," Toshiro said, swallowing hard. Unlike his father's distinguished executive style, Toshiro's navy Camoshita suit made him look like a young apprentice trying to prove himself and move up the corporate ladder.

But in Japan, there was a hierarchy. Subordinates did not raise their voices or challenge authorities by speaking their minds. And since Toshiro's father was also his boss, life was extraordinarily difficult for him. Out of respect, Toshiro had to do as he was told not only at work but also outside of it. Even so, compared to most Japanese, Toshiro was spoiled and got away with a lot more than the average Japanese son.

"It's the American, isn't it? She put you up to this," his father said, nervously tapping his pen on the desk.

"Her name is Tessa. And no, she didn't make me do anything. I choose to be with her."

"You're making a big mistake. She's all wrong for you," Riku said, throwing his pen on his desk, letting the gesture convey his anger.

"Yes, you've been telling me that for some time now, but I'm leaving with or without your approval. I'm sorry, but I love her."

"And what if I fire you for insubordination?" his father said, leaning back and crossing his arms in front of his chest.

Toshiro looked at his father nonchalantly, shrugged, and said, "So be it. I will find work after I get there." He had no idea what he would do once he got to Los Angeles, but he had plenty of money left to him by his maternal grandfather. Of course, he would need to work, but he wouldn't be destitute. He could take his time and find another job.

His father's nostrils flared as he let out a puff of air in frustration. If Toshiro wasn't his only child, he would have been much tougher on him. He popped his anxiety pills in his mouth like candy and pushed them down with a gulp of designer water from his personalized decanter. "Go ahead. Work at the Los Angeles office, but don't come crawling back to me when you realize that I was right."

No chance of that, Toshiro said to himself. For maybe the first time in his life, Toshiro felt strong and independent.

Over the next two weeks, Toshiro wrapped up his work, said farewell to his friends, packed his luggage, and had a chauffeur take him to the airport in a company car. On the way, his thoughts turned to Tessa. He wondered what she would do or say when she saw him. In a blue box in his raincoat pocket were two white-gold matching rings from Tiffany's that he had purchased with Souji's help. Because Tessa had made it clear that she did not want to get married again, the rings were not engagement rings. One of them had small diamonds, and the other was plain, both representing a symbol of their love and commitment to each other. The inscription on each read, "To my eternal love." Toshiro wanted to surprise Tessa and hoped that her reaction to him moving there would be receptive. They belonged together, he thought.

It was two days before Christmas, the first rain of the season was falling, and the streets were more slippery than usual. He stared out the car window at soaked joggers oblivious to the wet weather, pedestrians with see-through bubble umbrellas, and impeccably dressed women rushing for cover from the rain. Then in an instant, everything went dark.

Several ambulances arrived. Three people were badly injured and a fourth had minor injuries. The chauffeur was dead, and Toshiro was unconscious. The emergency response personnel immobilized his head, neck, and body and inserted a tube down his throat to give him oxygen. When the paramedics reached the University of Tokyo Hospital, Toshiro was taken to the ER.

The ER doctor requested a CT scan of Toshiro's brain and diagnosed him with mild, traumatic brain injury. A neurosurgeon read the CT report, examined Toshiro, and instructed the hospital staff to monitor his intracranial pressure as an increase in pressure could result in a more serious brain injury.

Toshiro's parents were informed about the accident and drove frantically to the hospital. They both were soaking wet when they came in and too preoccupied with Toshiro to think about removing their raincoats. Minako collapsed in a nearby chair, wringing her hands and staring vacantly at the pristine white floor tiles. Toshiro's father began to pace the floor between the restrooms and the nurses' stations. After a long, unbearable wait, the neurosurgeon finally showed up wearing his blue scrubs and a medical mask that had been pushed down to his neck.

"Hello. My name is Dr. Abe. Please have a seat," he said. On his left wrist, he wore a Doplr watch, which measured the pulse and respiratory rate of patients.

The Yokoyamas did as he requested, their eyes glued on the young doctor.

Dr. Abe took a seat on a brown leather chair facing them. "Your son was in a terrible car accident. There is some trauma to his brain. His skull and brain are intact, but when the driver crashed the car, your son's head hit the front seat, causing his brain to move forward and back, striking the skull."

"What does that mean? Is he going to be alright?" Riku asked, trying hard to hold it together.

"There is no bleeding or any major acute issues. There is a little swelling and there may be some memory loss. We're keeping him under observation and monitoring his intracranial pressure."

"Can we see him?"

"Yes. He is in the intensive care unit, but he is unconscious. You may see him for a few minutes. He needs quiet and rest."

Riku broke into tears. "Why? How did the accident happen? I know the chauffeur. He is an experienced driver."

Minako tried hard to control her emotions and stay strong for her husband, but her face betrayed her. Heaviness hovered over her like a thick black tarp, suffocating her. She tried to push her way out, but it was no use. She wondered if her son would ever recover. All those years of raising him, nurturing, him, and making sure that he was safe were gone in a blink of an eye.

"The driver had a heart attack. He slammed into several cars," Dr. Abe said.

"Where is he?" asked Riku

"I'm sorry, Mr. Yokoyama," the doctor shook his head, "He didn't make it."

"No, no, no, no, this isn't happening." Riku had known the driver for more than twenty-five years. He was a good man. He had a family to support.

"Your son was very lucky. Had he been on the freeway or in the front seat, he wouldn't have made it. Sitting in the back seat and wearing his seat belt saved him."

Minako felt goosebumps all over her body.

Riku took in a deep breath to regain his composure. "I would like to see my son now, please."

The doctor nodded and told a nurse to accompany Toshiro's parents to intensive care. There, they gazed helplessly at their unconscious son who was hooked up to wires and tubes, one finger connected to a pulse oximeter, and a white blanket over him from his feet to his chest. Riku covered his face with his hands. His wife wept, mascara running down her face, staining her raincoat. *It was all that stupid girl's fault*, they both thought. If it weren't for Tessa, Toshiro would have been at the office working, and none of this would have happened.

The next few days proved tiring as the Yokoyamas traveled back and forth between their home and the hospital. Toshiro's friends were notified, and Kaiya was devastated. She too blamed Tessa for this turn of the events. From the moment Tessa kissed Toshiro, she changed all of their lives.

On his fourth day in the intensive care unit, Toshiro opened his eyes when a nurse came in to check in on him. She noticed that Toshiro looked petrified and lost, so she notified the doctor, who showed up promptly.

"Do you remember what happened?" Dr. Abe asked. He was in his early 30s and as sharp as a razor.

"No," Toshiro responded, looking blank.

"You were in a car crash. Do you recall anything before or after it?"

"I, I, no," he answered, wracking his brain, but coming up with nothing.

The doctor lifted Toshiro's eyelid and used a bright light to illuminate the back of his eye and look for changes to his optic nerve. He wanted to better evaluate Toshiro's intracranial pressure.

"Any headache?"

He shook his head no.

"Blurred vision?"

"No."

"What is your name?"

"My name is … my name is … I don't remember." He was hollow, as though someone had erased his entire life from his memory. It was a horrible feeling.

When the doctor saw the look of terror on his patient's face, he patted his hand lightly and said, "Everything is going to be okay. Try to relax for now." He then told the nurse to increase his sedative so that he could rest.

The next day, after Toshiro's second CT scan, Dr. Abe reviewed the results and looked to see if there were any bruising, blood clots, or swelling. He looked for damaged areas of the brain before talking to Toshiro's parents.

"The scans we took show that there are no clots in Toshiro's brain, and the swelling has gone down," the doctor told the Yokoyamas in his office. "There are, however, some disturbances to the brain."

Using a monitor to point out specific areas of Toshiro's brain, he said, "Some of the neurons aren't functioning as they should, causing some chemical imbalance, but it is not severe. Toshiro will recover. There may be some short-term memory loss. It's too soon to tell."

"So, what do we do?" Minako asked.

"We have therapists at the hospital who will help with his rehab, and then there are outpatient therapies that would help him adjust to his home and work life."

"How long will all this take?" Riku asked.

"I don't know. He could recover in a few weeks or it could take months. We will continue to monitor his progress. That's the best answer that I can give you."

"Can we see him?" Toshiro's father requested.

"Yes, but don't pressure him to remember things. He will in time."

Toshiro felt better than the day before. He knew that he was in a hospital and that he was injured. He did not recognize anybody at the hospital. *Probably because I don't know any of them*, he thought. After the scan, he kept asking himself, "What is my name?" "What is my name?" And when his parents came to visit, he was surprised to recognize them.

"*Okaasan, Otousan?*" Mom, Dad?

"You recognize us! We were afraid that you wouldn't." Minako smiled for the first time since the accident.

"Yes, but I cannot remember my name."

"Your name is Toshiro."

"To-shi-ro, To-shi-ro, Toshiro," he repeated. Then a memory whizzed by him: He was at an office party and someone was calling his name, "Toshiro, Toshiro, come here. I want to show you something."

"You're okay, son?" His father asked.

"I think so. I'm just trying to remember what happened to me. I have no memory of it."

"The doctor said that you mustn't force it. It will come to you, and if it doesn't, we will help fill in the gaps."

After a week of therapy, Toshiro's memory was starting to come back, but there were still missing pieces. His parents filled him in about the accident and the driver's death. They also told him that he had been on his way to see a client when the car crashed. His father was hoping that Toshiro's memory of Tessa would never return. Not that he wished his son harm, but he felt that the accident had been a blessing to get Tessa completely out of their lives.

"You don't want us to talk about Tessa at all?" Souji, Kayia, and his friends asked Riku in the hospital waiting area.

"No. Not unless he remembers her." His rigid face and stern eyes said, *You do as I tell you.*

"But what if he remembers her?" Souji asked, running his hand nervously through his hair. "He …" *loved her,* he wanted to say but stopped himself. He understood full well the Yokoyamas' hatred of Tessa. And Kaiya, eyes teary, was sitting right next to him, wearing an ultra-feminine baby-pink skirt suit in case Toshiro woke up.

"Then you can all pin it on me for hiding the truth. I'm willing to take the blame because it's for his own good," said Riku.

They all looked at each other, not sure what to say. Souji unbuttoned his wool jacket. He felt suffocated. He would give anything for a puff of a cigarette.

"Look, that girl has been nothing but trouble in his life. You know it's true," Riku said when he noticed the uncertainty on their faces.

Kaiya nodded her head in agreement, but the others showed no reaction.

"So, we all agree to keep quiet?" Riku asked sternly.

Riku was a powerful man, and they were too afraid to cross him, so they all deferred. Souji didn't like the idea of lying to his best friend. Kaiya felt a deep sadness inside her because she wasn't sure if Toshiro would ever love her the way he loved Tessa. But if Tessa and the dolphins disappeared from Toshiro's memory, it would be possible for Kaiya to step in and try to rekindle the relationship.

CHAPTER 20

Three weeks into his hospital stay, Toshiro's long-term memory returned to normal. He recognized his friends and family and recalled most of his past except what had happened in the last six months. After a month, he was discharged from the hospital and started to see a therapist twice a week to help him with his memory loss. His father hired a live-in housekeeper-cook and an assistant, who accompanied Toshiro everywhere, making sure that he didn't get lost. Toshiro complained to his father that he really didn't need help. However, his short-term memory loss was still apparent. There were times when he didn't feel like talking to anyone. At other times, he was irritable and impatient. His body still hurt from the impact of the accident, but he didn't want to continue taking painkillers. Toshiro worked with a physical therapist and massage therapist several times a week to help alleviate his pain. By the third month, he reduced his housekeeper's hours to once a week and got rid of his assistant altogether because he wanted to be left alone. He remembered how to use the subway, he had no problem finding locations, and driving came to him naturally. At work, he was able to remember how to perform his job duties, and his life went back to normal.

His father had replaced the picture of him and Tessa in Toshiro's office with one of him and Kaiya, taken at a dinner party at his house before Toshiro had met Tessa. With the help of Souji, Toshiro's father found out that his nephew Hansuke needed to be informed of the scheme because he also knew about Tessa. Hansuke flat-out refused to lie to Toshiro. But after pressure from Riku, he promised to avoid the whole matter and not contact Toshiro. Riku went so far as to make sure that no one at work ever asked his son about Tessa. He had someone hack Toshiro's phone and computer to delete photos, phone numbers, emails, texts, search history, and anything else that would connect him to the American. He had Toshiro's home and office searched to eliminate any mementos of Tessa. Not only was his son's memory wiped clean of Tessa—so was anything that would help him remember her.

Unfortunately, Toshiro's short-term memory loss left a big hole in his heart. After four months, he became severely depressed. His therapist had been helping him adjust to his home and work life, but he still felt that something was not right and couldn't pinpoint what it was. One Sunday, while visiting Souji at his apartment, the two began reminiscing. Souji's place was small and looked more like an oversize hotel room than a home. He took out two beers and gave one to Toshiro.

"Thank you," he said, removing the gray scarf that Tessa had given him and laying it over his jacket on Souji's bed. Riku's cleaning crew had missed taking the scarf and a few other tiny items. He wasn't sure why, but he got a warm fuzzy feeling every time he wore that scarf. It had his name sewn on it. He assumed that he must have special-ordered it. Or did someone give it to him? He couldn't remember.

"You're welcome. Something on your mind?" Souji asked, plopping down on a cushy chair and propping his legs on the triangular coffee table that came with his furnished apartment. He noticed his friend was deep in thought.

"There are many things on my mind. I don't even know where to begin."

"Start with something small and work your way up," Souji smiled. "Chocolate?" he added, pushing a small bowl of individually wrapped patties toward his friend.

"Thanks," Toshiro said, unwrapping one and putting it in his mouth. "I've been getting emails and mail about fundraising to save dolphins. What is all that about?" he asked, playing with the green candy wrapper in his hand. Chocolate mint. It tasted familiar.

Souji gulped and tried to keep his cool. One false move and Toshiro could get suspicious. "You may have made a one-time donation somewhere. You know how those organizations work. You give to one and before you know it, your name is on the list of ten more charities."

"You think?" he asked, unconvinced. He felt like he had some kind of connection to the dolphins, but what? He had no memory of it.

"Yeah, absolutely. Once I donated to a dog shelter and before I knew it, I was getting all this mail about saving the elephants, African gorillas, wild horses, and so on."

"I guess you're right."

"What else is bothering you? Maybe I can clarify it for you," Souji asked, somewhat confidently. He was going to do his best to explain away as much as possible. Maybe he was starting to get good at evasion.

"Well, the dry cleaner gave me this," Toshiro said, reaching in his pocket and showing Souji a blue Tiffany's box. "They said that they found it in my raincoat pocket, but I don't remember buying it."

Damn! Souji thought. Toshiro must have been carrying the box with him the day of the accident. They had wiped all traces of Tessa, or so he had thought. But Souji had forgotten about the rings Toshiro had purchased. *What else had he forgotten to get rid of?* "Oh, that. You were going to give it to Kaiya as a Christmas present," Souji responded without a hint of deception in his voice.

"I was?" he asked, unwrapping the box, staring at the inscription on the rings, and frowning. *To my eternal love.* At what point did he fall in love with Kaiya and, more importantly, at what point did he stop loving her? He felt nothing toward her now. And why were the rings so simple? Wouldn't he have bought an engagement ring with a large diamond?

"Yes, we were together when you picked them out." Souji felt awful for lying.

Toshiro stared at him blankly for a few moments, searching his memory, but he recalled nothing. "You know the picture in my office of me and Kaiya?" he asked before chugging down his beer.

"Yes. It's a great photo of the two of you," Souji lied. He preferred that Toshiro have a picture of him and Tessa on his desk. Souji and Kaiya had become much closer since Toshiro's accident, and he had a notion that Kaiya's feelings for Toshiro had changed. Souji was no longer in a relationship and was waiting patiently for Kaiya and Toshiro to break it off so that he could make his move.

"I feel that there was, I don't know, a different picture on my desk."

"Oh?"

"I'm not sure which, but the one on my desk just doesn't feel right. We went out last night, you know."

Souji pushed back his feelings of jealousy and said, "How was it?"

"Awkward. My dad tells me that we were going to be engaged before the accident. Is that true?"

"I don't know. You never said anything about it to me." Souji did not want to confirm yet another lie. He still had trouble dealing with the first one. There had been so many times that he had wanted to tell Toshiro the truth, but was too frightened to break his promise to Riku.

"I think she cares for me, but I don't think she loves me and I feel nothing toward her except obligation. And these rings, I'm not quite sure what to make of them. I just don't see myself giving her something like this."

"If the rings bother you, I can hang on to them until you're ready to share them with her."

Toshiro pushed the box toward Souji. "I don't think I will ever be giving them to Kaiya."

Souji smiled on the inside. *Of course, you won't. You love Tessa*, he wanted to say, but instead, he said, "It's only been four months since the accident. You went through a life-changing experience. Give yourself time."

"True, but there are other strange things that are happening to me." Toshiro's face had aged since the accident. His skin lacked luster and he was no longer that vibrant boy Tessa had met seven months ago.

"Like what?" Souji asked. He glowed with contentment because he knew that he was close to having Kaiya all to himself, but he felt guilty for being so happy when his friend was struggling so much.

"I've been having these recurring dreams."

"About what?" Souji suddenly became anxious. *What if he remembered? What if he knew?* The clock was ticking and it was only a matter of time before Toshiro would figure out that everyone close to him betrayed him.

"In the dream, I'm with someone. It feels like we've known each other for years. We're walking by the Kamo River in Kyoto, holding hands."

"What? What does this, this person looks like?" he stuttered.

"That's just it, when I wake up, I don't remember her face. I just know she's not Japanese; she speaks English with an American accent."

Souji choked on his beer and started coughing. "Then what happens?"

"Then I'm somewhere else packed with crowds. I look for her as I push through, but people keep pushing me in the opposite direction."

"And?" Souji asked, wetting his lips. He felt turmoil inside of him. On one hand, he was scared that Toshiro would find out the truth; on the other, he wanted him to figure it out for himself.

"And nothing. Then I wake up," Toshiro said, looking at him with a sad expression. He felt lost and hollow.

"You have the same dream every night?" Souji asked, getting up for more beer.

"There are variations. You know, sometimes I'm with her in a place I don't even recognize, but we always end up getting separated."

Souji handed him another bottle. "You've been through a lot. You went to work right after the accident. Maybe you need a vacation"—*to Los Angeles*, he wanted to say, but he bit his tongue. Souji was scared that if Toshiro ever found out the truth, it would be the end of their friendship. He should've never agreed to lie to him.

"Sometimes, I have these flashbacks when I'm sitting in my office," he said, rubbing his eyes and sounding tired. "It hurts. It's like a sharp pain going through my head and I have a hard time dealing with it."

"What kind of flashbacks?" Souji asked, holding his breath. He couldn't let him go on like this. It wasn't fair.

"There's blood. A lot of blood. It's like it's underwater, and it's all red. I don't understand it."

Souji remembered Toshiro telling him about *The Cove* and the brutal way the fishermen slaughtered the helpless dolphins and separated the parents from the pups. Toshiro had told him that he had thrown up after watching it. He had told Souji that he had never seen anything like it. "You know, maybe you should talk this over with your therapist. Maybe he can help sort it all out."

"I already did. He told me there are probably some lost memories starting to resurface. Was there ever another girl in my life? An American, perhaps?" he asked, staring into Souji's eyes.

Souji looked calm and cool, but inside he was petrified. "Toshiro, you have dated many girls, some just briefly. It was always hard to keep up with all the women in your life."

"No, this isn't just any woman," he said, shaking his head. "There's some kind of deep connection between us."

The next day, at work, Toshiro studied the photo of himself with Kaiya. He was going to see her again in a few days. Something about the photo was off. Why did he have no memory of it ever being on his desk when he recalled almost everything else? He remembered his files, his office, the contents of the desk drawers, and everything on his desk, including the silver frame, but that photo was not in it. And why didn't he feel anything toward Kaiya? He had no answer. He was also bothered by employee discussions about the Los Angeles office at meetings. He felt as if that was where he needed to be, but his life was in Tokyo. He had no connections to Los Angeles. Why was he then pulled toward that city? What was so special about it? It wasn't beautiful like Paris or Rome. It wasn't a hub of business, like New York City. It wasn't serene and soothing like Hawaii. Why Los Angeles? He was tired of having so many questions and no answers. But there was one thing he *could* do to free himself: he could end his relationship with Kaiya. He called her.

"Can I see you tonight?" he asked, pacing his office. He wished that he could break it off with her over the phone.

"Tonight?" How odd, she thought, when they had just gone out two nights ago, and it hadn't been all that pleasant. He had been so quiet, so self-absorbed. She felt that they had been drifting apart for some time.

From the flat tone of her voice, Toshiro could tell that she didn't want him any more than he wanted her. "How do you feel about me?"

"I, um. …"

"I get it. 'I, um,' says a lot, already."

"Sorry," she said, wincing.

"Don't be. I feel the same way about you. Maybe we can just be friends."

"I would like that," she admitted. Too much had happened between them. Over the past few months, she realized that her feelings for him were not as deep as they used to be. She had become closer to Souji. The two of them shared a secret; a secret that Riku Yokoyama had imposed on them. Sure, in the beginning, she hated Tessa for coming between them, but as time passed, her hatred cooled. She realized now that Tessa had nothing to do with the car crash and that the accident could have happened at any point in time. It was destiny that Toshiro met Tessa and that Kaiya should be with Souji. Time was a funny thing. It twisted and turned and sometimes rolled back to where it all started. She had known Souji before Toshiro, and it took her this long to finally realize that she loved Souji and he loved her.

When his telephone conversation with Kaiya ended, Toshiro removed her photo and put it in his desk drawer. "Ugh," he uttered, feeling a sudden pain and more flashbacks. It was raining hard. He looked out the window at the pedestrians. Someone was driving. Where was he going? He couldn't remember. Someone tapped on his office door, bringing him back to reality. He collected himself. "Come in," he said.

His assistant, Ena, poked her head in and said, "The meeting is in five minutes."

"What meeting?" he asked, rubbing his temples.

"The monthly overseas conference call," she said and started to walk away.

Every month, everyone in managerial positions gathered in a large conference room so that management from the overseas offices could update them regarding stores, exchange ideas, and resolve problems.

"Wait! Please close the door behind you and have a seat," Toshiro asked Ena, pointing to an orange chair on the opposite side of his desk.

She did as Toshiro requested. She had been with the firm for two years, was meticulous, and adhered to strict rules.

"Would you tell me more about the Los Angeles office?"

"Not much to tell. It's fairly new. They are working to open a series of retail stores. One of our managers transferred there recently."

"Was I supposed to go there before the accident? I mean, was she my replacement?" he blurted.

She shifted in her chair. Riku Yokoyama had instructed everyone to not talk about two things: Toshiro's trip to Los Angeles and Tessa. She was just a subordinate and had no intention of getting fired. "You should ask Mr. Yokoyama, sir."

"I'm asking you. I'm tired of everyone tiptoeing around me," he yelled.

"It is not for me to say," she responded, sitting at the edge of the chair as though she were about to fall off of a cliff.

"Yes or no? It's not a difficult question," he demanded forcefully.

"I'm sorry, sir."

"Get out of my office," he ordered, and she scurried off. The flashbacks, the dreams, and the sense that those around him were hiding something made him feel unraveled and temperamental. He got up, threw on his jacket, and went to the meeting.

In the telepresence room, several rows of semicircular tables faced two curved 105-inch TV monitors, making it seem like everyone was in the same room, sitting across the table from each other. Toshiro sat in the front row with the heads of the manufacturing, finance, and innovative strategy departments. Also on the monitors were the general managers from the U.S., Germany, France, Australia, Switzerland, and Denmark. Toshiro, who was a regional manager, was covering for Japan's GM who was out sick with the flu.

"Vegan purses, wallets, and shoes are very popular here in Los Angeles. Toshiro, our factory in Tokyo should really consider making them," said the temporary L.A. general manager. She didn't want to be in Los Angeles at all. Since she was bilingual, she had been transferred from the Kyoto office right after Toshiro's accident.

She couldn't wait to go back to her old job as Kyoto's regional manager as soon as QZMZ could find a replacement for Toshiro.

"Are we talking about items made out of acrylic?" Toshiro asked. QZMZ made inferior leather goods for their customers to keep costs low, but they never used acrylic.

"Some, yes," she said. "But other items are also made of apple peels, cork, and recycled fruits. The industry has changed. You wouldn't be able to tell the difference between real and vegan leather by some of the new brands coming out. So what do you think? Is it possible to introduce vegan goods in our stores?"

Toshiro had this conversation with someone before. But who? A memory whizzed by him of someone saying, "It's faux leather. I like animals. I don't want to kill them and wear their skin."

"I don't think vegan leather would do well here," said the GM of France. "People here have a difficult time understanding why anyone would even want to be a vegan. They love their meats."

Another memory whizzed by Toshiro of someone saying, "Buddhist monks eat a vegan diet because they want to do no harm. Right?" Who had asked him that? A woman. Why couldn't he remember her face? Who was she?

"We would do very well with vegan products," Germany's GM said. "I think we should try it."

"So how about it, Toshiro?" asked the L.A. manager.

"How about what?" Toshiro asked. The entire time, his mind had been preoccupied with flashbacks.

"Vegan leather?"

"Is veganism big in Los Angeles?" Toshiro asked.

"Yes. There is a demand for ethical products. Vegan retail stores and clothing lines have been popping up everywhere," responded the GM of the L.A. office.

He remembered his dream. The woman he was with had an American accent. Maybe she was from L.A. "I know that this is off topic and I'm sorry, but didn't you used to be the regional manager at the Kyoto office?"

She shifted uncomfortably in her chair and said, "Yes, I was."

"And now you're the GM at the L.A. office?" he asked, surprised. "When did you get promoted?" None of it made sense. If anything, he should be the one who got the promotion because the Tokyo office was the corporate headquarters of QZMZ, and the regional manager of Tokyo had seniority over all the other regional managers.

She smiled nervously and replied, "Oh, the L.A. office is small. We opened not long ago, and my responsibilities are the same as before. It's just a title change."

"Why exactly did you move to L.A?" he asked, squinting and scratching his head.

Everyone looked uneasy, having been warned not to talk much about the Los Angeles office.

"Ba …umm … losing you. Reception is…" she said and went offline because she had no idea how to respond. How could she tell Toshiro that she hated being in L.A. because she missed her boyfriend in Kyoto? How could she tell him that upper management was in the process of interviewing qualified candidates for the L.A. office? How could she tell him that he was the Los Angeles GM before the accident? Her honesty would have incurred the wrath of Riku Yokoyama and landed her in the unemployment office. It was best to fake a poor telecommunication connection.

"I think we lost our L.A. connection. Apparently, they're having internet issues," remarked Australia's GM. "But anyway, I think we also would do well here with vegan leather. More people are shifting away from products that are made from animals and looking for sustainable solutions."

Toshiro listened to the heads of manufacturing and finance, who both said that it was possible and profitable to add vegan leather to their product line. "Okay, I'll look into it," Toshiro responded to them. He could tell by the managers' expressions and the sudden bad connection in Los Angeles that he was being played. He felt as though they were all hiding something from him. But why? Maybe the answer to recovering his memory loss was in Los Angeles—every time the subject came up, everyone looked uneasy.

After the meeting, Toshiro bumped into his father. "We need to talk," he said, following him to his office and shutting the door behind him.

"What is it? You don't feel well? You need time off?" his father asked with concern because Toshiro looked fatigued and distraught.

"No, thank you. I'm fine. But I would like to talk about Los Angeles."

His father's heart dropped. "Okay."

"I want to transfer to," he said and paused, puzzled by a feeling of déjà vu. He continued, "the Los Angeles office." It seemed that he already had this conversation with his father.

"I don't understand. Why exactly is it that you want to go there?" he asked, his hands in his pockets and his face red.

"I don't know. I just know I'm supposed to be there." Toshiro was looking for answers and his intuition warned him that the answers were not to be found in Tokyo.

"Nonsense. Your life is here. And what about Kaiya? You were going to marry her before the accident."

"Kaiya and I are finished."

His father stared at him in surprise. "Sit down, son. Let's talk this through."

"Whatever you want to say, I can hear you just fine standing," he responded with tightened lips, his anger boiling inside him.

"Fine. Please explain to me exactly why the two of you broke up," his father said, hoping that he could help mend their relationship. He wanted his son in Tokyo, beside him, married to a nice Japanese girl from a good family.

"There's nothing to explain. I don't love her, and she doesn't love me," he replied, clearly frustrated. He hated the fact that his father was so pushy and tried so hard to take over his life.

"What does love have to do with anything? What about duty and honor? Your mother and I and Kaiya's parents have been expecting the union between our families for some time, and if it weren't for the accident, the two of you would have been married by now."

"I don't care what is expected of me. I almost died, or don't you remember?"

"Don't you dare ask me if I remember." Riku wagged his index finger at him. "Your mother and I went through hell watching you. Waiting for you to wake up. Wondering if you ever be able to have a normal life. You are all we have."

"This life, this life that I've been living for the past few months is not me. It feels like I'm living someone else's life."

"Give it time. It's only been four months," he advised him with a gentler voice.

"'It's only been a month,' everyone said, and so I waited. 'It's only been three months,' you all said, and I waited. And now you're telling me it's only been four months. How much longer? Six months? A year? Two years? I'm not happy."

"Your mother and I, we need you. Hang in there a little longer," his father pleaded.

"I have waited long enough. We can always talk on the phone. And maybe once I have settled, you and Mom can come for a visit."

"You cannot do this. I will not allow it," he said forcefully, pushing to change his mind.

"Well then, I'm leaving with or without your approval." He knew that at some point he had said the same words to his father— he just couldn't recall when. He wondered if the accident had made him paranoid since he felt that everyone around him was lying. But why? Why would they all lie to him? No matter, he was leaving to make a new life for himself.

CHAPTER 21

Six months along, Tessa looked noticeably pregnant. Her breasts were enlarged, her feet were swollen, and her lower back hurt. She was apprehensive but overjoyed that her separation from Toshiro was nearing its end, so she took a couple of days off to get waxed and plucked. She also got a haircut, coloring, a blowout, and a mani-pedi. She purchased a pretty maternity floral-patterned wrap dress and pale pink sandals. They made her feel younger, feminine, and more attractive. She had her housekeeper clean her apartment until it was spotless. Her refrigerator, usually bare because she ate out most of the time, was stocked with food, drinks, and snacks that she thought Toshiro would like. She even bought his favorite mint chocolate patties. Tessa had her car washed and scented with citrus air freshener. She organized her schedule so that she could clear her calendar for the next few days. Fresh, multicolored tulips were arranged in a vase on her glass dining room table, and the sweet scent of orange blossoms wafted through the air. On this first day of spring when the two had promised to meet, she decided to leave her home early to make sure to get to Little Tokyo on time. On the way, she called her friend.

"How are you?" Bruna asked.

"Super-nervous. What if he doesn't show?" Tessa replied.

"He'll show. Stop worrying."

"I feel like a teenager with butterflies."

"How I envy you. I wish I had someone that special in my life."

"I'm about to pull into a parking structure and we may get cut off. You want me to call you back?"

"No, I need to wrap up my work at the office. Good luck!"

Minutes later, Tessa arrived at Japanese Village Plaza and found the Wishing Tree in front of a quaint shop that sold Japanese knickknacks. It was 4 o'clock. She looked around at the crowds, but there wasn't a trace of Toshiro. She wanted to have a look in the shop but was afraid she might miss him. Instead, Tessa started to read the messages written on colorful paper strips hanging from the tree. One person wished for a successful career, another to win a battle with cancer, and another to get a new car. Tessa looked around once more, but no Toshiro. She decided to keep waiting, and questions filled her head: Maybe his flight had arrived late? Maybe he was stuck in traffic? But as time passed, the temperature cooled, the crowds dispersed, and the sun began to set, she realized that he was not going to show up. At 6 in the evening, Tessa tried to comfort herself by purchasing a cup of hot herbal tea. Weak from worry, she sat on a nearby bench and nursed her drink.

She called Bruna, but there was no answer. She called both her parents, but no one picked up. She had told everyone close to her about her rendezvous with Toshiro. Tessa tried contacting a few more friends, but all she got was voicemails. It was chilly. She put on her sweater. A child licking a strawberry ice-cream cone sat down near her on the bench. A performer sang in various languages as patrons passed by and put money in his basket. The smell of baked goods from the corner bakery lingered in the air, and Tessa started to feel hungry. Tired, cold, and disappointed, she went into nearby Café Dolce to order take out. Inside, she could see the Wishing Tree. And again, no sign of Toshiro. She wrote a note on a strip of paper: "I hope that someday soon my broken heart will heal, and I will be happy again." She walked to the tree, tied her wish to a branch, and returned to the café. Her cellphone rang and she searched through her purse frantically, thinking that it was Toshiro calling to explain why he had not shown up.

"Mom!"

"Is everything okay? Sorry. I was in the shower when you had called and your father is in Santa Monica showing a house to a client. He forgot to take his phone with him."

"I'm fine, just waiting for my takeout."

"I thought you were having dinner with Toshiro."

"He, um, he never showed up," she said with a lump in her throat.

"I'm coming there right now," her mother insisted.

"No, I'm getting dinner and leaving. I want to go home and sleep."

"You shouldn't do that. You'll get stuck in terrible traffic and, in your condition, that's not smart."

"I just want to go home and forget about this day. He has probably forgotten all about me," she said, sounding shaken.

"You don't know that. Maybe something happened."

"No, I don't think so. I'm tired, cranky, and hungry," she said. Someone behind the counter called her name to let her know that her order was ready.

"It'll take you more than an hour in bumper-to-bumper traffic to get home. The Westin Bonaventure is near you. Why don't you spend the night there?" Carol suggested.

"Stay at a hotel?"

"Yes, it's better than sitting in traffic."

She contemplated it for a moment. It actually wasn't a bad idea. "You know, I think I'll do that. Thanks, Mom."

Tessa was in no mood to deal with heavy freeway congestion just to return to an empty apartment. Hating everything about her life and suffering from deep loneliness, she couldn't face the reality that she may never see Toshiro again and all that she had experienced with him was nothing but a big lie. Could one person have such a negative effect on her and push her into depression? No, she would not allow anyone to drive her over the edge. Tessa decided to pretend that she was on vacation and life was great.

At the Bonaventure, Tessa's room was quite comfortable except that with her expanding belly, she could not find a comfortable position when she lay down. But her bed had clean sheets and fluffy pillows, and the TV offered numerous channels. It was much better than sitting in traffic. At midnight she fell asleep sitting up in bed, watching television. The next time she opened her eyes, it was two in the morning and she had to use the bathroom. Tessa checked her phone. Bruna had called her five times. She texted Bruna to tell her where she was and asked if she wanted to play hooky and meet her for breakfast. Bruna, who had been worried sick about her, read the text and responded right away to let her know that she would meet her at ten.

Breakfast was served in the hotel's lovely lobby. Although the buffet was extensive, Tessa just had a cup of herbal tea. But Bruna brought them both a plate of eggs, fruit, and cheese.

"You have to eat. This is not just about you. Your babies need nourishment," Bruna said pushing a plate toward Tessa.

"I know, but I don't think that they're hungry either," Tessa said, brushing off a loose hair from her floral dress, wishing that she had a change of clothes. Even though she showered in the morning, she still felt grimy.

"Don't do that. Don't get stressed over Toshiro. Maybe something happened. You don't know. Why don't you call him?"

"No. We made a promise. He made his choice, and now I need to make mine. I was stupid to think that he actually loved me. He probably forgot all about meeting me. He's probably with Kaiya as we speak," she said, feeling the twins kick inside of her. She looked down at her belly. "Hey! You should be kicking your daddy instead of me."

"They kicked? I want to feel them."

"Don't encourage them."

"They're probably hungry, wondering why they're not being fed," Bruna said, eating a wedge of Brie. "Give yourself time before you make any decisions, and please eat something. I'm worried about you. You have dark circles under your eyes and you look pale."

"My mind is made up. We are done. I don't ever want to see him again," she said before angrily sticking her fork into a slice of honeydew. Maybe she never loved him. He had wormed his way into her life and she was mad at herself for allowing it. But she wasn't such a bad judge of character. No, he wasn't a deceitful person. There was so much goodness in him and that was precisely why she had fallen in love with him.

"It'll be difficult to raise the twins all by yourself. How is the house hunting?"

"My dad helped me find something that I like in West L.A."

"Where?"

"Culver City. I was waiting for Toshiro, but now, I'm just going to make an offer on it." Tessa could have bought a place somewhere posh because her parents had money, but she did not want to ask them for a handout. She planned to use some of her savings for a down payment on the house and mortgage the rest.

"What about work? Who is going to take care of the twins?"

"I get three months of maternity leave. My mom has offered to help out during the week," she said, trying her eggs. She started to feel better as she took control of her future.

"You'll be exhausted. Staying up all night, feeding them, getting them ready in the morning, going to work, and repeating. I mean, I'll help out whenever I can, but I'm not sure if that's enough."

"Thank you, but I'm going to look for a part-time nanny. And anyway, I should keep busy. I don't want to think about Toshiro anymore."

"Seems like you have it all worked out."

"No, not really, but I'm not going to worry about it right now," she said, feeling so overwhelmed and scared that she wanted to cry.

"I'm sorry that he ghosted you."

"You know, I waited for him for more than two hours," she said, angry at herself for having faith in him.

Tessa's feelings for Toshiro were complicated and changed depending on her mood. One minute she thought that she was in love with him and the next she thought he was too young for her. She was confident in all other areas of her life, but not when it came to intimate relationships. Her husband had done a real number on her when he dumped her, and now she had trust issues.

Bruna noticed the tears welling up in Tessa's eyes and handed her a tissue. "Forget about him. You'll meet a good guy. You'll see."

"I don't need anyone. I'm happy on my own. I didn't need him then and I don't need him now," she said, wiping her eyes. "I'll get over him."

During the next few weeks, whenever her cellphone rang, Tessa's heart skipped a beat, thinking that it was Toshiro calling to explain why he had stood her up. What would be his excuse? That he couldn't get away from work? That he had some kind of an emergency? The evening at the Wishing Tree kept replaying in her mind as she looked at the wallet-size photo of the two of them taken at *purikura*. Why had he ditched her? Kaiya. That was it. She never had a chance against a beautiful young Japanese girl who was better suited for Toshiro. Tessa was *gaijin*; Kaiya was loved by Toshiro's parents. She reflected on their time together and the promise they made to each other. She had kept her word, but Toshiro had not.

A month later, she was still wondering if her feelings of sadness would ever go away. *Will I ever stop missing him?* Tessa thought as she waited for Bruna to pick her up. They had planned to drive to Newport Beach, about forty miles south of Los Angeles in Orange County, to distribute materials for The Dolphin and Whale Guardians. She rubbed her belly. What if the twins looked just like Toshiro? She would be reminded of him every single day of her life. No, she needed to move on. She would continue with her work and her activism and make a life for herself and her children.

Once in Newport, Tessa and Bruna set up a table at the outdoor Irvine Farmers Market. They were both wearing jeans and pink T-shirts with a picture of a baby dolphin. The caption read: "They killed my mom and my family."

As Sunday shoppers passed their table, some slowed down to glance at the materials, others asked questions and picked up pamphlets, and a few purchased T-shirts emblazoned with "Save the dolphins and whales." Their best customer was a TV news journalist in his late 40s with blue eyes and medium brown hair with traces of gray. He introduced himself as Ben and told the women that he traveled all over the world to report news stories. Ben purchased twenty T-shirts to pass out to his friends, family, and coworkers. Tessa was ecstatic as she shared her trip to Taiji, her experiences with the authorities, and her deep interest in helping these voiceless mammals. Ben said that he was going to convince the AGA TV station where he worked to set up an interview with Tessa and took her number.

"He liked you," Bruna told Tessa after Ben walked away.

"What? No. His interest was purely in saving the dolphins," she said, touching her belly to remind herself of the twins.

"Say what you will, but he was a hunk. Hubba-hubba."

"Stop it. I'm pregnant. No man would want me," she said, thinking again about Toshiro ghosting her. She was still in love with him, or was she? She was mad at herself for waiting for him all this time without even considering dating someone else. She was disappointed that she had gone to the trouble of making everything perfect to please him. She was upset that each time her phone rang, her heart pitter-pattered, and she rushed to pick it up. But did these emotions signify love? How could she love someone that she had known for such a short time? Maybe she was just in love with the idea of him, having a home and family, and going on excursions.

"Are you crazy? A man would be a fool not to want you. Trust me, you have the whole package—looks, kindness, principles, and a great career."

"Well then, I'm sure glad you're here. I need you for my self-confidence. I woke up this morning feeling like shit, but you make me feel like a million dollars." Tessa was happy to be there, standing up for a good cause and keeping busy at the same time. At home and during work, she drove herself crazy thinking about Toshiro's love for her and if it had ever been real.

"Stick with me, and I will help you forget about all your troubles."

"In that case, I'm now absolutely determined to sell every single one of these shirts. Our cause will prevail," Tessa said, flagging down a passerby. "Hi. We're trying to raise money to protect dolphins and whales. Would you be interested in learning more?

So as the day continued, the two of them were able to sell half of their inventory. They did much better than the other activists who had tried to sell the same shirts the previous week.

CHAPTER 22

After his last conversation with his father, Toshiro decided to embark on a new life. Just like before the accident, he wrapped up projects at work, but this time he had no intention of returning to the Tokyo office. He put all his personal belongings in storage. Toshiro wasn't sure where he would end up, but there was one thing of which he was certain: He didn't want to live near his parents. He loved them very much, but it was time for him to spread his wings and fly away from the nest. Since his parents owned the house he lived in, he told them to sell it. When Souji asked Toshiro how he would feel if he dated Kaiya, Toshiro gave him his stamp of approval. Not only did this close a chapter of his past, but it also made his father realize that there was zero chance of Toshiro marrying Kaiya.

Afraid to lose his son for good, Riku Yokoyama came to terms with Toshiro's departure and arranged for him to work at the L.A. office. QZMZ paid for Toshiro's relocation and leased him a contemporary, furnished apartment in a downtown high rise, a short drive from the company's new U.S. headquarters.

Toshiro was given a company car, a black BMW, which he used to oversee six newly opened retail stores in Los Angeles County—three in the suburbs and three in the urban areas. As a general manager, he no longer could delegate most of his work as he used to. Since all the stores were new, he had to put in long hours until the employees felt comfortable with their responsibilities. Toshiro had changed since Tessa had first met him eight months ago. He was more responsible and preferred to occupy his time with work. There were plans to open up more retail spaces in Northern California, Seattle, and on the East Coast if the L.A. stores were successful. Toshiro was aiming to become the chief operating officer for U.S. operations.

In addition to his regular workload, Toshiro now had to study the competition by visiting other retailers to see what items they carried, what was popular with local customers, and if the QZMZ factory in Tokyo could affordably make goods to suit the brand. To keep up with trends, he visited the wholesale showrooms in the L.A. Fashion District. He was also in charge of a staff of seven— an accountant, merchandising supervisor, media manager, human resources director, executive assistant, administrative assistant, and shipping and receiving controller overseeing the downtown warehouse.

Toshiro started work the day after his arrival and immediately had to deal with the shipping and receiving manager to assess why the Santa Monica store hadn't yet received the requested viscose dresses and the cotton shirts. His executive secretary scheduled three candidates for him to interview for the job of office manager. The media manager wanted to know if Toshiro was interested in doing a magazine interview. He also had to review the profit and loss statements from all the stores.

The Yokoyamas were concerned for Toshiro, not only because he had a lot of work responsibilities but also because he might run into Tessa. They had family members who lived in Irvine, and they instructed them to introduce any suitable Japanese girls they might know to their son. And introduce, they did. A week after Toshiro's arrival, he started to date a 27-year-old Japanese-American girl named Piper, a lawyer at a prestigious firm in downtown Los Angeles. Unfortunately, Toshiro's nightmares and flashbacks were becoming more frequent. On top of that, there were references to dolphins everywhere he turned.

The first time it happened was on his first coffee date with Piper. A subscribed member of The Pacific Marine Mammal Center, which rescued suffering seals and sea lions, Piper was wearing a T-shirt that said: "Save the Dolphins and Orcas." When Toshiro asked her about it, she told him that she bought it at a booth in front of the Irvine Farmers Market. The second time he was reminded of dolphins was when he opened his forwarded mail and found a red flyer informing him of an upcoming protest in Tokyo. The third time was when he was seated at the ocean-side Duke's Malibu restaurant with his cousin, Ken. From their table, they could see a pod of dolphins jumping up high and dipping back into the water.

"Poke taco for you," the waiter said, placing a plate in front of Toshiro.

"Wow! Look. Did you see that?" exclaimed Ken, a Japanese-American with bleached blond hair, clearly enjoying the dolphins.

"Oh, we see them all the time," said the waiter, who looked like an aging beach bum. "It's so nice to watch them have fun here in their natural environment."

"True. They're free here," Ken said.

A man in a red baseball cap having lunch with his wife and two children overheard their conversation from a nearby table and inserted, "In search of that one perfect dolphin, a lot of them are slaughtered brutally, you know,"

"But why?" Ken asked, wondering who would do such a thing.

"Oh, some fishermen consider them pests because they eat all the fish, others kill them to eat them, and many are looking for show-quality dolphins."

"Really?"

"Oh, yeah. A show-quality dolphin can sell for about $100,000 to $300,000."

"I did not know this," Ken frowned.

"Yep. That's the way of the world. It all comes down to money."

Toshiro knew he had heard this before. Somewhere. But where? From someone. But who? He wondered why he kept encountering references to dolphins. What was their significance? He had no idea, but he wanted the dolphin images in his head to just go away and leave him alone. He wanted his nightmares to end. He wanted to stop seeing a faceless American girl in his dreams.

A couple of days later, Toshiro was in an outdoor courtyard lined with eateries in the downtown L.A. Financial District where many local workers met for casual lunches. It had been more than eight months since he had last seen Tessa and still, he had no memory of her. A variety of songs reflecting L.A.'s varied heritage and history—Mexican, surf music, Cuban, West Coast rap—played on the speakers. A majority of the men and women were dressed like executives—suits, ties, pantsuits, and conservative dresses, because they worked in finance, business corporations, politics, or law.

Toshiro was seated at an outdoor table with Piper, who worked nearby, and four of his coworkers. He was almost finished with his roast beef sandwich when he noticed an attractive woman seated a few tables away. Wearing a sunflower-yellow dress, she had dark blond hair, big gray eyes, and rosy lips. *What a beautiful woman*, he thought. His heart seemed to stand still and his eyes were glued on her when Piper nudged him and said, "Someone you know?"

He didn't hear her as he kept staring at Tessa, who was in the company of a handsome, broad-shouldered man with a full head of wavy blond hair.

Tessa was shocked. She stared right back at Toshiro. What was he doing here? Did he work there? Tessa was with her good friend Nick, whom she had met a few years back at a kickboxing class. He thought he could cheer her up over a pleasant lunch, but seeing Toshiro ended all that.

Tessa was not surprised to see him with a pretty Japanese girl. She knew from the first moment she saw him that he was a player. *I will not go to him*, she told herself. *If he wants to talk to me, he needs to come to me.* Yet at the same time, she didn't want him to approach her. It was over. He didn't even have the courtesy to call her and say that he didn't love her anymore. Not even a text to tell her that he had changed his mind. But then she remembered their agreement: "If one of us doesn't show, we don't need to call each other and explain. We will just part ways." But why did it hurt so much? Why did she expect so much more?

"Something wrong?" Nick asked Tessa when he noticed her staring out. Nick was also Tessa's new tenant. When Toshiro didn't show up on that fateful spring day, Tessa decided to make some changes in her life. She went ahead and purchased a three-bedroom house in Culver City, about seven miles south of Santa

Monica where she used to live. To help with the mortgage payments, she rented out one of the rooms to Nick.

Her friend repeated his question, but Tessa did not hear him. It was as though she and Toshiro were locked together, their energies completely in sync, and yet neither one was willing to get up to approach the other and say, "Hello. How the hell have you been?"

Enrique Iglesias' song "Nunca te Olvidaré"—which means "I will never forget you"— played over the speakers, but neither of them understood the Spanish lyrics and the irony of it all:

Three thousand years can go by, you can kiss other lips, but I will never forget you

They can erase my memory, they can rob me of your story, but I will never forget you

How to forget that I prayed, so that you don't leave, how to forget your craziness

how to forget that I still love you.

"Toshiro, we're leaving. Are you coming?" Piper asked when she noticed that he was just sitting there, staring at a stranger when everyone else was standing up and getting ready to return to work.

"I'm sorry, what?" he asked when Tessa broke her stare and looked away.

Tessa's eyes were moist, but she did not want to shed a single tear over a guy who had made a promise and abandoned her. What a terrible person he was. Whatever the reason he was in L.A., he hadn't even bothered to look her up just to say hi. How she had misjudged his feelings for her. The awful thing was that she still loved him. That day at the Irvine Farmers Market, she had convinced herself that what she felt for him was not real love because she had known him for such a short time. But today, right then and there, she saw that she was wrong. Logic dictated that she shouldn't be in love with him, but her heart betrayed her.

"Your friends are going back to the office, and I have a client in twenty minutes," Piper said, glancing at her watch and then at the woman in the yellow dress who captivated Toshiro's attention. Who was she? An ex-girlfriend, perhaps?

"You guys go ahead. I'm going to go get a cup of coffee," he said, his heart wanting to jump out of his body. For the first time since the accident, he felt alive. He couldn't explain the feelings churning inside him for this stranger. Who was she with? A boyfriend? Her husband?

"I'll go with you," Piper said, curious as to why he was behaving so peculiarly.

"I'll be fine. I'll see you tonight, yes?"

She hesitated before saying, "Okay." Things were still new between them, and she didn't want to come across as too demanding.

Toshiro picked up his trash and decided to deposit it in a trash can near the woman's table so that he could get a closer look. She looked so familiar. It was as though he had known her for years. Who was she? Why was he so drawn to her? And as he came closer, he realized that she was pregnant.

Tessa felt goosebumps all over as she stared back at him, wondering why he was acting so weird. It was as though he did not know her, had never kissed her, had never made love to her, and had never made a promise to her.

He mustered the courage to approach her. "I'm sorry, have we met before?" he asked. He was filled with affection for a woman he did not recognize.

Tessa was so mad that even in her late pregnant state she could quickly push herself up and slap him. But she refrained. What kind of game was he playing? "You're kidding, right?"

"So we have? Met, that is?" he asked, nervously.

Alright, so this is how the game is played, Tessa thought. "No, we have never met. Should we have?"

"I'm sorry. Excuse me," he gave her a slight bow and left.

She watched him walk away and couldn't believe her eyes. He didn't even have the decency to say hello or show any sign of recognition or remorse. After all this time. Her eyes began to sting.

Nick noticed Tessa's red eyes and asked, "Who was he?"

"No one important," she said, feeling a kick from one of the twins.

"He was obviously important. I saw the way the two of you were staring at each other," he said with concern. He was worried about her. Her face was pale and she looked like she was about to pass out.

"Drop it, okay? I don't want to talk about it," she replied, rubbing her belly.

Nick nodded. "Have some water." He pushed a bottle toward her. He didn't want to upset her more than she was. He didn't want to stress a pregnant woman who was due very soon. He knew that Tessa would tell him when she was ready.

Back at the office, Toshiro couldn't concentrate. Once again, he felt a deep hole in his heart. He had a terrible migraine and bits and pieces of his memory were coming back: Tokyo. Protests. Dolphin signs. Blood. Holding hands. Kamo River. Kyoto. Osaka hotel. Holding somebody.

Who was she? A dream? An ex-girlfriend? For some reason, he felt tremendous affection for her. He called Souji, forgetting that he was probably sound asleep in Tokyo. It was 1:30 p.m. on a Friday in Los Angeles, which meant that it was 5:30 a.m. on

Saturday in Tokyo. Souji didn't answer. Toshiro redialed again and again.

A groggy voice on the other side of the world finally responded, "You better be dying if you're calling me at this hour." He was in bed with Kaiya. She, too, was awakened by the ring of Souji's phone.

"Sorry." Toshiro winced. "What time is it now?"

"Never mind that. What do you want?"

"I feel as though the people around me haven't been honest with me."

"Why would you say that?" Souji asked, now more awake and uncomfortable as he sat up.

Kaiya whispered to him, "Who is it?" Souji whispered back, "Toshiro."

"I don't know. It's a gut feeling. Every time I ask my coworkers certain questions about Los Angeles, they change the subject."

"Hmmm," Souji replied.

"You even looked uneasy when I told you about the girl in my dream. I told you that I thought she was someone important from my past, and you said that you know nothing about her."

"And I don't." Souji bit his lips.

"Is there something that I should know? Something that you and those around me know, but are not willing to share?"

There was a long pause as Souji fell silent. What now? Toshiro was asking him directly if he knew something, and he didn't know how to answer.

"I met her."

Shit! "You met who?"

"A woman."

"Good for you," Souji responded coyly.

"You're playing games with me. Who is she?" He could tell from Souji's hesitation that he was hiding something big from him. All this time he thought that if anyone was loyal to him, it would be Souji. He trusted him, but now, he sensed that he had been deceived.

"How should I know? I don't know who you're talking about."

The phone went dead. Toshiro realized that Souji was not going to help him unless he had more to go on.

"Hello? Hello?" Souji repeated, but Toshiro was gone.

Kaiya sat up in her red nightie and said, "What did he want?"

"He ran into her."

"Who? Tessa?" A chill went down her spine. She had been fearing this day for a long time.

"Yes. He couldn't remember who she was. It's just a matter of time before he figures it out," Souji responded nervously. What now? He knew Toshiro would never stop looking for answers. Wearing only his underwear, he grabbed a packet of Winston Gold cigarettes from the nightstand and lit one up.

"You should tell him the truth," Kaiya suggested, taking the cigarette away from his fingers and putting it out in an ashtray. "Stop smoking every time something goes wrong. This isn't going to solve our dilemma."

"Are you crazy? He would never forgive me."

"If he finds out, and knowing Toshiro he will, he will never speak to either of us again. But if we're forthcoming, he may be more forgiving."

"No."

"Come on," she said, straddling him, putting her hands on his shoulders, and shaking him. "He has the right to be happy. We're happy. Don't you want that for him? He's your best friend."

Souji released himself from her grip and sat at the edge of the bed. He dropped his head and put his hands through his messy hair. "Let me think. Let me think."

Kaiya pushed back the blankets and went to use the bathroom. She could no longer sleep.

"This is all my fault. I should've never dared him to kiss her that day," he said, getting up and grabbing another cigarette.

"Don't you dare!" Kaiya yelled, staring at the cigarette in his hand when she stepped out of the bathroom. "It is all your fault, but if you hadn't done that, you and I would have never gotten together."

Souji smiled, got rid of the cigarette, pinned her against the wall, and kissed her.

Toshiro started scrolling through his contact list on his cellphone to see if he could find a name he did not recognize. He had no idea that he knew so many people. What with his Japanese, American, French, Australian, and British contacts, he had been quite busy. He remembered most of the names on his phone, and for the ones he didn't, he checked the note section where he wrote details upon meeting someone for the first time. He scrolled and scrolled until he got to the Zs and saw a name he did not recognize—Zekuu. He looked at the note section of his phone and couldn't find a single thing about this person. The area code and the number of digits indicated that the person's phone number was from the business district of Shinjuku.

Toshiro waited until it was 9 a.m. in Tokyo. He had to get to the bottom of this and was in no mood to go on a date that night. He worked for a couple of hours to keep busy, but his mind kept returning to Tessa. He called Piper and canceled dinner.

"Everything okay?" Piper asked, feeling jealous of the girl he had been staring at earlier.

"Yeah, sure," he said, getting up from his chair and pacing his office. "I just have a lot on my plate. It's a new office and we're all putting in long hours."

"Toshiro, if you have changed your mind about us, please be honest and tell me."

He fell into silence for a minute. Piper waited for an answer. Toshiro contemplated his situation. He wasn't himself, not when he was with Kaiya and not when he was with Piper. He needed to take a step back and be patient with himself until he could sort out the chunk of memory that had gone missing. "You remember what I told you about the accident and my memory?"

"Yes."

"I'm not doing so well, and it's not fair to you for us to continue dating. I thought I was ready to date again, but I'm not. I am sorry."

Piper was sad—she really liked him. But she also wanted to be with someone who would be there for her. "Maybe when you figure things out and get better, we can start over if I'm available."

"Thank you for understanding. Bye." A feeling of sudden relief came over Toshiro. He didn't want to make an empty promise and say sure, maybe we'll start over. He liked Piper and didn't want to lead her on. Maybe he was making a mistake by breaking up with her and maybe he wasn't. But being with her just didn't feel right, at least not at that point in his life when he was struggling so hard with finding out who he was.

He sat down in the white leather chair of his office and called Zekuu. By now, it was 5 p.m. in Los Angeles, which meant that it was 9 a.m. in Tokyo—a decent time to call someone.

"Hi, this is Toshiro Yokoyama. Am I speaking to Zekuu?"

"Hi Toshiro, how are you?" Dressed in an expensive gray suit, Zekku was seated in his office on the 32nd floor of an all-glass tower.

Toshiro got right to the point. "I found your phone number in my phone and I'm not quite sure how we know each other."

"Don't you remember?"

"Unfortunately, no. I was in a bad car accident about five months ago and lost some of my memory. I'm trying to figure out who some of the people are in my contact list."

"Sorry to hear that, but I have been sworn to secrecy by Toshiro Yokoyama. How can I be sure this is really you?"

"Do you know which company I work for?"

"Yes."

"Call them and talk to anyone. They will put you in touch with me."

"I will do that. You will hear back from me soon," he said. He hung up and looked up Toshiro's file on his computer. Zekku worked for a large firm whose motto was to digitize as much as possible. All documents were scanned into the company system and could be retrieved with a flick of the finger.

Five minutes later, Toshiro's office phone rang. It was Zekuu.

"It really is you. I apologize for all the secrecy, but you had insisted that I talk to no one about our deal."

"What deal? As I said, I don't remember many things."

"I am a lawyer. About seven months ago, you contacted me. You wanted to make two anonymous donations, one to Ms. Akira Nakano and one to Ms. Tessa Walker."

Akira Nakano. Tessa. Tessa Walker. What is your last name? What is yours? A newspaper photo. Dolphins. Singing. Otanjoubi omedetou, otanjoubi omedetou. *Happy birthday.*

"Hello? Toshiro? Can you hear me?"

"I, I, I'm sorry. I was having flashbacks," answered Toshiro. "Please, just bear with me. This is a difficult time."

"I can just imagine. Maybe I can be of some help?"

"Please tell me everything that we discussed."

Zekuu then told him about Akira and Tessa, their activism, the anonymous donations Toshiro had made, and how they were delivered.

"Do you know what they looked like?"

"I met Akira here in Tokyo. She has black hair with red highlights and bangs, nicely dressed, friendly, in her late 20s."

Toshiro tried hard to remember her, but nothing came to mind. "And Tessa?"

"I never met her in person. At the time, she lived in Los Angeles and I had someone in California deliver the donation to her."

"May I have the number of the person who made the delivery?"

"I can do better than that. I'll put him on a conference call. Hold on," he said and dialed Mike, a friend of his.

"Hey, dude. I'm working out on the treadmill. What's up?" Mike answered, breathing heavily.

"Mike, I have one of my clients on the line. Sorry, but I cannot give away the name. The client wants to know if you remember from seven months back the woman my client donated to for the dolphins?"

"The dolphins, the dolphins. Oh, yeah. The pretty veterinarian. Dark blond, big gray eyes, great figure."

"Thanks, Mike. Go finish your workout. I'll call you later and we'll catch up."

"Later, dude," he said.

"Do you recall anything else?" Toshiro asked Zekuu.

"That's all I know. You never explained what your involvement was with them."

"Thank you."

"I'll call you if I remember anything else."

"If you could get a phone number or an address on her, I'd appreciate it."

"Hang on. Let me have a look at her file," he said, scrolling through the notes on his laptop. "Ah, here it is. She works at Charles Avery Homeopathic Pet Hospital." He then gave Toshiro the address and the phone number.

"What about Akira Nakano? May I have her information as well?"

"Of course," Zekuu said.

Toshiro grabbed a bottle of water from his desk and collapsed on the leather sofa. Why the lies? Why had no one, not even his parents, told him anything? Why was there no trace of Tessa or Akira anywhere, not on his phone, in his house, or in his office? He called Akira and reached her voicemail:

"Hi. You have reached Akira Nakano. I'm away at a silent retreat in Tibet and cannot be reached. I will be back on June 7."

Her voicemail wasn't accepting any messages. It didn't matter anyway because he wasn't about to wait for two more weeks to find out the truth.

He called Kaiya.

Sitting at a café, Kaiya stared at her ringing cellphone. It was Toshiro, and she did not want to answer. Dread fell over her and she tried to calm herself before picking up. "This is a surprise," she said, when in fact she was not surprised at all. After overhearing Souji's phone call with Toshiro, she knew that he would not let this go. *Souji is lucky that he's at work and doesn't have to deal with this*, Kaiya thought.

"Who is Tessa?"

"I don't know," she mumbled.

"So, you never knew or met anyone named Tessa?" he shrugged, his face showing an expression of distaste as the corners of his mouth drooped.

"Stop it, you're confusing me," she said.

"I am confusing *you*?"

"Yes. Stop asking me questions I cannot answer." He could hear the deception in her voice from the way she stammered and her evasion.

He took in a deep breath and let it out. "Okay, let me ask you a different question. Were we ever engaged or was it all a lie?" He didn't want to ask politely. She didn't deserve courtesy and neither did Souji after deliberately misleading him.

Kaiya stopped breathing for a moment, closed her eyes, and tensed up. Her black silky hair was in a ponytail, but she was feeling a headache coming on, so she removed the band and let her hair fall. *This isn't happening*, she thought. *This is not my fault.*

"Are you there? Did you hear me?" Toshiro insisted.

"Yes, I heard you. What kind of a question is that?"

"Kaiya, I know you're not being honest with me. I can hear it in your voice. So, cut the crap and spit it out."

She rubbed her temples to relieve the pressure in her head. "What do you want from me, Toshiro?"

"The truth! That's all I ask for. Did you love me or were you just pretending for the sake of our parents?"

A lump formed in her throat and her voice shook. "Yes, I loved you. I loved you for a very long time, but you never loved me. It was always her, never me."

"Always who? Tell me, goddamn it."

"Tessa! Tessa! Tessa! We were happy, you and I, and then she came into our lives and ruined everything."

Toshiro felt cold and clammy. Was this real? Had his life since the accident been a lie? "I don't remember a whole lot. Just bits and pieces that are coming to me. Please? Explain to me how my life was before the accident."

Kaiya spilled everything about how he had met Tessa and how Kaiya had broken it off with him because of her. She told him about the accident and the request from his father.

"What else? What else happened? How did I get so close to her?"

"I don't know. We weren't talking at the time. Souji knows a lot more than I do. You should ask him."

"I've been betrayed by all of you," he shouted.

"If anything, you should be angry with your father. We had nothing to do with it. This was his idea," she said, wishing that she had refused Riku Yokoyama.

"But you all went along with it, didn't you?"

"I am so, so very sorry," was all that she could offer before he hung up.

Toshiro decided then and there that he would never speak to his father again. How could he do this to him? How could he ruin his life just to please himself? He had no right. Toshiro felt robbed of the past eight months of memories. He thought about the other day when he had seen Tessa, pregnant and with another man. Was the baby his or the other man's? Nothing made sense. He looked outside. It was dark now. A coworker knocked on his door.

Toshiro straightened himself up and went to his desk. He opened up a folder so that it would look like he had been working and answered, "Yes?"

It was Robert from accounting. "We're all going out for drinks after work. Would you like to join us?"

"Is it 8 already?" Although American corporations typically closed at 5 or 6 p.m., QZMZ was a Japanese company and, just like in Japan, the employees worked long hours.

"No, 6:30. I can get you when it's 8," Robert said, noticing his dark aura and thinking that Toshiro could sure use a drink.

"Thanks, but I'm good. I think I'll just stay here and finish up."

"If you change your mind, let me know."

"I will," Toshiro said, wishing that Robert would just go away. The last thing he wanted was to hang around a bunch of drunk office workers.

"If I don't hear from you, I'll see you at the 9 a.m. meeting tomorrow."

"Yes." *Now please shoo*, he wanted to say.

Once Robert left, Toshiro called Souji. He was at work, seated in a cubicle crammed with a computer, a framed photo of him with Kaiya, a hanging magnetic whiteboard, and piles of paperwork.

"We need to talk," Toshiro blurted before his friend even had a chance to say hello when he picked up.

"I'm at work. Can we do this later?" he murmured.

"We do this now," Toshiro pushed in a forceful voice that shook Souji.

"Okay. Let me call you back," Souji said reluctantly. "I can't talk here. Everyone will hear me." He passed a series of cubicles and offices, took the elevator down, and went outside.

Kaiya had warned him by text, so Souji already knew what Toshiro wanted. But before he could get a word in, Toshiro had already started the conversation.

"I spoke with Kaiya. Imagine my surprise when I found out that you all lied to me. I thought we were best friends. I thought we would never lie to each other. How could you agree to this? Help me understand," he said, leaning forward in his chair, waiting impatiently for Souji to answer.

"Your father is a difficult man to say no to. He has many connections. He could have made life very difficult for all of us," Souji explained, as he paced back and forth, biting a hangnail on his thumb. Oh, he could sure use a cigarette right then, but Kaiya made him promise to smoke no more than two cigarettes per day, and he had already smoked three. He rubbed the nicotine patch on his arm.

He reprimanded Souji. "You could've come to me. I would've helped you out."

"I made a mistake, okay? It happened so fast. We were all in shock about what had happened to you. We wanted to do all that we could to help your distraught parents. You weren't there. You weren't in our situation."

"I would have never done that to you," he said, tensing up. He wanted to punch someone.

"We weren't in the right frame of mind. We all blamed Tessa for the accident," he answered, sticking his hand in his shirt pocket, looking for his cigarettes. He found them, but his lighter was at his desk.

"Tessa?"

"Yes, Tessa. You were on your way to the airport to go to Los Angeles on the day of the accident. You were determined to leave that day."

"Yeah, Kaiya told me about the accident, but Tessa had nothing to do with it." His head throbbed and he frantically searched his desk for a bottle of aspirin. No luck. He had taken the last two earlier in the day.

Souji explained how much Toshiro had been missing Tessa and the promise they had made to each other.

"No wonder she was so angry at me when I talked to her. Tell me, how did we get so close so quickly?"

Souji told him everything about how he had dared Toshiro to kiss Tessa, about her activism, his participation in a protest, Kyoto and Osaka, spending the night together, and the fact that he wanted to spend the rest of his life with her.

"She is pregnant, you know," he blurted.

"I did not know that. I swear."

"Is it mine, you think? She was with this guy when I saw her."

"There's only one way to find out. Ask her."

"What she must think of me. She probably hates me."

"She may have met the guy you saw shortly after returning home, which would mean that she never waited for you by the tree. I don't know. I don't have all the answers. You need to talk to her and find out the truth," Souji said. But as soon as he said it, he regretted it. Toshiro and Tessa loved each other and no one could come between them. Souji decided to mail Toshiro an important piece of the puzzle missing from his memory.

"I also seem to have known someone named Akira Nakano. Who was she?"

"She was an activist friend of Tessa's. That's all I know. Sorry."

"I have to go."

"Go, but one day we need to sit together and clear the air between us. I love you, man. We've known each other since second grade."

"I need time to forgive you, Kaiya, and all of my friends, and I'm not sure if I could ever forgive my parents. Bye," he said.

He felt dizzy. He walked over to the sofa to lie down again. It had been one very long day. He shut his eyes and fell asleep from exhaustion. *They were together, in bed, making love. I want to come to L.A and live with you. Wait six months and see if that's what you really want. I will be there. I promise. Fighting with his father. Rain. The accident. The hospital.* It all jumped from scene to scene, like film snippets out of sequence.

CHAPTER 23

The buzz from the office phone jolted him awake. The sunlight streaming through the window onto his face felt unpleasant. Toshiro's head throbbed as though someone was tapping it with a hammer. He fought the urge to go back to sleep and forced himself off the sofa. Still wearing his wrinkled suit, he walked over to his desk and answered in a groggy voice, "What time is it?"

"It is 9:10, sir. They are all waiting for you in the conference room," an assistant answered.

Ugh! The meeting! He cleared his throat a few times before he responded, "I'm not feeling well today. Please ask Robert to take over the meeting and apologize to everyone on my behalf."

Toshiro's heart ached, his memories flooded back, and he knew he needed to face Tessa. He had no idea how he was going to approach her. So much time had passed. He still had strong feelings for her, but would he feel the same about her now as he did before the accident? Would she? The woman he saw was pregnant, and if the baby belonged to another man, Toshiro had no right to cause problems between them over a two-week relationship from eight months ago. Yet he felt a deep loss like when someone close dies. He had this hole in his heart and no idea how to heal it. Zekuu had given him the name, address and phone number of the hospital where Tessa worked. She must hate him for not even recognizing her.

Tessa was still seething from her encounter with Toshiro. For the last two months, she was obsessed with thoughts about why he didn't show. *How foolish I've been*, she thought, as she waited in her modest office for her next patient—a young cat named Oreo, who, according to its owner, had been experiencing lethargy for the past week. She got up and grabbed a small bottle of homemade green apple juice from her purse. Although it was lunchtime, she was losing her appetite as memories of Toshiro and her time in Japan tumbled around in her mind. On the one hand, she was glad she went because she accomplished her goals. On the other hand, she regretted her involvement with a stranger. Yet she didn't feel as though Toshiro was a stranger. They once loved each other. She was carrying his children. Why did he say, "Excuse me, have we met before?" What kind of game was he playing? None of it made sense, but she was glad that she hadn't contacted him when she discovered that she was pregnant. He didn't deserve to know the truth.

Her thoughts lingered on their time together. "I want to come live with you," he had said. "I will be there by the wishing tree, waiting for you," he had promised. She put her elbows on her desk, rested her head in her hands, and closed her eyes.

"Are you okay?" asked Brian.

Tessa lifted her head, "I'm fine, thanks. Is Oreo here already?"

"Not yet. There is a gentleman named Toshiro at the front desk asking for you."

Tessa had trouble breathing. "Bag, bag," she pointed at her brown-paper lunch bag and Brian gave it to her. She turned it upside down and a sandwich and a bunch of vegetables fell out. She began breathing into the bag to stop herself from hyperventilating. *What is he doing here? I do not want to see him, not after the way he behaved the other day.*

Brian stood there in fear—a pregnant woman breathing into a bag was not a good sign. "I'll call 911."

She shook her head no. And after two minutes, she removed the bag from her face and said, "Tell him that I have already left for the day."

"Alright," he answered with a look of concern.

"Oh, and inform the staff to make up an excuse for me if he ever comes by again, I do not want to see him. Ever! Is that clear?"

"Sure. No problem," Brian said, walking away. In all the time he had known Tessa, he had never seen her this upset. Frankly, he thought the guy was gorgeous, and if the man wasn't straight, Brian would have been more than happy to ask him out.

To Brian's disappointing news, Toshiro responded, "Would you please tell her that I stopped by and would like to talk to her?" He gave Brian his business card and left.

When Brian gave Tessa the message and business card, she ripped up the card and dumped it in the trash. The QZMZ logo, Toshiro's name, and an office address and number were embossed on it. *So he is in L.A. for work,* she thought. *If she hadn't run into him yesterday at lunch, would he have bothered to look her up? Probably not.* Her heart pounded hard against her chest, an uneasy feeling consumed her, and she wished that he had never entered her life.

Toshiro did not hear back from Tessa though he tried on several occasions to see her, only to be turned away by some excuse or another: she was in Laguna Beach operating on a sea lion, or she was at a school teaching kids about saving aquatic life, or she was out of town at a veterinary conference. The last excuse was that Tessa was performing surgery on a dog, and when Toshiro offered to wait, a staff member told him that Tessa had a full day ahead of her and that she would get in touch with him. After four attempts and numerous phone messages, Toshiro was certain that Tessa had no intention of ever seeing him. Although the reasons the staff gave sounded truthful, he thought that the people working at the front desk might have a variety of explanations written on a piece of paper, and each time, they cited a different one. He decided that since he could not get ahold of Tessa at work, he was going to follow her home.

Tessa ignored Nick's and Bruna's advice to meet with Toshiro and find out what happened to him the day he didn't show up at the Wishing Tree as well as the day he approached her in downtown L.A. and claimed he didn't recognize her. By this time, Nick knew the entire story about Tessa and Toshiro.

"What's up with the orange wig?" Nick asked as he walked from the hallway of Tessa's home toward the kitchen.

Seated on the sofa, Tessa opened up a box of crackers and said, "Oh, I forgot I even had it on. I got it from Tokyo. I thought that putting it on would make me feel better when I'm sad." She still remembered the day she purchased it on her outing with Toshiro like it was yesterday.

"And how's that working out for you?"

"I'm still sad," she said, removing the wig.

"I think you're making a big mistake, Tessa. Talk to Toshiro," Nick said, checking on his four-bean tomato soup on the stove.

"Is it ready yet?" Tessa asked. Feeling starved, she munched on saltine crackers.

"You are ignoring what I just said."

"Yes, yes, I am. I'm tired of you, Bruna, and my parents pushing me to hear his side of the story. I don't care what he has to say." Tessa felt heavy, grumpy, bloated, and tired. She wished that the twins would push themselves out already.

"Ugh. You are so stubborn, and if you weren't pregnant, I would put you on my knee and give you a good spanking."

"Promises, promises." She rolled her eyes.

"Oh honey, trust me, if you were at all interested, I would have made my move the first day we met." To Nick's dismay, Tessa never showed an interest in him, and now he was involved with someone else.

Tessa had no idea that Toshiro was following her home. Toshiro parked his BMW several cars away from her modest, 1960s-era beige house. It was raining as he watched her pull a white Audi SUV into the garage. From the back, she still looked like the woman in his dream. He waited, going over what he was going to say: "Hi, sorry to stalk you, no—hi. I followed you because, no—hi, we really need to talk." As he rehearsed, Toshiro realized that she was already in her house, and he hadn't budged from his car. The rain stopped, and he was about to get out of his vehicle when he saw the blond curly-haired man—the same one who was with her in downtown L.A. He was pulling a brown plastic trash can out to the street before returning to the house. *They are together*, he thought. *And worse, she is carrying that man's child. No, he couldn't do it. What would be the point? She had moved on, but when? How soon after she returned home from Japan? If that was the case, then she never loved him. But it couldn't have been so.*

He remembered how disturbed she looked when she saw him downtown. Did she still have feelings for him or did his presence upset her? He got out of his car and paced back and forth on the sidewalk, walked toward her house, and then walked away. Worried that someone would spot him, he got back in his car, turned around, and drove off.

Every time Toshiro thought about approaching Tessa, he lost his resolve. Today he decided to visit Little Tokyo's Japanese Village Plaza to see the Wishing Tree where they were supposed to meet. By then, he remembered everything and cursed the rain and the accident it had caused. Bad luck, that's what it was. There had been so many obstacles in his and Tessa's path that he wondered if they were ever supposed to be together.

Wandering through the plaza, he was impressed by the number of Japanese businesses—bakeries, restaurants, little markets, clothing stores, and offices that populated the area. The signs were all written in Japanese and, though the majority of workers appeared to be Japanese, people of all nationalities were milling about. A man who looked around Toshiro's age pushed a stroller. A pregnant woman who reminded him of Tessa slurped on a strawberry boba through a fat straw. An elderly couple walking hand in hand made him wonder if he and Tessa could be just like them and grow old together.

As Toshiro approached the Wishing Tree, he stopped breathing for a moment. He needed Tessa. He needed her to be there to share the moment with him. Except that his presence was two months too late. Toshiro tried to visualize Tessa waiting for him on that first day of spring, what she wore, how she looked, how she smelled. He put his hand on the tree, tracing its bumps and irregularities with his fingers. He looked at the strips of paper hanging from the branches, red, fuchsia, neon green, bright blue, and yellow—each with a wish written on it: "I want a cute girlfriend." "I hope that my daughter will get better." "I wish that my boyfriend would propose." "I want a house by the beach." "I hope that someday soon my broken heart will heal and I will be happy again." *How many people have passed by this tree over the years? How many disappointments have there been? How many wishes were granted?* he wondered. He sat on a nearby bench, not knowing that it was the very bench where she had sat waiting for him. What should he do? He called Souji.

Souji was getting out of the shower, wrapping a white towel around his waist. It was 5 p.m. on a Saturday in Los Angeles and 9 a.m. on Sunday in Tokyo. "Hello?"

"Oh good. You're up." Toshiro said.

"As if that would stop you from calling."

"Never mind that. I have something urgent to talk to you about."

"Go ahead," he mumbled.

Toshiro explained his dilemma and all that had happened since they last spoke.

"I guess this means you have forgiven me," he said, getting dressed—he was getting ready to meet Kaiya in the park.

"What?"

"Well, you are asking for my advice," he gloated, happy that he was back in Toshiro's good graces.

"Souji, this is important to me. I'm dying here. We can talk about us another time," Toshiro said, walking away from a group of noisy tourists so that he could hear better.

"Okay, okay. What are you so afraid of? Rejection?"

"Something like that."

"Remember how the two of you met?" Souji asked.

"Yes, I walked right up to her and kissed her," Toshiro answered with a smile, recalling how he had held her and how much he had enjoyed the kiss.

"You took a big risk. And then what happened?"

"She slapped me." He remembered it like it was yesterday.

"But you didn't care. You said that it was worth it and that you would do it again," Souji reminded him.

"This is different. She could be carrying this guy's child," Toshiro frowned and walked behind a brick wall so he wouldn't be disturbed.

"Toshiro, you're not going to see her with the intention of getting back together with her, are you?" Souji answered. He glanced at his watch and texted Kaiya to let her know that he was running late.

"Well. ..."

"Well, nothing. Too much time has passed. You need closure. Find her, tell her why you didn't show up, and move on. There are plenty of other fish in the sea." Souji knew that Tessa was not just any fish in the same way that Kaiya was not just any fish. But he wanted to take the pressure off of Toshiro so that he wouldn't be so nervous. If Toshiro wouldn't take the risk, he could miss a great opportunity.

When Toshiro got home from Little Tokyo, his apartment manager handed him a special delivery package. It was from Souji. *Strange*, he thought, opening the package. Inside was an iconic robin's-egg-blue box tied with a white ribbon along with a note from Souji: "A peace offering. I thought if things go well between you and Tessa, you would want to give her this. Again, I'm so sorry. Your dad made me clean all traces of her from your apartment."

Toshiro held the blue box in his hand, and wondered if it was too late to turn things around.

CHAPTER 24

On a late Sunday morning, Toshiro showed up at Tessa's house. Her Audi was parked outside. He rang the doorbell and a minute later, Nick answered.

"Hello," Toshiro said nervously, staring at Nick, whose sleepy eyes and unruly hair made him look like he had just woken up. "I was wondering if it is possible and not too much trouble. ..."

"You're here to see Tessa," Nick interjected. If Nick had waited any longer, Toshiro would have probably back-pedaled away in his perfectly polished black shoes.

Like most Tokyoites, Toshiro usually went to great lengths to look refined. For Tessa, he wanted to look impeccable because it gave him the edge and the confidence he needed to approach her. "As a matter of fact," Toshiro straightened his silk purple tie and continued "if I'm not disturbing you..."

"Come in," Nick interrupted him again, let him inside, and pointed him toward a worn but comfortable recliner that Tessa had brought from her former apartment. "I'm Nick, by the way," he introduced himself, without adding details.

"Nice to meet you. I'm Toshiro," he said, shaking Nick's hand before sitting down.

Nick knew that there was no way in hell that Tessa would want to talk to Toshiro, so he lied when he said, "Let me go get her," and then disappeared into the hallway.

He knocked on Tessa's bedroom door and she invited him to come in. She was getting ready to attend a demonstration to defend the rights of dolphins, so she was informally dressed in a pair of sweatpants, sensible, old-lady walking shoes, and an oversize black sweatshirt. "Who was at the door?" Tessa asked Nick as she applied her mascara.

"It's Bruna."

Tessa looked at her phone. "Already? She's not supposed to be here until noon."

"I guess she's a bit early."

"I'll say. An hour early! Fine. Tell her I'll be out in a few minutes."

"Is that what you're wearing?"

"What's wrong with what I'm wearing? I'm meeting up with a group of activists. No need to wear anything fancy," she said.

"Bruna is dressed up. She looks really good."

"She does?" Tessa crinkled her nose. She loved being pregnant but hated feeling ugly and fat.

Nick started rifling through her closet and said, "Why don't you wear this pretty pink dress and these shoes that go with it?"

Tessa looked at the pink heels in his hands but was in no mood to wear them. Her feet were a little swollen. "To an activist gathering? And since when do you care about what I wear?" she asked, pushing back her hair with a brown headband.

"Bruna looks really nice. Trust me, you don't want to be underdressed, do you?"

Tessa raised one eyebrow. "What's going on? You're acting weird."

"Suit yourself if you want to look frumpy. Don't say that I didn't warn you," he said and left. He could see that Tessa was already suspicious of his behavior and didn't want to push his luck.

Meanwhile, as Toshiro waited for Nick and Tessa to appear, he looked around. The house was nothing special: plain white walls, an old fireplace dividing the eating area from the sitting area, a tiny kitchen with white-and-blue-checked tile counters, and old appliances. He could see the backyard, which was mostly cement with some shrubbery and a wooden bench around the perimeter. There were no decorative pictures on the walls—no photos of Tessa and Nick. *Couples always display at least one photo together, didn't they? So odd*, he thought when Nick returned and announced, "She'll be right out. Can I get you something to drink? Tea, soda?"

Bourbon was what he needed. "Maybe a glass of water, thank you." Toshiro checked out his competition. With his fair hair and large build, he looked very American.

Nick went to the kitchen to get Toshiro's water.

"So ..." Toshiro said, feeling uncomfortable. He stared at Nick's hands to see if there was a wedding ring but only saw what looked like a college ring with a blue stone.

"So ..." Nick mimicked him and smiled, noticing that Toshiro was studying him. Nick too was measuring up Toshiro, a Japanese guy with perfectly layered and highlighted chestnut hair flowing to the nape of his neck. His natural hair color was probably black, Nick thought. That was Tessa's taste? In that case, Nick never would have stood a chance with her.

"Have the two of you lived here long?" Toshiro asked, trying to figure out their relationship. He gulped his water.

"About a month," Nick said, noticing that Toshiro's hand was shaking as he set his glass down.

"I guess you haven't had much time to fiddle around with that yard," Toshiro added.

"We were supposed to go to Home Depot last Sunday and get a few plants, but we were both too tired. Maybe next weekend."

Toshiro nodded and went outside to survey the yard.

Nick said, "Let me see what's keeping her."

What the hell are you doing here Toshiro? They are a couple and you need to leave, he told himself.

"Bruna is getting impatient," Nick said to Tessa through the bathroom door.

"Tough! She's the one who is early. I'm not ready yet." As her pregnancy advanced, so did Tessa's mood swings. One day she cried, another day yelled at someone, and on another occasion, she laughed uncontrollably.

Nick shook his head. What could she be doing in that bathroom? Tessa always got ready quickly. "I'm leaving to go have breakfast with my girl. At some point, you have to come out and entertain her yourself."

"Nick, wait! I'll be there in a minute."

"Hurry up, then." He rolled his eyes and left to talk to Toshiro.

Toshiro was waiting at the door, getting ready to leave. The butterflies in his stomach had caught up with him and he couldn't stand it anymore. "Thank you for the water. I should have called first. I'll come back another day," he said, twisting the doorknob.

Nick decided to lie: "Please stay. She has no plans today. She said that she'll be right out."

"No, I think I should leave," Toshiro said. He felt that the collar of his white shirt was choking him.

Up until then, Nick didn't want to butt in and say anything about his relationship with Tessa or about how much Tessa loved Toshiro. But he had to do something to keep Toshiro there. "Let me put your mind at ease. Tessa and I are not a couple. I'm renting a room from her to help her pay the mortgage. And I have a breakfast date with my girlfriend, who is probably really mad right now because I'm running late."

The look of relief on Toshiro's face made Nick happy. He felt he had done the right thing.

"Thank you!"

"You're welcome. I have to go. Please stay. She is coming out," he said. As he opened the door, he saw Tessa in the hallway. She had makeup on, her hair was soft and wavy, and she was wearing the pink dress and shoes that Nick suggested. Nick smiled and closed the door behind him.

"Sorry to keep you waiting, Bruna. It was Nick's fault. He made me change," Tessa said, without looking up. She was busy sticking a pearl earring in her pierced ear, but when she looked up, her heart skipped a beat. There he was, the love of her life staring at her with his warm brown eyes. "How did you? Who told you? Wait until I get my hands on Nick. I'll kill him," she said, seething.

"I followed you home a few days ago," he admitted, admiring her from head to toe. Even in her pregnant state, she looked beautiful.

"You followed me? How? When exactly? You know, it doesn't matter," she waved him off. "You need to go."

"Not until you listen to what I have to say."

"I don't care what you have to say," she said and opened the front door, trying to usher him out.

"I owe you an explanation," he answered and gently pushed the door closed.

"You owe me nothing. I understand. You changed your mind," she told him and walked away toward the sliding glass door that led to the yard. She wanted to leave the house and get as far away from him as possible, but he followed her outside.

Toshiro looked at her angry face and didn't blame her. They were both victims of his father. With a shaky, earnest voice, he said, "I have been sleepwalking through life for the past eight months. Nothing felt right. I felt empty. There was this hole in my heart, and no matter how hard I tried to push forward, I couldn't."

She eyed him with pity. They could've had a great life together. Life was all about timing, and she believed that he had missed the opportunity for real happiness. "I can't. I can't do this," she said, tears welling up in her eyes.

"Tessa, listen."

"No," she said, turning her head away and wiping a tear as it rolled down one cheek.

"There was an accident."

She turned to face him and sniffled. "An accident?"

"Yes. After three months of separation, I couldn't take it anymore. I decided to break my promise and come see you," he said. He stared at her red eyes. He wanted to hug her and make the pain go away. "I was on my way to the airport, you see, but the driver had a heart attack while driving."

"A heart attack?"

"Yes. He lost control of the car and we had a head-on collision with an oncoming car."

Goosebumps popped up all over and her body shivered.

"He died right there. Many people were injured. I was seated in the back and my life was spared."

"Why didn't you tell me this sooner? Why didn't you call me?" She didn't understand any of it. She should have been there with him. How could he hide this from her? But then again, she had lied to him when she was jailed in Osaka because she wanted to protect him.

"I was unconscious for three days. When I woke up, I was in a hospital bed."

"No!" Tessa said as more tears flowed down her face, blurring her vision. She wanted a tissue to wipe her face, but she couldn't move.

"The neurologist told me that I had a brain injury and that there would be some temporary memory loss, you see."

"You couldn't remember anything?" She asked, thinking how horrible it must have been to lose his memory and feel empty as though he had never existed.

"At first, yes. Then things started to slowly come back to me except for the last few months before the accident. I had no memory of you."

Her body went limp and she felt awful for being so angry at him for such a long time.

"My parents told my friends not to talk about you and to pretend that you never existed, and…"

"And you could not remember me," she said, finishing his sentence. The two of them had experienced so much bad luck since the first day they met.

"Not exactly. I started having these flashes of memories. There were dreams of dolphins. And blood. So much blood. There were also dreams about you and me. I couldn't make sense of any of it. I thought they were just dreams until the day I saw you," he said with deep sadness. He regretted all the time he had lost with her. It was going to take a long time before he could forgive his parents and friends for playing with his life.

"The first time you saw me, you didn't recognize me?" she asked, recalling his bizarre behavior.

"No. I was drawn to you. You looked familiar. But I couldn't figure out why."

"That's why you behaved so strangely," she said, closing the distance between them and hugging him. She wanted to make him feel safe. She wanted to never let him go. But he moved back, cupped her face, and gave her a long passionate kiss.

They still loved each other. Nothing had changed. They had lost precious time, but no amount of space or time could destroy their connection. "I'm sorry," he said.

"No, I'm sorry for doubting you. I gave up on us, but you never did."

"I knew something was off. My dad was trying to push me to marry Kaiya, but it just didn't feel right. In my gut, I knew that I was supposed to be with you."

She grabbed his hand, both happy and nervous as she said, "There's something you should know."

"The baby you're carrying is mine," he said, as though reading her mind.

"Yes, but it's not just one baby."

"Twins?" He asked with wide eyes, thinking how this day was full of surprises.

"Yes. I don't expect you to…"

He interrupted her and said, "I told you then, and I'll tell you now. I want to be with you. I want us to be a family." He grabbed her hand, walked with her to the bench in the yard, and sat down.

Tessa took a seat next to him, and said, "Yes, you did say that. I wish I had had more faith in us. I wish I had listened to those around me and talked to you when you reached out." As she told him this, Tessa realized that while Toshiro had always been certain about wanting her, she had often hesitated, too afraid to trust him and take a chance. Never again. From that moment, she would be more trusting, understanding, and loving toward him.

She once thought that he needed to grow up, but it was she who needed to do some growing up.

Toshiro reached into his pocket and gave her the box from Tiffany's. "I know that marriage is not your thing, but what do you think about these?"

She unraveled the white ribbon, opened the box, and found two simple couples rings. They were both white gold, hers with diamonds on it, his plain.

"There is an inscription inside each ring."

She looked at the diamond one and read the inscription: "To my eternal love."

"It's perfect," she said, crying and smiling.

He slipped the diamond ring on her, and she put the white gold one on him. And just like that, they were bound to each other without a piece of paper.

Tessa studied the ring, and with misty eyes, she lifted her head and said, "I would like you to meet my parents."

"I'd like that, but I'm a bit nervous, to tell you the truth," he admitted, fidgeting with his ring. *What if they didn't like him? What if they were just like his parents and didn't care for foreigners?* He remembered how nervous Tessa was when she met his parents.

"Don't be. My parents are low-key. My mom is super-friendly, and you and my dad have something very important in common."

"Oh? What's that?"

"Well, you both drink bourbon when you get upset," she said, trying to make him more comfortable with the idea of getting together with her parents.

"Ha-ha."

"Hello, hello?" Tessa heard Bruna calling out. Apparently, Bruna had been ringing the doorbell for some time.

"Shoot! Bruna! I forgot all about her," said Tessa, heading for the door. "Do you think you would be interested in helping us set up a table to protest the slaughter of dolphins?"

Toshiro followed her. "Will there be photographers?" he said, teasingly.

"Absolutely! Cover photo!"

And for the first time, Toshiro understood Tessa and why she had risked going to jail in his home country even if she was a *gaijin*. When he was separated from her, he had been traumatized the same way the dolphins were traumatized when they were taken away from their loved ones. When in captivity, they whistled in distress, hoping to hear their compatriots whistle back. During Toshiro's recovery, he was trapped by his brain's inability to function properly. Without the support of friends and family, dolphins get lonesome and depressed. Without Tessa, Toshiro was empty. Toshiro's separation from Tessa reinforced everything she taught him: dolphins are very much like humans.

"Hey, Bruna, this is Toshiro," Tessa introduced them.

"Nice to meet you." Bruna shook hands with him, noticing that both he and Tessa were wearing matching rings. *Well, no wonder Tessa wanted him back*, she thought. *The guy is irresistible.* Although Bruna was surprised to see him there, she tried to hide it.

"So you are an activist, too," Toshiro said, looking at her "Save the Dolphins and Whales" T-shirt.

"I am. Tessa has told me much about you and how you stole a kiss and her heart."

Toshiro turned red and didn't know what to say.

"Enough, Bruna." Tessa gave her a disapproving glance.

"I found this on your doorstep," Bruna said and handed Tessa a manila envelope.

"I wonder what it is! There is no stamp or address on it," Tessa said, examining the front and the back of the envelope. She tore off the top part of the envelope and reached inside. "My knife! I had lost it in…"

"Taiji," Toshiro finished. "Last year, the news in Japan reported that someone cut the nets and let four dolphins escape."

Tessa looked at her father's initials on the knife: JMW. She was remembering how she had gone to Taiji to help save the dolphins; in the end, it was the dolphins who had saved her.

"Was it you?" Toshiro asked, thinking that if it was her, she had put herself in grave danger.

"What are you guys talking about?" Bruna asked.

"It's not important. Let's just go." She couldn't talk about it, not to Toshiro, not to Bruna or anyone else. And she regretted telling her parents and her friend Karianne all the details of what had happened in Taiji because she had promised Jack not to talk about it to anyone.

What Tessa didn't know was that Jack was friends with Erica, and he had put in a word with his treasure hunting friends that if they ever happened upon a knife with the initials JMW in the cove, to give it to him because it belonged to a friend of his. It turned out that a few weeks ago, they were at the cove and found a wedding ring, earrings, money, a cellphone, an Apple watch, and a pocket knife. The problem was, Jack couldn't simply mail the knife because of government surveillance.

Government agencies around the world often coordinated with their country's post office to spy on activists by randomly opening their mail. Jack knew this and didn't want to take the chance of getting caught. He contacted Erica to see if she knew someone who could give the knife to Tessa. Erica told him that she had a friend in Osaka who was returning to L.A.

Tessa was curious as to who had found her knife and returned it. Was it Jack? The free diver? Another activist? And who had left it on her doorstep? It must have happened after Nick left but before Bruna arrived. She decided that this was one mystery that she would not try to solve because if she started to ask around and the person who found it was still living in Japan, he or she might get into trouble.

Toshiro decided not to push Tessa and let her tell him what happened in Taiji when she was ready. Even if she never wanted to talk about it, that was okay, too. He loved her and that was all that mattered.

"By the way, is that what you're wearing to the demonstration?" Bruna asked, looking at Tessa's pink dress and heels.

"Nick said that I looked frumpy in my other outfit and I can no longer fit in my Save the Dolphins shirt."

"I have just the thing for you," Bruna said, as she pulled out an extra-large shirt from her bag. It had a picture of a dolphin and her pup and the caption read, "Save us." "I ordered a bunch of them to give away. They arrived yesterday. I figured you had outgrown your old one."

"Thank you!" Tessa said.

"You're welcome. I think I have one for Toshiro too. I'll go get it," Bruna said and disappeared.

Tessa's cell phone rang.

"Hi, it's Ben. I'm not sure if you remember me. I'm a reporter for AGA TV."

"Hi, Ben. I know who you are. We met at the Irvine farmers market."

"Listen, I know that this is last minute, but I was wondering if you have time this Tuesday for a TV interview? We have a spot that opened up."

"Yes, absolutely," she said, excited.

"Wonderful. Text me your email. I'll send you more info with a list of questions that you need to answer and return before 3 p.m., tomorrow."

"Of course. Thank you," she said and sent him her email address.

"Who is Ben?" Toshiro asked when she was done.

"He is a reporter I met about a month ago. I'm surprised he remembered me. He wants to do a TV interview."

"You're a celebrity! May I have your autograph?" he asked, reaching in his coat pocket and pretending to be looking for pen and paper.

She nudged him, and said, "Very funny."

"May I?" Toshiro said, pointing to Tessa's tummy.

Tessa nodded, and he placed a hand on her belly. The twins shifted inside her, which brought him close to tears. "I want more of these."

"Forget it. This is it for me," she admonished him.

"We'll talk about it," he insisted.

"No, we won't. And by the way," she asked, with one hand on her waist, "it was you who made the donation, wasn't it?"

"I have no idea what you're talking about," he said with a poker face.

"Oh, c'mon. Who would send me and Akira an envelope full of money and not even expect a receipt?"

"You knew all this time?"

"I wasn't sure, but I had a feeling that I had finally brought you to the dark side. Thank you for supporting our cause."

"You bet," he said, feeling good that he could help.

"Chop-chop, you two. We're running late," Bruna said when she returned. She handed Toshiro a T-shirt.

Bruna helped herself to an apple from the basket sitting on the kitchen counter while she waited for them to get changed. Minutes later, she saw Tessa come out in her T-shirt, a red sweater, and leggings. She was holding hands with Toshiro, who looked sporty with his T-shirt tucked into his dress pants.

"You guys ready?" Bruna asked.

"I sure am," Toshiro said.

"Okay. Let's do this," Tessa said, as all three headed out to save the dolphins.

Also by the Author:

Lemon Curd: A Novel

The Dawn of Saudi: In Search for Freedom

Author's note and acknowledgement

The first time I saw the mistreatment of dolphins, I was on twitter. The Cove documentary had just come out and everyone was talking about it. I remember having a difficult time watching the snippets of the documentary. People all around the world were shocked and the international community started criticizing Japan. Activists everywhere took to the streets and foreign nationals flocked to Taiji to help save the dolphins, upsetting the townspeople. Flash-forward thirteen years, the brutal slaughter of dolphins continues. And with the exception of groups of activists who still care, the world has moved on to other topics such as the sluggish economy, exuberant gas and food prices, homelessness, and the war with Russia.

So, I thought why not bring back this important topic and also talk about the Japanese culture. Japan is a complicated society and to fully understand it, one needs to be a native Japanese. Obviously, I am not Japanese and my understanding of their culture before writing this book was minimal. But, after years of research and hiring private tour guides when I travelled there, I was able to get a better grasp of their culture and traditions. My goal was to bring attention to the plight of dolphins, and also, write a story about the Japanese culture.

Well, it wasn't as easy I thought it would be to work on this project. I really struggled with it more than I did with my first two books, and after going through hundreds of drafts, I was still not happy with it when I handed it over to my content editor, Heidi Dvorak. When I got my manuscript back and read all her comments, I thought you know what, I'm just going to scrap this manuscript because it's hopeless. Heidi basically told me that my protagonist was stupid and the story lacked depth. It was a difficult moment for me because I had put in many years of long hours, and I had nothing to show for it. But after weeks of brooding, I went back to work because I felt strongly about this topic and thought even if I could convince a few readers to care about these beautiful mammals, not all would have been lost. So, thanks to Heidi's harsh criticism of my manuscript and going through another in depth edit, I was able to come up with a better story. I also want to thank my copy editor, Kayla Kauffman, who helped polish the story, my brother who helped with the scuba diving scene, and my friend, Dr. Vivian Shirvani, who helped with the accident and coma scene. Without their help, this project would be sitting in my drawer.

I would like to express my gratitude to the hard-working activists around the world who risk their lives every day in order to make the world a better place. Many thanks to Ric O'Barry and his Dolphin Project, Japan's Life Investigation Agency, Action for Dolphins, DR. Dianna Reiss, People for the Ethical Treatment of Animals (PETA), and numerous other organizations and individuals whose wealth of information helped put this book together. I hope that readers will like the story enough to care about the truth and the injustice behind keeping any life form in captivity.

Born in Tehran, Iran, Homa Pourasgari spent hours in her father's home office, writing, reading and letting her imagination carry her to unseen worlds. She moved to United States at a young age. After graduating from Loyola Marymount University with a degree in business, she left for Paris to study literature at the Sorbonne. Her first book, Lemon Curd, was nominated Forward Magazine's Book of the Year Award finalist. Her second book, The Dawn of Saudi, won Reader Views Reviewers Choice Award. She lives in Los Angeles, California. When she is not writing, she is stumbling, miming and pointing to find her way in a foreign country. Her latest novel, The American Outsider, is based on her travels to Japan.

==

Visit the author's website at: www.homapourasgari.com

www.ingramcontent.com/pod-product-compliance
Lightning Source LLC
Chambersburg PA
CBHW060226030726

47499CB00004B/1208